Fake It

Till You

Bake It

ALSO BY JAMIE WESLEY

Body and Soul: Those Jones Boys Series

Make the Play

Camp Firefly Falls Series

The Time of His Life
Her Dream Come True

The Exclusive! Series

This Is True Love
The Trouble with Love

The One-on-One Series

Tell Me Something Good
Slamdunked by Love
The Deal with Love

Fake It Till You Bake It

Jamie Wesley

ST. MARTIN'S
GRIFFIN

NEW YORK

First published in the United States by St. Martin's Griffin, an imprint of St. Martin's Publishing Group

FAKE IT TILL YOU BAKE IT. Copyright © 2022 by Jamie Wesley. All rights reserved. Printed in the United States of America. For information, address St. Martin's Publishing Group, 120 Broadway, New York, NY 10271.

Designed by Jen Edwards

www.stmartins.com

Library of Congress Cataloging-in-Publication Data

Names: Wesley, Jamie, author.
Title: Fake it till you bake it / Jamie Wesley.
Description: First edition. | New York : St. Martin's Griffin, 2022. |
Identifiers: LCCN 2022003366 | ISBN 9781250801852 (trade paperback) | ISBN 9781250801869 (ebook)
Subjects: LCGFT: Romance fiction. | Novels.
Classification: LCC PS3623.E778 F35 2022 | DDC 813/.6—dc23/eng/20220128
LC record available at https://lccn.loc.gov/2022003366

Our books may be purchased in bulk for promotional, educational, or business use. Please contact your local bookseller or the Macmillan Corporate and Premium Sales Department at 1-800-221-7945, extension 5442, or by email at MacmillanSpecialMarkets@macmillan.com.

First Edition: 2022

10 9 8 7 6 5 4 3 2 1

To anyone who's ever had a dream

Fake It Till You Bake It

Chapter One

Donovan Dell was a professional football player who loved to bake.

Seriously.

He was used to the quizzical looks people gave him when they learned he, a man who made a living terrorizing quarterbacks, co-owned Sugar Blitz, San Diego's latest and best cupcakery. He didn't care, though.

Baking relaxed him. Running his own business thrilled him. His plans for his post-playing career were starting to take root. Exactly how he'd planned.

"Donovan, sales have declined for six straight weeks."

Okay, maybe not exactly how he'd planned. As his accountant had just noted with absolutely no attempt to spare his feelings. Their weekly business call was off to a rip-roaring start. He made a face at the cell phone lying so innocently on his office desk.

"Donovan, did you hear what I said?" His accountant's exasperation came through the phone's speaker loud and clear.

"Yes, Shana, I know profits have declined for the last six weeks," he answered. Better than anyone.

Business had been good—*really good*—when the shop first opened in January after his team was eliminated from the playoffs (which sucked, by the way), probably because people were dying to see their favorite football players up close and personal, hawking baked goods. After that first month, however, the number of customers had slowed from a flood to a steady stream to a damn trickle. He didn't know why. He'd done all the market research. Their product was top-notch. The shop's location was excellent.

Yet the sales figures on his computer screen did not lie. And if he and his business partners were going to follow through with their plan to hire a full-time manager, whose salary would be fully funded by the store's profits by the start of training camp in July, then sales needed to rebound. Soon.

He stifled his hundredth sigh of the day. "We're going to turn things around."

He was Donovan Dell. He didn't fail.

"I hope so." She didn't sound optimistic, which set his teeth on edge. Why had he thought it was a good idea to hire his big sister to be his accountant? Yes, she had a brilliant mind, but she would never respect their professional relationship. He was just her baby brother whose diapers she'd changed on way too many occasions, after all. "I told you I wasn't sure such a large storefront was the best option for the store."

"Yes, I know." He was proud of his cordial tone.

He'd bought the building, located in East Village, years ago as a real estate investment. He'd fallen in love with the wide-open space with its exposed brick and original fixtures. Then last year, his best friend and teammate, Nicholas, had suggested turning their mutual baking hobby into a business. Donovan had run all kinds of analyses on the best use for the property, but ultimately, he'd trusted his instincts.

"You've already invested so much money into this venture," she continued.

"Yes, I know," he repeated, maybe a little less cordially this time.

"You need to start turning a profit soon," she said. "Football isn't going to last forever."

"Yes, I know, Shana," he said through gritted teeth. Cordiality was no longer on his radar. If there was a person who could be counted on to keep things more real than he did, it was his sister. Growing up in a household with a father who had no interest in reality tended to do that to you.

Shana harrumphed. "I'm just looking out for you, baby brother. We can talk about your personal life if you want. You know Mama is dying to know when you're going to get married and give her grandkids."

Donovan groaned, the change of topic doing jack shit to improve his mood. "You already gave her two tiny humans to spoil."

He always considered the whole marriage-and-kids thing to be something he would think about in that nebulous time frame called the future. Maybe. His parents sure as hell weren't an example of wedded bliss.

"Pssht," his sister said. "Like she thinks that's enough. You know what she says."

"You can't give me grandbabies if you're working twenty-four hours per day," they said simultaneously. They chuckled for a moment, then went silent.

Shana sighed. "I'm really concerned about the shop, Donovan."

So was he.

"Have you considered—"

"Hold on, Shana. Someone's calling me." He loved his sister, but she'd been giving him advice his entire life, a lot of it good, but this was his problem. He'd figure it out on his own. Besides, he already knew what she was going to suggest—shutting the shop down and dividing the property into apartments he could rent at a premium thanks to the building's prime location. Probably because he'd contemplated the same thing before Nicholas proposed the cupcake shop. He never took chances. But he had this time.

As a kid, baking with his mom had offered joy and calm on the occasions when his dad made their lives unhappy and chaotic. He'd gone with his gut, instead of his head, for the first time in forever, and he was going to make the shop work if it was the last thing he did.

"Yeah, I'll be right there, Nicholas," he said loudly to his business partner, who was most definitely not standing in his office. "Shana, I gotta go."

"But what about—"

"We can talk about it next week. Love you." Donovan ended the call and dropped his head into his hands. He needed a stiff drink. But one wasn't available at the moment. Which left the next best option.

A cupcake.

A Sugar Blitz cupcake could always be counted on to make things better. Nicholas, the best baker in the group and the one who loved tinkering with new recipes, had been experimenting and put his newest flavor—apple crumble—on sale that morning. Donovan had meant to try one, but he'd worked through his lunch hour, staring at numbers that didn't get any better no matter how many ways he added them up.

He pushed away from his oversized oak desk and headed to the front of the building. The walk down the hall was a quick one. As he did each time he entered the storefront, he stopped for a second to inhale the intoxicating mixture of vanilla, chocolate, and buttercream frosting that filled the air. No other place in San Diego smelled as good, he was positive.

He tried not to notice how *not* busy the store was. A couple of the tables toward the back were occupied, but he'd always envisioned the bakery full of customers, all stuffing their faces with his cupcakes. Dreams could still come true, he supposed. No, they *would* come true.

He pushed in a chair at one table, grabbed an errant wrapper off the floor, and tossed it into the trash. He glanced around. No imperfections would thrive on his watch. But nothing else caught his eye. A keen sense of satisfaction swept through him. Everything was perfect again. Well, except for the lack of customers. And just like that, his shoulders tensed up.

He snaked his way around the tables and headed for the counter. He would be his own customer, damn it, and pay, instead of filching the product.

At least there were a couple of customers in line ahead of him eyeing the cupcake selection. Not a long line, but beggars couldn't be choosers and all that jazz. Except he'd never been good at setting his expectations low. He established goals, put in the work, and met them.

He settled in to wait, his mind turning to possible solutions. Maybe they needed to run a sale, do some more advertising . . .

"Girl, why do you come here?" the woman in front of him said to her companion.

Donovan's thoughts came to a screeching halt. Here? As in *here*? As in Sugar Blitz? As in the place he'd poured blood, sweat, and a hell of a lot of money into?

She'd said it in the bougiest tone he'd ever heard. Or maybe he was being sensitive. Maybe she'd said it in a completely neutral tone, and he needed to chill.

Donovan deliberately relaxed his shoulders and studied his new-found nemesis. Or at least the part of her he could see—namely, her back.

Cupcake Shop Critic was dressed casually in a red jumpsuit, but there were cheap jumpsuits you got off the clearance rack at Ross and expensive-looking jumpsuits like the one she was wearing. The garment was made of the finest raw silk that, if he were the fanciful type, he would say flowed like water across her body. A woman used to the finer things in life. He'd become accustomed to the finer things over the past eight years, but that still left twenty-two years of his life in which he'd shopped off those same clearance racks. The sleeveless outfit showcased toned arms and did amazing things for her ass. Not so much for her mouth, which was still running a mile a minute.

The other woman said something, but her voice didn't carry like her friend's. Too bad.

Donovan inched a little closer. He shouldn't be eavesdropping. It was rude and immature. And he tried to never be rude and immature. Practical and demanding, maybe—okay, always—but rude and immature, no. But she was talking about his pride and joy. And being loud about it.

"What is up with this ambiance?"

Ambiance? What the fuck was wrong with the ambiance? Who the hell used the word "ambiance" in normal, everyday conversation? Donovan took a quick survey of the space, although he knew every inch by heart. Sunlight streamed in through the wall-length windows. They'd gone with a modern, industrial look. Clean lines. Concrete floors, exposed ductwork, original brickwork. Modern splashes of color adorned the white walls. The interior designer he'd spent a fortune on assured him it was the latest and greatest design concept. The colorful frosting on the cupcakes would pop against the white and silver that dominated the area. Everything was neat and clean, just the way he liked it.

"It's so . . ."

So *what*? Bomb? Fire? Lit? *Awesome?* The only acceptable answers.

"Stale," she finally said, her dismissive tone making his insides curl in horror the same way it did whenever anyone suggested using carob instead of chocolate.

He should let it go. He was in a bad mood, and nothing good could come from confronting a woman who was entitled to her own opinion. Even when she was wrong.

"Stale, probably like the cupcakes," she added.

"Excuse me." Fuck letting it go. Nobody called his cupcakes stale. "Excuse me," he repeated, maybe a little too loudly given the way the two women jumped in unison and whirled to face him.

Shit. He forgot what he was about to say. The critic was beautiful. Stunning, actually. Skin the color of chestnut. A heart-shaped face. He was pretty sure he'd never noticed eyebrows before, but hers were perfect, arched flawlessly over large eyes that were the color of his favorite dark chocolate chips. Hell, her whole face was perfect. High cheekbones. Full, lush lips. She looked like she'd stepped off a runway. His gaze slipped lower. No, she was too short for that line of work. The black heels added at least four inches to her height. He lifted his head.

A hint of something—uncertainty, maybe—flared in her eyes.

He stepped back. *Damn.* He was used to his body. Used to how large it was and how he often intimidated without trying. Being six feet three, 265 pounds was an asset on a football field—not so much in real life.

"Can I help you?" The uncertainty had disappeared from her expression, making him wonder if he'd imagined it.

The bougie tone—and no, he hadn't imagined *that*—immediately grated on his already stretched nerves once again. He didn't care how beautiful she was. No one talked shit about his cupcakes and got away with it. "I overheard what you were saying."

She blinked in obvious surprise, but then her shoulders stiffened and defiance settled on her pretty face. "And?"

He gave her credit, reluctantly, for not backing down. "*And* I'll have you know we have the best cupcakes in the city."

Her skeptical gaze swept up and down his figure and lingered on the shop's logo on his teal polo. "You work here. I wouldn't expect you to say otherwise."

She thought he was a shopworker and not the owner. Which meant she had no idea who he was, even though he was one of the San Diego Knights' most visible faces. She thought he was sucking up to curry favor with his bosses. He caught the eye of Ella, an actual part-time employee standing behind the cash register. She was pretending not to listen while halfheartedly wiping away non-existent crumbs from the quartz countertop with a towel. Donovan gave a quick shake of his head. He wanted the critic's honest opinion and didn't want it swayed by his true identity. "Employee or not, I speak the truth."

A quick eyeroll let him know what she thought about that declaration. "Dude, are you really getting your boxers in a twist because I'm not rhapsodizing about your cupcakes?"

His boxers were *not* in a twist. "My cupcakes are stellar. We use the best and freshest ingredients and the best recipes. It's the only way to run a bakery."

Critic nudged her friend with an elbow. "Yep, totally in a twist." She tapped her chin, those lush lips pursing, then nodded as though coming to a decision. "I was wrong."

She was admitting it? Maybe his day was finally looking up.

"You're a boxer briefs kind of guy," she continued, spreading her arms wide in a whatcha-gonna-do move. "Practicality rules. Functionality meets comfort all the way for you, I bet."

He would not dignify her ridiculousness with a response. Even if it was true. Which it was. His Calvin Klein boxer briefs were the best. But he couldn't stop his teeth from clenching. She noticed, if her smirk was any indication.

They were entertaining their audience. Her friend's head swiveled back and forth between them like she was watching a riveting, fast-paced tennis match. Ella had given up any pretense of not listening. Any second now, she'd pull out a bag of popcorn. Thank God his partners weren't there. He'd never live this encounter down. But he should be polite. She was a customer, after all. He forced his lips into a smile. "Why don't you try one before making any more pronouncements? My treat."

Critic pointed to her companion. "She came to get a cupcake for herself. I'm good." The *eww* floated through the air, silent but deadly. She wheeled on those spindly heels like she'd been doing it her whole life, effectively dismissing him. His teeth ground together. Why did this woman he'd never met before know exactly the right thing to say to piss him off?

"That's fine. Unless you're scared," he said to her back. He ignored Ella's muffled snort of laugher.

The critic spun around with admirable quickness and agility. She could teach his teammates a thing or two. "I'm *not* scared."

Ooh, looked like he'd scored a direct hit. "Then you won't mind trying one."

Her jaw worked side to side as she glared at him. "Sure. Why not?"

Needling a customer definitely was nowhere to be found in the "How to Be a Good Business Owner" handbook. But he'd never claimed to be perfect. Driven, yes. And his driven ass had had a bad day. The least she could do was admit his cupcakes were damn good. He clapped his hands together and hurried around the counter before either of them could come to their senses. "What kind can I get you? You eat sugar, right?"

She gave a reluctant nod.

"Are you gluten-free?"

"No."

"Great. That means our entire menu is open to you."

"Can't wait."

He chose to ignore the sarcasm. "You look like a vanilla person."

Okay, maybe he hadn't ignored it.

Her lifted eyebrow said she'd caught the shot. "Is that the best this shop can offer?"

He deserved that. "It is the most classic of flavors, but we've worked hard to come up with unique flavors and put our stamp on the San Diego cupcake scene."

Her head tilted to the side. "The San Diego cupcake scene? I didn't realize that was a thing."

His lips quirked in spite of himself. "It is." Too much of a scene, actually. The competition was stiff, but it only drove him to be better.

She considered him, a wide, and if he was honest with himself—dazzling—smile stretching across her face. "Who knew? You learn something new every day."

"So what's your poison? Cherry chocolate? Cotton candy? Apple crumb?" Donovan was inordinately proud of the display. Variety abounded. The cupcakes were fresh, appetizing, and colorful. And most importantly, big. Sugar Blitz scrimped nowhere.

She tapped her index finger on her gloss-coated lips as she contemplated the choices.

"I get the cookies 'n cream flavor," her friend said.

That's right. They weren't alone. He'd almost forgotten.

Donovan flashed the friend a smile, grateful that *someone* appreciated the cupcakery's offerings. "Thanks for your repeat business. What's your name?"

"Olivia."

"Well, Olivia, I happen to know a fresh batch of cookies 'n cream cupcakes came out of the oven less than an hour ago. I'd be happy to buy you one."

He opened the case and carefully extricated a cupcake, making sure not to smudge the swirl of cream frosting or the Oreo crumbles adorning the top of the dessert. He handed it to Olivia, who immediately took a big bite. Her moan of appreciation made him do a Tiger Woods fist pump. He turned his attention back to her friend.

She was watching Olivia, but she still didn't look convinced. If he'd been in a more charitable mood, he would appreciate her stubbornness. He'd been labeled that more than once in his life. He owned it. Lots of people dreamed of becoming a pro football player. Few people made it happen. "My favorite is the chocolate chip chocolate swirl."

"Good for you. I'll take the strawberry shortcake," she replied with no hesitation.

A woman who knew her own mind, something he always appreciated. Maybe he could be charitable after all.

"Hard to mess that up," she muttered under her breath. Unfortunately, he heard every word.

Just like that, his appreciation disappeared like water from evaporated milk. But he could not, *would not* let her get to him. He consciously relaxed his jaw, then withdrew the dessert from the case and offered it up. "Good, safe choice."

Her brown eyes narrowed. But she reached for the treat without saying a word. Their fingers brushed. A spark of something electric, definitely pleasurable, zipped up his arm. What the . . . ? He could not be attracted to the customer from hell. A quick flaring of her eyes was the only indication she'd felt it, too.

"I hope you like it," he said. If his voice sounded huskier than normal, well, no need to overanalyze things. Even though that was the exact opposite of how he usually handled situations. Which he would not think about right now.

"What if I don't?" she challenged.

He blinked. He hadn't considered that possibility because it made no sense, and everything he did made sense. "You will."

She arched one of those perfect eyebrows. "But if I don't?"

He rounded the counter, drawn to her despite himself. This close, her scent drifted toward him. Soft, floral, more alluring than his favorite smells from Sugar Blitz. "Then I will publicly admit my cupcakes are stale."

Her nose wrinkled. "That's it? I'm gonna need more if I'm going to set aside my doubts and give your cupcakes an honest try."

He sighed. "Fine. I will also beg your forgiveness."

A grin played across her lips. "Beg, you say? I like the sound of that."

He ignored the way his blood thickened at the blatant flirtation. She was trying to distract him. And doing a damn good job of it. He couldn't let her. "Too bad it's not going to happen."

"We'll see." Her raspy chuckle sounded way too sexy to his sex-deprived self. A condition that was completely his own fault, as he'd put training for and playing football and then opening the cupcakery at the top of his priority list over the last six months.

She raised the dessert to her perfect lips. He watched intently, and if he was honest with himself, it wasn't just because he wanted to see how she would react to the cupcake. Her eyes drifted shut as she chewed slowly, like she was savoring all the dessert's flavors. At least she didn't spit it out. She went for another bite but got too close to the frosting. A streak of it ended up on her chin. And her nose. Her eyes flew open. "Crap!"

"Careful," he said. He didn't mask the laughter in his voice. The frosting in no way marred the perfection of her face, even if she did now look the tiniest bit like a clown.

She glared at him while swiping at the offending spot on her nose with her free hand.

He grabbed a napkin off the counter. "Here."

"I'm fine." She swiped again, spreading a trail of red cream across her chin.

"You missed a spot." Or two. "Take the napkin."

She snatched the napkin out of his hand and wiped her face. "Are you always this bossy?"

"Yes." He saw no reason to deny the truth.

Humor sparked in her eyes. "Did I get it all?"

After he nodded, she went back to delicately eating the cupcake. He should not be noticing how lush her lips were as she nibbled on the dessert. All he should care about, all he *would* care about, was her reaction to the cupcake. Her poker face gave nothing away.

"So do you say 'yes' to the cupcake?" he asked when she was halfway done. He couldn't wait any longer. "Do you want to marry it?"

She froze. "I say it's time for me to go." She thrust the cupcake at him, forcing him to take it or end up with cake and frosting all over his shirt, then jerked her chin at Olivia. "Come on."

Without another word, Critic marched toward the door, moving like she was made to walk the runway, the jumpsuit hugging her swinging hips in the best way possible.

"That means I won," he called after her. He resolutely ignored the panic that had unexpectedly surged through his entire body at proof of her impending departure. He never panicked. About anything. Besides, he only had time to care about football and the store, and an attraction to a woman who talked smack about his cupcake shop was neither of those things.

She halted, then spun to face him. "No, that means the cupcake was . . . decent." The bougieness was back in full force. Her gaze swept the space. "The atmosphere, not so much." She locked eyes with him. "I won't be back."

"We both know you don't mean that." He saluted her with her abandoned cupcake and a wink because why the hell not? He'd obviously lost his damn mind. "See you next time."

The snick of the closing door was her only response.

"Good going, boss," Ella called out from behind him.

Donovan groaned. Damn, he needed a cupcake.

Chapter Two

"Not a word," Jada Townsend-Matthews said to her best friend, Olivia Madison, as she strode down the sidewalk away from the cupcake shop. And that guy with a stick up his ass.

"I'm not going to say anything. I'm just going to enjoy the best cupcake I've had since the last time I stopped by Sugar Blitz." Olivia took a bite of the dessert and stared hard at Jada.

Jada's shoulders hunched defensively. "What? I didn't do anything."

Olivia's stare didn't waver.

"I mean I wasn't trying to do anything." Somehow, she just found herself in these situations.

"No, you were speaking your mind like you always do." Olivia grinned. "Which is one of the things I love most about you."

"Thanks." She needed to hear that, especially now. Olivia was her ride or die, the one who stuck by her side no matter what. Jada's mouth always got her into trouble. Always. One day she'd learn to control it. One day.

"At least he didn't know who you were," Olivia added.

Thank God for small favors. For a moment there, when he'd said "excuse me," she thought she'd turn around to find a phone in her face, either so the guy could take a picture and post it to his social media app of choice or show her the most humiliating moment of her life, a clip she'd seen, oh, a million gazillion times over the last two weeks since it had first been broadcast to the world.

Most people didn't have their most embarrassing moments recorded by a professional camera crew, then aired on national TV and then replayed over and over and over on the internet. She wasn't most people. Never had been. Never would be, apparently.

"It's not like I was lying," she said. "The place was like a mausoleum. Cold and sterile."

"Girl, I don't care what the place looks like." Olivia saluted her with the treat she'd had the good sense not to get rid of on her way out of the store. "The cupcakes are amazing."

Jada shrugged, then took a deep breath. She needed to relax. Being home, close to the beach, basking in the fantastic San Diego weather and the cool breeze from the nearby ocean was supposed to accomplish that feat. So far, mission *not* accomplished.

"More importantly, dude was fine," Olivia added.

Jada made a face. "Was he? I didn't notice. Not with that stern high school principal vibe he was giving off."

"You didn't notice those thick, hard thighs that could crack walnuts?"

A vision of Cupcake Guy and his aforementioned thighs crystallized in her mind. Jada shook her head, doing her best to dislodge the image, and took the opportunity to study the oh-so-fascinating cracks in the sidewalk. "Nope."

"The wide, broad shoulders and biceps threatening to break the seams of his polo?"

"Nope." That was her story, and she was sticking to it like Ariana Grande did with her ponytail.

"The scrumptious dark brown skin? The full lips? The deep, commanding voice?"

Jada rolled her eyes. "You mean the lips that I'm pretty sure are permanently pressed tight in disapproval? The how-dare-you-not-agree-with-everything-I-say voice?"

Her BFF snorted in disbelief. "Yeah, okay." Olivia's second snort morphed into laughter. "You called the man's cupcakes stale," she said through her cackling.

Jada's nose lifted. "I said they were decent." They were actually fantastic, not that she'd admit that out loud in a million years, especially not to him. Granted, she'd never see him again, but still it was important to take a metaphorical stand. *See you next time,* he'd said in that deep, commanding voice she'd just told Olivia she didn't think was deep and commanding.

"*After* you called them stale," Olivia corrected.

Jada tried not to squirm. "I mean . . . well . . . it's not like they were *his* cupcakes. He was toeing the company line."

Olivia scrunched her nose in reluctant disagreement. "No, I'm pretty sure he's the owner. One of them, anyway."

Oh. Oops. Her inability to keep her thoughts to herself had bitten her in the ass yet again. And she knew exactly who to blame. "You know, this is all your fault."

"*What?*" Olivia threw her hands up in the air, then cried out as her cupcake went flying. She made an impressive acrobatic dive to stop it from meeting an unfortunate end on the pavement. She landed in a crouch, saving the dessert a split second before catastrophe struck, cradled it in her palms, and rose back to her full height with a dramatic sigh. "If I didn't love you, I'd hate you for almost making me lose my cupcake." Her voice rose. "And how is it *my* fault?"

"Oh, I don't know. Something about how you can't hide out for the rest of your life, Jada," Jada answered in a singsongy tone. "Let's go to your favorite store, Jada. Why don't we stop in for a snack, Jada? Be the badass I know you are, Jada."

Olivia side-eyed her. "I meant every word. Admit it. You were miserable staying cooped up in your condo."

True. She'd always been social. Loved being around other people. Except now she'd become public enemy number one.

"Besides, you're the one who went all Joanna Gaines on the shop," Olivia continued. Ride or die did not mean not keeping it real.

"I was just talking. I didn't think anyone was paying attention to us. There *was* no one paying attention to us." Except the finest man she'd seen in forever. Wait. No. "He *winked* at me. Who *does* that?"

"I think he was being cheeky."

Jada squinted at Olivia. "Cheeky? Are you British now?"

"Must be all those episodes of *Doctor Who* and *Great British Bake Off*." Olivia swung an arm around her shoulders and squeezed. "Sorry he brought up marriage."

The sorest of subjects. Turning down a marriage proposal on national TV was how she'd ended up in this mess, although to be honest, messes were her specialty. She blew out a breath. "Yeah, well, he didn't know he was stepping into it."

Olivia took one last bite, then dumped the empty cupcake wrapper in a trash can. "Come on. We still haven't hit up the store."

"Now you're talking my language." Jada's step quickened. She loved retail therapy. Her favorite boutique, Perfection, was directly up ahead. She would *not* think about how that also meant it was right around the corner from that dude's cupcake store.

All thoughts of failed marriage proposals, cupcakes that weren't actually stale, and uptight, hella attractive cupcake shop owners who thought they knew everything fled her mind as soon as they entered Perfection.

Jada immediately zeroed in on a display at the center of the room. "Oooh."

Purple, her favorite color. She hurried over. She'd seen the dress with its long flowing sleeves and plunging neckline on a New York Fashion Week runway and had counted down the days until she could make it hers. Today was the day. Maybe her luck was starting to change. She didn't check the price tag. What was the point? That's what credit cards were for. Besides, when you were sad, you deserved whatever you wanted. Duh. Not that was she going to be able to fall back on that logic for much longer. Which she was not going to think about right now.

She quickly found her size and grabbed the hanger off the rack. "Mine. All mine. What do you think?"

"I approve." Olivia held up a cute green A-line skirt from a nearby rack. "I'm going to try this on."

Jada nodded. "Okay. I'll be back there in a minute. I want to look around a little more first."

While Olivia headed to the dressing room at the back of the store, Jada moved on to another display, where a pretty shirt was calling her name. This store really was her happy place.

"Jada!" A salesperson hurried up to her. The tall woman wore a cute wrap dress Jada recognized as one of the boutique's offerings because it also resided in her closet at home. The dress looked amazing on the saleswoman's lithe body. Man, what she wouldn't give for a few more inches to her frame. She loved her heels, but actual height would have been better.

Jada gave a quick wave. "Hey, Carrie."

"How are you doing?"

"Good." She injected some hearty, fake cheer into her voice. While she appreciated the concern in the brunette's eyes, she didn't do well with pity. Her pride wouldn't allow it.

Carrie nodded. "Great. Can I help you find anything?"

"No, I'm just looking, thanks."

"Well, let me know if I can be of assistance."

Jada's shoulders relaxed. "Will do."

Carrie nodded, then retreated to the cash register.

Jada returned her attention to the mannequin. The silk turquoise top would look amazing with her favorite silver heels and jeans. This shopping expedition was exactly what the doctor—or, in this case, the BFF—ordered. She'd have to buy Olivia a cupcake. But *not* from Sugar Blitz.

"Is that her?" someone behind her whispered. Jada's hand tightened on the shirt sleeve, crumpling the thin fabric. She had no doubt she was the "her" the woman was talking about.

"Yeah, that's her," someone else replied. Disgust infused the quick response.

Jada's heart thudded. Had what she'd done been so bad? According to Twitter, Instagram, various podcasts, and that old fave, Facebook, the answer was a resounding *yes*.

She should have slipped on her sunglasses before leaving the house. Even if they'd still recognized her, she could have used the extra layer of protection the Dior eyewear would have given her.

She had no doubt what was about to happen. What had happened every time she stepped foot out of her residence since the *My One and Only* season finale aired—well, until she finally gave up and stayed inside. She quickly deposited the dress she'd been so excited about on the nearest rack and scanned the store for Olivia. Damn it, she was nowhere to be found. Where the hell had her friend gone? Oh, that's right. She was trying on that skirt Jada no longer considered cute.

Still, she had to get out of here. She'd call Olivia from her car and come back to pick her up.

Jada made a beeline for the door. A woman stepped directly into her path before she got far. Only Jada's quick reflexes stopped her from plowing into the interloper.

"How could you do that to Dr. John?" the woman spat, bending down because she, too, was taller than Jada. Jada recognized her voice. The first woman to spot her. Her glare practically singed Jada's eyebrows.

Jada whirled. The other woman, whose skin was a shade of orange found only in tanning booths, was waiting. "He was the perfect guy, and you broke his heart!"

"Well, umm . . . I gotta go." She made another move toward the door, but the Darth Avengers weren't interested in letting her go. They crowded in on her. Jada automatically took a step backward, then stopped herself from taking another. She wouldn't let them intimidate her.

"What were you thinking?" Darth Avenger One asked.

"It's a blur, sir. Err, ma'am."

"What?" The avenger's face screwed up in confusion.

Jada waved her hand. "Sorry. Lyric from *Hamilton*."

Wrong. Thing. To. Say.

Jada had heard the term "spitting fire" before. She'd never witnessed it in person until this moment. Darth Avenger One's green eyes bulged, while her pale skin mottled with red blotches. "Really? Is everything a joke to you?"

Yeah, usually. That's how she got through life's disappointments and feeling like the ultimate disappointment to her brilliant parents.

Jada tried to dodge around the woman, but anger apparently gave a person the moves of a professional athlete who got paid to play defense, not offense. She blocked Jada's every maneuver. "Was it all a game to you?"

A game? No. A chance to have some fun and not think about her future? Yes. Until it all went to hell in a handbasket. *Hell in a handbasket?* What was up with that phrase anyway?

"You're a heartless bitch," Darth Avenger Two said with a derisive sniff.

Jada flinched, the insult punching her square in the gut and leaving her breathless. Showing emotion was the last thing she should do in this situation, but damn it, she was only human. A flawed, often aggravating human, according to her loved ones, but human, nevertheless. Words did hurt. Of course, her detractors would point out that actions hurt worse.

"Excuse me. Can I help you ladies with anything?" Carrie stepped beside Jada.

Jada took the lifeline. "No, I was just leaving."

"What's going on?" Olivia's voice carried across the store.

Jada waved her over. "Nothing. It's time to go."

Olivia gave the Darth Avengers a death stare, but followed Jada out of the store without further comment. Carrie blocked the avengers from following them. Still, Jada kept her head down and hurried to her car parked down the block.

"What did those bitches say?" Olivia said once they'd found sanctuary in the silver BMW.

Jada blinked back tears. "The same thing everyone says."

"I can go back and beat their asses." The freckles that dotted Olivia's sienna-brown skin belied her fierce nature.

Jada shot her a look. "No, you can't because then I'd have to call your parents and tell them their miracle child is in jail."

Olivia's scowl didn't lessen. Her red-tinted brown curls bounced as she twisted in the seat to peer out the back window. "Might be worth it."

"Ma'am, you have a job, a good job. You don't need to lose it because of me." Unlike Jada, Olivia had gone to grad school and got an MBA with concentrations in hotel management and HR. She was now an up-and-coming star for a successful hotel chain. Jada deflated. "I shouldn't have left my condo."

"You can't let those bitches ruin your day."

"I know. Or at least I'm trying to know that." And yet her voice shook and one, two, *damn it,* three tears slipped out.

"You look good though."

A punch of laughter bubbled up from her chest at the unexpected compliment. "Thank you." Her best friend always knew the right thing to say. Even if her life was a mess, Jada did her best to make sure her outside was always fabulous. If others were allowed to like comic books or sports or gardening or whatever the hell they liked, she could like makeup and clothes, damn it. The accoutrements gave her confidence and made her look good. Win-win.

Jada flipped down the visor and inspected her face in the mirror. No sign of the cupcake frosting, though the taste of strawberries lingered on her tongue. Eyes only a little bloodshot. Mascara and eyeshadow on point. Foundation still making her skin look luminous and blemish-free. That new makeup setter was doing its job. She should make a YouTube video review.

Except social media was no longer her sanctuary. People had left all kinds of "fun" messages on her various pages. She'd shut off notifications. Only pride had stopped her from locking the pages, or, worse, deleting them altogether. If people wanted to show their asses on someone else's page, then let them. Jada sighed.

Olivia squeezed her arm. "If you want to talk, I'm here."

"I know, and I appreciate it. I'm talked out though." Olivia had heard all the thoughts rioting through her head since filming ended and even more once the show started airing. No need to regale her with them for the thousandth time.

Time to move on. Literally. She dropped off Olivia at her place after declining her friend's offer to come in for dinner and some Netflix relaxation time. Right now, she needed to decompress from the afternoon's festivities alone.

A few minutes later, her shoulders drooped in relief as she entered her condo. Well, not *her* condo, exactly. Her family owned the property in Mission Hills, but since she was the only one staying there at the moment, it was hers.

She kicked off her black patent leather stilettos. They were her favorite pair, the ones she wore when she needed a little extra confidence booster, but she'd reached the end of her daily limit of heels wear. Looking effortlessly chic was a lot of work.

Dinner was next. Thank God for food delivery apps. Cooking was *so* not her forte. Her phone buzzed as she dug it out of her purse. She groaned at the name that appeared on the screen. She only hesitated a half second before answering. "Hi, Grams."

"Oh, so you do know how to answer the telephone?" her grandmother, one Mrs. Joyce Townsend, replied.

Jada dropped her head into her free hand. "I love you, Grams." And she did. So much. She would never say her grandmother was her only family member who loved her because that wasn't true. Her parents and only sibling loved her deeply. They also didn't understand her and wanted to change her into someone they *did* understand. Grams had never done that.

Grams's sniff came through the phone loud and clear. "Hmmph. I wouldn't know it considering this is the third time I've called you in the last twenty-four hours."

Jada swallowed as guilt grabbed her by the throat. "I texted you."

"*Texted?* I want to hear your voice. But I know you young people have a bad habit of thinking texting equates to an actual conversation, which is the only reason I didn't call the police."

Jada headed for the living room, suppressing a sigh. "I know."

"Well, I'm glad you finally came home."

Home. As in San Diego. At eighteen, college in New York had offered the perfect excuse to leave. Since then, she'd only made infrequent visits home to see her family and friends.

"I'm sorry." She said that a lot. She was used to saying it.

"Did you have a good day?"

Unbidden, a man and his cupcakes popped into her consciousness. Not the crazy Darth Avenger ladies, strangely enough. "It was fine."

"Are you okay?"

The genuine concern in her grandmother's voice almost undid her. Jada sank down on her couch. "I've been better, but I've also been worse."

Grams sighed. "I told you I didn't think doing that show was a good idea. I might be old, but I know reality TV producers are nothing but vultures."

"Live and learn." And it wasn't like it had been awful. Not until the end when she'd turned the whole thing into a poopshow, which the producers had *loved.* Well, after they'd gotten over their shock and horror that she'd ruined their carefully constructed plans.

Lila Patterson, the show's creator and executive producer, ran a tight ship and made it her business to know what the show's participants would say almost before they said it. She'd been the main one pressing her on why she'd turned down John's proposal.

Jada had had no idea what to tell her, so she blurted out the first thing to come to mind—that she'd said no because there was someone at home she couldn't stop thinking about. The TV exec had changed her tune slightly when the finale aired and the show received more attention than it had in years, but Jada knew Lila was currently unhappy with her because she'd declined to do any interviews.

After listening to the first few voice mails and Lila's cajoling tone, which did little to disguise how pissed she was, Jada now sent all her calls to voice mail and ignored her texts.

Grams sighed, thankfully interrupting that upsetting train of thought. "Not like this, Jada. I worry. How can I make sure you're okay if you won't even come see me?"

Jada side-eyed the phone before lifting it back to her ear. "We've moved on to guilt, I see."

"Is it working?"

"Yes."

Grams's voice lightened. "Then I haven't lost my touch."

Jada shook her head. Like there was any chance of that happening. Her grandmother was the smartest, sharpest person she knew. Her parents and sister were all certified geniuses and Grams left them all in her dust. "You're too much."

"Thank you! You know I love a compliment. Since I know you feel the same, here's one for you. I see your potential."

Gratitude swept through Jada. Her grandmother often had a sixth sense for saying exactly what she needed to hear. "Thanks, Grams."

"You're welcome," Grams said. "Remember what we talked about before you went on that show?"

At the indirect mention of her trust fund, Jada's heart stuttered. She'd always counted on that money to act as her safety net if her parents ever went through with their threat to cut her off if she didn't "grow up" and join their business. They'd asked one more time after the finale aired. She'd turned down the offer because a., working for her parents sounded like hell on earth, and b., she knew she could always ask Grams for early access to her trust fund if it came to that. They'd informed her that on the first of the month, a mere ten days away, they would close her credit card accounts and no longer pay her bills.

She was supposed to take control of her trust fund at age twenty-six, but only if her grandmother deemed her ready. She'd planned to ask if she could receive it early, but now . . . She swallowed. "Yes."

Grams sighed. "I want *you* to see the potential inside of you. You're smart."

Her grandmother was the only person to say that. Jada was used to being described as fun. Unpredictable, too. But smart? Nope. "Thanks."

"Have you thought about your next steps?" her grandmother continued.

"Yes." She just hadn't come up with anything. She was twenty-five years old and had no idea what she wanted to be when she grew up. Awesome.

School had been hard. Not impossible, but hard. Most people would think it would get easier once she was diagnosed with dyslexia. Her parents had seen it as their personal failing. They'd overcompensated with tutors and doctors galore, which did help her academically, at least.

Even if she didn't have dyslexia, the odds still hadn't been in her favor that she could keep up with her genius parents and sister. She thought quickly on her feet but making scientific breakthroughs like her parents and sister did would never be her calling.

That didn't mean she didn't want to please her parents, which led to an unfortunate detour into a legal studies major in college. They'd been thrilled. She hated it. She graduated with a degree in humanities—by the skin of her teeth, but she'd done it out of sheer stubbornness, if nothing else.

Her parents had not been pleased. Their practical, scientific minds couldn't fathom majoring in something as "flimsy" as humanities. They'd pressured her to join their medical research firm. According to them, she could work as a receptionist, and they would hire the best tutors available if she went to grad school and got a "real degree." She'd escaped to Europe instead.

"So you've found a job?"

The eagerness in her grandmother's voice yanked Jada out of her trip down hellacious memory lane. She cleared her throat. "Not yet."

There was no point in lying to her grandmother. Grams always saw right through her. But Grams didn't know what her parents had done, and she didn't want to come in between her mother and her grandmother.

"That's okay," Grams replied immediately, ever supportive. "I don't expect you to have your dream career picked out, and I understand you don't want to work for me or your parents."

Jada's stomach fluttered with nerves. Why did she sense a "but" coming?

"But you do need some direction," Grams continued.

Something that had eluded Jada since graduation. While in Europe, after traveling a bit, she'd dabbled in deejaying. Who didn't like dancing in the club to fun music? Except it wasn't as glamorous as she'd imagined it to be. Weird hours. Unfamiliar, sometimes unsafe, settings. Unsteady, unreliable pay. She'd quit after being grabbed by one too many sweaty, sleazy, gross club owners who thought she was using the job to meet them. The last guy had gotten a nice knee in the balls for his trouble. He'd also badmouthed her to every owner of every noteworthy club throughout Europe.

After her overseas adventures, she'd spent the last few years in L.A. trying to make it as an actress. Everyone said she was dramatic, so why not tap into her natural state of being? Unfortunately, wanting to be an actress and making a living at it were two entirely different things. There had also been her brief stint as a stylist's assistant, but the less said about that, the better.

The reality TV dating show, *My One and Only*, had been a last-ditch effort to gain a potential career. At the very least, she thought she'd emerge from the show with certified credentials as a social media influencer, like so many of the show's previous contestants. Instead, she'd panicked and broken Dr. John's heart on the season finale because her gut was screaming that something wasn't right about their relationship. In the process, she'd become public enemy number one. You couldn't influence anything if the people you were supposed to be influencing hated your guts.

"I expect you to be able to hold a job for a decent amount of time," Grams continued. "If you can do so for six months until your birthday and get rave reviews from your supervisor, the trust fund is yours."

Six months?

There it was. The ultimatum she'd been dreading and avoiding. Jada pressed a shaky hand to her roiling stomach. If she couldn't keep a job for six months, Grams wouldn't hesitate to follow through with her decision not to give Jada her trust fund. She wasn't a bullshitter. Then Jada would truly be on her own, her only options to go crawling back to her parents or end up on Olivia's couch, which Olivia would be okay with, but Jada would not.

Too bad she'd never found that *thing* that was hers. She didn't even know if it existed. She wasn't that great at anything. When she thought about it too long, that grating voice inside her head never failed to whisper, "You're dumb, that's why."

Panic welled up inside her, seizing every muscle in her body into a tight-fisted clench, cutting off her ability to breathe, but she beat it back. Barely. She forced her lips to move. "I understand."

"Great." Grams's voice softened. "I'm not doing this to punish you. I want the best for you."

Jada squeezed her eyes shut. "I know." The ultimatum sounded mean, but Jada understood. Grams did believe in her. She just didn't understand the pressure she'd unwittingly placed on her granddaughter.

"We'll talk tomorrow. I expect you to have a plan. If you don't, one will be provided for you. See you at 10 A.M., my office."

That wasn't a request.

Jada's grip on the phone tightened. She needed the anchor, any anchor, even as small as it was. "Of course. I can't wait to see you."

"Hmmph. You have a funny way of showing it." That was Grams. Show love, but take no shit.

"I love you, Grams. I'll be there in the morning." Jada ended the call and pressed unsteady palms against her eyelids.

She had less than twenty-four hours to come up with a life plan that would satisfy the person she most wanted to make proud and keep herself from becoming penniless. No biggie. Collapsing against the sofa cushions, she let out a loud, gusty sigh. Oh, God. Where was a cupcake to stuff her face with when she needed it most?

Chapter Three

A slow movie clap greeted Donovan the moment he stepped through the Sugar Blitz front door the next morning. *Oh, fuck.*

"Y'all can cut that shit out any time now," he said to his two best friends/business partners.

Thankfully they did, but their twin smirks remained.

"Well, well, if isn't the ambassador of customer goodwill," Nicholas Connors said.

Donovan glared at the man he'd known for the past seven years. They'd officially met when the hotshot running back showed up to training camp, positive he was going to run roughshod through the league—until Donovan had laid him flat during his first play in practice. "Good morning to you, too."

Nicholas spread his hands wide and laughed. "Hey, I'm just repeating what I heard. And what I heard was ah-ma-zing!"

"I can only imagine." Donovan transferred his glare to Ella, who became engrossed in filling napkin holders at the front counter. He turned to the other member of their best friend triumvirate. "Do you have anything to add?"

August Hodges shook his head. "Naw, man."

Donovan wasn't surprised. August was a man of few words who truly believed and lived the adage that actions spoke louder than words. There was no one else Donovan would rather have watching his back. August was the team's fullback, the one who went in headfirst after the ball was snapped to block for running backs. He'd been through some tough shit, but still stood tall and came to work his ass off every day, first for the team and now for the cupcake shop.

They'd met as college freshmen football players, both anxious to prove they belonged, and immediately bonded. During those early days, Donovan had been an offensive lineman responsible for blocking for fullbacks like August before the coaches realized his talents would be better served on the other side of the ball. Then, four years later, they'd both been drafted by the Knights.

"He might not have anything to say, but he definitely has something to do." Nicholas held out his palm toward August.

Donovan knew what that meant. They'd made a stupid bet. He knew because he partook in the practice himself on the regular with these two. That didn't mean he liked it when he was the subject of a wager. "What the hell did you two bet on?"

"Whether you would show up on your day off," Nicholas answered, glee infusing every word. Donovan rolled his eyes while August pulled out a black leather wallet from his back pocket, took out a twenty, and slapped it into Nicholas's waiting hand.

That matter settled, August turned his attention back to Donovan. "We can handle things," he said, his voice filled with its usual gruffness, like he was unused to speaking. An accurate description, really.

"I know," Donovan said. And he meant it. "I only planned to stop in for a few minutes to fill you in on what happened yesterday, but obviously *someone* beat me to it." August had the day off and

Nicholas had already left after spending the early morning baking before the *incident*. "I'm going to see Mrs. T and get some advice about how we can boost sales."

"So you're not taking the day off." Nicholas sighed his disgust. Not that he wasn't a hard worker. He was the best running back in the league. Talent alone hadn't gotten him there.

When Nicholas was drafted by San Diego a year after Donovan and August, he'd glued himself to August's side, wanting to build a rapport with the man who would make his life easier on the football field. Which meant he was always there whenever Donovan turned around. Donovan had eventually warmed up to him when he saw his commitment to the team and dedication to his family and community. Now, he couldn't imagine life without the man others had dubbed "Pretty Boy Nick."

"We promised each other we would take one day a week for ourselves," Nicholas added.

With his smooth mocha skin, sharp jawline, gray eyes, and ever-present grin, Nicholas looked like a damn *GQ* model, even dressed in the standard Sugar Blitz polo and khakis. There was a reason they made him work the counter when he wasn't baking. August was stockier, a few inches taller than Nicholas's five feet ten. August didn't give a damn about chasing the spotlight or records, leaving that up to his business partners. Jeans and a decades-old T-shirt with his black locs pulled back into a low ponytail and a perfectly groomed beard that covered the mahogany skin on his face was his preferred look when he wasn't playing football.

They both crossed their arms, united in their exasperation with Donovan.

He refused to feel guilty. There would be no relaxation for him until the shop was consistently turning a profit again and they could afford a full-time manager and more part-timers. Yesterday, after Cupcake Shop Critic had waltzed out, he'd gone back to his office and scrutinized the sales numbers some more. Maybe if he stared hard and long enough, they would change. Or maybe he would develop some magical powers to make it happen. Why the hell not?

When he'd realized he'd ventured into hallucinogenic territory, it dawned on him that he knew someone who did know how to make magic. Who had turned an underachieving team into a major success story. He'd put in a call. "Look. It's just a meeting. Then I'll relax."

Nicholas's brows lifted. "You mean go work out for two hours?"

Damn it, why did his friends know him so well? His spine stiffened. "Owning a cupcake shop is—"

"—no excuse not to stay in football shape," his best friends finished for him.

He gave them the only response warranted. He flipped them the bird.

"Mature," Nicolas intoned. "But enough about that. Tell me about this mystery shopper. I want to hear the dirt straight from your mouth."

Donovan glared. Nicholas remained unfazed. Donovan sighed. Why didn't his glare work on his best friend? Or Cupcake Shop Critic? "Okay. Fine. She was talking shit about the store and said our cupcakes were stale. I wasn't in the mood to hear it, so I offered her a cupcake. End of story."

Nicholas rocked back on his heels. "Wow. I want to meet the woman who made you forget to be polite at all times."

Donovan's chin lifted. "I was polite."

A loud snort sounded from behind Donovan.

Donovan whirled toward the counter. Ella cleared her throat, gesturing toward her face. "Sorry. My nose. Allergies. Must be some pollen in the air."

Donovan glared. "Aren't there some dishes that need to be washed? Some inventory that needs to be taken?"

"Yep. On it, boss." She said it with a giggle, not in the least intimidated. That's what happened when you hired kids you'd babysat when you were a pimply faced teenager. No respect. She rounded the corner and slowly, *very* slowly, headed to the back of the building.

"Any chance the mystery shopper makes a return visit?" Nicholas asked, clearly not interested in being deterred from his gossip-gathering mission.

"Hell no." He ignored the sting of disappointment that swept through him, just like it had yesterday as she walked out of the store.

"Too bad," August said. Donovan shot him a look. *Now* he chose to speak?

Nicholas shook his head. "Man, I am so sorry I missed the show."

Donovan wasn't. It had not been his finest moment. More witnesses would have only made it worse.

"Was she cute at least?" Nicholas pressed.

A crystal-clear vision of stunning chocolaty brown eyes and perfect red lips filled his mind. Donovan threw up his hands. "Man, I don't know!"

"Yeah, she was," Ella tossed over her shoulder. She'd made it as far as Donovan's office down the hall, which was to say, not far at all.

"Something must be wrong with you if you didn't notice a pretty face." A considering light entered Nicholas's eyes. "Maybe you *did* notice."

"But you didn't like noticing," August said.

"Yep, sounds about right," Nicholas said. "Which makes the situation even more interesting." He and August nodded in unison.

Donovan pinched the bridge of his nose. Damn it, he needed new friends. Today. Right now. His phone dinged with the familiar appointment reminder tone. Thank God. "As much as I'd love to stay and continue this riveting conversation, I have somewhere to be. See you fools later."

He strode toward the door.

"Chicken," Nicholas called after him. Donovan kept walking, shooting his friends the deuces over his shoulder as he exited. He rounded the building to the parking lot and climbed inside his black Mercedes SUV.

Yeah, he'd engaged in very un-Donovan-like behavior yesterday, arguing with Cupcake Shop Critic, then thinking about her at random times since. But he'd returned to his senses. It was time to seek out the advice of someone he trusted implicitly.

Some might question his loyalty to the team owner. Football was a brutal sport with brutal economics. Those economics rarely, if ever, worked out in favor of the players. Yeah, they got paid well, but not as well as athletes in other sports. Worse, though, their contracts weren't fully guaranteed. But Mrs. T had always been straightforward with him. She said what she meant and meant what she said.

Her late husband had bought the team twenty years ago, and after he passed away five years later, she hadn't sold the team like all the experts had expected her to. Today, the Knights were one of the league's most successful franchises and worth over three billion dollars.

In other words, there was no one else he'd rather get advice from. If anyone knew how to beat the odds, it was her.

Twenty minutes later, he greeted the petite woman with a hug.

She always smelled like expensive perfume. She cared not one iota that her most famous employees towered over her and outweighed her on average by 130 pounds. He stepped back. She wore her salt-and-pepper hair in its customary I-mean-business bun, along with a sleek designer black dress. "How are you doing, Mrs. T?"

"I'm fabulous as always, Donovan." She gestured for him to follow her into her office that overlooked the practice field at the team's state-of-the-art training facility. "I can evaluate the players and coaches while getting other work done at the same time," she liked to say.

The office was actually a suite. Yes, it had the prerequisite working area of desk and chair, but it also housed a separate sitting area with a loveseat, several armchairs, and a minibar. A huge TV dominated one wall above a mantel, while shelves crammed with books lined the opposite wall. Photos of her family dotted the room, along with Knights memorabilia. He spotted a helmet he'd signed on his draft night on the mantel.

"Can I get you some coffee?" She gestured to the bar. "Or maybe something stronger?"

He thought he should refrain from pointing out that it was nine thirty in the morning. "Thanks for asking, but I'm good."

"Suit yourself." She picked up a black ceramic mug emblazoned with HBIC in red on one side and the Knights' silver shield logo on the other. Donovan chose not to worry about what else filled the cup besides coffee. She gestured for him to take one armchair while she sat across from him. She crossed her legs and leaned toward him. "How are you doing?"

Donovan rubbed the back of his neck. "I have some things on my mind."

"Are you sure you don't want something from my stash?" she asked with a smile and nod toward the bar. "I only supply the best."

He sighed. "It's tempting."

A concerned expression replaced her smile. "Are you sure you should be here without your agent? He'd have your hide if he thought you were negotiating a contract extension without him."

Donovan chuckled. "I can handle Adam. But, no, that's not why I'm here. It's not football-related. But we're both looking forward to the team's offer." He had one year left on his contract. Contract extension talks had already started between Donovan's agent and the team, but nothing was imminent. That's how contract negotiations went. He was used to it by now. Or as okay with it as a player could be.

This might be his last contract, certainly the last one guaranteed to come with a big payday, since he was an "aging" player at thirty. The NFL was wild that way.

"I'm sure you are." She settled back against the cushion and studied him. "Then what's troubling you?"

He sighed. "It's about Sugar Blitz."

She nodded, familiar with his latest venture. "Okay. What about it?"

He quickly explained the bakery's declining sales. She nodded, sipping her coffee while he spilled his guts. When he finished, he blew out a breath. "Maybe I will have that coffee." He stood and walked across the room to pour a cup. As he made the return trip, he prayed she'd come up with some words of wisdom during the delay.

"I'm sorry you haven't had the success you anticipated. I know how hard you work, so that's not the cause of the problem." She was quiet for a few seconds. "When I took over the team, I quickly realized I couldn't rest on my husband's laurels. I had to put my stamp on the team and impress the league, which was not interested in having a woman, a Black woman at that, running one of their precious franchises.

"I asked myself, 'What do I bring to the table? How can I make this team stand out—to fans and to players looking for a new team to play for?' The answer came to me right away. My listening skills are top notch. I listened to players, coaches, fans, league officials. Anyone who had an opinion on how to improve the team. I went from there."

Donovan nodded. "I thought I figured that out. Our cupcakes are the best in the city."

Her lips spread into a grin. "I know. That's why I have a standard weekly order for the front office staff."

"And it's greatly appreciated." He smiled for what felt like the first time since—well, since a certain cupcake shop critic visited his shop.

Mrs. T took another sip of coffee. "But it can't just be the cupcakes. People love cupcakes, but there are a lot of businesses supplying them. What makes people want to return to *your* store?"

He always appreciated her honesty. That's why he'd sought her opinion. She wasn't going to tell him what she thought he wanted to hear. He nodded. "I don't know, but I'll figure it out. I'll do whatever it takes to make Sugar Blitz successful."

She studied his face, then nodded. "I believe you will." She paused, her head tilting to the side in contemplation. She spoke slowly. "Yes, I do believe you will." She refocused on him, her expression now sharp and determined. "I have a favor to ask."

What was she plotting? Donovan set aside his mug, granting himself a precious second to respond, then gave the only answer that made any sense. "Anything you need."

She nodded as though his assent had always been assured. "You have your head on straight. You realize football doesn't last forever. You're focused. I admire your smarts. I always have. You know that."

He sensed there was more to her flattery than, well, flattery. "Thanks, Mrs. T."

Mrs. T set her mug on the end table next to her chair. "My granddaughter has recently moved back to town. She's struggled to find her place in the world, and I really believe she could benefit from learning from an entrepreneur. A go-getter like you."

The tension melted out of his shoulders. That was the favor? A job for her grandkid? "She doesn't want to work for the team?"

Mrs. T's lips quirked. "That comes with its own set of expectations and pressures that she doesn't need right now, and no, she doesn't want to work for the team. Crazy as it sounds, she's not much of a sports person. Neither is her mother, actually. It kills me, but it happens. I think she'd learn a lot from you."

He smiled. "We'd be happy to have her at Sugar Blitz."

What harm could it do? They could always use an extra set of hands at the shop. And hey, giving in on this matter might help in the upcoming contract negotiations. Nothing wrong with a little quid pro quo.

She clasped her hands together. "Wonderful. I'll pay her wages, of course."

Donovan's voice tightened. "I can pay my employees." Sugar Blitz might not be able to pay a manager out of its current profits, but he could and would pay any part-timers—out of his own pocket, if it came to that.

She nodded. "Pride and stubbornness. Qualities I understand all too well. I didn't mean to offend, but I'm know I'm foisting a new worker on you."

He shook his head. "You're not foisting anyone on me."

"Thank you, but I'm sorry nevertheless." Her apology was genuine. She was genuine. That's why he looked up to her.

He smiled. "Apology accepted. But I'm paying her."

She chuckled, patting him on the arm. "You're a good man, Donovan."

A sharp knock sounded on the door.

Her eyes brightened. "That must be her. Come in," she called out.

Donovan rose alongside her as Stacey, Mrs. T's longtime assistant, entered. Someone, presumably the aforementioned granddaughter, stood behind her, but Stacey blocked Donovan's view. Granddaughter was no taller than grandmother, it seemed.

"Mrs. T, Jada is here," Stacey said. "On time," she added in a stage whisper.

"I can hear you, you know," Jada said dryly.

Donovan froze. That voice . . .

"Sorry." Stacey stepped aside, giving Donovan his first clear view of his newest employee. Who just happened to have perfect lips and eyes the color of dark chocolate chips.

His mouth dropped open. So did the granddaughter's.

"You!" they cried out in unison.

Chapter Four

An all-consuming rush of embarrassment swept through Jada. Had he known who she was after all? Or had he figured it out somehow and come here to blackmail her grandmother or something?

"Do you know each other?" Grams asked, a confused yet interested glint flickering in her eyes.

There was no way she was going to relive yesterday's fiasco with her grandmother with the cause of said fiasco standing right there, giving off his stern principal vibes. In her extensive experience, vice principals tried to be your friend, while principals were the disciplinarians. It wasn't like she could ignore him, though. Grams's office was large and roomy, but he still took up too much space. Her eyes were drawn to him, as was his to hers, apparently.

Grams cleared her throat, obviously not interested in being ignored.

"No," Jada quickly replied.

"Yes," Donovan said at the same time.

Jada tried not to squirm as Grams let those contradictory answers linger in the air for a few seconds. "I see," she finally said. "Or maybe I don't. Is there something going on here I should know about?"

"Nope." Jada gave her grandmother the best "I'm innocent, nothing to see here" smile she could muster. All those professional acting lessons had to pay off at some point, right?

"Are you sure?" Grams lifted an eyebrow while crossing her arms and leaning against her desk.

Not good. Grams was a smart woman and could and would start asking really excellent questions any moment.

That crisis needed to be averted more than kitten heels. *Think, Jada, think.* "What I meant to say is that no, we don't know each other, but we did meet briefly yesterday when I stepped into that cupcake shop by the stadium. Such a funny coincidence."

She even ended on a slight chuckle. She ignored the slight snort from the dude. What was his name anyway? Who was he?

"Sugar Blitz." Grams clasped her hands together, her eyes opening wide. "That's terrific!"

"It is?" Her grandmother had heard of the bakery, which was okay. What was *not* okay? Her grandmother's excitement that Jada had heard of the bakery. And why was Stern Principal Dude in Grams's office looking way too comfortable? Her gaze flicked his way once again. Massive shoulders were still massive. Thick thighs were still thick. His jeans and Henley did nothing to hide those irrefutable facts.

A sinking feeling rumbled in her stomach. He wasn't large just because he was large. He was large because . . .

"Donovan plays for the Knights, honey, so yes," Grams said. "You'd know that if you took an interest in the team, which is part of your legacy."

Yeah, add that to her list of shortcomings. She didn't care much about football and felt little to no shame about that fact, but sticking her foot in her mouth was a whole 'nother matter. Oh, God. Spontaneous Jada had struck again. The rumbling in her stomach increased in agitation. "Oh."

"I also own Sugar Blitz, by the way," Donovan added. Yeah, she'd figured that out, too. Insult the man's cupcakes, insult the man. She was batting a thousand or scoring a game-winning touchdown, to use football lingo. But he still had that disapproving look on his face, so she didn't feel one hundred percent bad. More like ninety percent. His frown deepened as her gaze lingered. Okay, make that eighty-five percent.

His jaw worked side to side before he spoke, the deep timbre of his voice filling the air. "Did you come to the store on some type of reconnaissance mission? Get the lay of the land?"

Jada's mouth fell open. "What? No! Why would *I* do that?" Add arrogant to his list of attributes.

His lips twisted in a self-satisfied grin.

Jada swallowed a growl. Barely. He was messing with her. Trying to get a rise out of her. And damn it, it was working, and he knew it.

"I'm so happy you've been there. You liked the product, I presume?" Grams interjected.

Oh, great.

Now Stern Prin—no, *Donovan*—was studying her with unvarnished interest. She couldn't go with "decent" again because that would only arouse Grams's interest, and he knew it. Was it too early to declare Donovan her nemesis? She'd known him for less than twenty-four hours, after all.

Ignore him. Jada turned to face her grandmother. "I did like them."

"Oh, really?" he marveled from behind her.

Her eyes cut to him. He was laughing at her. Jada's teeth

clenched. No, it wasn't too early to declare him her sworn enemy. It was right on time, actually.

"I'm so happy to hear that because I had the most marvelous idea." Grams beamed, clearly clueless to the undercurrents of dislike flowing in her office.

"What's that?" Jada managed to push out of a dry throat. Her stomach was still heaving. Grams looked way too pleased with herself. Where was a bottle of extra strength Pepto-Bismol when she needed it?

"Donovan has agreed to let you work at Sugar Blitz for the next six months." Right when she would turn twenty-six. Grams had thought of everything.

The roller coaster of her stomach dove straight down to her knees. Jada blinked. "I'm sorry. What?"

"You heard me. Wasn't that nice of him?"

Calm was currently out of reach, but she grasped for it anyway, even as she felt it slipping through her fingers like grains of sand. "Grams, you can't ask him to do that."

"Why not? You need a job. He has a job." Hurricane Grams had struck again with her infallible logic.

Jada sputtered. "Be-because . . ."

"If she doesn't want to do it, I certainly don't want to force her," Donovan said, all superior principal talking to a recalcitrant student's parent. And just like that, Jada opened her mouth to exclaim her eagerness to accept a job with the great Donovan. She caught herself in the nick of time. Only a small *meep* escaped. "Grams, really, I don't think this is . . ." Her voice trailed off as Grams's eyes narrowed.

"Hmm," her grandmother said. "Donovan, do you mind if I speak to my granddaughter alone? We'll be in touch later today."

Donovan's gaze met Jada's briefly before he nodded. "Of course, Mrs. T. I look forward to working with you, Jada."

The way he said her name, with a hint of mockery in the soft drawl, made her want to pop him in his smart mouth. But she wasn't a violent person, or so she'd always believed. She forced her lips into a replica of a smile instead. "Have a nice day."

That was the best she could do. No way could she say she was looking forward to working with him. 'Cause it wasn't going to happen.

He nodded once more, then departed.

"Would you like to tell me what's going on with you and one of my favorite players?" Grams asked as soon as the door softly clicked shut behind Donovan.

Damn, Grams never missed anything. "Nothing, Grams. Like I said, I went into his store yesterday and bought a cupcake. That's it."

Grams didn't look convinced. "What did you think of the cupcake?"

"Like I said, it was good."

"Then you should have no problem working there."

Jada threw up her hands. "Oh, my God, Grams, what did you tell him? He must think I'm pathetic if I need my grandmother to find me a job." A fresh wave of mortification smacked her square in the face.

Grams lifted her chin, the only sign she may have thought she'd overstepped. "He thinks no such thing. I simply told him you were looking for a job and I thought you could learn a lot from him."

"And what did he say when you brought up this proposal?"

"He said he'd love to hire you."

"Because he had no other choice. You sign his paychecks." Jada groaned.

"Be that as it may, he's a very nice man." Jada caught herself before a snort escaped. "More importantly, he recognizes how fleeting a career in professional football can be and has set himself up nicely to continue to succeed after his playing career ends. I wasn't wrong. You *can* learn a lot from him."

Jada's shoulders slumped at the reminder of her aimlessness even though Grams hadn't meant it to be a slight. "I told you I could find a job by myself."

Grams's eyebrows lifted. "And have you?"

Jada glanced away. "No. But we just talked last night!"

"I know, sweetie. I'm not doing this to punish you. I actually think it could be fun. It's a cupcake shop. That should be—what's that word you young people like? Oh, yes. *Lit.*"

Jada groaned. "Grams, please never use that word again."

Grams shrugged. "Why not? I own a football team. I have to be able to communicate with my players."

"Grams . . ."

"This is my final offer. It's time for you to apply yourself. Time to stick to something for longer than a month."

Jada knew that. Had known that before she went on *My One and Only.* That didn't mean she wanted to work with *him.* But she couldn't voice that opinion without rousing suspicion. So she went with her next best option. Facts. "I don't cook. I can't cook."

"Luckily, you'll be baking. I'm sure Donovan will be more than happy to give you some pointers."

No, that was the last thing she wanted or needed. Spending more time than necessary with Principal . . . "Grams, what's Donovan's last name?"

Grams sighed in clear despair about her granddaughter's lack of knowledge about her life's work. "Dell. His name is Donovan Dell. He's only one of the best defensive ends in the league."

Whatever that meant. She had a full name now. Donovan Dell. She rolled the name around in her head. A strong name to go with a strong-minded and physically strong man. Not that any of that was important. "I'm sure Mr. Dell has more important things to do than look after me."

"You'll be working in his business. I'm sure it will be fine."

Grams had an answer for everything. Now Jada was desperate. Grasping at straws. "As true as that may be, Grams, do I look like the type to wear a polo and, God forbid, a hairnet? That's not really my style." She waved a hand down her figure. A visit with her grandmother was no excuse not to look cute. Casual, but cute. A red-and-white-striped romper paired with some cute Jimmy Choo sandals. She'd pulled her hair into a sleek high ponytail and gone for a natural makeup glow. A perfect look for a sunny San Diego day.

Grams leveled a hard look on her. "I know you like fashion, and I've always encouraged that interest, but spare me the ditzy routine. I know you are anything but."

Jada's shoulders deflated.

"Haven't I always had your best interests at heart?"

Jada nodded, unable to deny that claim. Her grandmother had always had her back.

"What's really going on here?"

"I guess I thought I could figure things out on my own." She hadn't expected Grams to actually have a plan in place before Jada stepped foot in her office. She also hadn't been positive that her grandmother had been serious. She'd thought she could cajole Grams into giving her early access to her trust fund. But Grams was deadly serious.

"And you still have time. You're only twenty-five. This is temporary. When your six months are up, you'll have your trust fund and fully become the captain of your own ship. I have faith in you."

Jada wasn't so sure. She'd rarely succeeded or stuck with anything for long. She didn't know how this situation would be any different—not working for that man, anyway. But she did want her trust fund. She stifled yet another groan. Who was she kidding? She needed a job *now,* forget the trust fund. Money was money, and in less than two weeks, she wouldn't have any coming in. She couldn't tell Grams what her parents had done. She didn't want to be the source of a potential rift between her mom and her grandmother.

What was a little flour, hairnets, and a polyblend polo compared to all that? It was only for a few months. Donovan couldn't be the only person who worked at Sugar Blitz. She'd hang out, ignore him, make enough money to buy groceries and pay her bills, and collect her trust fund at the end of her sentence, thank you very much.

Great. It looked like her nemesis had become her mentor. Absolutely freaking great.

* * *

Donovan jumped like a skittish cat when the bell over the front door chimed. His shoulders slumped when a harried man in a business suit rushed inside. "It's my daughter's day to bring in snacks to her first-grade class, and I completely forgot."

Donovan smiled. "No worries, man. I got you." He welcomed the distraction. He'd been antsy since he woke up that morning.

Not that he was counting down the minutes until his newest hire, Jada Townsend-Matthews, arrived. He just didn't know what to expect, that was all. He liked order and sensible actions. Jada promised neither of those things.

He'd been more than a little surprised to get the email from Mrs. T's assistant last night letting him know Jada couldn't wait to start at Sugar Blitz.

No message from Jada herself, of course. Not that he'd anticipated one. But today was a new day, and she'd be walking through the door any second now. In any case, he needed to pay attention to the most important person in this shop. "What's your daughter's favorite flavor?"

He was working the front counter by himself this morning. Nicholas was in the kitchen working on a new cupcake flavor, August wasn't scheduled until the afternoon, and Ella was running late.

The proud dad smiled. "Chocolate with sprinkles."

"Sounds good. Why don't we go with a mixture of chocolate and vanilla?"

The guy's face relaxed with relief. "Perfect. I'll need a dozen."

After grabbing a to-go box, Donovan opened the display case and extracted the agreed-upon goodies. As always, his stomach rumbled as soon as the intoxicating scents of chocolate, cream, and sugar hit his nose. He knew from extensive taste-testing that the cupcakes were spectacular. Nicholas had perfected the simple but incredibly important recipes during his first year with the Knights, when he'd been a nervous rookie looking to blow off some steam.

The customer handed over his credit card. "Thanks, again. You're a lifesaver. I never thought I'd say this, but I'm not talking about what you do on the football field. I am a huge fan, but this tops that by a mile. I'm going to be the coolest dad in first-grade history thanks to these cupcakes."

Donovan smiled. "Glad I could be of service. Be sure to come back."

"I absolutely will." The dad headed to the door while Donovan reached under the register and grabbed more to-go boxes to restock the counter.

"Oh, hey, sorry," the dad said. "I was in such a rush I didn't see you there."

"It's okay," a soft, bougie voice answered. "No harm, no foul."

Donovan's head snapped up. Jada stood just inside the front entrance. She was smiling at the dad. Donovan sucked in a breath. A perfect face had, somehow inexplicably, become even more perfect with the simple action. That he wasn't the recipient of said action meant nothing. Hell, he hadn't even known she knew how to smile.

The dad held up the box. "I'm in a rush. Got to get these to my daughter's school before snack time." Yet he didn't move, obviously mesmerized by the stunning woman in front of him.

Delight spread across her face. "Oh, that's so nice. I would have loved if my dad had brought cupcakes to my class. Your daughter's so lucky."

The dad, who clearly wasn't in that damn big of a hurry, fucking preened. "Oh, it's nothing. You're too kind."

Okay, yeah, that was enough of the mutual admiration society. Donovan cleared his throat. Jada's gaze swung his way. The smile instantly faded away from her expressive face. He would not feel some type of way about how she'd gone from joy to annoyance in a nanosecond thanks to him.

The dad looked his way, his giddy grin sliding away once his gaze landed on Donovan's face. He nodded at Jada one more time and *finally* departed. Leaving Donovan alone with his newest employee. His boss's granddaughter. Who'd stood in this very shop two days ago and called his cupcakes decent and the ambience stale.

A tension headache pulsed behind his right eye.

FML.

"Nice to see you're still rolling out the red carpet for customers," Jada said, strolling into the shop like she owned the place.

"You're an employee, not a customer," he said, even as he inwardly winced. Damn, he needed to get it together. He was never like this. He sounded like a curmudgeon. And he sounded even more like a curmudgeon for using the word "curmudgeon." Damn all those crossword puzzles his grandfather liked to rope his grandson into helping him solve.

Her perfect eyebrows arched. "Indeed I am. Thanks for the reminder."

"I wasn't sure you would show up." Donovan walked around the counter to stand by her.

She mock gasped. "But then I wouldn't be able to see that grumpy puss look on your face, especially those scrunched-up eyebrows."

"There's nothing wrong with my face." Donovan immediately worked to smooth his features, balling his hands into fists at his sides to keep from checking his eyebrows. He would not give her the satisfaction. Make that *more* satisfaction, since she was already smirking at him.

"I'm sorry. Can we start over?" He held out his hand. She stared at it like it was an alien tentacle and if she deigned to touch it, he would swoop her up and take her back to his lair on some faraway planet. "Never mind."

She grasped his hand as he was retreating. Their palms met. A dizzying electric charge shot up his arm, shocking him literally and figuratively. His gaze locked on to Jada's. The shock, the awareness was easy to identify in her gorgeous brown eyes.

He needed to say something. Do something. Their hands remained clasped. Her skin was soft, and he had no inclination to let go.

"No, you're right," she said, sliding her hand away and stepping back, leaving him feeling oddly bereft. He'd forgotten what she was agreeing to.

"Let's start over," she added when he didn't speak.

"Right. Okay," he said slowly, his brain still whirling, his hand still tingling. They still maintained eye contact.

The bell above the door jingled. "Donovan, I'm so sorry I'm late," Ella said in a rush as she came in. "I needed to make sure my paper was perfect before I turned it in, and I fell asleep without setting my alarm. It won't happen again." Her torrent of words stopped when she spotted Jada. Her eyes widened in recognition. "Hi. Nice to see you again. What are you doing here?"

Donovan marshalled as many brain cells as he could. "She's our newest hire. Ella, can you show her around for a bit? I have to do . . . something, yeah, something, in my office."

He left her with Ella and escaped. He didn't run. If his gait was a little faster than normal, it was just a coincidence. He definitely was *not* running.

* * *

An hour later, Nicholas stuck his head into Donovan's office. "I'm done with the latest batch of s'mores cupcakes. I think I'm almost there with the recipe. The marshmallow isn't overwhelming the chocolate and graham crackers anymore. I'm going to need you to do a taste test."

Donovan spread his hands apart. "A hard job, but someone's gotta do it. Hey, Nich—"

"Can you hold that thought? I want to give Ella the heads-up, too. The last time I didn't tell her about a new flavor taste test, I didn't hear the end of it for two weeks." Nicholas disappeared before Donovan could object. His business partner returned less than thirty seconds later. He shut the door behind him and leaned against it, crossing his arms. His eyes squinted in confusion. "Um, who is that out there with Ella?"

Donovan sighed. "Our newest employee."

Nicholas blinked. "We're hiring?"

Donovan nodded. "Yes, especially when she's Mrs. T's grand-daughter."

"Oh, okay. Sure. I guess your meeting with Mrs. T was fruitful." His head tilted to the side. "I only got a quick look at her, but she's fine as fuck."

Donovan held up a hand, studiously ignoring the flare of . . . something vaguely *greenish* temporarily blurring his vision. "One, no, you're not dating an employee. Two, you're sure as hell not dating our boss's granddaughter." He hesitated. "Three, she's also the woman who came in the other day, you know the one who had a lot to say about the shop."

Nicholas's mouth gaped open. "Noooo. Tell me more."

Damn gossipmonger. "There is nothing more."

A hard knock sounded on the door. Nicholas moved out of the way as Donovan told the newcomer to enter.

A second later, August walked in. "Why is there a strange woman behind the counter with Ella?"

Nicholas closed the door. "Good timing. I was about to get the scoop."

"There is no scoop," Donovan said through clenched teeth.

"You mean hiring the woman who talked shit about the shop doesn't count as scoop? I don't know about that," Nicholas said.

"You hired the woman who talked shit about the shop?" August chimed in, his puzzlement clear.

"Yes," Nicholas said eagerly. "And we're not allowed to date her because he already put in his claim."

Donovan's teeth ground together. "There is no claim. She's a grown woman who can do what she pleases. Regardless, you need to keep your hands to yourself." Nicholas could and had charmed the panties off countless women. Undoubtedly, Jada would respond to Nicholas's approach better than she had to Donovan's brusque, argumentative, combative demeanor. Which wasn't his usual state. He was usually thoroughly logical and calm. Not that it mattered what his state was. He wasn't interested in her. She wasn't interested in him, and even if those statements weren't true, they still wouldn't date. Jumping into a relationship would only distract him from his goals.

"So she works here now?" August asked, still clearly confused. "You sure that's a good idea?"

"Yes." Donovan quickly explained the situation, ignoring the way his business partners' facial expressions cycled between amusement, confusion, astonishment, understanding, and in Nicholas's case, utter giddiness. "Don't worry. She'll report to me, and I'll train her."

Nicholas nudged August with his elbow. "Told you. He already put in a claim."

Donovan glared at his best friend. "Get out of my office."

Chapter Five

Jada hung back while Ella helped a customer. She didn't know what else to do. She was so out of her element.

Ella kept staring at her like she was a bug under a microscope, only pausing her inspection when she had to help customers. Two men she assumed were Donovan's business partners and teammates, based on their physiques, had taken one look at her and disappeared around the same corner as Donovan had earlier.

Jada was mostly just trying to stay out of the way. She didn't want to drop the merchandise or accidentally give the wrong product to a customer or any other of the limitless possible calamities running roughshod through her brain.

If her gaze kept sliding to the hallway, where her erstwhile boss had fled like the hounds of hell were chasing him, well, that was simply because he was the only person she knew here. It wasn't like she missed or anticipated their antagonistic banter or anything.

But the latest customer was walking away from the counter carrying a to-go box, and Ella was back to staring at her, twirling one of her shoulder blade–length box braids around her finger. She was a cute girl, a few inches taller than Jada, with curious brown eyes, a round face, and medium-brown skin.

"How long have you worked here?" Jada asked to break up the awkwardness.

"Well, the store's only been open a little less than three months. I've been here since the beginning. I've known Donovan my whole life. My family lived next door to his in Oakland. When I moved here for college, I needed a job with flexible hours, he needed the help, so here I am." Her eyes widened. "Don't worry. He's old, and he's basically my big brother."

Jada chuckled. Donovan couldn't be a day over thirty. Then, the other part of Ella's response registered. She blinked. "Worry?"

"I was here the other day when you came in."

"Oh." For some reason, she had a hard time remembering any-thing other than her umm, *spirited,* exchange with Donovan from that encounter.

"I also saw y'all when I walked in today," Ella added, like that explained everything. "It was kinda hot," she continued when Jada stared at her blankly.

How to respond to that? "Umm . . ."

Ella snapped her fingers. "Now I remember where I know you from. It's been bothering me. I saw it on Instagram. You're that girl from that show!"

Every muscle in Jada's body froze.

"I can't believe you did that," Ella continued. "It was so cool."

"It was?" No one had said that to her. She'd been the recipient of so much online vitriol, it hadn't occurred to her that some-one could be sympathetic to her decision to decline the offer of marriage.

Ella nodded. "Oh, yeah. If you weren't feeling him, you shouldn't have accepted his proposal, and you didn't, and it was dope!"

It took a second for the compliment, an actual compliment, to sink in. "Thanks."

Ella scrutinized her for a second, then nodded. "Want to take the lead with the next customer?"

"Um, sure." Guess Ella had decided to cut her a break. Jada took the lifeline. For the first time that morning, she began to relax.

The bell dinged, and a woman with her natural curls pulled into a puff on top of her head, black leggings, and a T-shirt proclaiming BOOKS R YOUR FRIENDS! walked in. She practically bounced to the counter. To have that much energy must be exhausting.

Ella gave Jada a look. Her time was now. Jada took a deep breath. She could do this. And she wanted to do this. This was her job, and she didn't want to screw it up. Besides needing a paycheck, she wanted to prove she could do what it took to make her grandmother proud. She wanted to prove to *herself* that she could stick to something and see it through to the end. This was her chance to be a better Jada. A less impulsive Jada. More mature. She filled her lungs with air, then exhaled. "Welcome to Sugar Blitz. How can I help you?"

The customer stopped her perusal of the display case to look up. "Hi, I've never seen you here before."

Jada smiled. "Today is my first day."

"I'm Kendra. I own the gym down the street." She adjusted the tortoiseshell glasses on her nose. "How's your first day going?"

Jada shifted from one foot to the other. "It's going. I'm just trying to get the lay of the land."

"Well, Sugar Blitz has the best cupcakes in the city. I'm a cupcake aficionado. I know these things. I stopped by out of curiosity right after they opened, and I've been making at least three visits per week ever since."

Jada laughed. "How long have you owned the gym?"

"A little over five years. Do you like romance?"

"Um, well . . ." She didn't hate it exactly, but given the state of her love life before, during, and after the show, the less thought given to that topic, the better. Was the question a segue into asking about the show?

Kendra waved her hand. "I'll take that as a yes." She pointed to her book-lovers shirt. "I run a monthly romance book club, we have a meeting coming up, and we can always use more members. Different, new viewpoints are always welcome. So you'll come?"

Jada blinked at the rapid-fire invitation. "I'll think about it."

Kendra grabbed a napkin off the counter and reached into her purse, pulling out a pen. She quickly scribbled on the paper. "The book we're reading this month is called *No Cowgirl Left Behind*. I don't expect you to remember that, so I'm writing it down. We want to encourage reading in whatever capacity feels right for the reader, so you can do physical book, ebook, or audio if that's better for you, or check it out of the library." She gave the spiel all without taking a breath.

Jada took the paper because she didn't know what else to do. "Oh. Okay."

"I'm going to also take that as a yes." Kendra winked. "That's how I've managed to be successful for five years. I'll take three strawberry vanilla cupcakes and two chocolate peanut butter. It's one of my staffers' birthdays and the chocolate peanut butter is her favorite. We work out and then we treat ourselves." She stared at Jada expectantly.

Jada started. "Right. Three strawberry vanilla and two chocolate peanut butter coming right up." Earlier, while she'd loitered behind the counter, she'd also studied Ella intently. She grabbed a box first, then scooped the desserts up and placed them gingerly in the box, snapping the box closed with a jaunty gesture. Kendra paid with a credit card, a payment type the cash register made easy to accept.

When the receipt printed without delay, Jada did a little shoulder shimmy. Hey, maybe she wouldn't be so bad at this after all.

"Perfect." Kendra pointed to the napkin Jada had set aside. "See you here tomorrow and next week at book club. The location is a little up in the air right now, but we should have a place nailed down soon. And no, 'no' is not in my vocabulary." She winked. "I can't wait to get to know you better, Jada Townsend-Matthews." She exited the store like a whirling dervish.

Jada's mouth dropped. Kendra had known who she was. But she didn't have much time to think about it because more customers entered. Ella let her handle them all, and she quickly fell into a rhythm, welcoming them to the store, taking orders, not dropping cupcakes, and taking payment with Ella there to guide her when someone asked for a special cupcake only available on Wednesdays.

She enjoyed talking to the customers, learning about how their days were going and why they chose the flavors they did. If the next few months went like this, her trust fund would be hers in no time, giving her the freedom to chart the course of her life on her own terms with no interference from her loved ones.

As she wiped some crumbs off the counter, her motions stilled. The atmosphere in the room had changed. Become charged. Electric. Exactly like when she'd touched Donovan's hand earlier. Her eyes zeroed in on the spot where Donovan was rounding the corner, followed by the other two men. They were a striking group, all large, fit, and each attractive in his own way, but she only had eyes for the one she'd met. He stopped in front of the counter and stared at her.

She lifted an eyebrow. She wasn't intimidated. She couldn't be.

She was Jada Townsend-Matthews, even if she had a hard time figuring out what that meant on any given day. But he didn't know that. He'd been coerced into having her here. Oh, well. She wasn't going to act desperate to have a job. Even though she totally was. Besides, it wasn't like he could fire her. Her grandmother would have his hide. At that thought, her lips split into a grin.

His shoulders stiffened, his spine going ramrod straight. Poor dude. If he didn't stop doing that, he would end up frozen in that position, and oops, there would go his football career. Her smile widened.

He cleared his throat, no doubt expecting everyone in the room to give him their undivided attention. Just like a principal at a school assembly. "Jada, I'd like to introduce you to my partners, Nicholas Connors and August Hodges."

She squinted at them. "Let me guess. You guys play for the Knights, too?"

Nicholas sidled up to the counter next to his teammate. "What gave it away? Our aura? Powerful physiques?" His gray eyes twinkled. Flirting was obviously his natural state of being. He probably flirted with every woman who came into the place. And while he was definitely good-looking, she felt not an ounce of attraction to him. He was harmless.

Playing along was no hardship and equally harmless. She tilted her head to the side. "Powerful physiques? I hadn't noticed."

Beside her, Ella snickered. "Jada, you're my new best friend."

Nicholas side-eyed the teen before returning his gaze to Jada. "Oh, wow. Ruthless. Dagger to the heart, lady." He slapped a hand over his chest.

Jada laughed. "It's the only way I know how to be."

He leaned an elbow on the counter, shot a quick look over his shoulder at Donovan, then winked at her. "I like you. You're the woman of my dreams."

Jada laughed, recognizing the joke for what it was. She liked him. He clearly didn't take himself too seriously, and she'd missed laughing. Had almost forgotten how good it felt to indulge in the activity.

"Chill, Nicholas," Donovan said, that stern principal voice making a reappearance. "Don't you have some baking to do?"

Nicholas winked at her again, clearly not fazed by his business partner, and stepped aside. "I just finished, as you know. I'll be right back. Yes, Ella, I was going to tell you I'd finished my latest test batch, not that you deserve to taste my latest culinary effort." He turned back to Jada with a hand over his heart. "Please promise you'll still be here when I return."

Jada nodded solemnly. "I promise."

While he departed, the other man, who'd been silently observing the scene, held out his hand. "Nice to meet you. I'm August." His voice was gruff and deep and slightly hesitant.

She shook his hand. Unsurprisingly, his large hand swallowed hers, but his shake was surprisingly gentle. "Nice to meet you. I'm Jada."

August nodded once and said nothing else. Obviously, he was a man of few words, but he had kind eyes. Curious, too, but his quietness worked in her favor there, so she'd take it.

Nicholas returned a few seconds later, carrying a tray of cupcakes. Jada's mouth watered. She could smell the marshmallows all the way across the room. Her stomach rumbled when he reached the counter and she got a good look at the desserts.

"Be kind, everyone," Nicholas said, wringing his hands. "I'm close to perfecting the recipe. I'm almost there, but not quite yet. They're gluten-free, so we can offer them to a wider clientele." The flirt had turned into a nervous, yet serious baker. "Jada, as our newest employee, you get first taste." Maybe not completely serious. A flirt was gonna flirt.

To her untrained eye, the cupcakes looked perfect. They smelled delicious. He handed her one, and she took a big bite. The perfect combination of milk chocolate, graham crackers, and fluffy, sweet marshmallows burst onto her tongue. She couldn't stop a moan from slipping past her lips. She was officially in love.

"Better than decent, I take it?" Donovan drawled in her ear. Jada froze as a treacherous yet delicious shiver raced down her spine, then turned to face him. He'd come around the counter and was standing right next to her, the heat from his body seeping into hers.

She lifted her head to meet his challenging gaze. She took another delightful bite and swallowed. "Yep. They're terrific. You didn't make them, did you?"

There went his spine again. She should stop baiting him. He was her boss, after all. But he made it so easy, and it was so much fun. And she hadn't had much fun lately. She deserved some fun. And he'd started it. This time, anyway.

Behind him, his co-owners snickered. He glared at them over his shoulder, then returned his attention to her. "Let me give you a tour of the place."

"Done with the *something* in your office?" She really was going to stop. Probably. She would try.

"Let's go." He turned on his heel, undoubtedly expecting her to follow him. She did the only thing she could. She followed him.

And stuck her tongue out at his ramrod-straight, retreating back. While trying not to notice how his tucked-in shirt drew attention to the way his wide shoulders tapered into an eye-catching vee. And to how his pants cupped a world-class butt.

Jada bit her lip.

Yep. Totally not noticing.

* * *

Donovan headed to the kitchen. Even without Jada's reminder, he felt guilty for abandoning her earlier. He knew, without looking, that she followed him. He just knew. He felt her presence. His skin tingled whenever she was near. He was almost getting used to it.

He pushed the door open and held his breath as she slipped past him. Despite his action, an intoxicating hint of the light, floral scent she wore slipped through his defenses. It was delicate but alluring all the same. It was doing its damn job, making him want to lean in and find out if it smelled the same that way all over her body.

"So you were talking to your boys about me?"

Her voice jarred him out of his dangerous musings. He focused on the cause of his distraction. She was leaning against the refrigerator, her red-painted lips twisted into a taunting smile.

His feet, clearly working on their own accord, moved closer to her. "What makes you say that?"

She held up her index finger. "Well, you didn't deny it, first of all." Another finger went up. "Second clue was the way Nicholas came around the corner, saw me, immediately turned around, and disappeared." One more finger joined the party. "Third, the way August walked in, saw me, and kept walking."

Donovan crossed his arms over his chest. "Oh, you noticed all that?"

"Kind of hard not to see." Her nose wrinkled, and though he would never tell another soul, it was kind of cute. Adorable even.

"Sorry about that," Nicholas said from behind him. Donovan whirled. Where had he come from?

Shrugging his apology, Nicholas held up an empty tray. August and Ella had obviously cleaned him out of the remaining test kitchen s'mores cupcakes. "I'll be out of your hair in second." He turned the smile women never resisted on Jada. "Unless you want me to stick around. I'm a better tour guide than he is."

She laughed, the soft lilt filling the air. "I appreciate the offer, but don't let me hold you up. I'm going to gird my loins and take my chances with your teammate here."

Nicholas laughed. "I can't believe you're Mrs. T's granddaughter. She's the best."

"She is. I'm lucky to have her." She smiled at Nicholas. Again. She had yet to smile at Donovan like that, not that it mattered. It was just something he noticed. Nicholas smiled back.

Donovan growled. He couldn't stop himself.

"You okay?" she asked.

Nicholas slapped him on the back. "He's fine. Just missing some fiber in his diet. And I'm going to leave before he decides protein is more important and throws me in the oven to roast. I've got to get a nap in before my big date tonight anyway. I'll see you tomorrow, Jada." He pointed at Donovan. "Don't destroy my kitchen."

Donovan rolled his eyes, but finally, his teammate was gone. He didn't expect any more interruptions. Ella had to watch the front counter, and August avoided people as much as possible.

Leaving Donovan all alone with Jada. Which was nothing to get excited about, his pounding heart notwithstanding. Everything was fine. They could get through the next hour without killing each other.

"Nap?" she asked, her brow wrinkling. "It's barely noon."

"He gets here at 6 A.M. to prep for the day, and I'm not sure of the last day he had that didn't end with a date. He definitely needs a midday nap." He held his breath. How would she react to that news?

"Busy boy," she said casually. "I've had a few exes like that." She shrugged. "Fun for a while, but then . . ."

He so did not want to hear about her previous relationships. "What do you say I give you a baking lesson? I do know how to bake, you know."

Her lips curved again. "That got to you, huh?"

Yes. "Nicholas is the lead baker, but we all bake. We have to in order to keep this place going."

Her pretty, chocolaty brown eyes twinkled with excitement—and challenge. "Then show me what you know."

Chapter Six

Jada loitered while Donovan gathered the necessary ingredients and equipment to make cupcakes. She'd never given it much thought, but now she knew. A guy who knew what he was doing in the kitchen was hot as hell. But that was just a general observation. Nothing to do with Donovan specifically.

She turned in a slow circle to survey the kitchen, which took up a large portion of the back of the building. A light and bright area filled with multiple stainless steel counters. Clean, high-end equipment. Donovan and his business partners had obviously spared no expense.

A grunt had her eyes returning to her new boss. Just because she noticed the way his biceps flexed in mesmerizing fashion, thanks to the polo's short sleeves, meant nothing. That little crease that appeared between his eyebrows as he concentrated wasn't cute at all.

"What?" she asked.

Donovan's head was bent low. He pointed at her feet. "What are those?"

"Shoes." Very cute shoes, actually. Jimmy Choo sandals, to be exact.

"They're heels." Uh-oh. Stern Principal had reappeared. His frown deepened. "We work in a bakery. We're on our feet all day."

Her morning had gone well, all things considered. She would not let him get to her. She used her friendliest tone. "I thought about that, so I wore my most comfortable wedges."

They were only three inches. She usually stuck to a minimum of four inches, but concessions and all. She'd already relented enough. Donovan had instructed, through Grams's assistant, that she wear a plain white button-down shirt and either khakis or black pants. She'd gone with slacks because who in the world owned, let alone *wore*, khakis. Eww. The shoes were a must.

She loved clothes, but she absolutely *adored* shoes. They took any outfit from good—or, in this case, positively boring—to great and gave her an extra boost of confidence whenever she looked at her feet.

"I'm assuming wedges is a synonym for heels." He didn't look or sound impressed by her ingenuity.

"More *type* than synonym," she said, wiggling her hand back and forth.

His frown deepened, which she hadn't thought was possible. What was his deal?

"Don't worry. I'll be fine. I mean we all can't pull off plain black sneakers with two-inch soles." Oops, she hadn't meant to add that last part.

He shot her a look that clearly said he was tired of her shit, but luckily said nothing more about her footwear. Good, because the shoes were starting to bother her just a little. But she'd never admit it, not to him anyway. Yes, she was used to wearing heels, but usually she had breaks here and there or could count on a chair magically appearing, but today, not so much. But at least the black wedges were cute.

He strode over to a tall cabinet, reached inside, and pulled out two brown aprons with the store's logo emblazoned on them, then returned to her side. "Here you go."

Their fingers brushed as they completed the transfer. She studiously ignored the frisson of heat that raced up her arm at the contact and the way she drew in a breath at his closeness. The way her fingers trembled as she tied the apron strings around her waist under his intense gaze. "Not sure brown is my color."

"You look fine." He turned away before she could process the compliment, if she could even label his statement as such. He sounded almost resentful.

"Thanks. I think."

A beep chimed through the air. Donovan dug his phone out of his pocket and stared at the screen for a few seconds, his face going blank, the ticking muscle in his jaw the only sign he wasn't as calm as he appeared.

"You okay?" It wasn't her place to ask—she barely knew him— but she recognized when someone was being affected by something he didn't want to affect him.

He slid the phone back into his pocket. "Never better."

She didn't believe him, but again, she didn't know him, so she simply nodded.

He rubbed his forehead like he was trying to erase whatever thought was crowding his brain, then pointed to the bowls on the table in front of him. "Let's start with something simple. Vanilla cupcakes are our biggest sellers, even as boring as they are."

Jada froze. Should she be flattered or horrified that he apparently remembered every word she'd said to him?

He shot a quick grin her way. She exhaled. He wasn't going to hold that quip against her. Okay, starting now, she'd do better and stop messing with him.

He pulled a tablet out of a drawer underneath the table and tapped on it a few times. "I'm pulling up the recipe so you can follow along more easily," he said by way of explanation.

Jada offered up a tight smile. He might ask her to read the recipe. She'd been dealing with her dyslexia forever and wasn't ashamed of her diagnosis, but she never knew how people would react to it. Then again, no one could be as bad as her parents. "How did you get into baking?" she asked to distract herself.

He glanced up. "My mom taught me and my sisters. I took to it more than they did. Do you bake?"

She snorted. "That would be a solid no. I'm a wiz at ordering all kinds of delicious food in restaurants, but that's as far as my culinary skills extend."

That line was starting to appear in his forehead again. She'd seen it plenty of times from her parents. Disappointment. Consternation. "But I'm eager to learn," she quickly added.

He squinted. "Are you? You didn't seem too eager in your grandmother's office."

How much to reveal? She didn't know this guy, and what she did know didn't suggest he'd be understanding. "Working here was my grandmother's idea. I wasn't prepared to see you."

He studied her like he knew there was more to the story, but then he nodded like he'd decided not to press. "Let's get started."

She braced her legs apart. "What do you want me to do?"

His lips twitched. "Not stand like a linebacker before a play starts, for one. No tackling will be happening in this kitchen, I promise."

Wait. Did Mr. Uptight have a sense of humor? Nooo, couldn't be.

He lifted his eyebrows, his lips twitching again. Oh, right. She was still standing like a linebacker. She'd been exposed to just enough football to know a linebacker was a football player, so whatever she was doing at the moment was not right. She was nervous, okay. Sue her. This was a new, weird situation she hadn't asked to be in.

"Relax," he said.

Did he read minds, too?

"I'm not going to grade you and send a report card to your grand-mother," he continued, his voice gruff and slightly aggravated. Ahh, that was exactly what she needed to relax. The reappearance of Principal Dell. Earth had returned to its rightful position on its axis.

He handed her the tablet. If she made sure their fingers didn't touch, well . . . whatever.

She tapped on the screen a few times to change the font to Comic Sans and enlarge the font to sixteen. Much better. She'd learned numerous ways to compensate for her dyslexia. Her parents had made damn sure of that.

One crisis averted. Now she had to follow the recipe. That was way more terrifying. Her attempts at so-called easy dishes like scrambled eggs or spaghetti always ended up as a runny, yellowy, inedible mess or mushy noodles in burnt sauce—i.e., disaster. It wasn't her fault her busy (and okay, wealthy) parents had hired a chef. There had been no need for her to learn how to cook.

"What are you doing?" he asked.

Jada hesitated, but she had nothing to be ashamed of. If he acted like an ass, that was on him. "Changing the font. I have dyslexia, and certain fonts really help."

He nodded. "Oh, okay. If there are any modifications you need, just let me know."

That was it? "Oh, I should be fine, but thanks for the offer."

"You're welcome. Follow my lead," Donovan said. Guess that was it. It was a bossy command, but he sounded almost . . . nice.

She gave a brisk salute. "Aye aye, captain. So how many cupcakes do you bake per day?"

"Roughly twelve dozen. It used to be . . ." His voice trailed off, a
discomfited look settling on his face.

"Be what?"

"Nothing." His tone made it clear he wouldn't be revealing anything else.

Okay, then. Looked like she wasn't the only one who had no
desire to bare their soul today.

"Wow. Almost a hundred fifty. That's a lot of cupcakes." One of
the ways she'd learned to cope with dyslexia was a lot of memorization. She could do multiplication tables in her head like nobody's
business.

"We offer the special of the day, along with our basic flavors and
a seasonal favorite. At least that's the goal." A shadow crossed his
handsome features. He rolled his shoulders and sent a clearly forced
smile her way. "Let's get to these cupcakes."

He handed her a glass mixing bowl identical to the one on the
counter in front of him.

"Do you ever improvise?" she asked after he studied the recipe
for at least ten seconds like he was committing the steps to memory.

"No, I leave that to Nicholas. I like having a formula to follow."

Her lips cracked into a smile. "You mean a recipe?"

Despite not knowing him long, she wasn't surprised by his answer. He struck her as someone who liked logic and order. Someone who was stuck with her illogical and disorderly self for the
next few months. No wonder that crease seemed to have taken up
permanent residence between his eyebrows. Not that it mattered.
She was here to work so she could gain access to her trust fund and,
subsequently, full control of her life. Not become besties with him.

He rolled his eyes. "Yes. Whatever. I like knowing if I follow a *recipe,* the result will be exactly what I want and expect."

He cracked two eggs into the bowl with precision and minimal movement of his hand and wrist.

Jada took a deep breath. She could do this. She just had to follow exactly what he did.

One tap on the lip of the bowl, two. *Crack!* The shell split and the yolk splattered on the counter. "Crap!"

The yellow liquid slid in a slow but nonstop blob, spreading across the pristine counter and then down the side. Oh, no. Panic dogged her heels as she spun in a circle, frantically searching for a towel. She spotted a red one and swiped at the mess she'd made. She moaned as more of the yolk slipped over the side in a race to the tiled floor. "I'm so, so sorry."

"Hey, it's okay." Donovan's hand landed on her shoulder, sending a jolt of sensation through her. She turned. He nodded, his face and voice equally calm. "Don't worry. It's just egg."

"I didn't want to mess up this beautiful kitchen." She didn't want to see the same disappointed look on his face she'd seen so often on her parents' faces every time she screwed something up.

He squeezed her shoulder, his gaze a mesmerizing combination of concern and sympathy. "We all start somewhere. Don't worry. We have a refrigerator full of eggs and a supply closet full of cleaning supplies. I can handle any mess you make. But yes, please remember the eggs go *in* the bowl."

His deadpan delivery surprised a snort of laughter out of her. They shared a grin. "When you put it that way." As her heart slowed to a more normal rate, Jada turned back to the counter. A few swipes and the mess was gone. She exhaled. "What's your favorite flavor?"

A brief smile touched his lips. "Out of our staples, peanut butter chocolate. It's like a Reese's but a million times better. My mother made them for my birthday whenever she could."

"Whenever she could?"

His shoulders tensed. "Money was tight some years. When it was, cupcakes were the last thing on her mind, but those years when we were okay . . . those were the best." He glanced at her. "Stop procrastinating."

"Okay, fine." She took a deep breath and followed his directions. Or at least, she tried to. Flour was a slippery sucker and liked to create a plume, but she kept going, even if she did spend more of her time cleaning up spills than doing anything that could reasonably be called baking. And there was the unfortunate moment when she added four cups of sugar instead of two and had to start over for the third time. Through it all, Donovan was patient. Mostly. That crease in his forehead never disappeared, but he didn't yell at least, so she took it as a win.

"Time for the mixer." He gestured toward the massive shiny stainless steel piece of equipment on the opposite counter.

Jada swallowed. The machine was intimidating. Forget sugarplums. Visions of ingredients flying across the immaculate kitchen if she screwed up the timing or whatever settings were on the mixer danced in her head. The nerves she'd battled back returned with a vengeance.

"Push this button." Donovan showed her what to do. She mimicked his movements precisely, holding her breath. She released the button. Miracle of miracles, disaster didn't strike. The ingredients whirled and stayed in the bowl. She let out a little squeal and tried to turn it into a more dignified cough when Donovan side-eyed her, but then something got caught in her throat. She ended up doubled over, hacking up a lung.

He whacked her on the back. "Are you okay?"

She stumbled forward. Too bad she couldn't stumble away from her embarrassment. "Yeah, yeah, I'm fine. What's next?"

He eyed her, his face impassive. Jada sighed. At least he wasn't laughing at her.

"Time to bake." He showed her how to scoop the mixture into the baking pans. A good fourth of the sticky, liquidy mixture ended up on the counter, and the part that did end up in the baking pan cutouts looked nothing like Donovan's evenly spread-out version. But she did it. She just had to accept the mess.

The heavenly scent of vanilla rent the air. Her stomach called out for a cupcake. If she wasn't careful, she was going to have about ten cavities when her time at Sugar Blitz was done.

"How long?" she asked.

"Twenty minutes." He stepped closer, bringing his heat and woodsy, tempting scent with him. She ordered her feet to not move. "What?"

"You have some flour on your—" He gestured toward her face.

Oh, great. This was the third time she'd been in Donovan's presence, and the second time she ended up with something on her face. Fantastic percentage. She swiped at her nose. "Better?"

His lips crooked. "No, not really." The soft pad of his thumb stroked across her cheek. Air lodged in Jada's throat. He was close. The heat from his body rolled over her, creating a cocoon of delicious warmth she wanted to snuggle up into. "There. Got it."

Her lips parted, air escaping in an unsteady rhythm as she tracked the movement of his thumb with greedy eyes. He rubbed his thumb and index finger together like he was savoring the touch of her skin, but perhaps she was projecting. He hadn't stepped away, however. Nor had he taken his eyes away from hers. Her gaze slipped lower. His lips, too, had parted. The moment built . . .

lingered. His eyes darkened with awareness. Her pulse pounded in her ears.

"There's a guy at the front insisting on speaking to the manager. I think he's a fan, and he's not taking no for an answer."

Jada whirled. Ella stood there, eyes darting between the two of them.

Donovan recovered first. "And we can't afford to say no." He pinched the bridge of his nose and hurried toward the door. He stopped. "I'll be back in a minute."

She waved her hand. "Don't worry about it. I got it." She needed as much alone time as possible to recover. Her breath was still coming hard and fast, her pulse racing. What was that? Had they almost . . . ? *No.*

The air rushed out of her lungs in relief when he exited with Ella close on his heels. Okay, time to restore her equilibrium. What had they been doing before they . . . looked at each other? She turned in a circle, taking in her surroundings. Oh, right. They were in a kitchen baking cupcakes. Her gaze landed on the pans they'd poured the mixture into. All that was left was putting the pre-baked cupcakes into the oven. Even she could handle that.

* * *

A loud screeching sound rang through the cupcakery. *Beep, beep, beeeeep!*

Jada froze. What was that? It sounded like the . . .

"Fire alarm!" Ella's eyes widened. She hurried around the counter. Jada followed close at her heels. Donovan's office door flew open and he and August joined them in their mad dash to the kitchen. Jada started coughing before Donovan pushed the door open.

When he did, she gasped. Wisps of gray smoke filled the air.

Tendrils of dread, much like the smoke irritating her eyes, began to curl in her stomach and sting her from the inside out. Even worse, the room's other occupants began to cough. Embarrassment scalded her, hurting ten times more than the smoke.

Jada's gaze cut to the oven, where the plumes of smoke were originating. "Oh, no," she whispered. She ran to the oven and yanked the door open. Thick whirls of smoke blew directly into her face. "Oh, no." Her incantation was a little louder now.

She stared at the black, hard lumps that could masquerade as the coal Santa put in the stockings of naughty children. What had she done? That was her handiwork. "I'm so sorry."

She felt like a misbehaving child who'd disappointed her parents. Nothing new there. They needed to go in the trash. Now. She grabbed the red towel on the counter, reached into the oven, and yanked out one of the pans with too much force. She stumbled back and the pan slipped, hitting her forearm.

"Ouch!" She dropped the pan on the counter with a clatter as a shooting pain sliced up her arm. Tears sprang to her eyes. At the moment, she didn't know if the pain firing through her owed more to the physical or emotional pain double-teaming her. She bit her lip to keep a whimper from escaping, but she wasn't entirely successful.

"Are you all right?" Donovan barked the question at her. "What are you doing?"

She couldn't get her lips to work to answer him. He grabbed her forearm and turned it over. The press of his thick fingers against her flesh enthralled her. His lips were downturned. He drew—well, more like *yanked*—her over to the sink. He turned on the water and thrust her arm under the spray. The sting of cold liquid caused her to yelp and try to pull away. He didn't let her, holding her arm under the stream.

"Ella, get the first aid kit," he barked, never taking his eyes off her reddening skin. His eyes were dark and focused. Ella handed him the red-and-white box a few seconds later.

"I can do it," Jada said, trying to tug her arm away. She didn't like him touching her. It made her feel unsettled. Warm.

"I got it," he said simply. "I can get a better angle than you."

So orderly. Logical. Of course. No real worry for her. Which was fine. Not that he had to. They barely knew each other. "I'm fine," she muttered. "Nothing to be concerned about."

"You were hurt in my business, so yeah, it is my concern." His voice remained flat. He ripped open a packet of burn cream with his teeth.

Right. Of course. She gave one more experimental tug on her arm. He tightened his grip and fixed his principal glare on her. He was officially tired of her nonsense. His look said "One more move, and I'm sending you to detention, young lady."

She sighed and dropped her gaze. For such a large man, he had a light touch when he wanted to, his blunt fingers barely caressing her skin as he squeezed the cream on her arm and massaged it into her skin slowly and methodically, covering the entire wound. The cool, clear liquid calmed her stinging flesh immediately. He looked up, and at her nod, he inspected several sizes of bandages before selecting one that apparently met his approval. He unwrapped it, then covered the mark on her arm. He'd selected correctly because every inch of the mark was covered.

His nearness affected her. He smelled good even through the acrid air of charred cupcakes. That same scent from earlier. A light touch of vanilla underlined by soap and something woodsy. None of which were important.

She refocused on what he was doing. He turned her forearm

back and forth a few times, examining his handiwork. "Good?" he asked. His gaze, dark and intense, clashed with hers.

"Yes," she said, her mouth now dry thanks to something other than the smoke.

He released her and scrubbed a hand across his scalp. "Then what the hell happened? What the hell were you doing?" he barked, his glare getting darker and darker. "Did you not start the timer?"

"I did." She looked closer at the digital display. *Oh, no.* "I must have accidentally set it for two hours instead of twenty minutes."

A muscle ticked in his hard jaw. "Look at all this smoke. You've only been here three hours and you almost burned down the kitchen. This isn't going to work."

The statement, full of barely leashed anger and annoyed certainty, tore through her like a rip in the fabric of her favorite silk shirt. She was a failure. Again. And she'd barely started. Not that it mattered. This is the way things were always destined to go for her.

"I'm sorry." Averting her gaze, she hurried out of the room. She ignored Ella's call to wait. Bursting into tears in front of an audience wasn't part of today's plan.

Chapter Seven

D onovan threw back his head and let out his aggravation with himself in a long, gusty groan. Fuck. What was that?

His heart was about to fly out of his chest, it was beating so hard. Chaos. Too much chaos. He lived his life with order and calm. He'd done his best to eradicate all unpredictability and uncertainty.

August looked at him but didn't say a word. He didn't have to. Donovan felt like a piece of shit all on his own. He never lost his temper like that. Shit.

Ella came rushing back into the kitchen. She was alone. She did not look pleased with him. "She left, thanks to you. What was that? We've all burned cupcakes before. Don't you think you were a little hard on her?"

Donovan scrubbed his face with a shaky hand. The adrenaline driving his actions for the past few minutes seeped out of him like the air out of a popped balloon. "I screwed that up, didn't I?"

She gave him the look all younger sisters and pseudo younger sisters gave older siblings when they realized they could screw up like everyone else. "Yep. Sure did."

The excuses of the past few days, with the mounting evidence of slowing sales, the mounting evidence that he didn't have everything under control in *any* aspect of his life, weren't enough. He shouldn't have lost his cool like that.

Concern about Jada's well-being, an adrenaline rush all on its own, had consumed him. First, he entered the room full of smoke, unsure if the room was on fire. Then, Jada cried out in pain. The only way to control it was to focus on the task at hand. But then that task had come to an end. And he'd gotten worked up about something really inconsequential. So no, not his finest moment. As much as Jada drove him up the wall, she didn't deserve that.

He offered up a half smile to Ella. "Love you too, kid."

She didn't look appeased by his admission. "What are you going to do to fix it?"

He sighed. "I'll figure something out."

He nodded to August, then made his way back to his office. He had to make this right. Somehow. He pulled up the email from Mrs. T's assistant. Great, there it was. Jada's cell number.

He dialed quickly, but she didn't pick up.

That didn't mean she was *actively* ducking his call. Donovan rolled his shoulders, seeking some relief from the guilt twisting his muscles into knots. A lot of people didn't answer calls from strange numbers. He snapped his fingers. Texting. Yes!

What should he say? He tapped out a message.

Hey, it's Donovan.

Not great, but it got the job done.

She left him on "read."

He tried again.

I'd like to talk.

No response. Damn. What now?

Then it hit him. His fingers flew across the phone. He sent her a message that would undoubtedly get her to do his bidding.

"What's with the evil smile?" Ella called out as she passed his open door.

Donovan's grin widened. Evil genius more like it.

* * *

Be here tomorrow morning at 9 A.M. Or else.

Jada stared at her phone, willing the autocratic text message to change.

Or else?

What did that mean? How dare he? That uppity, starched-shirt principal! Nobody talked to her that way. Well, except for her parents, but she'd put distance between them. Everyone else got a piece of her mind. So she would give him a piece of her mind.

"Except he's kinda your boss, so I'm not sure that's a good idea," Olivia said after Jada ranted for a full ten minutes. She'd come over right after work after receiving Jada's SOS text.

"I thought you were on my side," Jada countered with a huff as she took another lap around her living room.

Olivia sent her a look. "I am on your side, which is why I'm telling you not to go full G.I. Jada on him."

"But he's so insufferable! Did you see his text?"

Her friend's curls bounced as she nodded. "Yes, you've shown it to me approximately twenty times since I arrived. You also told me he took care of you after you burned yourself. Maybe he was worried about you and didn't know how to express those emotions in a positive way."

"Hmmph." Would she be a terrible person if she ignored that logic and stayed mad? Jada crossed her arms, not really caring. "Why didn't you tell me he played for my grandmother's team?"

Olivia arched an eyebrow. "I was about to until you said your *encounter* with him was my fault and then I almost lost my cupcake and got distracted."

Jada groaned, dropping her head into her free hand. "This is a disaster."

"Well, at least you get to eat the product."

Jada stopped pacing to side-eye her BFF. "Really?"

Olivia shrugged. "I'm trying to find the bright side." She snapped her fingers. "Oh, wait. I thought of another one. You get to work for three fine-as-hell men, one of whom really wants to talk to you and knew exactly the right thing to say to catch your attention. Maybe you should listen."

Jada made a face. "Maybe you're right, and I don't like that." This is why she'd called Olivia. Her friend always had her back and could be counted on to set her straight.

Olivia rose from the sofa and swung an arm around her shoulders and squeezed. "But you're going to listen, right?"

Jada sighed. "I guess."

Which is why she entered Sugar Blitz at 8:58 A.M. on the dot like the boss she hoped to be one day. Not that she had any idea what she would be the boss of, but you know, fake it till you make it. Or break it. Or burn it, in her case. Whatever, she was here to face the music, in whatever form it came in. She'd synchronized her watch to global standard time, which seemed like something Donovan would appreciate.

To her surprise, he wasn't standing in the store tapping his foot and the face of his watch simultaneously. Ella, however, rushed up to her. "Jada! You came back!" The teenager threw her arms around Jada and squeezed hard. "I was soooo worried."

Ella's unabashed enthusiasm and genuineness seeped into Jada. She greatly appreciated it even though she had no clue what she'd done to engender Ella's loyalty so quickly. She stepped back and studied the other woman. Her confusion must have shown on her face because Ella laughed.

"I've known Donovan my whole life. No one gets to him. I mean *no one*. He's Mr. I-Have-a-Plan-and-I-Stick-to-It. You shake him up."

A surprised snort of laughter bubbled out of Jada. "And that's a good thing?"

Ella's nodded enthusiastically, sending her braids swinging. "Absolutely."

"I'm not sure he would agree." And speaking of . . . "Crap. I'm supposed to be meeting him right now."

She hurried toward his office, quickening her strides as she got closer. After a short, brisk knock, he bade her enter in that professorial voice. Oh, yeah, she was definitely the misbehaving kid sent to the principal's office. No matter. She wasn't a kid. She would say her piece and ask, not beg, him not to fire her.

When she entered the office, he sat imperiously behind his desk like the ruler of his kingdom, waiting to see his loyal subjects. Great. He'd upgraded from principaldom. Worse, he was tapping the face of his watch, so she hadn't been completely wrong. Yay for small victories.

"You're late," he intoned.

Her teeth immediately went on edge. "It's 9:01."

"That's late." The gleam in his eye gave him away. He was trying to get at her. Give her a taste of her own medicine.

Her eyes narrowed. "You're a diabolical bully."

Crap. That's not what she meant to say. He leaned back in his chair. The only sign he was surprised by her outburst was a raised eyebrow. She focused on it like a talisman while biting her lip. She wasn't going to say anything else. She'd promised Olivia she would be good.

He gestured for her to take a seat. Since her knees were threatening to collapse, she didn't hesitate to take him up on the offer.

"Running out of your job on the first day was quite the move. So was not answering the calls and texts from your boss."

"Don't you think my actions were justified? Need I remind you of what you said to me before I left *and* after? Be here at 9 A.M. or else. Who says that?" Wait. Oops. Those weren't the words she was supposed to be saying. She was supposed to be conciliatory. More mature. But his supercilious raised eyebrow egged her on. Besides, she always spoke her mind. She couldn't help herself, so it really wasn't her fault. She was a work in progress.

"I say that." He straightened in his chair, his spine going straight and stiff, and studied her intently for a few seconds. She lifted her chin. She wouldn't squirm and give him more ammunition. His lips curved into another diabolical grin. "Wanna know why?"

"Sure." She went for nonchalant, even throwing in a one-shouldered shrug for good measure, even though she wasn't sure she pulled it off. He could be getting ready to toss her out on her ass and demand that she never step foot in this shop again. And she would have to take it. Unless she decided to beg, which would be horrible and humiliating and heave-inducing.

"Because that was the only way to ensure you would show up today. I knew you wouldn't be able to resist putting me in my place."

"Oh." He knew her that well already? Looked like Olivia had been onto something. She wasn't sure that was a good thing. Maybe that meant she was boring and predictable. Gross.

"I needed you to show up today for a specific reason." He stood and came around his desk.

The blood flowing through her veins slowed to an agonizing crawl. Here it came. The ol' heave-ho. The pink slip. The relieving of duties.

He dropped to one knee in front of her like he was going to *propose*. What the hell?

"What are you doing?" Her voice came out shaky.

She almost kicked him in the face when he cradled her foot and slipped off her Ferragamo flat. She'd searched the depths of her closet because of a deep, long-buried memory that she owned shoes that weren't heels. Just when she was about to lose all hope, there they were—ballet flats collecting dust. They were red, her favorite color, and now he was taking them off. "No, seriously, what are you doing?"

"I have to see if the slipper fits." He looked up at her, a smile playing at the corner of his lips.

Wait. Was he being *charming*? Did he even know what that word meant?

"I'm sorry. What?" Thank God she'd had a pedicure last week in her quest to cheer herself up. He reached under the chair next to the one she was sitting in and pulled out a blue shoe box she hadn't noticed. Surely he hadn't. Surely not. "You bought me . . . shoes?"

"I did." He sat back on his heels and looked up at her.

She could get used to having this large, ridiculously handsome man on his knees, his thigh muscles straining against the fabric of his pants, trying to please her in whatever fashion she so desired. She shook her head. Those were dangerous, fantasy-inducing thoughts she needed to exorcise from her brain and never think of again. "Why?"

"Because I noticed that after standing on your feet for hours yesterday, you were hobbling a little bit. And as much as you loved those shoes, I could tell you were cursing them."

He'd been paying attention to her state of being *and* acted on what he'd seen? She would not smile. She would not. "Oh."

He took a deep breath. "And also because I need to apologize for how I acted. I've been feeling a little overwhelmed lately, and I took it out on you. You didn't deserve that."

Thank God she was already sitting down. He'd shocked every ounce of tension out of her body. She would have melted to the ground in an ungainly, undignified heap. "Oh."

He flashed a killer smile that sent her heart catapulting in her chest. "That all you have to say?"

She tried to wrestle her brain matter back into a cogent being. "No, it's not. I'm just shocked, but thank you for the apology. I wasn't expecting it, but I appreciate it." She paused. "Does this mean you're not firing me?"

"Yes, although you did almost burn down my kitchen."

"I did not burn down your kitchen!"

He held up a finger. "I said almost."

"It was just a little smoke!" That was the mantra she'd been repeating to herself since she ran out of the place. It was really the only reason she showed up. Okay, and because of his "or else" text. Fine. She could admit it to herself. Not him, of course.

He reached for a pen and writing pad on his desk and made a mark.

She frowned. "What are you doing?"

"A demerit for insubordination. I think it's in my best interest to keep a tally." He said it like it was the most natural thing in the world for him to be doing. "I like statistics. Speaking of statistics, I didn't know your shoe size, which is partially why I chose these."

Her eyes dropped to the box on her lap. There weren't many

identifying characteristics on the box besides a size, indicating it was a men's shoe box. She really hoped he hadn't bought her men's shoes.

He gestured, a soft smile playing around his mouth. "Open it up."

Jada took a deep breath and lifted the lid. She reached into the box and pulled out . . .

Crocs?

She stared at the rubbery black clogs. "What are these?"

"Crocs."

She huffed her frustration. "Yes, I know that, but why these shoes specifically?" She'd seen other people—people deprived of all fashion sense—wearing them occasionally, but it had never occurred to her to buy some for herself.

"Because I didn't know your size and these are a little forgiving in that regard."

"Oh, okay." She could still be shocked and touched. Who knew? She'd guarded her emotions so much over the years that she'd almost forgotten she had the capacity to be affected by a kind gesture. A kind gesture from Donovan Dell, of all people. "Thank you."

"I know a WTF meme is flashing above your head right now, but try them on. If you don't like them, I'll look the other way when you hand them over to Ella."

Jada laughed. Dude had a sense of humor. Who knew? She'd indulge him by trying on the shoes, but she was positive her flats would do the trick. She slipped on the clogs, trying not to wince at how they made her feet look like they belonged to Mickey Mouse.

Donovan stood, holding out a hand. She grasped it and let him pull her to her feet. She flexed her toes.

"Oh. My. God." The shoes were like little plush pillows that cradled her feet and felt amazing. Angels in heaven were weeping with joy. She was never taking them off. Like ever ever. Crocs were *life*.

"Good, huh?"

She wanted to wipe that smug grin off his face, but she couldn't. "Thank you. As much as it pains me to admit it, you were right. I do like them. I guess this means you weren't just being nice when you said you weren't trying to get rid of me."

"Don't sound so surprised."

Jada studied him. "You're not going to rat me out to Grams."

His lips pursed. "I did think about telling your grandma. That was the 'or else' part of the text."

"I knew it!"

"But I never had any intention of following through on it."

Her hands landed on her hips. "You really were just trying to rile me up to get me to show up."

"I was."

"Impressive. A word to the wise, though. Never ever refer to her as Grandma. She's much too grand for that title, as she reminded me, my sister, and my cousins repeatedly growing up. Grams is the only acceptable term she would allow. According to her, it is the perfect combination of stately and comforting."

He smiled. "I do love that woman."

Genuine admiration shone in his eyes. Any person who could appreciate the force that was her grandmother was okay with her. "Me, too."

"So, truce?" He held out his hand. His large hand engulfed hers.

She sucked in a breath at the innocuous contact. Jada forced a smile to hide her reaction. "Truce."

She was going to ignore that weird, quick flare of something wicked and pleasurable that flowed through her every time they touched. It was . . . nothing.

He aggravated her. She aggravated him, and that was just the way it was. She was not going to repeat the mistakes from her past, like falling for guys too hard too fast, no matter how not right they were for her.

She was here to make sure she gained control over her trust fund so she could fully take control over her life. That's all that mattered. Well, not completely.

Now that she was here, she wanted to prove she was capable of more than almost (even though not really) burning down a kitchen. She hadn't asked for this job, but now that she had it, she wanted to prove she could do it. She didn't want to see that disappointment on his face again. She'd seen that same disappointment on too many other faces throughout her life. Operation: Jada Gets Her Life Together was officially on.

She squared her shoulders and met Donovan's gaze. "I promise to do better."

That's all that mattered.

Chapter Eight

Donovan studied Jada out of the corner of his eye while he made a fresh pot of coffee. She was across the room chatting and laughing with a table of customers. They hadn't spoken since their meeting in his office an hour earlier.

"So look," she'd said, wrinkling her nose. "I don't think *baking* is for me."

Had "baking" ever been uttered with such distaste and mistrust before? "Giving up already?"

Her shoulders deflated while a shadow crossed her face. "Quitting while I'm ahead."

And he felt like shit all over again. Damn. "Hey, I really am sorry for yelling at you."

"I know," she'd said with a brief smile that didn't quite reach her eyes before escaping.

Instead of going after her, he'd stayed in his office because what else was there to say? Besides, he had work to do—ordering supplies, paying invoices, staring at yesterday's dismal sales numbers, and not thinking about how the simple act of touching Jada's ankle had made him hotter than he'd been in too long to contemplate. Her ankle. Good Lord. Had he transported himself to the Victorian era? And then she'd smiled at him—really, *smiled*—after the comfort and amazingness of the Crocs had sunk in. He'd felt like he'd been sucker punched.

But it was all nonsense. Inconsequential nonsense. He didn't deal with nonsense, inconsequential or otherwise. He'd made that promise to himself years ago, and his life had improved exponentially. In regard to Jada, they were temporary colleagues, and that's where it needed to start and end.

So why had he made his way to the front counter long before his official shift was supposed to begin? Oh, right. Because Jada was his employee, and he needed to monitor her progress. Make sure she didn't try to burn the place down again. And maybe because he'd heard Nicholas's voice followed by her laughter after Ella's shift ended. Nicholas had given him a shit-eating grin when he spotted Donovan before retreating to the kitchen.

"Gonna break your neck if you keep staring at her like that," a grumpy voice drawled from behind Donovan.

Donovan spun to face the counter. "What?"

The graybeard staring at him didn't flinch. "You heard me. I've been standing here for a while now, and you didn't notice. I might be old, but I'm not foolish. You might be though if all you do is stare without making a move."

He was getting killed by a man old enough to be his grandfather. Awesome. Donovan cleared his throat. "Welcome to Sugar Blitz. How can I help you?"

The old man snickered while he studied the menu board. "Well, I don't know. Give me some time to decide."

Hadn't he just said he'd been standing there for a while? But

Donovan decided to keep that fact to himself. He was in no position to antagonize customers, even if he spoke the truth.

His shoulders straightened when Jada joined the geezer at the counter. "Hi, Mr. Till. Good to see you again."

"Oh, hi, Ms. Jada." Old Guy hitched up his pants and sucked in his paunch before patting his head, where a crown of gray hair circled a shiny brown bald spot.

Donovan blinked. "Wait. You know him?"

Jada turned those amazing chocolaty brown eyes his way, hitting him square in the solar plexus. "Oh, yeah, we're old friends, right, Mr. Till?"

"Yep. Met yesterday." He beamed at Donovan, sure he held a higher place in Jada's affections than Donovan.

"I told him to come back today after he was done playing chess to try out our red velvet cupcakes." Her smile and tone were both bright and authentic. "He said red velvet was his favorite, but we were out."

"Yep, I play chess with the fellas at the park and my sweet tooth was cutting up yesterday. This was the closest place I could get something." But not the preferred place, based on his tone.

Donovan infused his voice with his best "happy to have you here" customer service tone. "Well, we do have a fresh batch of red velvet cupcakes. They're a crowd favorite."

Mr. Till sniffed. "I'll be the judge of that." Yeah, Donovan could see how he and Jada had bonded. He tapped his fingers on the counter while Donovan completed his order. "You play chess?"

"A little." Donovan slid the box across the counter.

"Good to know." Mr. Till gave him a look that said maybe Donovan wasn't a total loser.

"Mr. Till said if he liked the cupcakes, he'd bring his chess buddies in," Jada said.

Mr. Till pointed a gnarled finger at her. "I said I might, young lady. You've got a long way to go before that happens." He paid for his purchase and shuffled to a table in the corner of the shop.

The bell over the front door dinged. A woman wearing an expensive-looking, sleeveless, black-and-white-striped dress entered.

Jada raised her hand in a wave. "Carrie!"

Donovan blinked. "Wait. You know her, too?"

"Yes," she hissed out of the corner of her mouth.

"What are you doing here?" the fashionable woman asked when she reached the counter.

"I work here," Jada answered cheerfully.

"Oh, cool." Carrie's brow furrowed. "Are you okay after what happened the other day?"

What happened the other day?

Jada waved away Carrie's concern. "Oh, yeah, I'm fine."

Her smile and tone were so chipper, Donovan almost believed her. Almost.

Carrie glanced over her shoulder, then leaned forward and lowered her voice. "Did you see that interview Dr. John did with *Extra*? He says he misses you."

Who the hell was Dr. John?

"No, I missed that," Jada said, her voice still so sunny Donovan almost believed he'd misread the stricken look that had flashed across her face at the mention of that John guy. "How can we help you?" she added quickly, stepping around behind the counter to stand next to Donovan, bringing her gentle and always intoxicating scent with her.

Carrie flipped her long brown hair behind her shoulder. "I'm not sure. I usually go old-school and get chocolate, but today I thought I'd try something different to celebrate some good news. What do you suggest?"

Jada eyed the case for a second. "Well, we do have a new s'mores flavor today that gives you the comfort of chocolate with a little extra flavor."

The woman's eyes brightened. "Ooh, that sounds delicious. Give me half a dozen to take back to the store."

Donovan gave himself a mental fist pump. Jada packaged up the cupcakes while he rang up the sale.

"Now that I know you work here, I'll make sure to stop by more often and spread the word," Carrie said. A minute later, another satisfied customer, who hopefully would keep her promise to bring more, left. If only there were more satisfied customers. He looked around the store. Still too many empty tables. Business was steady, but slow. Slow and steady was not going to win this race. He sighed.

"You okay?" Jada asked.

"Yeah, I'm fine." Sharing his problems wasn't his way to begin with, and burdening someone he'd known for less than a week didn't strike him as fair. Hell, maybe she would think a slow trickle of customers was normal and wouldn't ask any questions he didn't want to answer. "You really liked those s'mores cupcakes, huh?"

"I did. They were so good." Her head tilted to the side in contemplation. "But I think in addition to how delicious they were, they made me remember how every summer, my parents would pack my sister and me off to camp for two weeks. I loved those weeks. I was just Jada there with none of the expectations that came with my everyday life." A soft smile touched her red lips. "I remember the first time I made a s'more. It was messy and fun. I got marshmallows and chocolate everywhere. I burned my marshmallow to a crisp—*don't* say anything—but no one cared. It was charred but so good because of it. Then the graham crackers broke in half and I just scooped everything up and stuffed it all in my mouth. Good times."

She'd lived with expectations so high that making s'mores

counted as one of her favorite memories? Wow. What was the story there?

"So yeah, I'm going to hand-sell these bad boys to anyone who will listen," Jada said, pointing to the case. "Nicholas promised to make me an extra batch so I can gorge on them in the privacy of my own home." She held up a hand. "And yes, I'm going to buy them."

Was he that obvious? Well, he was trying to run a business, so no apologies would be forthcoming. Her smile—natural, wide, and bright—stunned him. She was teasing him. Maybe they had turned a corner. And why did the thought of that make him feel like he'd conquered a mountain? That he could accomplish whatever he set his mind to?

* * *

"How can we help you?" Jada asked the blond woman who stepped up to the counter a few hours later. The customer was dressed in a slim skirt with a button-down shirt tucked into the waistband.

Jada was falling into a rhythm. Ella had done a good job training her. It wasn't that hard pulling cupcakes out of the case, but she enjoyed talking to the customers about why today was the day they *needed* a cupcake and helping them select the perfect flavor. She did have the gift of gab, if nothing else. The blonde, who'd spent a little too much time in the tanning booth, stared back at her through wire-framed glasses.

"Hi," she said again after a few seconds of silence with an awkward wave to catch Staring Lady's attention.

The woman blinked.

Jada offered up her most charming smile. "Any of our cupcakes catch your eye?"

The blonde blinked again like she'd forgotten they were indeed in a cupcake shop. She stared at the menu board, then dropped her gaze to the display case. "I'll take a vanilla cupcake."

"Coming right up." Jada decided that it was for the best if she kept the conversation to a minimum. The lady was still staring at her. She boxed up the cupcake without asking if the woman wanted it to go or eat in store, which technically was bad customer service, but Donovan wasn't there, so he couldn't give her any more demerits. He had reluctantly left her alone only after she pointed out that she had demonstrated a reasonable ability to remove cupcakes from the display case and press a few buttons on the computer screen attached to the cash register. But not before he'd stared at her with a *not-at-all* insulting mixture of suspicion and reluctance.

The customer paid for the dessert and then detoured to one of the tables that had a clear view of the front counter, i.e., exactly where Jada was. Great. Luckily, a few more customers came in back-to-back, which kept Jada busy. Nevertheless, every time she looked up, Staring Lady was taking an infinitesimal bite of her cupcake while keeping her eyes locked on Jada. Did she recognize her from the show? Jada suppressed a sigh. Probably, but there was nothing she could do about that.

Jada took a lap around the store to check on the customers. Mr. Till was happily munching away on his cupcake. Everyone else was doing good and didn't need anything. Too bad. She meandered as much as she could, swiping the crumbs off one table, picking up an errant wrapper, bringing extra napkins to an excited four-year-old, but finally she admitted there was nothing else she could pretend held her attention. She forced herself to stop at Staring Lady's table. "Are you finding everything okay? Can I get you anything?"

"No, but I do have a question. Are you Jada Townsend-Matthews?"

Jada nodded slowly. Her shoulders tensed. She deliberately

relaxed them. She had nothing to be ashamed of, and if this lady started giving her crap, she would handle it. Somehow.

Staring Lady's eyes widened. "Oh, wow. I heard the rumors you were working here, but I had to see it for myself. I couldn't believe it."

Jada shrugged. "Well, I am."

"I just thought with your family connections you'd be working somewhere . . ."

"Somewhere what?" Jada was just about tired of the bullshit. No, this wasn't her dream job—not that she had any clue what her dream job was—but this was a more than decent place to work. She was annoyed Grams had orchestrated this work assignment for her, but she wasn't embarrassed to be here.

The woman paused, clearly sensing she was treading on thin ice. "My name is Tamara McCarthy. I work for celebinfo.com. We should do an interview. Get your side of the story."

Oh, crap. She should have ignored her. Great move, Jada. Again. "I'm not really doing press." Even if she did have to continuously ignore the calls and emails from Lila, *My One and Only*'s executive producer, asking, then demanding she reconsider. She wanted the story and her involvement with the show to go away as soon as possible. Her fifteen minutes of fame wasn't worth it.

"That was such an interesting decision you made," Tamara continued like Jada hadn't spoken.

"Thanks. Did you need anything?"

"Did you know you were going to turn Dr. John down before that last ring ceremony? Was that your plan the entire time?"

"Nope. I gotta go." Jada about-faced and headed back to the sanctity of the front counter. Surely that waist-high barrier would protect her. The screech of what sounded like chair legs sliding against the floor filled the air behind her. Jada didn't turn back to see what was going on. The clattering of heels on the concrete floor behind her confirmed her suspicion anyway. She quickened her stride instead. Almost there. A strong hand on her arm stopped her. She wanted to fling the woman's hand with her perfectly manicured fingers off, but that definitely wasn't in the good customer service handbook, and she'd promised Donovan and herself that she would do a good job. She turned and forced her lips upward. "Can I get you something?"

"Yes. Tell me everything." The blonde's eyes were gleaming. She was a vampire ready to suck the life out of Jada. Terrific.

"Nothing to say."

Tamara gave her a get-real look. "You've got to give me something. I'm the first person to make contact with the most notorious woman in America."

"That's a bit of an exaggeration, don't you think?"

Tamara shook her head. "No, not really. *My One and Only* is the number one show among women aged eighteen to thirty-five in America. There aren't any current celebrity scandals to divert attention away from you. You're it, kid."

Effing great. Would she ever stop making mistakes that led to nowhere good? "Well, I don't really have anything to say."

"Everyone is caught up in how you turned down his proposal, but I'm much more interested in your side of the story."

Jada just stared at her. She refused to give the intrepid reporter any encouragement.

"You said you turned him down because there was someone else you couldn't stop thinking about and you were hoping to reconnect with him when you got home."

Jada ignored the way the bottom fell out of her stomach. "Right."

"The internet has been abuzz with speculation about who this mystery man is."

"Has it? I hadn't noticed."

"Only because your social media accounts have been strangely quiet. People have scoured your accounts to see if they could figure out who this mystery man is." Tamara's eyes gleamed with that vampire look. Pretty soon, her bloodthirsty grin would spread too far, revealing sharp bicuspids. "So who is it? He does exist, doesn't he?"

Oh, shit. She couldn't say he was purely a figment of her imagination. Then she really would be a dead woman walking. "Of course he exists."

"Then who is he? I mean I'm going to write this story either way. I'd like to have a quote from you to give it balance."

Oh, wasn't she a champion of journalistic ethics?

"I don't want to talk about him. I didn't mention his name on the show for a reason." Namely, because he didn't exist, but that wasn't important at the moment.

"Well, have you talked with him since you've been back? Surely he's seen the show. He must know that you couldn't stop thinking about him."

"Umm, well . . ."

"Has he reached out to you?"

"Umm, well . . ."

"He hasn't said *anything*? Surely you didn't make him up, did you? That would be an even crazier story." Tamara was standing way too close to Jada, her beady green eyes bulging with a desire to get a scoop, any scoop. Jada could smell the vanilla frosting from her cupcake on her breath. Jada had never given much thought to the smell of icing, but its overwhelming sweetness was going to make her gag in the very near future. She forcefully tamped down the sensation.

"What? No, of course not."

"Because I would *hate* to report that." Hate, love. Love, hate. Same difference.

Jada forced a smile. "Then don't."

"Give me something, Jada. Everyone wants to know who this mystery guy is. I don't want to assume you made him up. That would be really embarrassing for you."

Embarrassing. A simple word that carried so much weight for her. She'd always been an embarrassment to her parents. She'd strived not to be, but hadn't ever really succeeded. Humiliating. Demoralizing. She was already a national villain. She wouldn't, couldn't become a national laughingstock.

Her parents would never, ever let her hear the end of it. The sighing and disappointed looks would never cease. Neither would the demands that she get a real job and stop disappointing them. She couldn't go through that. They hadn't forgiven her for going on the show, which is why they'd decided to stop paying her bills. This extra humiliation would give them all the ammunition they needed to harangue her at will. She didn't know if she could survive their special brand of concern mixed with bewilderment, overlaid with embarrassment that she wasn't like her sister. What was she going to do? What *could* she do?

"Jada? Is everything okay?"

Oh, no. Donovan had appeared at her side. She'd been so focused on Tamara the intrepid reporter she hadn't noticed him walking up.

Tamara swept her gaze up and down his admittedly impressive physique, then turned back to her. "Is this him?"

"Him?" Donovan asked.

"Yep, this is him. Hi, honey." Jada stepped toward him and covered his mouth with hers before he could blow up her spot. That was her initial reason for kissing him. But that thought quickly gave way to "wow, his lips are nice." Thick and firm and lush. Perfect, in other words. Perfect lips that were frozen solid underneath hers.

Jada stiffened. What the hell was she doing? She couldn't just *kiss* somebody without their okay.

Then she felt a slight movement of his mouth against hers. A delicious bit of friction that sent a shiver cascading down her spine. A slight parting of the lips, a slight tilt of his head for a better angle. He was kissing her back. Expertly, his masterful lips gently sliding against hers, savoring her, then there was a nip—just the tiniest bite against her bottom lip, just enough to make her crave more. Her breath caught in her lungs, then she was free. She barely registered the faint cheers from the cupcakery's other occupants.

She stared up at him, her chest heaving. His eyes, always so dark and piercing, mesmerized her with their intensity and heat. Oh yeah, he'd felt it, too. Was still feeling it. *It* being an intense attraction she'd done her best not to acknowledge. And she'd just blown that all to smithereens.

Chapter Nine

"Oh, my God, that was terrific," Tamara loudly proclaimed, jarring Jada out of the dazed trance she'd stumbled into. She lowered a phone she'd whipped out from somewhere. "I'm going viral with this footage. That was great. I can't wait to watch it again and post it. What a scoop!"

"Jada?" Donovan asked, his voice low and dark, demanding answers.

"Oh, is that why you're working here?" Tamara asked, thankfully not picking up on the dangerous vibes swirling in the air.

Jada took the unintentional lifeline. "Yeah, I wanted to do something low-key while everything died down, and he suggested I come work here. I was going a little stir-crazy being cooped up in my condo. Isn't he the greatest?" She turned her back on Tamara and pleaded with him with her eyes. *Please go along with this. Please. I'll owe you forever and ever.*

"You own this place, right? And play for the Knights?" Tamara asked.

"Yes," he answered, his voice short and clipped. He was suspicious and wasn't giving any more info than was required. Her shoulders relaxed marginally. At least he hadn't decided to sell her out. Not yet anyway. A muscle in his hard jaw was ticking at a steady, angry rate.

Tamara looked at her with new respect. "Girl, if this is who you were coming home to, I wouldn't have said yes either. I can see why he was on your mind when you were on the show."

"Jada," Donovan warned.

"What can I say? I'm a lucky girl," Jada said. She had to get this Tamara person out of here before Donovan blew a gasket. His whole body, pressed against hers, was vibrating with suppressed tension. His fingers pressed hard into her waist, anchoring her to his side. He sensed she might make a run for it, and he wasn't entirely wrong.

"Some of your luck has rubbed off on me. I'm so going viral. I've got to go write this story and upload the video before anyone else can. Thank you for the scoop!" And just like that, Hurricane Vampire Tamara was gone. Jada's shoulders sagged in utter relief.

"Jada. My office. Right now." Donovan's tone—stern, angry, furious—immediately sent her shoulders skyrocketing up to her ears again. Uh-oh. So much for thinking she'd survived the storm. He turned on his heel. She wanted to stick her tongue out at him, but she had no right. Not after what she'd done. But she shuffled along as slowly as she could in her cool new Crocs. They made an absurd squeaky noise against the hard floor. *Squeak, squeak.*

"Now, Jada."

Yeah, Stern Principal was back. She took a deep breath and lengthened her stride a tad, but he didn't bark any more orders.

"What the hell was that?" he asked as soon as the door clicked shut behind her. At least he didn't yell. But he didn't have to. Clearly, he was used to people answering any question he had. The quiet command in his tone, his unflinching focus on her were just as effective. Probably more so.

She opened her mouth to answer. "I . . . well . . . it's just . . ."

"Speak, Jada." Yeah, he was tired of her crap.

"Have you ever heard of *My One and Only*?"

His eyes flashed. "No." He inclined his head. *Continue.*

"It's a reality show."

"And?"

She squeezed her eyes shut for a second. "And it's one of the most popular reality shows in the country. It's a dating show. I was on it. I made it to the end, but I declined the proposal."

"Get to the part that ends with you *kissing* me and declaring me your *boyfriend*." He hissed the entire sentence, which was kind of impressive, considering there weren't a ton of *s*'s in the sentence. He was still pissed, in other words.

Jada swallowed. "Right. I'm almost there. When I declined the proposal, I said the reason I did was because I was missing somebody at home."

"And?" he asked, his exasperation clear.

"That person doesn't really exist."

"So?"

Jada lowered her eyes, then raised them. She'd gotten herself in this mess. She had to own up to it. "Look. I've become a villain."

"A villain? After you were on a silly reality show?"

"Yeah, the internet hates me."

"You've got to be kidding me. People actually give a shit about what happens on reality shows?"

She shrugged. "I mean sports are the biggest reality shows out there, so yeah."

"Jada." The thunderous look on his face would have been hilarious if they weren't talking about her life.

"Right. Back to the point. No, I'm not kidding. You can check my social media pages. I stopped a while ago. The hate is real."

"Because you turned down a marriage proposal on some ridiculous TV show? People still watch TV?"

"Yeah. And they stream. Which extends the time people can get worked up and want to express their very important opinions on a variety of social media platforms, which then catch the attention of media outlets, who report on it, extending the life of the scandal."

Donovan rounded his desk and sank into his leather chair, once again looking like the king of the manor. "Back to the point, Jada."

"Right. She recognized me and started asking all these questions, and people already hate me, and I didn't want even more to hate me and she was pressuring me and all of sudden you were there."

"So you kissed me?"

"Yes! I started talking before I could think. I'm sorry, okay!"

"She said she planned on going viral with that video of us kissing."

"Maybe she's joking. Going viral isn't guaranteed. It's organic. Most times." Sometimes.

He threw his hands up in the air. "You just said you were a national villain! You don't think people are going to care?"

"I don't know," she said in a small, hopeful voice, her eyes downcast.

"We're not dating."

"I know that, Donovan," she said through stiff lips. That brief, yet scorching hot kiss notwithstanding.

"I don't do reality TV. I do as little social media as possible."

"You don't?" What must that be like? "Are you eighty?"

That muscle in his jaw jerked again. "No, I'm someone who has a lot going on and made a decision to concentrate on more important things."

"Oh." Right. Some people did make that decision.

"In other words, I don't care what she posts."

"Yep, got that." She reached across the desk, clutching his hand. "But you have to."

He stared down at their clasped hands for a second before raising his eyes, now inscrutable, up. "Why?"

"Because I know how powerful social media is." She closed her eyes for a beat. This was not the time for pride. "And I'm asking for your help."

"Which means what exactly?"

"That you won't blow up my spot."

The muscle in his jaw ticked again. "Which means what exactly?"

"That if someone asks if we're dating, you don't look at them like they've asked if Sugar Blitz's cupcakes are nasty."

His lips twitched, just a little, but she caught it. "So you want me to lie."

"You know, the word 'lie' has such weight attached to it."

His dark eyes flashed. "As it should."

"I'm not asking you to lie, just don't . . . deny it."

"Oh, my God, this is ridiculous. I'm seriously worrying about some strange woman coming into my store claiming she's going to go viral with a video of me kissing my newest employee who said I was her someone special. Do I have that right?" For a moment, he looked overwhelmed by what she'd put him through over the past few days.

Jada's shoulders hunched forward. Her vision blurred for a second. Here it came. He really was going to fire her now. "Yeah."

He sighed. "Jada."

Yep, it was coming. She'd heard that sigh her entire life. Her parents had mastered it, but she'd heard the same from teachers, friends, employers. And now Donovan. But could she blame him?

First, she'd burned his cupcakes, now she'd invaded his personal life. Speaking of . . . she gasped. "Do you have a significant other or a spouse?" Her stomach twisted at the thought. But only because she never wanted to be a party in adultery, not because the thought of him touching someone else, *loving* someone else bothered her.

Now he did look at her like she'd asked him if he thought the cupcakery's offerings were gross. "No. Do you think I'd kiss you, sad, puppy dog eyes be damned, if I had someone waiting for me at home?"

She shrugged. "I mean . . . I don't know."

"Exactly. We don't know each other. Which is why it makes no sense for us to pretend to date or whatever you have in mind. We literally met three days ago." He paused. "Were you serious about not having a special someone at home?"

She nodded. All of her exes were exes for a reason. All disasters better left in the past. She didn't have any close male friends who she could call to help bail her out of her latest mess.

"Oh. Well." He sighed again. "No, sorry, can't do it. It doesn't make sense and is ripe for disaster. I have too much going on to be courting disaster. I run my life to be orderly. I have a plan to be successful. I've stuck to the plan—mostly—for the past fifteen years, and the plan is working. I can't be distracted. I won't be distracted. I'm not going to worry about some strange woman coming into my shop saying she's going to go *viral.*"

Jada lifted her chin even as her hopes plummeted to the soles of her Crocs. "Okay, then. I understand."

And she did, but that didn't change facts. Looked like she was on her own. Nothing new there. She knew something about survival. This was yet another obstacle in a lifetime of obstacles. If she felt a little more alone this time because she'd felt a bit of connection when they'd kissed, then faced nosy Tamara together, then it was all in her head. And he was right. She was a big distraction.

She'd gotten herself in this mess. She'd get herself out. Without Donovan's help. Somehow.

* * *

At 7:15 P.M., Donovan walked into his house. August was closing Sugar Blitz tonight. Donovan huffed out a breath. Thank God. He was beat. He wanted nothing more than to pop one of the high-protein, nutrient-rich meals his chef prepared for him into the microwave and eat it on his patio as he listened to and watched the ocean waves crashing against the beach. He headed to the kitchen, ready to put his plan into action.

At 7:18 P.M., right when he'd made the decision to go with steak over pasta carbonara, his phone rang. He gave a moment's thought to not answering, but it was his baby sister, Sloane. He'd always looked out for her, especially given the chaos they'd grown up in, and he'd never been able to stop even though she was now an adult. He dropped into a dining table chair and answered. "Hey, what's up?"

"What's up with me? What's up with *you*?" she screeched into his ear.

He yanked the phone away before he suffered any permanent hearing loss, then gingerly brought it back to his ear. "Sloane, can I get you to bring it down an octave? Dogs are howling as we speak."

"Sorry," she said in her normal, steady tone. "I'm just so excited."

"Excited about what? Did you get a promotion?"

"No, I didn't get a promotion and don't try to distract me."

Distract her? From what? "What are you talking about?"

"I'm talking about the fact that you're trending on Twitter."

Donovan stifled a groan. It couldn't be. That lady couldn't go viral just because she wanted to. It didn't work like that. Did it? He'd been truthful with Jada. He didn't do social media. He had social media accounts, of course. He wasn't that out of touch. But the main reason he had them was to prevent randos from pretending to be him and posting crazy shit under his name. He didn't do anything with the accounts, however. Which didn't really endear him to his baby sister, who made her living as a social media assistant. Soon to be manager, according to her, though apparently not today.

He asked the question he didn't want the answer to. "Why am I trending on Twitter?"

"Because you were kissing Jada from *My One and Only*!" There went the screeching again, but that was the least of his problems.

His stomach cratered. Shit. Thank God he hadn't eaten yet. Okay, that was dramatic, and he didn't do drama. He needed to chill. He'd listened to his sister enough to know trends on social media were just that. Trends. Trends came and went. In thirty minutes, some attention-seeker would do or say something truly outrageous, and he would soon be ancient history. "Can you forget about that please?"

His sister gasped. "No! I'm calling Shana."

"Please don't." His big sister would undoubtedly love to add her opinion to this matter. She had an opinion on every aspect of his life. This would be too juicy to pass up.

"Too late."

Yeah, he'd figured that out. The phone was already ringing. His older sister answered a second later. "Hello."

"Sloane, did you see that Donovan is trending on Twitter? Because he was kissing *Jada*?" She made Jada sound like some scandalous, two-bit hussy. And now he sounded like some old biddy from a western from the fifties.

"Girl, I did!" Sloane answered. "Can you believe it?"

"Hello, I'm right here," he interjected before they could really get going.

"Oh, you're on the call, Donovan. Perfect," Shana said. "You always were my favorite sibling, Sloane."

He rolled his eyes and stifled a sigh.

"Now tell us everything," she continued.

"Don't leave anything out," Sloane added.

His sisters were tag teaming him. Why had he not been blessed with a brother or at least a sibling who didn't love teasing him or digging into his personal life? He took the only option available to him—stalling. "There's nothing to tell."

"Don't try that with me, little brother," Shana said, sounding exactly like their mother.

"You're lucky Mama hasn't found out yet," Sloane said, no doubt thinking along the same lines as him. "She'd be on you like white on rice."

Wasn't that the truth? A little tug of guilt pinched near his heart. Jada hadn't wanted him to tell anyone they weren't dating, but he'd told her he couldn't promise her that. And these were his sisters, who he trusted more than anyone else in the world. If he asked them to keep their mouths shut, they would. Yet he felt like he was betraying Jada, which was the height of ridiculousness. He didn't do ridiculousness. So the truth it was, but first he had questions. "Tell me about this show."

"It's so great," Shana said. "Drama-filled. It's like potato chips. Once you eat one, you can't stop."

Sloane murmured in agreement. "Basically, there's the lead, and he goes out with a bunch of women. Every week, the contestants vote on which two women they don't want to get a date. They form coalitions. The lead has the right to veto one objection per week in his quest to find his one and only. He eliminates a few women each week after all his dates."

Donovan clutched his phone. "What about Jada?"

"Jada was the best, or so everyone thought until the finale," Sloane said. "She was funny and always spoke her mind with the lead, Dr. John, and the other contestants. She and John had great chemistry."

"Dude was smitten," Shana said. "Viewers loved him. He was genuine and there for the right reasons."

"Finding love on a reality show? Yeah, okay." Donovan had his doubts.

"It's true. He was the sweetest guy. Funny and kind, but not easily bamboozled by antics. Some of the other contestants didn't like how well Jada and he got along and tried to split them up, but it didn't work. They were always together."

He swallowed around the lump in his throat. "So they what? Fell in love with a bunch of cameras in their face recording their every move?"

"It seemed like it. They were like the Black Ken and Barbie. Gorgeous, funny, photogenic. All the viewers thought we were getting a fairy-tale ending with a proposal."

"And then she dumped America's Favorite Bachelor—that was the headline on the *People* cover—instead," Sloane said. "The fans went crazy."

Shana concurred. "Some of the other contestants said she was playing him the whole time and they were right."

That didn't sound like the woman he knew. Granted, he hadn't known her very long, but the look of devastation and resignation on her face at the shop was real. He'd bet his entire net worth on it. And maybe that made him as much of a sucker as the dude on the reality show. "What happened next?"

"She stopped posting to all her social media accounts," Sloane said. "No one knew where she was—until tonight. Tweet's up to twenty-three thousand retweets, by the way. Why was she at the shop wearing the uniform?"

Donovan sighed. "Because she works there."

"Since when?" Shana asked, her voice full of breathless disbelief. At least she didn't screech like their little sister.

Donovan blew out a breath. "Since yesterday."

"And you're already kissing her. You move fast, big brother. Who knew you had it in you?" Sloane teased.

He groaned. "That's not how it went down."

"Then tell us the truth, the whole truth, and nothing but the truth. How did she go from reality TV villain to Sugar Blitz employee to Donovan Dell's girlfriend?"

"She's not my girlfriend," he said through clenched teeth.

"But you did have your tongue down her throat," said his logical, straight-shooting older sister who would never be intimidated by him.

"No, I didn't," he said over Sloane's snickers.

"Then tell us what's up," Shana said, clearly pleased with herself for maneuvering him into a corner.

Donovan started with how she'd come to work at the store and ending with the reason Jada had kissed him. "That's it. She needed a temporary stand-in and I happened to be the guy standing there. No more, no less."

His explanation was met with a few seconds of silence.

"Oh. That's it?" Shana finally said.

"Yep." Mostly. He'd left out the details about how that was the best first kiss he'd ever had. How her soft lips had clung so temptingly to his that he couldn't help but respond. How the taste of her haunted him hours later and he could still taste her, especially if he closed his eyes and replayed the frustratingly short embrace in his mind. Which he'd done approximately fifty times since it happened. Yeah, his sisters didn't need to know any of that.

"You're not really dating."

"Nope." He ignored the twinge of disappointment that zapped him.

"Even though you're trending on Twitter, and people are commenting that you two looked like soulmates as you gazed into each other's eyes?"

Jada had the most amazing eyes he'd ever seen.

"Donovan?" His sister sounded way too hopeful.

He groaned. "No."

"Oh. I was hoping what she said on the show was true. I really liked her and didn't understand why she would go on a show just to humiliate somebody. Didn't seem like her vibe."

"We're not dating." He said it because it was true and maybe to remind himself. Just because he'd felt something new and sweet and hot during the kiss and had temporarily lost himself in the taste and scent and feel of her didn't mean anything.

"Do you want to date her?" Sloane asked, apparently still hopeful. "Sounds like she could use a guy."

"And dating her could boost your sales given the reaction tonight on Twitter," Shana, the pragmatic accountant, added.

"No, I don't, and really, Shana?" If there was a little tug of something near his heart that felt like regret, then whatever. He and Jada were not destined to be anything other than temporary boss and employee. No matter how soft her lips were or how good her body felt against his. "I have two focuses: making Sugar Blitz successful—without dating someone for the sole purpose of making that happen—and winning a Super Bowl next season. I don't have time for anything else right now." Especially someone who drove him crazy.

Chapter Ten

At 8:45 A.M., Jada made the right turn onto Sugar Blitz's street. *What the hell?*

Even from a block away, she had no trouble identifying the scene unfolding before her. A line of people started at the front door and extended down the sidewalk all the way to the stop sign at the end of the block. Were they here because of her? That was an arrogant assumption, but why else would so many people be here on a random Thursday morning *before* the cupcakery opened?

Shit.

Olivia had called her last night to let her know she was trending on Twitter and was the talk of Instagram. Jada had politely thanked her, ended the call, climbed in the bed, and chose to block out reality by binge-watching *Nailed It!* Low-stakes good times involving people who baked about as well as she did were all she could handle at the moment.

She didn't want to think about Tamara's video and the reactions to it. Apparently, that wasn't the best decision. She should have been coming up with a game plan to handle the fallout of the Kiss instead. Jada blew out a breath. Oh, well.

Fortunately, Donovan had given her the code to come in through the back entrance. She drove around to the parking lot behind the store and pulled into a spot, thankful for her car's tinted windows. Back here, everything was quiet. Normal.

She flipped down the visor and inspected her face in the mirror. At least her hair and makeup were on point. No need to mention the polo shirt and khakis she wore. Or the Crocs. And that was enough stalling.

Still, she kept her head down and entered the store as quickly as possible. Reality TV show fans could smell fear.

"I assume we have you to thank for that crowd out there."

Jada's head jerked up. But it wasn't Donovan standing there. It was August, who'd just uttered the most words she'd ever heard from him. She offered up a weak smile. He nodded, his small smile sympathetic, and disappeared into the kitchen.

Jada loitered in the hall, indecision rooting her to the spot. Going out to the front of the store meant seeing all the people standing outside, who'd be staring at her through the windows. She could follow August to the kitchen, but that meant returning to the scene of the baking fiasco. Smoke probably still lingered in the air, undercutting the smells of chocolate and vanilla. She shuddered. And August was in there. Nicholas, too, most likely. They would have questions about the Kiss, assuming Donovan hadn't filled them in.

Her stomach lurched, the strawberry cereal bar she'd forced herself to eat that morning rolling around in her stomach like a drunk uncle on the dance floor at a wedding. Oh, God, her mouth had gotten her into trouble yet again, figuratively and literally this time.

But she was a grown-up. Right? Right. She could do this. She threw back her shoulders and headed to the front of the store. She kept her eyes straight forward.

"Jada," Donovan called out through the open door of his office.

Jada's heart seized. She stopped mid-stride and swallowed. Forced her feet to turn to face him. "Yes?"

"Come in, please," he said, gesturing with his hand. His face was impassive, as was his voice. She'd take that over anger or annoyance. She nodded. "Close the door," he added when she crossed the threshold. She swallowed again, following his order.

Maybe he was going to fire her. He'd had a night to think it over, after all. Surely, he knew that he, she—*they* had been a hot topic of discussion on social media last night. She collapsed in the chair in front of his desk in a rather undignified heap, her legs unable to support her any longer. Maybe he didn't notice. She raised her head. His eyebrows were nearly touching his hairline. Her gaze skittered away. He'd noticed. Whatever. Dignity was overrated, anyway.

"Looks like we're in a predicament." His voice was calm, nonjudgmental. "How do you want to handle this?"

Jada caught herself before her mouth fell too far open. He wasn't firing her. Her shoulders deflated. Or maybe he wanted her to fire herself?

"There's a line of people outside the shop who've undoubtedly come to gawk," he continued. "You can work the front counter or you can stay in the kitchen and help Nicholas with food prep. August is leaving soon to run some errands. You can go with him if you want."

"You're not mad?" she asked in a rush.

He sighed. "No, I'm not mad. Although usually the only time anyone on Twitter cares about what I'm doing is during a game when I do or don't make a play. People speculating about my love life isn't ideal, but I plan on ignoring it. They'll get bored and move on if they haven't already."

She blurted out the question that had been buzzing in her head since he demanded to speak to her. "Why are you being nice to me?"

He leaned back in his chair. Studied her with his intelligent dark eyes, giving nothing away. "Do you want me to be mean to you? Yell at you?"

"No, but I'd understand if you did. I did put you in a weird position yesterday."

"You did, but it's a temporary thing that will go away." He shrugged. "I don't care about social media. It'll be easy for me to ignore. Besides, I promised your grandmother you could work here, and I do my best to live up to my promises."

Right. He didn't care about her specifically. She needed to remember that. She was a duty, nothing more, nothing less. "I want to work out front. That's where I was headed before you ordered me in here." She shrugged. "We both know I'm a disaster in the kitchen."

He nodded. "You are."

"Thanks," she said dryly.

His eyebrows lifted. "People are gonna stare."

Jada was proud of herself for not flinching. "I know. Let them."

"You've got gumption. I have to give that to you."

Gumption? Did people really still use that word? "Wait. Is that a compliment?"

"Don't let it go to your head." His voice was calm and measured, but if she wasn't mistaken, a smile was striving to make its presence known on his normally impassive face. His lips, those same lips she'd seen and tasted over and over again in her restless sleep last night, stretched the slightest bit.

"I'll try." She stood and crossed to the door, resolute in her mission, although her legs were still a little unsteady.

"You'll be fine," he said to her back. More effusive praise. If she wasn't careful, her head would start swelling any second now. She continued on her way to the front of the store, smiling to herself.

"There you are," Ella squealed when she spotted her. "One half of #JaDon."

Jada groaned. "Really?"

The teen nodded enthusiastically. "Oh, yeah. The folks who don't hate you now ship you with Donovan. It took them about two-point-two seconds to come up with that name."

"Awesome."

Squeals penetrated through the windows and doors. The crowd outside had spotted Jada. She did her best to ignore them as she rounded the corner to join Ella at the cash register.

Ella jerked her chin toward the entrance. "I think they're going to rip down the door if we don't open soon."

Jada busied herself by pouring a cup of coffee and took a sip of the hot brew. "They probably want to rip my throat open."

"They'll have to go through me first." Ella's fierce voice was matched by her facial expression.

Jada blinked back unexpected tears. What had she done to deserve such loyalty so quickly? Her parents had certainly never felt that urge. Again, she squared her shoulders.

"Thanks, but I don't think that will be necessary. We're here to work and serve some cupcakes."

Ella nodded. "Then let's get to it."

Jada took a moment to enjoy the sweet, sweet quiet while Ella walked to the door like she wasn't about to open the portal to hell. Jada bit her bottom lip. Maybe that was a little dramatic. Maybe. In a few seconds, her entrée into impolite society would effectively commence. The flip of the lock, followed by the ding of the overhead bell as the door opened, offered a ringing one-two punch of a sonic boom to her nerves.

The hordes from outside streamed in, gawking at the store like they'd never been inside a bakery before they turned their hawk eyes to Jada. She lifted her chin. She couldn't stop the bead of sweat sliding down her temple, but she wouldn't squirm.

"How can I help you?" she asked the first person to reach the front counter, a petite woman with a long ponytail, who looked like she came straight from her yoga class and was all limbered up and ready to rumble.

She practically bounced on the balls of her feet. "Wow. It really is you, Jada. You work here?"

Jada pasted on her brightest smile. "Yep. How can I help you?"

The woman stared at her like she expected Jada to say more. Jada stared back. Finally, the woman sighed. "I'll take two vanilla cupcakes."

Jada retrieved the desserts and sent the woman on her way. One down, a million more to go.

The stares were a lot. The not-so-quiet whispering, too. But as long as they bought cupcakes, she didn't care. At least her impulsive decision to declare Donovan her boyfriend had done some unintended good. They were way busier than they'd been during her first two days. Just when the line slowed down, new arrivals came to take their place. The customers sat at the tables and stared at her as they ate their cupcakes and drank their juice or coffee while also pretending they weren't taking photos of her with their phones. But whatever. She'd put herself in this position. She'd live with it.

The questions were another story.

"Where's Donovan?"

"He's busy." Said with a pleasant smile. Where was her Academy Award?

"How long have you two been together?"

Jada pretended she didn't hear. Donovan had been clear he didn't want to lie about them dating and she would respect his wishes. She'd done enough damage by opening her mouth and declaring him her boyfriend to Gossip Barbie.

The chatter increased in volume. Jada looked up from the cash register. Donovan and Nicholas had rounded the corner. Nicholas, who Jada had come to realize loved attention, headed straight for the masses. Donovan came toward the front counter. The women in line quieted as he neared, then started furiously whispering to each other. He nodded at them and rounded the corner.

"What are you doing here?" she muttered out of the corner of her mouth.

"I do own this place," he murmured close to her ear. A shiver lanced her body. Whatever. It was cold. "But really, Nicholas told me the line hadn't slowed for the past hour, so I had to come see for myself."

"Makes sense." She looked up and was caught by his dark eyes. "But you're adding fuel to the fire."

"Am I?" He didn't seem concerned. Is this what happened when you weren't part of a reality show/pop culture fandom? You didn't understand how fierce and interested in every detail of your life said fandom could be?

By coming out here, he'd put himself directly in the line of fire, and it was her responsibility to protect him because he wouldn't be there if it wasn't for her—although he could've taken a page out of his friend August's playbook and found some errands to run. But he hadn't.

They worked in tandem for a few minutes, fulfilling orders and taking payment. She watched him out of the corner of her eye. He smiled and chatted with the customers like he actually knew how to be charming when he put his mind to it. He was playing everyone's favorite teacher now, instead of the crusty principal. He actually seemed . . . human.

He didn't even lose his focus or cool when the more emboldened clientele put their phones right in front of his face and snapped photos.

"Oh, my God, can I get a photo of you two?" one customer asked.

Jada immediately shook her head. "Sorry, but that's not possible. We have a line."

"We don't mind," the woman behind her said. The other people in line quickly added their assent.

With a Herculean effort, Jada forced her lips upward. "Okay." She inched closer to Donovan. She didn't look at him because, well, this was awkward enough.

The woman lowered her phone. "Seriously, guys, you can do better than that. You look more like middle schoolers on their first date than America's hottest new couple."

Beside her, Donovan stiffened even more. Oh, God. Any second now he was going to give her up. Tell the women she was a liar and that she was only working there because her grandmother had begged him, her employee, to give her flighty granddaughter a job. That they were in no way, shape, or form *dating*.

"Not a problem." Donovan shocked the hell out of her by wrapping his arm around her waist and pulling her against his side. Good Lord, the man was built. Like a brick wall. A warm, really interesting to the touch, I-wanna-explore-every-ridge-and-nook-and-cranny brick wall. She looked up. His eyes were trained squarely on her.

Just like that, the memory of their kiss from yesterday played like a movie in her head. Crystal clear in 4K. The decadent glide of his lips against hers. Her soft sigh. Despite its brevity, the powerful impact it had on her couldn't be denied. The desire to reexperience the embrace again nearly overwhelmed her. His eyes darkened, revealing the truth. He remembered, too. Wanted to experience it again, too. She was barely aware of the quick *click-click*s of the cameras.

"Can we get a kiss?"

Yes, fantastic idea. Wait. What? Jada forced out a laugh and broke away from his hold, the slide of his hand warming her even through the cotton of her shirt. What would it feel like with no barrier? Wait. No. That wasn't going to happen. She didn't want it to happen. Right? Right.

Donovan coughed into his hand like he was floored by the request. Jada returned her attention to the customer. "No, you can't, sorry. One viral kiss is one more than we bargained for."

The woman pouted for a second. "Oh, all right. What about a selfie?"

"Sure," Donovan said and made a move to step around the counter. Who was this man? Where had austere, everything-needs-to-make-sense Donovan gone?

"Jada." Mr. Principal had returned.

Oh, right. They were waiting for her. She hurried around the counter to stand on the right side of the customer while Donovan stood on the left.

"Say cheese," the customer said, then snapped. She lowered the phone. "Oh, this is so cool. I'm going to post this on Facebook and Insta right now." She wandered away. Jada moved to return to her rightful place behind the counter, but the next customer stopped her.

"Oh, I want a picture, too," she said.

And so began the avalanche of selfies. Eventually, Jada relaxed, her smile becoming more natural. Maybe she could make a living as an influencer after all.

"Does it bother you that your girlfriend is a heartless bitch?" the next customer asked.

And just like that her smile withered away to nothing. This was the response she'd expected. Had experienced before she got smart and stopped checking her social media accounts. The ball of anxiety in her stomach that had started to calm began to twist and turn and bounce around the small space again.

"Excuse me." Donovan's voice carried through the room, quiet, forceful in its intensity, snaring the attention of all occupants.

Jada laid a hand on his bare forearm. "It's okay."

"No, actually it's not. No one talks about my girlfriend that way."

Jada's jaw unhinged itself from her face and fell straight to the floor. She couldn't hear anything else over the buzzing in her head. When she stumbled out of her stupor a few seconds later, Donovan was marching the woman to the door and gently but firmly pushing her out the door while the other customers cheered. Well, the ones who weren't recording the spectacle.

He came back and held up his hand for silence. Such a principal move, but kinda cool. *And so fucking hot.* "Thanks, everyone, but the applause isn't necessary. We're happy to serve anyone who wants cupcakes and a photo, but I won't tolerate rudeness."

His message was received loud and clear. For the next thirty minutes, they sold cupcakes to very eager, but polite customers.

Jada kept sneaking glances at him out of the corner of her eye. Who was this person? Had he been body snatched? Was she dreaming? Would she wake up and be reminded that he had no desire whatsoever to be associated with her in a romantic way? He barely tolerated their working relationship. But she didn't wake up. He didn't contradict anyone who commented on their "relationship." In fact, he smiled and went along with it. The other shoe would drop soon enough, but for now, she appreciated knowing no one was going to scream at her and call her a horrible person when she least expected it.

Finally, the line began to dissipate and he said goodbye and disappeared down the hall, no doubt to his office to do whatever he did on his computer for hours at a time. Not that she paid much attention to what he did. She worked there. It only made sense to know what was happening and who did what.

Still, she was thrilled when August came to take her place when her shift was over. As far as she knew, she hadn't made any serious mistakes, but her mind had only been half attached to her work. The other part had been preoccupied by the man who'd stood next to her and said what he'd said. Declared. That she was his girlfriend. Which made her feel like she was in high school, wondering if the boy she'd gone on a date with liked her enough to want to be official. Not that she wanted that with Donovan. Jumping into a relationship made no sense when everything in her life was so uncertain and unsettled.

She was free to leave. She should leave, but for some reason she stopped outside his office door. It was closed, which was good. He couldn't see her standing out here looking like a fool. Bright side.

"Everything okay?" Nicholas asked. He'd come out of the bathroom, which was two doors down.

Jada coughed. "Yeah, I was about to go talk to Donovan."

He pointed at the door. "Don't let him intimidate you. I don't think he realizes his, uh, starchy nature can be a little discomfiting for other people. His bark is way worse than his bite."

Jada lifted her chin. "I'm not scared."

He winked. "Good to hear it." He made a right, heading back to the kitchen.

She hadn't lied. She wasn't scared. She was *terrified*. Which was ridiculous. He'd had every opportunity to send her packing, to never hire her in the first place, and he hadn't. No, he'd declared to the whole world that they were dating, and she needed to find out why. So yeah, time to get it together. She knocked briskly, her hand only trembling slightly on the doorknob at his commanding "come in."

She opened the door and rocked back on her heels. For once, he wasn't sitting behind his desk like the principal waiting to give a misbehaving student detention. He leaned against the desk, his arms crossed across his wide chest, the material of his polo pulling against his mouth-watering biceps like he'd been waiting for her. His eyebrows quirked. "You going to come in or just stand there?"

She lifted her chin. Show no fear. Brazen her way through this, just like she did every day of her life. She stepped forward. Toward him. Toward the man who could torpedo her already-shredded reputation with barely any effort. Toward the man who studied her with a hard, unwavering gaze.

"I was wondering how long it would take for you to show up." His voice, deep and mesmerizing, sent a thrill racing through her. But she had to ignore that.

She let out a little laugh. "It's not every day a man who declared that he wouldn't lie and say we were dating did exactly that less than twenty-four hours later. I was thrown for a loop." She took another step forward, drawn to him. "The question is why. Why did you do it?"

Chapter Eleven

That look on her face. She tried, but she hid nothing. Every emotion showed. When that woman had called her a heartless bitch, before she remembered to school her features back into a calm, unbothered veneer, he'd seen the devastation, the hurt on her face. And the words had flown out of his mouth.

Again, she was trying to hide what she was feeling, but it was there, swirling in her eyes—confusion, uncertainty, and a glimmering, flickering hope. She wanted people to think she was a worldly, sophisticated character—and she was—but that wasn't all she was. She was a red-blooded woman with insecurities and hopes and dreams like everyone else. Like him. And she didn't want anyone to know. Just like him. He coped by making his life as orderly as possible and staying as even-keeled as possible. She made it through with some good old-fashioned gumption, even as she took it on the chin.

He couldn't be the one to let her down. He reached for some papers on his desk. "Do you know what these are?"

Her head tilted to the side as she stared at him like he'd lost his damn mind. Maybe he had. "No. Should I?"

He smiled. She made him smile like no else had in a long time. "They're analytics tracking our website for the past twenty-four hours. We haven't seen traffic like this since the opening week of Sugar Blitz."

"That's great." She bit her lip like she didn't know what else to say. And he wouldn't think about what it felt like if it were his teeth biting that plump lip. The lip that he now had irrefutable evidence was utterly kissable, undeniably biteable.

He shook his head. That wasn't important. It was never going to be important. They were two different people who needed to make the best of this weird situation. Which was the only reason he was excited that she'd stopped by his office instead of leaving for the day. Yep.

He took another step toward her. Underneath the vanilla and chocolate scents that permeated the shop and now clung to her, he caught a hint of something floral. Something intoxicating. Lilies, maybe. "It is great, which is why I've given some more thought to your proposition."

Her perfect eyebrows rose. "Is that why you declared that we were dating?" The mocking was subtle, but clear. He was amused. Whatever uncertainty he'd detected she'd felt had disappeared. This was the Jada who'd basically said his cupcakes weren't all that the first time they'd met. The same woman he'd dreamed about that night, though he wouldn't admit that to anyone, especially to himself.

He took another step forward. He couldn't help it, really had no desire to try to stop himself. "Yes, and that's why I want to continue to do it."

Her mouth fell open. "You're joking, right?" she sputtered.

"Now, Jada, I know we haven't known each other long, but I get the sense that you think I don't have a sense of humor. If we go with that premise, then of course I'm not joking."

"But you said, and I quote, 'I run my life to be orderly. I won't be distracted.'" She'd put some bass in her voice in a horrible attempt at imitating him. He struggled to keep his lips from twitching.

Did he really sound like he had a stick up his ass? "I did say that. However, I can't ignore the line outside that door. My sister tells me we've gained ten thousand fans on our Instagram account since yesterday. Online orders have increased three hundred percent since yesterday. All because of interest in our love life."

"But we're not dating. There is no 'our love life.'" Her eyes were big and wide.

He couldn't, wouldn't get lost in them. This was a logical move, nothing more, nothing less. "I thought you'd be jumping at this opportunity. It was your idea, after all."

"Yeah, but I've had time to think. I'm trying to turn over a new leaf. Not be so impulsive. Really take charge of my life." Her hands twisted together at her waist, her perfectly manicured nails painted a pretty lavender.

He shouldn't be noticing such a small detail about her, but he did. He noticed everything about her, if he was being honest with himself. "I understand that desire."

Her head lifted. "You do?"

He nodded. "I didn't grow up in the most stable environment, so I sought to make my life as stable as possible once I became an adult." He spread his arms wide. "Opening a cupcake shop is the most impulsive thing I've done in years, even if I did run all kinds of analyses to make sure it was a sound investment."

"Until now. When you want to date me." Her lips, painted a deep red, curved. His blood stirred. He knew how that gloss tasted and had loved it.

"Fake date." He needed to remind himself of that fact, if no one else.

She chuckled. "Yes, my bad. Fake date."

"I need this shop to be a success, to stay on the stable train, and the only way to make that happen is to have more customers. I've thought this through."

She crossed her arms. "And what evidence-based and orderly conclusions have you come up with?" Jada was back to silently laughing at him. You could knock her down, but she would always get back up, ready and willing to put him in his place. He ordered himself not to smile.

"That we don't have to do much more than what we did today." He ticked the points one by one on his fingers. "We work here together. We don't argue."

Her nose wrinkled. "Aww, really? That doesn't sound fun."

He continued like she hadn't spoken. "We don't deny it when someone claims we're dating. We take photos when asked. If someone asks us to kiss, we decline like we did today."

"No kissing, huh?" She tapped him on the chest with a single finger. It was the briefest of touches, but it sent his heart rate skyrocketing anyway. He needed to get a grip. Like right now. It was also a reminder why kissing was out of the question. He liked order. He liked to stay in control. And yesterday, he'd lost control temporarily when he'd kissed her back. He didn't need any distractions, and she practically had a neon light above her head that spelled out DISTRACTION.

Then why are you trying to convince her to do this, dumbass? Because it made sense given their predicament. He needed to increase store business so he could hire a manager soon. If people showed up because they thought they were dating, it didn't matter as long as they bought cupcakes, which would help him meet his goal. That's all it was.

She was shaking her head. "I'm not dragging you into my mess. I was impulsive. I have to work on that."

He ruthlessly reined in the panic trying to sink its claws into him at her attempt to back out of his proposal. This was all about reason. "That's why we have these rules. It should be pretty simple. We'll ride the wave while we can. I don't expect the attention to last long, but if it increases our brand awareness and gains us some new customers, then it'll be worth it." He tipped her chin up because really, why shouldn't he take his chance to touch her? She'd scalded him through his shirt, after all. "Need I remind you that this ruse will help save your reputation and give you some armor to protect you from the arrows shot your way? I haven't forgotten what that woman said out there. Or what you said yesterday. There are more people out there like her, aren't there? People who delight in being mean to you, who don't hesitate to call you all kinds of names?"

Her eyes widened. She nodded. He nodded back. Yes, he knew, and he was here to help. It was the truth. Yes, he was a selfish bastard for using her for his own purposes, but that didn't mean he liked seeing that look of pain in her eyes.

Then she glanced away. "I'm still not sure this is a good idea. If there's one thing I've learned, it's that not all attention is good."

"That's why we're in this together. We'll rely on each other. We'll control the narrative." He held out his hand. "Are you in?"

Her teeth snagged her plump bottom lip while she considered his offer. He suppressed a moan. He would not let an unintentionally sexy action get to him. He was in control. He was always in control. He could handle one inconvenient attraction, especially since the source of the attraction lived to drive him up the proverbial wall. This was what was best for Sugar Blitz.

And him?

"It'll be an adventure," he added.

"Is that so? I can never resist an adventure. I'm in." Her eyes were twinkling. Her soft hand slipped into his, the slide of their palms against each other sending a zap of pleasure up his arm and down his spine.

Donovan swallowed past the lump in his throat. What the hell had he gotten himself into?

*   *   *

"Hey, Kendra, what can I get you today?" Jada asked with a friendly smile.

The woman dressed in khakis and a button-down shirt pointed at the display case. "Those are calling my name. I'll take two."

"Excellent choice." Without another word, Jada retrieved two pumpkin spice cupcakes from the display and boxed them up. This was Kendra's third time in the shop this week. "How's your mom doing?"

"Better. She got the cast off her arm and is now back to climbing ladders like nothing happened. It's driving us crazy, but she insists it was only an accident and she won't change her lifestyle. We have no choice but to go along with it. My dad holds his breath every time she moves, but whatcha gonna do?"

Jada shook her head in commiseration. Grams was known for her stubbornness.

Kendra handed over her credit card. "You gonna make it to book club on Thursday?"

Jada swiped the card, then handed it back. "I'll try. I haven't finished the book yet, but I'm trying."

"Girl, don't let that stop you. Half the people show up for the free booze and snacks."

Jada laughed. "I'll remember that."

Kendra made a face. "I'm not sure how much longer we'll be able to meet."

Jada settled her hip against the counter. "Why not?"

"The restaurant where we meet says they want their room back on Thursday nights. They can make more money from food sales than from our puny room rental. We haven't been able to find a place that's big enough and cheap enough that's as centrally located." She shrugged. "It sucks though, but it is what it is. I'll probably see you tomorrow when I need to not think about the situation. Bye."

Jada stilled. What if . . . ?

Her fingers tingled with excitement.

Nope. None of her business. Literally not *her* business. *Keep your mouth shut.* Jada bit her lip because surely that would stop her.

Kendra's hand pushed against the door.

"Wait!"

* * *

"How do you know what her usual is?" Donovan asked several hours later. He'd been observing Jada for the past few minutes. Ostensibly, he was waiting for Nicholas and August so they could have a meeting. That didn't explain why he needed to do that at the front counter instead of the table he'd commandeered in the corner of the shop. He'd told himself he was merely making sure his newest employee was settling in. Soon thereafter, he'd told himself he was a mf-ing liar. And yet he hadn't stepped away.

She shrugged. "I'm good at memorization. It's kinda second nature at this point. She comes in here every morning. I mean the baristas at my favorite Starbucks know what I like. I thought I'd continue the practice here." She tilted her head to the side. "Do you know what any of your regulars like?"

"No. That's more Nicholas's territory." He frowned. That was something he'd never thought about. He was more of a numbers guy. If they offered world-class products, people would return and they'd make money. Easy peasy.

She tsked. "Okay, dude. Since he's spending more time in the kitchen perfecting his recipes, I guess it's up to me to pick up the slack on that front. I think it's good for business. Terry likes vanilla with sprinkles. Bobby from the drugstore around the corner likes red velvet." She studied him. "Did you need something?"

Why did the question make him feel like an interloper in his own business? "Uh, no. Just checking in."

She smiled. "Oh, okay. I'm good. Nothing new to report."

Which should have been his cue to retreat to his table and reports and prepare for his meeting. But he didn't want to leave. He liked talking to her. Which was fine. There was no harm in admitting that.

Before he could come up with a non-embarrassing excuse for why he was still standing there, a customer approached asking for a photo. He should be used to it. In a way, he was. As a high-profile pro athlete, selfie requests were pretty standard. But standing next to Jada, often with his arm around her like they were a true-blue couple, was unsettling.

She settled against him, her back to his front, like this was a natural position for them. Like they'd done this a million times. Like they fit, two connecting pieces in a puzzle. His hands hung at his side, but they tingled with the urge to lift her shirt and touch her soft skin. The light scent of her perfume wrapped around him, the same scent that haunted him in his dreams. She looked up at him and smiled. All he had to do was lean down to taste those perfect lips. Her tongue peeked out like she too was remembering their one entirely too brief kiss.

"Hey, Donovan, you ready?"

Jada sprang away from him. He instantly missed the press of her body against him. Her heat. Her. Which was completely illogical.

Donovan ignored the smirk on Nicholas's face and joined his business partner on the other side of the counter. "Yeah. Where's August?"

"Right here," August said, entering the shop from the back.

Donovan clapped his hands together, determined to ignore the way the blood in his veins continued to pump at ten times its normal rate. He marched to the table in the corner and took a seat.

Nicholas held out his hand as he sat. "Gimme my money, August."

Donovan groaned. He didn't want to know, but he needed to know. "What did you bet on this time?"

Nicholas smirked. "That you would change your mind about the fake dating thing."

Donovan glared at the both of them. "Really?"

"Yeah," Nicholas said as August opened his wallet. "I knew you'd give in, but August had his doubts."

August shrugged while he slapped the twenty-dollar bill into Nicholas's palm. He lowered his large frame into another chair. "I thought you'd stick to the orderly and true like you always do."

Nicholas slid the bill into his pants pocket. "I knew better."

Donovan rolled his eyes. He wasn't surprised by either of their stances. Even though he'd deny it to the ends of earth, Nicholas was a closet romantic. August, on the other hand, knew up close and personal the downsides to love.

"Can we get to the actual reason for this meeting, please? How are we going to boost sales? We're running out of time to get to where we want to be before we have to hire a manager," he said.

"Does anyone have any ideas? The floor is open." Donovan gestured toward his two business partners.

August and Nicholas stared back at him with twin blank expressions on their faces.

Donovan leaned back in his chair. "What?"

"Isn't the whole point of you 'dating' Jada to boost sales?" August asked, using two fingers for air quotes.

"Or are you doing that to get close to her?" Nicholas chimed in. "I mean I recognize a moment when I see one."

"Moment?" August echoed.

"No, you don't, asshole," Donovan answered. "There was no moment."

Nicholas snorted. "Maybe it's been too long since you got laid if you don't recognize a moment with a beautiful, smart, charming woman."

Donovan craned his neck to make sure Jada hadn't overheard, then glared at Nicholas. "One, shut up. Two, yes, the point of Jada and I pretending to date is to boost sales, but we can't rely on that. Something new and salacious will happen tomorrow to divert people's attention, and we'll be yesterday's news. We need something a little more substantial to keep the momentum going. I don't know about y'all, but I like sales. That's one thing the last few days have taught me. I can show you the reports." He made a move to hand out his color-coded spreadsheets with their meticulous charts and figures.

"No, we're good," Nicholas quickly returned. August held up his hands in rejection. Donovan laughed and set the papers down. His partners counted on him to tell them what was what with their finances, but neither liked getting involved in the nitty-gritty world of numbers on a daily basis. Monthly was all about they had time for. Twice a month if they were feeling frisky.

August lifted a shoulder. "A sale?"

Nicholas nodded. "That always helps."

Donovan made a face. "It does, but I was hoping we could come up with something that will have a bigger payoff, a longer payoff. We need to think bigger."

Nicholas leaned back in his chair. "We need to post more on social media. We're too sporadic there."

Donovan sighed. He didn't hate social media, but they were all too busy to devote a lot of time to it. Before Sugar Blitz opened, he'd asked Sloane if she'd be interested in the job, but she'd been steadfast in her refusal, saying she wanted to establish her career out of his shadow. As a result, they'd hired a firm to maintain their website and social media accounts, and they posted regularly, but he'd never seen the posts move the needle.

Someone cleared their throat behind him. Not someone. Jada. Donovan turned in his seat. "Yes, Jada?"

"I overheard y'all talking."

She had? *Everything?* Nicholas snickered. Donovan was going to kill him. What would take the longest time and cause the most pain? He'd have to do some research. Good thing he loved research.

Jada sat in the only open seat at the table. Right next to Donovan. "You've gotten a bump thanks to our little scheme, but I think we both knew that it won't be sustainable forever. We haven't really done anything to feed the gossip beast, so to speak."

Nicholas spoke. "Maybe you should."

Donovan frowned. "Maybe we should what?"

"Feed the beast."

"Which means what exactly?" If his friend suggested he and Jada have a full-on make-out session for the cameras, he was going to kick his ass today, right now.

"Go out on a date. Be seen. You spend all your time here. There are other places in San Diego, or so I hear."

Donovan rolled his eyes. "You date enough for the both of us."

Nicholas inclined his head. "I do, but everyone expects that from me and no one bats an eyelash. No one posts videos from my dates on Twitter. If you and Jada went on a date at a very public place, I guarantee you they will."

Go out with Jada? On a date? Act couple-y? No way. He couldn't. They couldn't. It was a ridiculous idea. He turned to August, but his first best friend only shrugged. Effin' great. That meant he didn't think it was a terrible idea. Donovan shook his head. "No."

"Well, how about a television appearance?" August asked.

"What?" Where had that come from? Had his friends been conspiring behind his back to come up with the most outlandish plan to torture him?

August gave a casual shrug, like he hadn't dropped a huge bomb on the proceedings. "Well, one of us has to monitor the business email, and we—well, you and Jada—received a request today to appear on *Good Day, San Diego*."

Nicholas leaned forward, his eyes gleaming with the desire to cause mischief and add to the mayhem. "I like it. Go make some cupcakes, mention the shop a million times, act lovey-dovey and get us some business. Positive press. It'll be like five minutes." He snapped his fingers. "Or you could go with my original idea of a fake date in a very public place—I'm thinking a kiss cam at a basketball game."

"San Diego doesn't have a team." Technically true, but Donovan was grasping at straws, and he didn't care. He needed to stop this train from further derailing.

"L.A. is right up the freeway." Apparently, Nicholas was determined to keep the train spinning off the tracks. "They have two basketball teams. And they have paparazzi. Even better." He smiled the smile of a smug bastard. Donovan was going to kill him.

Jada held up a hand. She looked slightly panicked, like Nicholas and August's ideas had spooked the hell out of her, which he wouldn't take personally. One of their rules was to do the bare minimum. The bare minimum did not include going out on a date or appearing on a TV show as a couple.

"Um, guys, as interesting as those ideas sound, I was thinking more along the lines of hosting the neighborhood book club," she said. "Their usual place is kicking them out."

Donovan frowned. "We're not a bookstore or a library."

"No, but you do have a big enough space with comfortable chairs. They need a space. A lot of them have probably never been in here before, and if they have, it never hurts to remind them what a great place this is. And . . . uhhh . . ."

"Spit it out." Whenever she started prevaricating like that, it never meant good things for him.

She wrinkled her nose. "I *may* have already told them they could use Sugar Blitz. I'm sorry. I know I should have asked, but Kendra looked so sad and this place is perfect and don't be mad please. I really do think it will be perfect."

"You did what?" A pulse began to throb behind his right eye.

"You know, you should have a doctor look at that vein in your forehead. Check it out to make sure everything's okay."

The pulse beat harder. "Jada."

"I was going to tell you after my shift was over, but you called this very important meeting with your business partners, so I couldn't. But then I overheard what you were talking about."

"Because you were hovering," he bit out.

Nicholas cleared his throat. Right. He was sounding like an ass. Donovan waved his hand. "Please continue."

Jada took a deep breath. "I can handle everything. You don't have to do anything."

"Which is great, but we're not ready. We're not prepared to host a book club meeting. We can't just open our store to chaos."

"Dude." That was August.

Donovan caught himself again. Right. He needed to chill. He sounded like a buzzkill, and he had been the one to ask for ideas. He held up a hand. "What kind of book club?"

"Romance," Jada said.

He could handle that. How bad could it be? He sighed.

Jada sat up straighter, eagerness spreading across her expressive face. "Is that a yes?"

He side-eyed her. "Didn't you already tell them yes?"

She glanced away for a second. "Yes, but I don't own this place."

"Oh, so now you remember that." He ignored his friends' disapproving looks. Hey, he was who he was. Sarcasm was going to be the result when his world was thrown out of order.

She hopped up, now bursting with energy, clearly no longer fazed by his attitude. "I'll get in touch with them to set everything up."

"You're going to plan it."

She spun back toward him. "I mean yeah, if that's okay." There was that vulnerability she tried so hard to hide. The vulnerability he found impossible to resist.

Fighting the urge to reach for her hand, he nodded. "It's okay."

"I promise not to burn down the place." A smile, stunning in its intensity and beauty, spread across her face.

Unable to resist, Donovan stood, moving closer to her like she was a magnet. "Of course you won't. I'll be there." He gestured toward his business partners. "We all will."

He ignored Nicholas's and August's twin groans.

Chapter Twelve

Jada caught Kendra's gaze and gave what she hoped was a crisp, authoritative nod. It was time. Sugar Blitz's first ever after-hours event. Which Jada had coordinated in less than two days. No biggie. Oh, God, she was going to hurl. Jada wiped sweaty palms on her dress.

Kendra stood and cleared her throat. "First of all, I'd like to thank Jada for recommending we move our meetings here and Sugar Blitz's owners for allowing us to use their space and for providing cupcakes and drinks for us to enjoy while we're here." Kendra spread her arms wide, merriment twinkling in her eyes. "And also for gracing us with their presence tonight."

The other eight women applauded and tittered while shooting glances at the three men in attendance. Nicholas waved, hamming it up per usual, while August held up the wall at the back of the room, no doubt wishing he could disappear into it. Donovan sat with his arms crossed, surveying the situation, like he couldn't wait for his chance to declare the night an unparalleled disaster.

Or maybe that was just Jada's overactive imagination. Nerves battled with hope in the pit of her stomach. She wasn't sure which side would win out.

She wanted tonight to go well. She really, really wanted tonight to go well. This was her idea, after all. Her chance to prove she wasn't a screwup and had something to add to Sugar Blitz other than her notoriety.

At least the place looked nice. Less sterile. With August's silent help, she'd added a few festive touches, including placing posters of the books the club had read over the past year on easels all around the room. Vases filled with red and purple flowers to mimic the cover of tonight's pick acted as centerpieces on every table, along with a few lamps to warm up the space. She'd wanted to do more, but she'd been in a time crunch.

She'd carefully studied the Sugar Blitz catering menu before putting in an order with Nicholas. She wanted a variety of cupcakes so people could try fun, new flavors while having the fallback of familiar favorites.

Nicholas had upped the ante, decorating the desserts with horses and cowboy boots and hats. The women had oohed and aahed at his attention to detail. Nicholas, of course, had taken the opportunity to flirt with the club members, much to their delight, when he delivered the baked goods. The bakery had also supplied lemonade, juice, coffee, and, most importantly, wine, because according to Kendra, "What were books without wine?" Infallible logic, really.

The club members were already indulging while mingling and complimenting each other on their outfits before the meeting started. They had all worn their best western gear, which varied from plasticky cowboy hats from Party City to real cowboy boots and western shirts with suede fringe.

Jada had a wide and varied wardrobe, but western wear wasn't really in her wheelhouse. She wore a denim dress that hit her at mid-thigh and brown suede high-heeled boots that could qualify as western if someone squinted really hard. Donovan had taken one look at her, scanned her figure from head to toe with his inscrutable dark eyes, and then plopped down in the chair next to her. He hadn't spoken a word since. She was trying not to take his silence personally.

"We're happy to have you," Donovan said in reply to Kendra, his deep voice a counter to the majority of the other voices in the room.

Kendra nodded and held up her copy of *No Cowgirl Left Behind*. "Did we all have a chance to read the book?"

The club members nodded. And so did Donovan. Wait. What? Jada leaned over. "You did?" she whispered.

"Wasn't that a stipulation of attending?" he murmured, turning his head, putting their faces, their *mouths* millimeters apart. She drew in his clean, fresh scent as a shiver of desire slid down her spine. His eyes were trained on her, like there was no one else in the room. "Look at that. I do have the power to surprise you."

He had no idea. He had the power to make her long for things, feelings she'd denied herself for so long. Her breathing quickened.

"Now, now, there will be time for that lovey-dovey stuff later," Kendra said to more titters from the book clubbers. Her heart racing, Jada jerked back, settling into her chair. The distance did absolutely nothing to stop her from sensing every shift of his body or inhaling the faint aroma of his cologne.

"I'm so glad you read the book, Donovan," Kendra continued. "We're always eager to get a male perspective, but it only happens every now and then when a male significant other joins us. That's you this time!"

Donovan held up his hands, looking slightly uncomfortable, which she would not find adorable. "I'm not sure I have much to offer, but I'm happy to be here."

"We love a man who shares his love's interests, don't we, ladies?"

The women, by universal decree, all beamed at him. Jada pressed her lips together to stop a groan from escaping. Not only would they have to keep the charade going tonight, the women were looking at the skeptical principal like he was some conquering hero returning home.

And she couldn't exactly blame them?

That was *not* in the plan, and she needed to get her head on straight right now. She hopped up. "Does anyone need any wine?" she asked when everyone turned to stare at her.

She sighed in relief when a few women held out their wineglasses. She'd done some hard-hitting "research" to find the best wines to pair with cupcakes. According to the internet, it was more about the effort than the execution. Any wine was good with cupcakes as long as it was plentiful and free-flowing. She'd gone with a nice Moscato. The women seemed to have no complaints. They downed it liberally in between bites of cupcakes.

Jada scanned the room one more time. Overall, everything looked good and the women seemed satisfied. Granted, they were just happy to have a place for their discussion, but she wanted them to have fun and be comfortable as well. A home away from home. Maybe tell their friends and come back.

Kendra nodded. "Let's get started. This story follows Becca, a horse ranch owner, and Carlton, who had the misfortune of being named after a character on a sitcom, but has overcome that giggleworthy fact to become a successful owner of several boutique hotels. He comes to stay at her ranch because he's thinking about buying it and turning it into a bed-and-breakfast dude ranch, and shenanigans ensue, as they often do in romance novels. So Becca and Carlton meet cute when he literally falls at her feet."

"Which is the exact opposite of what usually happens in romance," said a woman named Cara, according to her name tag. The other women nodded.

"Thank God. What woman doesn't want some fine-ass man at her feet?" said Alex, another club member.

"Yes, girl, yes," another woman named Lydia said, holding up her hand for a high five.

"When Carlton arrives at the ranch, he doesn't tell Becca why he's there," Kendra said. The group groaned in unison. Jada didn't blame them. Every romance reader knew when a love interest kept secrets, doom was sure to follow.

"What do you think about that, Donovan?" Kendra asked.

All eyes turned to him. To his credit, he didn't wilt under the attention. He'd clearly regained his footing and, unlike her, wasn't obsessing about that moment when they'd been close enough to kiss. "Well, I'm usually a fan of honesty is the best policy. However, he had just accidentally overheard her conversation saying she would never listen to anyone trying to buy the ranch and would throw them out at the first opportunity. He's also not sure he wants to buy the ranch. He was only there to get the lay of the land."

Jada had heard enough. "Dude, come on. He wants to buy the ranch. We all know that."

"He knows he doesn't want to get his ass kicked before he can even say hello."

The women laughed. Of course they did. Jada rolled her eyes. She would not be taken in by his charm. She didn't even want to admit he had charm.

"Have you always been honest with your girlfriends, Donovan?" Lydia asked.

He nodded without hesitation. "Yes, I have."

"Is that true, Jada?"

She considered him. Considered how he'd treated her from day one, and how he'd never been less than forthright with her. And how she appreciated it. "Yep, he's never been afraid to let me know what was on his mind."

He didn't even try to hide his smirk. Her eyes narrowed. Then they rolled when the club members sighed as one. Now they'd have visions of Prince Charming dancing in their head. *And maybe so do you.*

Jada shook her head. Okay, again, that was enough of that ridiculous thinking.

Thankfully, Lydia turned her attention elsewhere. "What about you, Nicholas?"

"I believe that honesty is the best policy," Nicholas said, rubbing the back of his neck, "which hasn't always served me well when it comes to ending a relationship."

Kendra's eyes narrowed. "So you're the love 'em and leave 'em type?"

"Well . . ."

"Yes," Donovan chimed in. Everyone laughed.

Discussion continued with Donovan and Nicholas giving their male point of view about the story, with the women good-naturedly boo hissing every time they defended Carlton for not admitting the truth even though he had several opportunities to do so. They all agreed that Becca and Carlton were perfect for each other.

Inch by inch, tension melted out of Jada's shoulders and hope beat back the nerves in her stomach. The wine flowed and the cupcakes were downed with unbridled appreciation. Success was officially within her grasp.

As the discussion came to a close, Kendra clasped her hands together. "Jada, in addition to imbibing wine and having a book discussion, we like to do a different activity each month to really make our book club stand out from other groups."

"Oh, okay." Unease skittered across her skin. Why didn't she know what Kendra was about to say? They'd been in constant contact over the past few days.

She ignored Donovan's intense gaze boring a hole into the side of her face. He liked order. He wanted to know everything before it happened.

Kendra's leaned forward. "Rose is a photographer who does custom photo shoots." She pointed to a waving woman seated at a table a few feet away from Jada. "We've been interested in the science behind cover photo shoots, and she promised to show us how they go down. However, the male model pulled out at the last minute, so we thought we'd have the book club members pose individually as Becca with a western, cowboy ranch–themed background."

"Okay," Jada said slowly. That didn't sound too bad. It's not like she didn't like having her photo taken—well, before the whole reality-TV-villain thing happened, anyway.

Kendra's voice rose with way too much excitement. "But with Donovan here, we'd love it if you two re-created the cover. We can display the photo on our website and social media accounts and hopefully attract more members. Y'all are both so good-looking, it makes perfect sense."

The blood in Jada's veins crystallized. Good thing, because running screaming into the night wouldn't send the right message, and it would probably lead to yet another social media viral moment. Beside her, Donovan's face had gone completely blank.

"You have amazing chemistry. You'll be great," Kendra continued like she had to convince them, clearly attributing their silence to being shy about stepping in front of the camera, and not to the fact that they weren't actually dating.

Jada shook her head. "I'm not sure . . ."

"Oh, no, you have to do it," Nicholas chimed in. August stepped away from the wall to finally join the group and nodded his approval at this new development.

Donovan glared at his friends. Nicholas and August beamed in return, clearly not intimidated by their best friend. She added her glare to the mix. Their grins slipped a tad, but they didn't retract their endorsements.

While Rose moved to set up the impromptu photo shoot, Jada's gaze dropped to the book on her lap. The cover was pretty tame compared to a lot of other romance novels. The male model wore a buttoned-up shirt, which, well, was not a problem. She would not fantasize about—wait, no—*think* about a shirtless Donovan and being able to ogle his wide chest up close. Just because she recalled with crystal-clear clarity how his chest felt under her hand during their totally *not real* kiss meant nothing.

What *did* mean something was the look between the two people on the cover. They stared into each other's eyes like they'd found their soulmates, their parted lips a breath apart. But the cover models were just that. Models. They were acting, and if they could do it, so could Jada. She'd been an actor once upon a time. An unsuccessful actor, but whatever.

Kendra clapped her hands together and stood. "Okay, gang, let's get going. Donovan, your shirt isn't the best, but we did spring this on you, so it will have to do. The shirt we have is way too small." She reached into the bag at her feet and pulled out a black cowboy hat. "Hopefully, this will fit."

Donovan took the hat from her and settled it on his head. He turned to Jada with his hands out as if to say, *How do I look?*

Damn good. Okay, yeah, this look worked for her. Who knew she had a thing for cowboys? What would he look like on the back of a horse, thigh muscles bulging? Hot. So fine. She cleared her throat. "You look all right."

Kendra snorted. "Girl, please. He's the perfect choice for the photo shoot. Now you, put this on. It will fit over your dress." She held out a red-and-blue-checkered flannel shirt. Jada took the shirt and slipped it on without comment. Nerves had risen from the dead like a phoenix to whip hope's ass in her stomach. Any second now, she would be in a clinch with Donovan.

But so what? She needed to chill. It would be fine. They'd take a couple of photos, laugh, and that would be the end of it. Memories of their kiss bombarding her brain would stop any second now.

Rose directed them to stand together in front of a background that featured a horse and a cactus. Totally authentic western details. "Arm around her waist and pull her in tight, Donovan. Jada, tilt your head back slightly and lay your hand against his chest."

Jada swallowed and followed orders. She watched as her hand seemed to work independently of her brain. It lifted itself, then landed on his chest, directly over his right pec. Warmth seeped through his shirt to her hand. She snatched her palm away. It felt like she'd been burned, like she was doing something naughty. But that was ridiculous. Slowly, her hand lifted again, then settled over his heart. His hand around her waist tightened, catching her off guard. She stumbled forward, then yanked herself back. "Sorry," she mumbled.

"No worries." He didn't sound affected at all. Of course, he didn't. Not Principal Dell, who kept his cool at all times.

"You two are so ridiculously attractive," Kendra said. "It should be illegal to look as good as y'all do together."

The other women laughed, calling out their agreement.

"Okay, I'm ready," Rose said, raising the camera to her face. "Let's get to it."

Jada kept her gaze glued to his Adam's apple and tried not to flinch at every click of the camera.

Rose lowered her camera. "Oh, my God, guys, you look so stiff. What's the deal?"

Oh, right. They were supposed to be a real-life couple. Jada exhaled and deliberately relaxed her shoulders.

Donovan's arm around her waist loosened as he turned to the photographer. Jada missed the connection immediately. "I know it sounds crazy, but we've tried to keep our relationship private, and I'm not used to cameras and people staring at me when I'm with my lady."

He was taking the blame? Why did he insist on being a standup guy?

The book club members sighed as one.

"That's certainly understandable," Rose said. "Y'all are so pretty, I forget you're not professionals. Donovan, tilt the hat back so we can get a better look at your handsome face."

Jada sucked in a breath. The hat had been hindering their connection. No longer. "Stare into each other's eyes like you were doing earlier. Pretend I'm not here. There you go. Jada, touch his jaw, raise on your toes, tilt your head back."

The hair of his five o'clock shadow was surprisingly soft. She continued to caress him, unable to stop herself. Her eyes drifted down. Their mouths were so close, so achingly close. She felt lightheaded. He felt it, too. His eyes had darkened, his breathing coming shallower. He remembered. She remembered. What would it be like to have more? For real this time? *Spectacular,* his eyes answered.

Jada inched up on her toes. Closer, closer, almost there . . .

"That should do it, you two," Rose said. "Much better."

The book club members cheered, jarring Jada back to the present. The quick *click-click* of the camera had stopped. Donovan's arm, so strong and sure, fell away from her waist, leaving her bereft. Their romance cover shoot was over.

Back to reality. Reality where they weren't dating. Reality where they had no right to kiss each other.

* * *

"So, the book club party went well," Jada said after all the book club members had cleared out. Nicholas had hustled August out of there too, mouthing "you got this" on his way out. Donovan rolled his eyes. His friend couldn't be more obvious if he tried. And he sure as fuck did not *have this*.

"Did it?" He was still trying to find his equilibrium. Despite all his admonishments to himself, his attraction to one Jada Townsend-Matthews wasn't fading. No, it was raging out of control. That photo shoot had nearly done him in. The hitch in her breath as their mouths nearly touched, the way he'd longed to delve under her shirt and dress to touch the skin underneath, to determine if it was as soft and fragrant as he imagined it to be.

She bumped hips with him in a playful motion, but touching her was never innocent. Never without meaning. Never without unfulfilled promise.

"Yes, it did, and you know it," she said. "Donovan, thanks for letting me do this. And for reading the book. And for taking this seriously." She sat and unzipped her boots and eased the shoes off, giving him a brief, tantalizing glimpse of her shapely thighs.

He wiped at his chin to make sure drool wasn't showing. "You miss the Crocs, don't you?" he asked when she looked up at him with a raised eyebrow.

Her smile, so smooth, so natural, so beautiful, spread across her face. She looked around the room to make sure there weren't any spies hiding in the corner, then leaned toward him. "Since it's just you and me, I'll admit it."

He laughed. She made him feel good. Damn good. And carefree like the whole world wasn't counting on him to make a success of everything.

She bit her lip, drawing his eyes once again to the delectable flesh. "So, I've been thinking."

Oh, God. Donovan couldn't stop a groan from spilling past his lips.

Jada held up her hands. "I deserve that. However, I'm growing."

He crossed his arms over his chest. "I'll be the judge of that. Continue."

Jada rolled her eyes. "I was thinking that maybe we should make that appearance on *Good Day, San Diego*."

He blinked. That's not what he'd expected her to say, but he should have known to expect the unexpected from her. "Why?"

"Because it will generate interest in the shop, and that's the whole point of this ruse."

He reached for her hand, pulling her to her feet. "Are you sure? You know if we do the show, they'll ask about your time on *My One and Only*."

She squared her shoulders and lifted her chin, ever the warrior. "I know, but I can handle it. It's time for me to stop hiding." She turned her hand to absently draw light circles in his palm. The air caught in his lungs. Why did her touch affect him so damn much? "Besides, I'll have you there for backup." A teasing grin pulled at her lips, drawing him deeper into her web, a web he was finding harder and harder to resist.

"And that's not all."

He grinned. Jada was gonna Jada, and he was starting to . . . appreciate it. "Why am I not surprised?"

"Tonight was a huge success." She spoke in a rush, like she'd practiced the speech and wanted to get it out before he objected.

"I was thinking we should do more events. Stay open so we can get the folks traipsing home after the bars and clubs close. Who needs tacos when you can have sugar to soak up the alcohol?"

He pointed at his chest in mock indignation. "I need tacos. Never say no to tacos. It's my life motto."

She laughed, rolling her eyes. "Okay, I stand corrected. But my point stands. We need to make this place a destination, a neighborhood hangout spot. I have to assume you opened the shop here because of the prime location. We need to take advantage of that. Can I be candid?"

"When have you ever not been?" Determined Businesswoman Jada was the sexiest Jada.

"You like numbers. You see your customers as statistics, the cupcakes as inventory, but that's really shortsighted."

His eyebrows rose. "Is it?"

"Yes," she said, her chocolaty eyes sparkling with determination and conviction. "There are too many other cupcake shops around to solely rely on the numbers to keep you ahead. You need more. Hosting special events and opening after hours gives you the perfect opportunity to lure your neighbors in. This is the perfect place to sit back, relax, get high off sugar, and bond. What more could they ask for?"

Donovan couldn't take his eyes off her. "I don't know, but I assume you're going to tell me."

"Yes, I am. Why don't we use this abundance of wonderful space—"

"Didn't you call it stale the first time you were here?"

She waved away that truth. "That's not important, even though the place could use some new decor, if I'm being honest. What is important is that we need to host events here."

Donovan studied her. "You keep saying 'we.'"

Jada's chin lifted. "Yes, because I want to plan the events. As you said, I did a good job tonight. I believe this can be my way to bring value to Sugar Blitz." A soft smile touched her luscious lips. "We both know it won't be with my baking." She squared her shoulders. "So yes, I want to plan the events."

Determination, along with a dose of uncertainty, swam in her eyes. She bit her lip, waiting for his answer. Bracing for him to turn her down. Let her down.

That wasn't going to happen. His way of doing things hadn't panned out exactly. Tonight had been a success. Her enthusiasm was certainly contagious, her determination admirable. He wouldn't be the one to disappoint her. "What do you suggest?"

She let out a little squeal that was frankly too cute for words, which he couldn't believe he was admitting to himself, and clapped her hands. "Let me handle that."

Chapter Thirteen

*D*onovan sniffed. Something new was in the air. Something other than sugar and chocolate. Something familiar. Something terrifying.

His mother's perfume.

"Donovan, are you okay?"

He barely registered Jada's question. Not when . . .

Donovan whirled, then blinked, hoping, praying his eyes were deceiving him. He blinked again. Nothing had changed. *Shit.*

And there was absolutely nothing he could do to avert the up-coming disaster.

With outstretched arms, his mother bore down on him with his two sisters trailing close behind. His mom wrapped her arms around him, humming the way moms did when they hadn't seen their child in a while, and squeezed for all she was worth, even though she barely came up to his chest.

He dropped his head and breathed in the comforting scent of roses. His mom called it her signature scent. He called it home.

But why was she here? More importantly, how could he get her to leave before she wreaked havoc? She squeezed one more time, then released him.

"Donny, my baby." She patted his cheek with a soft hand, a proud smile spread across her lips. "It's been so long."

He couldn't help but smile. "We had dinner a week and a half ago."

His mother stepped around him like he hadn't spoken. "And who do we have here?"

He'd sent a telepathic message to Jada to abandon ship, but apparently she hadn't gotten the message. Or maybe she had and simply decided to ignore it based on the look of utter joy on her face. "Hello, I'm Jada Townsend-Matthews."

No. This could not be happening. He didn't bother trying to stifle his groan, not that his mother or sisters were paying him any attention. Not when his newest employee/fake girlfriend was standing there talking to his mom like this was the most natural situation in the world.

"Sorry," his sister, Shana, mouthed behind his mother. Yeah, right. She'd driven their mom down here, he had no doubt. As the eldest, she'd always seen it as her responsibility to support their mother in whatever scheme she came up with, good or bad. Not that he could count on his younger sister, Sloane, to avoid disaster, either. In her own words, she "loved a hot mess."

"Nice to meet you, Jada. I'm Sandra Dell."

Jada held out her hand, but his mom had never met a stranger. She waved that polite gesture away like the inconsequential nuisance she thought it was and stepped forward to wrap Jada in a tight squeeze. "Oh, baby. A handshake is so formal, don't you think?"

Jada slowly lifted her hands and patted the other woman on the back. "I do."

His mom stepped back, beaming. "I had to come meet the woman who's stolen my baby's heart."

Donovan pinched the bridge of his nose and groaned again.

Jada laughed, still ignoring him. "I'm so happy you did. Donovan looks just like you, so I can only assume you're his mother."

His mother considered her for a moment, then nodded. "I like you. You didn't go for the bullshit response of saying you thought I was his older sister. You kept it real."

Jada laughed. "Well, I do try."

His mom sent a disapproving sniff his way. "I am disappointed I had to hear about the relationship from some relatives who spend way too much time on Facebook."

Donovan stepped forward. "Mama, you know I only introduce the most important people in my life to you."

"Are you saying I'm not important?" Jada asked, her eyes sparkling and her lips twitching with the obvious struggle to hold in laughter.

"Of course not, dear," he said through clenched teeth.

He could tell his mother the truth. That was an option. It wasn't a *good* option, but it was an option. He and his sisters had already agreed to keep her in the dark because his mother was not known for her ability to keep a secret. If she knew the truth about his "relationship" with Jada, she'd be on the phone with her sister spilling the beans before he could say "fake." However, he and his sisters had *also* agreed that they wouldn't bring their mom to the shop, so he could keep the lying to a minimum, but that plan had obviously flown the coop. He took a moment to side-eye both his sisters.

His mother clasped her hands together. "In case Donny hasn't told you, I love love. When I saw that video of you two, I knew I had to meet the woman who put that look on my son's usual stoic face. Come, come, sit."

She headed for a table, obviously expecting Jada to follow. He hung back with his sisters. "Really? Neither one of you could stop her?"

Shana sent him a get-real look. "When has anyone ever been

able to stop her when she makes up her mind? Aunt Darlene sent her that video and that was that. She said she was coming down here whether or not we brought her."

"And you know we had no intention of missing that fun," Sloane added, glee coating every word.

Donovan sighed. What was done was done, and he needed to run interference before his mother whipped out his naked baby pictures or asked Jada's thoughts on providing her with more grandchildren. His step quickened when his mother started scrolling through her phone. He exhaled when he reached her side and saw she was showing pictures of his niece and nephew, and not him, to Jada.

"Family is very important to us," his mom said. "What about you?"

Jada's smile dimmed just the slightest. Most wouldn't have noticed it. He wasn't most people. Not when it came to one Jada Townsend-Matthews. Donovan's eyes narrowed in contemplation. "Well, my grandmother owns the Knights," Jada said.

His mom gasped. "You're Mrs. T's granddaughter? Then, you're even more family than I thought. She's been wonderful to Donny and all of us, really."

Jada nodded. "She is the best."

"And your parents?" His mother wasn't satisfied. Of course, she wasn't. She was nosy, but she was also very protective of her children.

Jada's voice lost some of its usual vibrancy. "My parents and my sister are all here in San Diego. My parents own a medical research firm. They're all doctors and scientists."

His mom shrugged. "Good for them, but we all have to find our way in this world. Now on to the good stuff. How did you meet my son?"

Jada glanced his way, a smile teasing at her red lips. "I stopped in here for a cupcake on a whim."

"And it was love at first sight?" his mother asked, all eager hopefulness.

"No, it wasn't. She insulted my cupcakes," Donovan said. They'd agreed to keep their "love story" as close to the truth as possible.

His mother squealed. "I love it! My son can be a little uptight. Eh, a lot uptight. I knew the woman who stole his heart would have to be someone who pierced that stodgy exterior."

He threw his hands up. "Stodgy? Really, Mama? I'm right here."

Sandra waved away his objection. "You'll be all right. You know the truth when you hear it."

"So do I," Jada said, shooting a grin his way. "And you are absolutely right, ma'am, but he has some good points, too."

Sloane leaned his way. "Where are your business partners?" she asked casually, looking around.

"Nicholas is in the kitchen." Donovan checked his watch. "August should be here any minute." The bell over the front door rang. "Speak of the devil." He waved August over.

August ambled over in his unhurried fashion. "Mrs. Dell, it's always good to see you."

She hugged him like he was one of her children. "It's good to see you too, baby. How have you been?"

He ducked his head. "I'm all right."

Shana waved. "Good to see you, August. My kids can't wait for you to babysit them again and show them how to fix another leaky faucet."

He offered up a small smile. "Love to. Just let me know when." He sent a brief nod Sloane's way before continuing on his way down the hall.

She snorted at his retreating back. "Good to see you, too, August. I'm fine, by the way."

"Sloane," Donovan warned. Once upon a time, August had

treated her like his younger sister. Their relationship had cooled years ago, although neither would say why.

Her eyes widened. "What? I didn't do anything."

"Both of you, stop," Sandra said. "I haven't finished talking to Jada yet. What do you think about football players owning a cupcake shop?"

Jada glanced his way before answering. "I think it's fantastic and fun."

His mom nodded approvingly. "I agree. Did you know this isn't his first business?"

Donovan groaned. "Mama."

He didn't talk about his past. There was no point. Learning from the past and making the present and future the best they could be was important. It's how he lived his life. How he'd gotten through the tough times.

Jada leaned forward. "No, I didn't know. Tell me more."

"When he was eight, he overheard an argument I was having with his father. His father had gambled away the money we needed to pay the rent. I was not happy. I was upset and worried and let my husband have it. What I didn't know was that Donovan was outside the door listening.

"When I went to check on my kids, I couldn't find him in the house." Her voice softened with the memory. "I finally found him outside selling lemonade. He said he was going to stay out there until we had enough money, so we didn't have to move."

Donovan dropped his gaze to the table. He'd never forget how he'd felt listening to his parents hurling insults at each other. At his father offering up excuses and promises that, even then, he knew were bullshit. Helpless, yet determined to fix things. Determined to make his mother feel better. In that moment, control had become very important to him. Donovan gripped his thigh as he tried to hold those old yet familiar emotions at bay. A hand—Jada's hand—covered his. She squeezed. The comfort she offered so selflessly immediately calmed him. He ignored the knowing glance his sisters exchanged.

"That's the sweetest thing I've ever heard," Jada said.

His mom nodded. "I've never been prouder of him than I was at that moment. I knew what kind of man he was destined to be, and he's done nothing but prove me right. He's been taking care of his family and friends ever since, including opening this store because it's what his friends wanted and needed." She glanced down at their entwined hands, then stood. "Well, I think we've monopolized enough of your time."

Donovan walked his mom and sisters to the door. At the entrance, Sandra stopped and patted him on the cheek. "I found out what I came to find out."

His eyebrows lifted. "Which was?"

His mom touched his arm, her voice and face going serious. "If Jada is good for you. She is. She has a good sense of humor and cares about you. Makes you think about something other than your contract negotiation and shop sales. There is more to life than money. Don't let her get away."

With unerring accuracy, Donovan zeroed in on the woman in question. She was standing at the counter, laughing at something Ella had said, her whole body involved in the endeavor, head thrown back, shoulders shaking. Holding back wasn't Jada's way. His lips quirked. For good or bad. She'd certainly turned his world on its head. Maybe that wasn't such a bad thing.

Chapter Fourteen

What the hell? Donovan wasn't sure his jaw could be picked up. It had to be permanently cemented to the ground.

When he'd agreed to hosting events to bring in new business, he'd had no idea that would lead to pearls, dildos, vibrators, and fake penises hanging on the Sugar Blitz walls. Jada. This new decor had her fingerprints all over it.

Where was she?

He about-faced and headed to the kitchen, where he'd last seen her.

On his way, Donovan paused outside the supply closet. Light spilled from under the closed door. He cocked his ear toward the door. Maybe someone was inside, but he didn't hear anything. Nicholas had probably forgotten to turn off the light. But Donovan paid the bills around here. There would be no wasted energy on his watch.

He grabbed the key from his office, unlocked the door, stepped inside, and felt along the wall for the light switch as the door shut behind him. His fingers had closed around the switch when a flash of movement flickered in his periphery. Donovan turned, peering into the room.

Jada was huddled in the back corner, looking for all the world like she was trying to disappear into the red brick wall behind her.

He frowned, moving closer to her, unable to stop himself, a fate that was becoming all too familiar to him. "What are you doing in here? Are you okay?"

She stepped away from the wall, lifting her stubborn chin, clearly determined to give a convincing performance. She threw a defiant look his way. "Yes."

Too bad her voice quavered.

Worry and concern urged him closer. "For some reason, I don't believe you. Are you hiding?"

She lifted her chin higher. "Of course I'm not hiding."

He glanced around the room. "So you were looking for something?"

"Yep." Quintessential Jada, always determined to brazen her way out of any situation.

He gave her the look that always sent pro athletes scurrying for cover. "Then what are you looking for?"

Her throat muscles worked up and down before she swung her gaze wildly around the room. "Um . . . sugar."

"It's right there." He pointed to the shelf containing bags upon bags of sugar.

"Oh, thanks." She tried to move around him, but he stopped her with a hand on her arm. She sucked in a breath at the light touch but didn't pull away. Good, because he didn't want to let go. But he made himself, his fingers sliding across her soft skin until he grasped nothing but air.

He peered deep into her eyes. "What's going on?"

She shook her head, averting her gaze, obviously still unsure telling him was the right course of action.

"We could walk out of here without talking about it. Or you could use the sanctity of the supply closet to unburden yourself."

That brought a small smile to her lips. "What happens in the supply closet stays in the supply closet?"

He spoke straight from his heart. "Absolutely. You can tell me anything."

* * *

Jada opened her mouth to tell him it was nothing. But the look on his face stopped her. Like he cared and was ready to slay dragons for her. When was the last time anyone had looked at her like that? "Well, it's just that I got to thinking about how the next event, *my* next event is starting in less than an hour, and what if it's not successful?"

A vee appeared between his eyebrows. "The book club meeting was a success."

Jada was already shaking her head. "That was a last-minute thing, so I didn't have much time to let the nerves and what-ifs eat me alive. This is different. I've been planning this for a week."

This was a bachelorette party/sexuality seminar for a professor from a local university, who apparently had a million friends, who were all set to descend on Sugar Blitz in thirty minutes. The professor, a frequent customer of Sugar Blitz, wanted to combine the shenanigans of a bachelorette party with a pseudo-conference designed to make sure her friends and loved ones were fully attuned to their own sexuality, and Jada had been tasked with making sure that happened.

Oh, God. Her vision dimmed for a second. She paused for a moment to suck in some oxygen. But only for a moment. She needed to get this off her chest, and he'd offered to listen, so he was going to get the full Jada experience. "What if no one has a good time? If they don't have a good time, they're going to tell their friends, who are going to tell their friends, and then no one will step foot in this place again, and then you will fire me and I couldn't even complain because it would totally be my own fault."

She was rambling. She could hear herself. But since her thoughts had started rioting ten minutes ago when she looked at the clock and decided a trip to the supply closet was desperately needed, that was okay. He wanted to know. Well, now he knew.

He cocked his head to the side, clearly waiting to see if she would catch her second wind and go again. When she remained silent, he nodded. "Jada, I'm not going to fire you."

"You might!" Her hands twisted together.

He reached for them and squeezed. "I'm not, and the reason I know I'm not is because I haven't done it already. I didn't do it when you almost burned down my kitchen. I didn't do it when you kissed me and declared that I was your boyfriend. I didn't do it when you rented my business out as meeting space for a book club without asking me first. I didn't do it when I got roped into posing as a cover model while a room full of boozed-up women whooped and urged me to show them how it's done at said book club meeting."

When he put it that way . . . Oh, God. Why *hadn't* he fired her yet? Panic started shredding the lining of her stomach again. She shook her head. "But this time might be different!"

He squeezed her hands again. "Jada, look at me." She looked up from where his hands, so large and scarred, cradled hers like they were precious cargo. His eyes were steady and calm and sure. "It's not going to be different."

She shook her head, the doubts crowding out his assurances.

She'd failed before. She'd been riding the high of a successful book club meeting when she'd suggested hosting other events. When would she learn not to be so impulsive? Why would this time be any different? "How do you know?"

"Because I've seen all the hard work you've put into this. You saw a hole in the market and are looking to fill it. I've seen the results of your hard work—more people in the shop and more making return visits. The place looks, umm, interesting tonight though."

Jada giggled at the discomfited look on his face. He was really cute when he was being earnest.

"Not only that, her guest list keeps growing. You've already told her what you have planned, which means they're excited to come and experience it. They're going to love being here, having our amazing cupcakes and drinks, and then they're going to come back. We all win."

When he put it that way . . . Her stomach began to settle. Just a bit. "How are you so logical?"

The corner of his mouth lifted. "You mean how do I manage not to be impulsive?"

"Yeah, I guess," she mumbled.

A wide smile spread across his face. Whoa, he was fine. Like whoa. Which was not the point. Yes, it was a good distraction, but it was not the point. He shrugged. "It's just the way I am." He looked away. Just the way he was? She wasn't so sure. Before she could travel down that potentially fraught path, he released her hands and pointed at her.

"There are going to be a bunch of hungry folks here in the near future. You got us in this mess, and you're going to get us out of it."

The last of her nervousness released its grip on her stomach. She nodded in appreciation. "Bullying. Okay, that's a technique one could use, I suppose."

He nodded. "Coaches love to use it. Look, you obviously thought it was a good idea, and you're nervous, which is understandable. That means you care. Everyone gets nervous."

"Even you?"

He rolled his eyes. "Yes, even me, Mr. Robot. Every time I step on a football field."

What? "You're one of the best defensive players in the league, or at least that's what all your fanpeople say when they come in here to buy cupcakes and end up gushing in your face." He side-eyed her. She shrugged. "What? It's true."

"Are the nerves as much as when I was in high school or college and knew scouts were watching me? No. I've been playing football a long time. But I still want to do a good job every time I step out on the field. Knowing I've done everything in my power to prepare calms me."

She nodded. "Take comfort in my preparation."

"Exactly."

"Anything else make you nervous? And be honest! What happens in the supply closet stays in the supply closet," she reminded him when he looked like he might object.

He quieted and leaned against the wall next to her, his shoulder brushing hers before he put another few inches between them. She bit her lip before an objection could slip past.

She was becoming a greedy little witch when it came to contact with him. She would take it whenever and however she could. She would examine why later. Right now, she wanted to know what made him tick. What made him Donovan. She would also examine the why for that later. In this moment, she just wanted the knowledge.

"Failure," he said simply.

She wasn't surprised by the answer. He set a high bar for himself.

The question was why? But she didn't reply, sensing he was still struggling with how to continue or if he even should.

He gripped his arms, his eyes closing for a moment. "Growing up, financial stability was nonexistent. You already know about the lemonade stand. My father was—*is*—addicted to gambling. He was always searching for that next big hit, certain it would happen on his next bet."

"Did it?"

Donovan let out a wry chuckle. "Yeah, occasionally. Just enough for him to hunger for the next win, making an even bigger bet. My mom did her best to hold down the fort, but that's hard to do when you never know when your husband is going to empty out the bank account." He turned toward her, leaning his right shoulder on the wall. "I don't take risks. I think logically. I was good at football and knew it could give my entire family a financial stability we could only dream of if I stuck to it and made the pros. So I did, and it did."

"You succeeded." She reached for his hand, needing to offer the comfort he so willingly gave her. Needing that connection, as simple and pure as it was, to him.

He squeezed her hand in return. "I did, which allowed me to take a chance, the first chance I've really taken since I was a kid, when my best friends convinced me to open a cupcake shop. I want Sugar Blitz to succeed, but it's been tougher than I anticipated and I'm learning all over again that nothing is guaranteed."

Jada groaned. "And here I am adding to the uncertainty and messing stuff up."

Another wry laugh slipped out. "Yes and no."

She inspected the sharp, fascinating angles of his profile. "What does that mean?"

"It means I'm not going to let an impulsive woman who thinks nothing of telling me exactly what she feels whenever she feels it to destroy my business."

"Hey!" She reached out to push his chest.

His hand caught hers before she made contact. His palm surrounded hers. Her breath stuttered when he tugged her closer, his heat surrounding her. "Jada the worker doesn't make me nervous. But Jada the woman does."

She searched his eyes. They were dark and serious. Focused solely on her. Not that she needed to. He could be feeding her a line, but her gut told her he wasn't. The butterflies in her stomach started dive-bombing again. "How do I make you nervous?"

"Well, in case you hadn't noticed, I like logic and order. Calm. And none of that enters my orbit when you're around."

Jada swallowed, searching for words. "I'm . . . sorry."

His lips quirked. "Don't be. It's not your fault that you tilt my equilibrium off its axis. Every day, I try to figure out how I'm going to handle it. I'm not like you. I like spreadsheets and SWOT analyses. Every day, I fight my instincts."

She swallowed. She couldn't look away. His draw was too strong. Too powerful. "What do your instincts want you to do?"

He didn't answer. Not with words.

The kiss was sweeter than spun sugar. Gentle. Coaxing. Jada's eyes fluttered shut as she instantly became lost in the embrace. Lost in him. Kissing Donovan was quickly moving up the list of her favorite activities. Right now, she couldn't think of anything that topped it. She could soon become addicted to him. To feeling like this. Cared for. Desired. Liked for who she was.

She didn't know how it happened, but her back was against the wall, his hard chest pressed against hers, and he was taking the kiss deeper, deeper, deeper like he couldn't get enough of her. She understood how he felt. She was quickly slipping under his spell. His tongue twined with hers in long, sensuous, decadent slides. A perfect, sensual mating that drugged all her senses. The kiss gentled as he slowly backed away, giving her a moment to inhale. Right when she was about to beg for more, he was back, groaning as he sucked on her bottom lip. He was hungry. Hungry for her.

No more than she was for him.

She lifted on her toes, desperately seeking a stronger connection. He chuckled. His laughter came to an abrupt stop when she mimicked his action and bit his bottom lip. Oh, yeah. She liked that. It was soft and plush. Perfect. She repeated the action, her teeth sinking into the plump flesh and tasting him.

"It's like that?" he murmured, his voice teasing.

"Yes," she moaned.

Then the kiss got hotter. Wilder. Necessary. Teeth clashed. Tongues battled. Lust rampaged through her system. She wanted more. Needed more of Donovan.

Arousal pooled between her thighs. He rocked against her, his hardness pressing into her stomach. Jada gasped into his mouth. He was just as affected as she. Wanted it just as much as she did. She clutched his shirt, needing the anchor.

It wasn't enough.

She wanted his hands on her. "Touch me."

The need in her voice startled her, but she didn't take it back. Couldn't.

Jada groaned in deep appreciation when his hand worked its way under her shirt and pressed against her stomach before sliding upward toward her breasts.

In the recesses of her brain, she recognized that the rhythmic pounding she was hearing wasn't only coming from her racing heart, but she ignored it. This kiss with Donovan was all that mattered. She never wanted to leave this world they'd built only for the two of them.

But the pounding only increased in volume.

"Jada, you in there? Folks are starting to show up." The voice came from right outside the door. Nicholas.

They sprang apart. Jada's heart raced like she'd just completed a 10K. Donovan stared at her with wild eyes, his chest heaving.

"What was that?" he muttered, clearly more to himself than expecting her to answer.

The doorknob began to rattle. Donovan's eyes widened. Add that to the things she'd dwell on later. "Yeah, I'm in here," she called out, forcing her voice to cooperate. "I'll be out in a bit. Just looking for some poster board."

The doorknob stopped rattling.

"Good deal," Nicholas said. The sound of his footsteps faded away.

Donovan still looked shook. Which made her feel *awesome*. Was kissing her so bad? Kissing him was the absolute highlight of her day. Hell, her year. But he looked dismayed, if not outright horrified.

On unsteady legs, she stepped around his motionless figure and headed for the door. She paused with her hand on the knob and closed her eyes for a moment, gathering all the dregs of composure she could muster. She'd been here before, having to pick up the pieces after terrible, impulsive mistakes with other men. He said nothing. So it was up to her. "Hey, don't worry about it. What happens in the supply closet stays in the supply closet, remember."

Chapter Fifteen

The next day, Jada stared hard at the photo of her and Donovan on her phone screen, committing every pixel to memory. Like the fool she so obviously was.

"Jada."

She dropped her arm and pressed the phone to her side like she could force the device to meld into the cotton of her dress if she tried hard enough. "Hey."

Donovan narrowed his eyes. "You okay?"

"Yep." She pushed her lips up for extra emphasis.

He continued to study her for a second, but then he finally nodded. "All right. Ready to do this?"

"Sure." Jada followed him outside to his SUV. She opened the car door and pulled herself up to the seat. She stared straight ahead as Donovan opened the driver's side door and slid behind the wheel. She absolutely did not think about that photo. She absolutely did not think about how fantastic his mouth felt on hers yesterday. Nope. She did think about how he'd looked poleaxed after the incident and how they'd been avoiding each other since last night, only speaking when necessary.

But they couldn't do that any longer. Not today, anyway.

They'd agreed that it made sense to drive to the news station together for their *Good Day, San Diego* appearance because they were "dating" and going to the same place, after all. No big deal. It made perfect sense.

Except for the unspoken third party that took up so much room in the vehicle. And her hormones that apparently had no pride and didn't care that Donovan wasn't exactly thrilled about being attracted to her.

There was no place to run. At the bakery, at least, she could escape by checking in on a customer or helping Nicholas clean or do other mundane, nonbaking tasks in the kitchen.

He took up so much space. The width of his seat was no match for the width of his shoulders. Her gaze dropped to his hands. He gripped the steering wheel and handled the car expertly. Would he handle her body in the same way, instinctively knowing how to please her? As she stifled a moan, she shifted in the leather bucket seat. What was wrong with her? Where was her pride?

He broke the silence first. "What were you looking at on your phone?"

He *had* noticed. Crap. She could lie, but lying made no sense because she'd done nothing wrong—well, other than starting this whole farce.

She forced out a totally lighthearted, totally casual laugh. "You remember Rose, the photographer from the book club? She texted me a few photos from the shoot." She hesitated. "Do you want to see them?"

He took a moment to answer. "Sure."

Jada could read absolutely nothing in that one syllable. There was no inflection. No hesitation. Just resolve.

At the next red light, she handed the phone to him. He silently scrolled through the images, his face as impassive as ever. He studied the last one, the same one that had captured her attention. It had to have been the last frame. Their mouths were temptingly close. His grip on her waist was tight. Possessive. But it was the look in his eyes, the look on her face that had arrested her. Mutual longing. Desire. Connection. "What do you think?"

His gaze collided with hers. "They're nice. Rose is a talented photographer." He handed the phone back to her and pressed his foot to the gas as the light turned green.

Jada gripped the phone and stared straight ahead, hoping she projected calm although she was feeling anything but.

According to the car's GPS, they were seventeen minutes away from their destination. Seventeen minutes to inhale his scent, underscored by the light yet alluring aftershave he used. Seventeen minutes to watch his thigh muscles stretch and bunch as he navigated the streets of San Diego. She should have insisted on driving. Anything to keep her mind from wandering down a dangerous path.

Not that it mattered, even if she'd thought about the kiss a million times today. She and Donovan were faking. The beginning, the middle, the end.

She was still running Operation: Jada Gets Her Life Together, and starting a relationship or fling or whatever would only act as a distraction. She could not, would not jump into something with him just because her hormones went haywire whenever he was near. Just because he made her feel good about herself meant nothing.

She always fell too fast too soon. She was turning over a new leaf. There was no room in her life for a man. Not right now. Not to mention the fact that he was her boss and played for her grandmother's team. That was a complication she did not need.

And hell, she hadn't even gotten to the part where he'd said nothing as she left the supply closet. Or that horrified look on his face.

"The event went well last night," he said. "You did good. Nicholas said people were asking how to book events as they were leaving."

"Thanks," she said. Her saving grace. Somehow, someway, she'd pulled herself together to focus on the task at hand. She'd enjoyed herself, knowing others were having a good time, partially as a result of her hard work. It helped that Donovan made himself scarce for the night. His compliment warmed her even as the temperature in the car remained frigid.

Silence, that familiar foe, descended again.

"We should talk about what happened last night."

Oh. Guess he'd decided spending the next fifteen minutes in strained silence wasn't the best strategy. Jada looked out the passenger-side window. She saw nothing of the scenery. "What's there to talk about? We kissed. It was a mistake. The end."

Donovan sighed. "Jada."

"Don't Jada me. You're the one who wouldn't even look at me." She cringed, hearing the hurt and confusion in her voice.

He sighed again. "I'm sorry. I wasn't expecting . . ."

Jada turned his way when he didn't finish his thought. She needed to know. "You weren't expecting what?"

His scarred hands tightened on the steering wheel as he stared straight ahead. "My intense reaction to you. I haven't felt anything like that in a long time, and it threw me. And when I get thrown, it takes me a minute to get it together."

Jada sighed. "I get it." And she did. She was still having a hard time accepting that she'd felt *everything* while locked in his arms. That had never happened to her before.

"I'm sorry that it came across as callous. That was never my intention."

Jada's heart took a tumble. How could it not? His sincerity rang true. He'd never been anything but a stand-up guy, even when she was driving him nuts. If he could be honest, then so could she. "Thank you for the apology. I was feeling a little hurt because of your reaction, but what you said makes sense. It was a moment, and it's over. It's not like either of us are looking to start anything, right?"

"Right." He sent a shy, uncertain smile, and yet so devastating, her way. "So . . . friends?"

Jada nodded. "Yes. I can't promise not to do something in the future that makes you sigh in despair, but yes, we're friends."

And if she thought she'd like more? Well, she'd already reminded herself of the various reasons she and Donovan shouldn't be more. Those reasons were still valid, which left only one viable outcome. Friends only.

He chuckled, lightness finally returning to his eyes. "There's no doubt that'll happen."

Jada rubbed her hands together. "I can't wait . . . Donny."

"It's Donovan," he said through gritted teeth, his nostrils flaring.
Score!

Jada snickered. This was way better than strained silence. "Your mama calls you Donny. I'mma call you Donny."

Meeting his mother and sisters had been eye-opening. It was easy to cast Donovan as the staid stick-in-the-mud. Easier for her, at least. Anything to keep her emotions and feelings in check. Easier not to think of him as a living, breathing, caring human being. But she couldn't pretend anymore. Not after seeing the loving and close relationship he shared with his mother and sisters. Not after hearing the story about a young Donovan trying to step up to take care of his family. She'd imagined a determined and resolute Donovan gathering his supplies and heading outside to set up a lemonade stand, and her heart had melted.

He shot her the same unamused look he'd undoubtedly fixed on passersby who declined to buy his lemonade when he was a youngster. "I was named after my grandfather, so she calls me Donny in order to avoid confusion."

She studied his profile and tried her hardest not to get distracted by his razor-sharp jawline and how she hadn't taken the opportunity to caress it in the supply closet. "I'm going to bet you were eleven when you first asked to stop being called Donny."

"Ten, actually," he mumbled.

She laughed. She could totally do this friends thing. Totally.

* * *

Jada flipped open her compact and studied her appearance in the mirror. The sweat she could feel beading at her hairline hadn't slipped down her face, thankfully. She blotted anyway. She never left home without her invaluable tools. Makeup was armor, and she needed to make sure her equipment was in tip-top shape at all times.

She pursed her lips. No lipstick on her teeth. She loved this shade. It was the lipstick she wore when she wanted to feel confident. Fenty 67. A bold berry that highlighted her skin.

"You look fine," Donovan said, sitting next to her on the couch in the green room where they waited for a producer to lead them to the studio for taping.

She snapped the compact closed. "With compliments like that, I'll be surprised if my head can fit through the door."

"You don't need me to tell you you're a beautiful woman." He said it plainly without a hint of mockery. Like it was a simple truth that couldn't be argued.

He also didn't sound happy about it, and yet her heart, that stupid muscle, stuttered in joy. "Thanks. I think."

His phone beeped with an incoming message. He took it out, frowned at the screen for a second, then jammed the phone back into his pocket. A sigh full of frustration accompanied the gesture.

"Bad news?" Jada asked.

"It's nothing."

It didn't sound like nothing, but before she could decide whether or not to press her new "friend," the door opened, and a woman in her thirties appeared, wearing a headset. "Hi, I'm Jenny, one of the producers. Are y'all ready to go to set?"

Jada took a deep breath and slowly stood. "As ready as I'll ever be."

She and Donovan followed Jenny single file down the hall. The walls were lined with photos of guests over the years and stills of the more infamous moments from the show. Would she and Donovan end up on the wall? She hoped not. She wanted to get in and get out without a new scandal. Or the urge to beg him to kiss her again.

Jenny introduced them to the host, Kayla Ruiz, a stunning brunette, while two production assistants miked them up. Unfortunately, that task didn't take long and soon they were sitting on two high-back metal stools next to Kayla, waiting for the show to come back from a commercial break.

Why did she think this was a good idea? She should have kept her mouth shut. But nooo, she'd wanted to thank Donovan for letting her host the book club meeting and get the store more customers.

From behind the camera, Jenny counted down. "Three, two . . ."

Kayla instantly transformed into a professional TV show host. "Welcome back to *Good Day, San Diego*. Today, we're lucky to have

Donovan Dell, one of the stars of the San Diego Knights, and Jada Townsend-Matthews, who you may recall starred on the most recent season of *My One and Only*. She's also the granddaughter of the Knights' owner, Joyce Townsend. But all that is old news. What you may not know is that Donovan co-owns Sugar Blitz, San Diego's newest buzzed-about cupcake shop, and Jada works there with him, and they are San Diego's newest, hottest couple. Welcome, Jada and Donovan."

Jada threw back her shoulders. *Here we go.*

* * *

"Thanks for having us," Jada said confidently while Donovan waved.

He could only assume the gesture looked as awkward as it felt. He wasn't used to being on camera with numerous hot lights shining on him. On the football field, he ignored, then completely forgot about the cameras once the game started and he became engrossed in the action on the field.

As for Sugar Blitz, Nicholas usually handled their media. He'd never met a camera he didn't like. Donovan had been more than happy to cede the spotlight. Too bad there was a spotlight currently shining directly on him, turning the studio into a literal hotbox.

The host beamed at the audience at home. "Today, Jada and Donovan are going to show us how to bake the perfect cupcakes that will have your family and friends begging for more."

"Or at least come down to Sugar Blitz for more," Jada quipped.

A bubble of laughter bursting from his chest surprised him, helping to put him at ease. Jada grinned at him like they were sharing a private joke. Like the moment in the supply closet hadn't happened. *But it had.* Her shining eyes and bright smile dazzled him. Nothing new there.

Anchor Kayla cleared her throat and stared at him expectantly.

"Right." He clapped his hands together and gestured to the ingredients set on the table in front of them. "We're going to make vanilla cupcakes. They're our number one bestsellers because of our secret ingredient, which I'm going to reveal only to the people watching and then all the people who will undoubtedly watch later on YouTube and Facebook and Twitter."

Kayla laughed. "Just a few, right? Jada, are you a baker?"

"I am not," she said emphatically. "Donovan is going to be doing all the work today. I'm here to cheerlead. But I will say Donovan is a great teacher." Her gaze shifted to him. "He was super patient with me."

"Is that what attracted you to Donovan? His patience?"

Donovan cut his eyes at the host. Ooh, she was smooth. He had to give her credit for segueing into gossip so seamlessly.

To her credit, Jada rolled with it. "Absolutely. I knew he was special when I made a mess of things in the kitchen and he kept encouraging me."

"How long have you two been seeing each other?"

While Kayla talked, Donovan started mixing the ingredients.

Jada absently handed him the bottle of vanilla before answering. "I met him before I went on *My One and Only*, and I couldn't stop thinking about him while I was on the show. When it was time to make that final decision, I had to be honest with myself."

Kayla nodded like she was conducting a hard-hitting news interview. "That honesty led to an interesting reaction from the show's fans. Donovan, have you seen the abuse Jada has taken online?"

He nodded. "I have, and it's total BS."

Beside him, Jada jerked, clearly surprised he'd sought out the vitriol spewed her way. He shrugged. He hadn't mentioned it because he wasn't sure she wanted to talk about it.

"I'd use stronger language, but I recognize this isn't a late-night show on premium cable or streaming service," he added.

Kayla made an "aww" face at the camera. "Jada, you're a lucky woman to have someone defending you like that." Her expression hardened. "Of course, there is some speculation that all that glitters isn't gold."

Donovan froze. Did she know they weren't actually dating?

"There's been some speculation that Donovan is dating you to get a better contract with the Knights," she continued.

Fury rose in Donovan so fast it damn near obscured his vision. A loud guffaw stopped him from setting Kayla so straight she'd never look askance again.

Jada slapped her hand on the table. "Are you serious right now? He's dating me to get a better contract? That would be a big fat hell no. He's the most upstanding man I've ever met and the last person to ever do something so underhanded. He didn't even know who I was when we first met. Please apologize to him right now or I will walk off this show."

Jada was deadly serious. She looked for all the world like a warrior ready to defend her family. He was touched beyond belief. Despite everything that had gone down between them, despite the way he'd hurt her feelings in that supply closet, she still had his back.

Kayla's eyes had widened. "I'm sorry. I didn't mean to offend. I just wanted to get your thoughts on some of the rumors that are out there."

"That rumor is false, I assure you," Donovan said, his voice quiet and steady with resolve. Jada reached for his hand, silently offering comfort.

Kayla considered them both. "Yes, I can tell it is. My sincere apologies." She turned to the camera with a smile. "And before I get fired for running off our guests, why don't we get to the baking? Jada, since you're not baking today, do you mind directing traffic by reading off the ingredients?" She jerked her chin toward a guy in his early twenties, one of the production assistants, who was holding cue cards.

Jada hesitated, then cleared her throat. "Sure, no problem. Well, actually, there might be a problem. I'm dyslexic, so if I hesitate or mispronounce something, that's why."

"Oh, if you want, I can do it," Kayla said.

Jada held up a hand. "No, I want to do it. Dyslexia isn't the end of the world. I've learned to compensate and muddle through when the situation calls for it. It can be hard, but I don't want to give the impression that I can't do something because of it."

She didn't look at him the whole time she spoke. Why? Did she think he would make fun of her? Did she think he was that much of an asshole? Is that what all their interactions had led her to believe?

"You're absolutely right," Kayla said. "Whenever you're ready."

Jada held out her hand toward him, signaling her okay with him going forward.

"We add the butter and sugar, then add two eggs, our secret ingredient, and the flour," Jada said while Donovan and Kayla demonstrated in their respective bowls.

Just like on the football field, he soon forgot about the cameras and became engrossed in the task at hand. He and Nicholas had premade portions of the cupcakes so they would have time to get through the whole process in the five-minute segment. He whipped the sugar and butter into a frothy mixture in the glass bowl while Jada watched.

"Good job, Donovan. You might be able to make a living at this someday." Jada winked. "Now it's time for the special ingredient."

She looked left, then right, then leaned forward and mock whispered, "Yogurt."

Donovan laughed. She was a natural. He could see why viewers had been drawn to her on that show. At her direction, he poured the mixture into the cupcake baking dish. It was a six-hole dish, unlike the two-dozen pan they used in the shop. He smiled. It brought back memories of baking with his mother during the less tumultuous times of his childhood, or the times when they'd both needed a distraction from said tumultuous times.

Kayla looked into the camera. "Through the miracle of television, our cupcakes are ready." She pulled the pan out of the oven and gasped. "These look amazing, Donovan."

"They are," Jada said. "And let me tell you, the icing really is the icing on the cake."

"Then let's get to it." He and Kayla grabbed their icing utensils. "You too, Jada. The hard part's over now."

She stuck her tongue out at him, while Kayla laughed. Jada picked up the icing bag. "What flavors are inside, Donovan?"

He winked. "It's a surprise. Squeeze gently." He waited while the two women squeezed softly, letting out a small spurt of frosting. He would not think about how cute Jada looked, her brow furrowed in deep concentration, her tongue peeking out between her slightly parted red lips. That was the lipstick she'd worn when they kissed. He'd bet everything he owned on that fact.

He still remembered the taste of her lips. He'd watched the clip of their first kiss too many times to count. If Nicholas and August knew how high the number went—hell, if Jada knew—he'd never hear the end of it. He told himself that and then he pressed play again anyway. And those photos? Donovan shook his head. No, he needed to stop.

They'd agreed to be friends less than an hour ago, so that's what they'd be, no matter what his libido or his heart wanted.

"I got strawberry," Jada said, her joy clear. Her delight delighted him. The shop had become a business for him, money and spreadsheets and expenditures. He'd lost sight of the reason he'd said yes to the shop in the first place—those memories from his childhood, the simple pleasure of baking with his mom. Jada was bringing back all those good feelings.

"I got chocolate," Kayla said. "Which is great, but I feel like I'm going to screw up."

"It's all about the wrist action," he said. "Press gently on the bag and move your wrist in a circle to spread the icing evenly."

Just as he finished, a large plop of frosting fell out of Jada's bag. The cupcake looked like a bag of blood had exploded all over it.

"Crap," she muttered, her head dropping.

"Hey, hey, none of that," he said. "We all started off as beginners. Some of us stay in that phase longer than others."

Her eyes widened, her sadness clearly forgotten. "Hey!"

He shrugged, his lips twitching. "I call 'em like I see 'em."

"Why don't you show me how to do it, Mr. Smarty Pants?"

Before he could think it through, he stepped behind her and grasped her wrist. He recognized his mistake immediately. She fit against him perfectly. Her skin was soft and supple. He'd be a fool not to notice the way her pulse sped up under his seeking fingers. He bent to whisper in her ear. "You've got to have patience. Slowly." He guided her hand as she spread the frosting over a different cupcake. He released her as soon as it made sense to save himself from turning her in his arms and kissing her like he longed to do, though he was having the damnedest time remembering why that was a bad idea. "See, that's just average, not horrible. I knew you could do it."

"What?" She whirled. Before he could blink or think about taking cover, she swiped the red frosting off the cake and dabbed it on his nose. Her head cocked to the side. "How you doing, Rudolph?"

His eyes narrowed as he struggled to contain his laughter. "You're going to pay for that."

Her eyes danced with mockery. "Yeah, how? I'm not scared of you."

"You two are adorable," Kayla said, jolting Donovan back to the present. They were in a TV studio, not a private world of their own making. Unfortunately.

"Thank you for being here today." Kayla turned to address the camera. "If you'd like to try these terrific cupcakes for yourself, visit Sugar Blitz. Donovan and Jada will be waiting. We'll be right back."

"And we're clear," Jenny called out, sending the show to commercial.

"I can see why you left that other guy in the dust and why you have your own hashtag," Kayla said. "People respond to true love. Y'all are lucky to have each other. You two are the perfect couple."

Donovan caught Jada's eye. The perfect *fake* couple. That was their agreement. He needed to remember that undeniable fact.

Chapter Sixteen

"Overall, that went well, don't you think?" Jada asked when they were back in Donovan's car. "I mean besides those thirty seconds when I thought I was going to have to fight in these heels." She had to say something to break up the lingering silence. Something to exorcise the memory of her heart jumping when Kayla said they were the perfect couple. They weren't the perfect couple. They weren't even a couple. They were . . . coworkers, or, more accurately, employer and temporary employee. Friends, even. Yet the phrase lingered. *The perfect couple.*

He glanced her way. "Yeah. Kayla gushed over the cupcakes, and I think she actually meant it and wasn't saying it out of fear she'd stuck her foot so far down her throat she'd never be able to extract it. Sugar Blitz got some great publicity. Our ruse is working. It's great." He didn't sound great. He sounded distracted.

"Are you worried about what she said about you dating me to get more money from Grams?"

He shook his head. "No. We both know that's not true. But I do have a confession to make. When your grandmother asked me to hire you, I did think agreeing might put me in a better position with my contract negotiations."

Jada snapped her fingers. "I knew it. I knew you had nefarious motives." She laughed at the stricken look on his face. "Donovan, seriously, it's cool. I know my grandmother. I have no doubt that she ran roughshod over you and gave you no real option other than to hire me, so it makes total sense that you were thinking about what you could get out of the deal. You are like the most upstanding person I've ever met, and if I didn't admire you for it, I'd hate you for it."

"Yeah, I guess." He didn't crack a smile.

Jada studied his profile. What was he thinking? Was he regretting their deal? Regretting her working at the shop? Well, that part didn't make sense. They were getting along, and she hadn't set off the fire alarm again.

She chuckled.

"What's so funny?"

"Just thinking about how I almost burned down your kitchen."

"So you admit it!" There was humor in his voice. *Finally.* She didn't want to examine too closely how good that made her feel.

Jada put on her haughtiest tone. "I do no such thing. I was simply using your words to describe the situation."

His eyes twinkled. "Riiiight." He quieted for a moment, then looked her way. "That was cool how you handled her asking you to read the cue cards."

The muscles in Jada's shoulders locked. There it was. She'd been wondering how long it would take him to bring that up. "I was kinda hoping you would forget that."

Donovan's eyebrows drew into a deep vee. "Why? A learning disability is nothing to be ashamed of."

Her shoulders relaxed marginally. "I know that, and yet . . ." She shrugged.

"And yet what? People have given you shit for being dyslexic?"

Jada looked out the passenger-side window at the passing scenery to give herself a few extra seconds before responding. She hated talking about this. But he'd revealed a part of himself in that supply closet, and no matter how far things had gone left afterward, she'd never forget that. "Mainly my parents."

"Are you serious? Why would they do that?"

She shook her head, like that simple act could dislodge all the painful memories that had collected there since childhood. "Dyslexia didn't fit into their narrative of the perfect, intelligent elite family."

"Dyslexia has nothing to do with intelligence." He sounded so forceful, so shocked people would peddle that type of bullshit. Having this man in her corner gave her a strength she hadn't even known she was missing.

She shrugged. "They expected effortless perfection. A learning disability kind of got in the way of that, and I don't think they ever forgave me for it."

"That sucks."

Jada looked his way. "Yeah, as far as they're concerned, you're either a genius who gets straight A's or you're not bright. Not much room for a gray area." Her voice trailed off as she remembered all the times they'd unintentionally made her feel like shit. Like she was unworthy of love because of something she had no control over.

"I'm sorry." His deep voice brought her back to the present. "I get it. Well kind of. It's not exactly the same, but my whole life, when people hear athlete, they tend to automatically think 'dumb jock,' even some of the coaches, who regard us as muscled game pieces they can move around at will on the chessboard known as the football field. I got a degree in business admin even though my college coaches didn't want me to."

"What did they want you to major in?" Yes, she was happy to

move on, but mostly, she wanted every piece of info she could about him. She wanted to know everything. She wanted to know *him*.

He lifted his wide shoulders. "Basket weaving. I don't know. Whatever wouldn't take away from my focus on the field. Business economics requires a much too strenuous workload for student-athletes."

Jada harrumphed. "Student-athletes? Seem like they didn't care too much about the student part of that phrase."

"Nope. That's not what they're paid to care about. It wouldn't have been so bad if one of my coaches hadn't told me he didn't think I was smart enough to pass the classes."

Her jaw dropped. "Are you serious?"

"Oh, yeah. His so-called concern backfired. I became even more determined to be a business major."

Jada nodded. "People judging and underestimating you. I totally understand that."

She met his eyes. He did understand what she'd gone through. Warmth spread from her heart through her veins.

"I know you do, and I appreciate it. Seriously though, it's hard, I know, but try not to let your parents get into your head or stay there."

"Thanks. And not that it matters, but I know you're not dumb. No one is. You *are* a little uptight." She wrinkled her nose. "A lot uptight."

Donovan chuckled as he pulled up to a red light. "You're right."

Jada perked up. "I am?"

"Yes, about no one being dumb. But that's not all. You're also impulsive. A lot impulsive, actually. A regular troublemaker who creates mayhem wherever you go."

He didn't say it like he was annoyed by that fact. He sounded almost okay with her state of being. Dare she say he sounded almost . . . impressed? She grinned. "Thank you."

He raised his hand for a high five. With a laugh, she slapped palms with him and did her best to ignore the zap of electricity that traveled up her arm.

* * *

"If it isn't the conquering hero and heroine returning," Nicholas called out when Jada and Donovan stepped into the shop.

"You're ridiculous," Donovan said, shaking his head.

"I'm right." Nicholas spread his arms wide. "Most of the people here saw the lovebirds on *Good Day, San Diego* and came to see y'all in person. Or at least that's the word on the street."

And since Nicholas was the head gossip, Donovan didn't doubt the veracity of his statement.

"Y'all did a great job," Ella said. "Everyone's been asking when you would get back. I think it's going to be a selfie parade."

Jada looked slightly panicked, like she was having a hard time believing the customers had actually come in peace.

Right. "Before we do that, Jada, can I talk to you for a second in my office?"

Her brow furrowed. "Um, yeah. Sure."

"We'll be back in a few minutes," he called out to the room at large. He placed a hand at the small of Jada's back and reluctantly dropped it when they reached his office door. Which was ridiculous. They were friends. Nothing more. They'd agreed less than two hours ago.

He opened the door and followed her inside.

"What's up?" she asked, taking a seat.

He sat in the other chair next to her. "You looked worried out there, so I'm thinking we should check social media. Or at least text messages to see how our appearance was received."

Jada rubbed her forehead. "I guess I need to work on my acting skills."

"Not with me you don't."

Her lips stretched into a brief smile. "Thanks. You're right. Social media and I don't have the best relationship right now, so I've been keeping my distance."

Anger welled up inside him. He wished he could obliterate the hurt she'd endured from people hiding behind their keyboard through the sheer force of his will alone. "I'm sorry."

Jada blew out a breath. "It's not your fault. Social media giveth and taketh away. If I'm looking on the bright side, all that hate led me straight to you. I wouldn't have panicked and kissed you and introduced you as my boyfriend."

He wiggled his eyebrows. "And in the process, discovering what an excellent kisser I am."

She rolled her eyes, the dark light in them now replaced by humor. "Oh, my God. You are so ridiculous. I am not going to inflate your ego by agreeing. Check social media, please. I've got texts galore that will tell the tale." Her phone vibrated, underscoring her point. "First one is from Olivia." She laughed. "She said that I looked like a supermodel, my shoes were fab, and we gave the best #JaDon energy. That's why she's my bestie."

Donovan glanced up from his phone. "What else you got?"

"Let me see. Carrie, she works at the boutique up the street. Kendra and the rest of the members of book club." Jada laughed. "They all said we did great. Oh, wait. Here's one from Lila, the producer from *My One and Only*. Not reading that one. She's been bugging me to do interviews, and I know she's going to be pissed I did one on my own." She sighed, her shoulders slumping.

"You okay?" Donovan asked, laying a hand on her shoulder. "What's wrong?"

She lifted her head. Disappointment swam in her gorgeous eyes. "I guess I was expecting a message from my parents or sister." She let out a little chuckle. "I don't know why. *Good Day, San Diego* isn't their usual TV fare."

But she was hurt all the same. It was written all over her face.

Jada lifted her chin. "It doesn't matter. All the texts I read were positive. I'm relieved."

He didn't believe her, but the look on her face warned him not to press, so he simply nodded instead. "As far as I can tell, social media is going well. The only negative stuff I can find is some people telling us not to flaunt our relationship all over the place. It's unseemly or something."

Jada laughed. "Didn't I say something about being unable to win? What else did they say?"

He lifted his phone to eye level. "Jada and Donovan's chemistry is off the chain. No wonder she left Dr. John in the dust. Where can I find my own Donovan, a man who's not afraid to show his softer side and let us know how much he appreciates his woman?"

Jada snorted. "Of course, you'd read a tweet praising you."

"Kinda hard not to. There are so many of them."

She picked up a pad of sticky notes off his desk and threw it at his head. He easily dodged the hot-pink missile, and it harmlessly bounced off the white wall and slid to the floor.

He shrugged when she growled at him. "You gotta try harder than that if you're going to beat the king."

* * *

Donovan picked up a napkin that had fallen on the ground, then used a towel to wipe away crumbs some recently departed customers had left behind. His phone buzzed in his back pocket. Another congratulatory call? Or something else? His shoulders stiffened as he dug the phone out and sighed when he saw the name on the screen. Adam, his agent. He moved to the farthest table in the shop. "Hey, man, what's up? Got some news on the contract extension?"

Adam's Brooklyn accent drifted through the speaker. "That's actually why I'm calling. I saw a clip of you on *Good Morning, San Diego* this morning."

Donovan leaned against the wall. "Okay. What about it?"

"Are you sure it's a good idea to be dating your boss's granddaughter?"

Donovan looked around to make sure no one could hear him. Luckily, no one was paying him any attention. "How is that any of your concern?"

"I'm your agent, and anything that affects your contract is my concern. The court of public opinion matters. If people think you're dating her to get more money, it doesn't look good. We want the public on our side when we're asking for millions of dollars. Maybe you should end this relationship or whatever it is."

He'd rather chew off his arm. Wait. No. He'd promised Jada. That's why the thought of ending their "relationship" made him nauseous. "That's not going to happen."

Adam sighed. "I suspected you would say that. You looked like a besotted fool."

Donovan's jaw clenched. "Do I need to hang up?"

"No, no, no. Fine. How about you ask your new girlfriend to sweet talk her grandmother into giving you some more favorable terms in the contract?"

Donovan's hand tightened around the phone. "I'm not asking Jada to do that!"

"You're not asking Jada to do what?"

Shit. He'd been so busy trying to tamp down his fury he hadn't seen her come up to him.

He met her concerned eyes. Shit. "Adam, goodbye. Do your job or I'll find someone else to do it."

"What's going on?" she asked as soon as he pressed the icon to end the call.

Truth was always his calling card. "My agent is an asshole." He quickly relayed Adam's thoughts and how he'd rejected them.

Distress spread across her face. "I don't want to put you in a position where you're at odds with people in your life because of me."

Donovan shook his head. "Don't worry. You're not. Adam cares about money, which is why I hired him, but he can go too far. It's not the first time. Won't be the last. But I set him straight." He touched her arm. He couldn't help himself. "I got you. This isn't your fault."

She nodded, but doubt lingered in her gaze. What had happened to her to make her doubt herself? Solving the puzzle that was Jada had become his number one goal in life.

* * *

"Are you really going to make us do this?" August asked, his disgust clear.

"This" being binge-watching *My One and Only*.

"Sure am," Donovan cheerfully replied from his kitchen where he was gathering snacks and beer. "And you came, so you can't complain."

He'd ordered August and Nicholas to show up to his place after Sugar Blitz closed for the night, but who cared about the details?

"The hell I can't," August muttered. But he didn't move from his perch on Donovan's sofa.

"Won't do you any good," Nicholas called from where he was sprawled across the love seat. "I already tried."

Donovan crossed into the living room and deposited the chips, popcorn, and drinks on the coffee table before slapping Nicholas on the back of his head. He two-stepped out of the way before his friend could retaliate. "My man here is correct."

And he knew they would have his back, no matter what. They would support him in any way he needed. Even if that included watching a reality TV dating show. Also, they were nosy mother-fuckers. Well, Nicholas was, anyway.

He definitely needed their support as he tortured himself by watching Jada fall in love with another man in 4K. Still, Donovan was resolute, if a little queasy.

He needed to understand Jada. It was no longer about wanting to understand her. He *needed* to understand her like he needed air to survive.

The need—the desire—to fully understand her and all she'd been through weighed on him.

Which is why he'd enlisted his boys for this mission. He trusted his best friends' opinions and knew they would likely pick up on something he wouldn't. He was logical, went with the facts, which he didn't consider a problem, but according to the people closest to him, his mindset made him unmindful to the whys and hows people made the messy decisions they did.

All those facts didn't stop the doubts and the "what the fuck was he doing?" from sounding on a loop in his brain, however.

"This better be good," Nicholas said. "I canceled a date to be here."

Now, that was brotherhood. "Thanks, man."

He joined August on the couch. He'd already pulled the show up on the streaming platform on his TV. All he had to do was press play. He stuffed some chips in his mouth and passed Nicholas a beer instead.

"Stop procrastinating," August said.

Damn, sometimes it sucked having friends who knew you better than you knew yourself.

"I'm not—"

"You are." Nicholas pointed to the TV.

"Fine."

Showtime. He pressed play. The season was only six episodes long. He could get through this, and hey, if he needed to fast-forward through some scenes, then oh well.

The opening credits played with a light, upbeat musical beat that was undoubtedly supposed to put the audience in a good mood. Too bad it had the opposite effect on Donovan. But this was his idea, so he'd see it through the bitter end.

"Who is this douche?" Nicholas asked, in between bites of popcorn, about the host.

The guy oozed smarm with his too-wide grin and veneers and fake "aww, shucks" manner. Donovan made a face. "Vince Baker."

Nicholas and August burst into laughter when the lead of the show, *Doctor* John Timmerman, esteemed anesthesiologist, was introduced. "Is there a reason they need to take video of him showering to prove what a good doctor he is?" Nicholas asked.

Donovan didn't care. The show had moved on to introducing the contestants. Twenty women would be vying for Dr. John's heart, and Jada was one of them. Knowing she'd ultimately turned down Dr. John's proposal didn't stop jealousy from flaring deep in his gut.

And there she was. Looking as beautiful as always. She wore a floor-length black gown shot through with gold thread. Her hair cascaded over one shoulder in waves. That fool, Dr. John, smiled at her and kissed her hand like the prick he clearly was.

Donovan growled.

"You going to make it through this?" Nicholas asked. "The fun hasn't even started yet."

Right. He needed to chill. He settled in to watch Jada fall in love with another man.

Two hours later, he hadn't moved from his seat.

"Damn, this is getting good," Nicholas said. "I mean, we already know how this ends, but I am *invested*. Like Candace is the villain, but is ol' dude ever going to notice?"

August pointed at Nicholas. "Right! And who is he going to choose to kick off this episode, Angela or Destiny? I need to know. We need some more popcorn."

"Clearly, the right choice is Angela. They have no chemistry, but it's not going to happen if he keeps listening to Candace."

Donovan barely paid them any attention. He only had eyes for Jada. Even in the scenes she wasn't in, he wondered what she was doing. Was she thinking about John? About falling in love with him?

When she was on camera, she was Jada. Funny, smart, observant about the strengths and shortcomings of her fellow contestants and her place in John's affections.

She wasn't afraid to voice her opinion, but was encouraging of the other contestants. She kept her cool. Not afraid to crack jokes. She was herself always. And that was a sweet, well-meaning person who occasionally got herself into hot water because of her impulsive decisions.

But, if he didn't know better, he would say there was a strain around her mouth. The twinkle in her eyes wasn't quite as strong as he was used to seeing. Was she feeling the stress of the moment? She and Dr. John did have good chemistry. He'd taken her to play miniature golf on their first date and hadn't been able to stop smiling. "I love your competitive spirit." Jada had laughed and pumped her fist every time she sank a putt. It was the laugh he'd come to crave hearing, so full of life and joy. Then, he'd followed up with a picnic on the eighteenth hole. The other women hadn't viewed her as a threat until then.

"You okay, dude?" Nicholas asked.

"Yeah, why wouldn't I be?" He squirmed to find a better position on his couch, which he'd bought because it was the most comfortable piece of furniture he'd ever come across.

"Because your woman is kissing another man as we speak."

Donovan glared at his friend. "She's not my—" Breath whooshed out of him. They'd gone to the next scene. It was over. Thank God.

She wasn't his woman, but he wanted her to be. And it wasn't the jealousy talking. He wanted to be the one to put a smile on her face. He wanted her to defend him. He wanted to defend her and know that it was real. That *they* were real. That they didn't have an expiration date.

"Nerves, right? It's just nerves," she said in an interview. "Everything's moving so fast, but he's the perfect guy. Any girl would be lucky to have him." She never said she'd be lucky to have him.

That blind look of panic in her eyes was obvious to see as Dr. John declared his love for her during the season finale. Donovan wished he'd been there to comfort her. Tell her everything was going to be okay.

Donovan sat up straighter. He could be there for her now.

And he was going to tell her that. Fuck the fake dating. He wanted it to be real.

For so long, he'd held on so hard to a plan and who he believed he should be and being perfect for everyone else that he'd lost sight of who he was.

He wanted the lightness she brought to his life. He hadn't had so much fun in a long time. He liked who she was. She brought chaos and he wanted more of it. The chaos came from Jada being unabashedly Jada. She wasn't trying to be somebody she wasn't. And he loved that.

He wanted more of her. He wanted her to be his. He wanted to be hers.

It should have been obvious to him. Why else would he spend an evening watching *My One and Only* with his two best friends?

Had she gone on the show looking for love? He didn't know, but he knew he wanted to be the one to give it to her. He wanted to be the one to comfort her when she feared no one would.

Did she feel the same? Only one way to find out.

Chapter Seventeen

Jada smiled at the two women stepping up to the front counter. "Hey, nice to see you again, Gwen and Tracy. How can I help you?"

"By serving us the best cupcakes in the city, of course," Gwen said with a wide smile.

Tracy gestured toward her outfit of yoga pants and a tank top over a sports bra. "What better way to reward ourselves for a good workout than with a cupcake from the best cupcakery in the city?"

Jada grinned. "Makes perfect sense to me."

Tracy had attended the sexual healing bachelorette party and mentioned she worked out at the gym two blocks over, but she'd never known Sugar Blitz existed.

"How you doing, sugar?" Tracy asked.

"Good." And she was. The appearance on *Good Day, San Diego* had gone better than she could have imagined. Her relationship with Donovan was in the best place it had ever been in. Not that they were in a *relationship* relationship. If she sometimes thought about how he made her laugh like no one had in a long time, or how he'd quietly supported her in the supply closet or on the show, or how he'd kissed her in said supply closet, well, then . . . nothing. They'd agreed that they were friends only, and that was that.

She wasn't going to tip over the proverbial apple cart for someone who hadn't indicated he looked at her as someone other than an annoying friend or fake girlfriend. They were friends, and that was okay. She needed friends, and he'd been there for her as she embarked on this new chapter in her life. Operation: Jada Gets Her Life Together was still in effect. And that was that. She focused on her customers. "What are you in the mood for?"

"I'll take a pumpkin swirl," Gwen said.

"I'll have a peanut butter chocolate," Tracy said. "Give me the biggest one in the case. If I'm going to add back all those calories I burned off working out, I'm going to do it in style."

Jada laughed and rang up their order. "Enjoy, ladies."

They took their goodies and headed to one of the few available tables.

Jada scanned the store with eager eyes. Most of the tables were filled with customers happily munching on cupcakes and sipping coffee or lemonade. A stark contrast from her first few days at the shop. And it was due, in large part, to her—some unintentional, but a lot intentional. Her work had brought in new customers who were turning into repeat customers. In addition to the book club meeting and bachelorette party, they'd held a singles night, pairing people based on their favorite cupcakes, and a couple of birthday parties, all fun and successful. This weird feeling flowing through her veins, giving her energy, was pride.

She lowered her head to check the display case. They were running low on vanilla cupcakes. Today's special—mocha fudge—was selling briskly, but they'd restocked less than an hour ago, so they should be good for a while. Only five peanut butter chocolate cupcakes left. They needed more of those, too, or else Katrina, who came in every day to buy cupcakes for her workers at her design firm as an afternoon treat, would not be happy.

Jada froze. Something was different. Maybe even wrong? The quiet din of conversation permeating the shop a few seconds ago had died a sudden death. Jada raised her head. And gasped.

Dr. John Timmerman, the star of *My One and Only*, was standing at the entrance of the store, surveying the interior. And everyone had noticed. The quiet disappeared as quickly as it had appeared. Loud whispers and clicks of camera phones filled the air.

John's perusal stopped when he spotted her. A confident smile spread across his handsome face and he marched toward her with long, purposeful strides. There was no doubt he was a striking man. The other contestants had all flipped when he was introduced to them, delighted the show had managed to secure such a photogenic star. He was about six feet tall, a few inches shorter than Donovan. He had the muscular physique of a man who spent plenty of time in the gym and lived off boiled chicken and rice.

His teeth were white and perfect. His face was perfectly symmetrical. A sharp nose hovered over lips that were neither too thin nor too full. Dark brown skin stretched over high cheekbones. He had long eyelashes plenty of women, including Jada, paid plenty of money to replicate.

He was perfect.

She'd rejected him on national TV.

And he was here.

Her heart, which had stopped beating when she first spotted him, started pounding again at three times its resting rate.

What was he doing here?

"What are you doing here?" she blurted out when he stopped in front of the counter.

He laughed the booming laugh that sounded so great on camera. "There's the Jada I've missed so much."

What was he doing here? Had he come to curse her out for dumping him on national TV now that the shock of her rejection had worn off? She offered up a smile, though the muscles in her face mightily resisted her efforts. "You know me. I'm a riot."

Her lunch roiled in her stomach. Sushi was not a good choice when you were about to experience major upheaval. But maybe that wasn't about to occur. She needed to remain positive.

His smile hadn't faded. "I drove down from L.A."

Jada blinked in surprise. "Aren't you from Minnesota?" He'd talked often about his All-American Midwest upbringing on the show and how much he loved the Twin Cities, snow and all.

He propped a hip on the counter like he planned to stay there for a while. "I moved to California a few weeks ago. Gotta take advantage of the opportunities that come with being on the show. I took a leave of absence from my practice. I can always go back if things don't work out."

"Oh. Right." She couldn't blame him. After all, "exploring opportunities" had been her primary reason for going on the show.

John hadn't stopped blinding her with his white teeth. Of course, he could just be waiting to lure her into a false sense of security before dropping the hammer. Yes, there was nothing in her contract with the show that said she was obligated to accept a marriage proposal if asked, but it was expected. The lead didn't go on the show to be embarrassed.

She gripped her hands together behind her back, while she struggled to think of something else to say. There was no one to rescue her. Ella's shift hadn't started, and the owners were in other parts of the bakery. Yelling for help seemed uncouth. She dropped her hands and squared her shoulders. Besides, she didn't need any help. She was Jada Townsend-Matthews, hear her roar. Or something. "How can I help you? Did you want a cupcake?"

He didn't look at the display case. "You're really working here, huh? Wow. Social media knows all, but some part of me still found it hard to believe."

She lifted her right shoulder in a shrug. "Yep. I'm working here."

"That's great. The last month has been kind of a whirlwind for me with interviews and TV appearances." He didn't seem fazed by the incessant clicks of the cameras in the room behind them. She wished she could say the same. It took everything in her not to flinch at every click.

"You look wonderful," he continued, scanning her figure.

Jada blinked. "Oh. Thanks. You look great, too." Maybe the hammer was coming down now. There hadn't been much time to talk after the rejection. Producers whisked her away for an interview, and she hadn't sought him out. Why would he want to talk to the woman who dumped him on camera, in front of millions? As far as she knew, he hadn't asked producers to see her either.

John straightened to his full height. "Can we go somewhere and talk?"

"Not now. I'm the only one watching the store." But the cameras were still clicking, so maybe they should.

Over his shoulder, Jada saw Donovan coming around the corner. He came to a halt when he spotted everyone with their cameras up, all pointing in the same direction, not trying at all to be subtle. His gaze swung her way. His eyes narrowed, then widened as he spotted John. His strides were purposeful as he made his way to them.

He rounded the counter and wrapped an arm around her waist. She leaned into the embrace, letting his strength seep into her. Seeing John had knocked her off-kilter. Donovan inclined his head, with his natural regality, toward John. "Funny seeing you here."

Such a Donovan statement. He wasn't one to hide behind bull-shit and pretend he didn't know who her ex-almost-fiancé was.

John, for his part, showed no sign of intimidation. No one ever said no to him. He always got what he wanted. She'd picked up on that aspect of his personality early on, and the producers had only continued to cater to him during filming. "Hey, how you doing man? I'm John." He held out his hand for a handshake. Donovan made no move to take it. John cleared his throat. "I came to see Jada. Check on her."

Jada broke Donovan's hold and turned to face him. "Do you mind watching the counter for a few minutes?"

Donovan's expression didn't change. He studied her face for a few seconds. His voice remained steady. Steadfast. "Of course. Take your time."

Without another word, Jada led John toward the door to an ac-companiment of camera clicks. No doubt someone was live tweet-ing the whole encounter and/or contacting TMZ as she walked. But there was nothing to do about that. She hadn't done anything wrong, except unexpectedly dumping the star of a reality TV show during the season finale and then lying about having a significant other at home, but other than that, she was perfectly innocent.

Once outside the store, Jada turned in a circle. She needed to get him away from the windowed walls of the storefront. She spotted a bench farther up the block and headed that way. John fell into step beside her. He seemed to understand she wanted a modicum of privacy before resuming their conversation. Thankfully, they didn't pass any other people, and the bakery's customers had all stayed inside. Or maybe they had telephoto lenses and didn't need to be within twenty feet to get decent photos. After all, everyone was an amateur paparazzo these days.

She arrived at the bench and dropped unceremoniously onto the wooden seat. Closing her eyes, she lifted her face to the sky, where the sun shone high and bright, and let the rays soak into her and give her strength. It was a lovely day, nothing to indicate that her world had been turned upside down less than ten minutes ago.

The bench shifted slightly. John had sat next to her. Her eyes drifted open. He watched her with curious and—if she were full of herself—keen interest. Okay, this wasn't a time to be modest. She knew what a man's interest looked like, and John was definitely giving off the vibes. But maybe not. Hopefully not. When they'd had time together on the show, tingles of attraction had filled her belly. Now that space was reserved for nerves. It felt nothing like when she was near . . .

Jada shook her head. "What are you doing here, John?" Her voice came out craggier than she would have liked, but that was a small price to pay. She needed to take control of the situation.

His lips, full and sensual, curled into an amused smile. She'd first been attracted to his smile. When he turned up the full voltage, it could be devastating. But then she'd noticed he employed it on everyone from cast to crew whenever he wanted his way.

"I came to see you," he said with his smooth, baritone voice.

She couldn't help but compare it to Donovan's drawl, with its rough edges. She found it lacking in authenticity, if she was being honest with herself.

"Why, though?"

He threw back his head and laughed. "That's why. I missed your particular brand of brutally honest communication."

"Glad I could oblige. How have you been?" She really wanted to know. Reaching out to him in the aftermath never seemed right. Why would he want to hear from her? *Hey, it's me, the woman who rejected you on national TV. Seen any good movies lately?* Yeah, no.

"I'm good." He laid a hand over his heart. "Truly."

"Have you kept in contact with the *My One and Only* team?"

He nodded. "Yes. Lila has checked on me a few times, making sure I'm okay."

Jada hadn't received the same consideration, but that was to be expected. The only thing she got were emails and calls asking, then demanding she do interviews. "That's great. And you're not angry with me?" She searched his eyes for the truth.

"I've found that anger is usually a manifestation of hurt. For me, anyway."

Ouch. She felt that deep in her soul. She winced before she could stop herself.

He touched her arm. "Hey, don't do that. I'm just being honest. I wasn't trying to shame or embarrass you. When you turned me down, I cycled through the stages of grief. I can't say I've gotten to acceptance, but I'm trying. I was so angry and confused. I racked my brain trying to figure out what went wrong."

He looked away for a moment. "Then the show started airing and I was doing press. It was a lot. I thought I was doing okay, and then I saw you on social media with that guy, and I couldn't believe it." His eyes narrowed. "But really, that guy? Jock meets the Grinch."

A surprised laugh spilled from her chest. He'd always been able to make her laugh. "Interesting description, but he's a good guy."

"But is he the right guy? I know you said you couldn't stop thinking about him while you were on the show, but I'm hoping you couldn't stop thinking about me once the cameras stopped rolling. We had some good times, Jada. You have to admit that."

The hand he'd rested on top of hers squeezed, then turned her palm over and lightly ran his thumb up her palm in a sensual gesture. *Danger, danger* started flashing in bright red letters in front of her face. She casually withdrew her hand. "John—"

"Jada. Can you at least admit we had some good times?" His dark eyes pleaded with her.

She sighed. Current predicament aside, lying really wasn't her style. "We did."

"Have you thought about me at all since taping ended?"

She had. After all, she'd had no real reason to turn him down, just something in her gut telling her something wasn't right. So many questions had crowded her mind in the aftermath. Had she made a mistake? Had she really devastated him? He'd claimed to be in love with her. Though, after watching the show, she now knew he'd said the same thing to the other two finalists as well. But she was the one he'd chosen. And hadn't love been missing from her life for what seemed like forever?

She gave a momentary thought to lying, but that wasn't fair to either of them. She'd done enough lying. She nodded.

He pumped his fist. "I knew it!"

"But that doesn't mean I want to hop back into something with you. I'm . . . seeing someone." Even though it wasn't real. Her stomach cramped in protest at that truth.

He nodded like he'd expected her answer. "I get that. If I had my way, you would dump him right here, right now, but that's my version of the fairy tale. I don't want to put you in a bad spot, but I do want you to know that there's another option out there for you." He chuckled. "How the tables have turned. I was the guy with multiple women after me and now you have your choice."

Jada offered up a weak smile. Talking was a little beyond her capabilities at the moment. He'd shocked the crap out of her. *He wanted to get back together? Like for real?*

He squeezed her hand again. "Don't forget about us, that's all I'm saying. I've surprised you. Just think about it. Think about how good we were together." He gestured with his free hand. "I can take you away from all of this. You don't want to work at a cupcake shop for the rest of your life."

Right. The store. Her job. The current iteration of her life.

"Uh . . . yeah. Wow." Jada stood on trembling legs.

John rose and gathered both her hands. "We can be the total media darlings we were meant to be. The new Bonnie and Clyde."

"They killed people, so . . . no, we can't, but I get your point."

He laughed, an action beyond at her right now.

Her mind was whirling in a spin cycle. Her heart was sprinting faster than a toddler who'd spotted Mickey Mouse at Disneyland. This was bananas. What a twisted web she'd woven. She'd dumped an almost-fiancé with the excuse she had someone at home, and the man who'd stepped in to rescue her from her lie was starting to mean more to her than she ever thought possible. But she had no idea if he felt the same way, and now the almost-fiancé was back, professing that he hadn't ever stopped loving her.

John lowered his head to peer directly into her eyes. "So what do you say? What's it gonna be?"

Chapter Eighteen

"Donovan. Donovan. Donovan!" Nicholas tapped him on the arm. "Donovan, what's going on?"

Donovan barely registered the question or the divine smell of the freshly baked desserts Nicholas carried. He was too busy thinking about that fool who'd had the nerve to show up here at his business, smiling that fake, toothy grin with his too-big veneers. But he wasn't Donovan's biggest concern.

Was Jada okay? He didn't know, and it was killing him.

Nicholas set the batch of cupcakes on the counter. "Why is everyone looking out the window, acting like they've spotted Beyoncé and Jay-Z? Now that I think about it, we should work on that, figuring out how to get them in the store. Or maybe the Mandalorian and Baby Yoda. The green one loves cupcakes."

"Yeah, sounds good. Whatever you want." Donovan craned his neck, trying to spot Jada walking back, but there was no one there. Just an empty sidewalk. When was she getting back? Was she okay? Maybe he should go look.

He jerked back when snapping fingers appeared less than an inch from his face.

"Earth to Donovan. Are you there?"

Donovan pushed Nicholas's hand away. "Yeah, yeah."

Nicholas cut him a look. "You just agreed to strip naked in front of the whole store and sing karaoke."

"What?" Donovan squinted, then shook his head. "No, I didn't!"

Nicholas lifted an eyebrow. "You sure?"

Donovan searched his brain, trying to recall what Nicholas said. He came up with nothing. "What do you want?"

Nicholas opened the case and deposited the cupcakes inside. He looked over his shoulder. "I want to know why you look like you discovered Santa only left you a lump of coal underneath the Christmas tree."

"John Timmerman came in a few minutes ago."

"What? Dr. John?" The gossipmonger leapt to his full height and almost broke his neck scanning the store. "He did? Where is he?"

"He left with Jada." Donovan grabbed a towel and scrubbed at the counter with all his considerable might. This was some bullshit. Every last bit of it.

Yes, Jada could take care of herself, but he hated seeing her unsettled. And there was no denying she'd been shocked to the soles of her Crocs to see that blast from the past.

What did that ass want? And maybe he wasn't an ass, but any guy who showed up to his ex's *job,* a job where she also happened to work with her current boyfriend, qualified as an ass in his book. And no, it did not matter that technically they weren't dating. Fuck technicalities. He didn't like that dude showing up. He smelled like bad news with his overpowering cologne that was only slightly better than Axe. "Whatever he's up to isn't good."

"You sure that's not just what you want to believe?"

Donovan jumped. Where the hell had August come from?

He scowled. "I'm going to kick your ass one day if you sneak up on me like that ever again."

"You've been saying that since freshman year and you haven't done it yet, so . . ." August's massive shoulders lifted in a shrug.

Donovan rubbed his temples in a futile attempt to hold a headache at bay. His shoulders and stomach were tight. His skin was itchy. He didn't like that John guy showing up out of the blue. What if Jada wanted to get back together with him? Before he could tell her how he felt? He'd planned to invite her out for drinks when her shift was over. He'd wanted to play it cool, not make things awkward at work. Look where that had gotten him. Fuck.

"You seem awfully bothered by something you say isn't bothering you." Nicholas poured himself a cup of coffee, took a sip, and studied Donovan over the rim.

"I'm not bothered. I'm worried about Jada. She's out there by herself with that dude."

"Jada has traveled all over the world by herself. Pretty sure she can take care of herself."

"Of course she can take care of herself, but I have no idea what he's saying to her. She's been through a lot. If he's messing with her head or playing on her vulnerabilities, I will kick his ass. Full stop. Damn it. Where is she?" He looked at the clock on the wall. She'd been gone seventeen minutes. Plenty of time for that dude to say what he wanted to say and get the hell out. He threw the towel on the counter. "I'm going to go find her."

As he hurried around the counter, the front door bell jingled and Jada stepped back inside Sugar Blitz. Immediately, every conversation in the bakery went mute. None of the nosy customers had left. After a suspended second, more camera clicks filled the air.

Jada took it all in stride, or at least she did her best to give that appearance. Donovan was starting to know her well. She squared her shoulders, lifted her chin, and plastered a smile on her beautiful face. But the smile wasn't genuine, her gait wasn't steady, and she gripped her hands together in a tight vise.

Donovan took the three steps needed to get to her and wrapped an arm around her waist, which he was now realizing he'd done when he first spotted John. She sagged into his side. Fuck. She wasn't okay. He needed to get her out of here.

He walked with her to his office and shut the door on the outside world. Jada collapsed against the wall and closed her eyes. "Jada, are you okay?"

She didn't respond. Her chest rose and fell rapidly.

"Jada." He'd done his best to offer her comfort, but now he was panicking. And he never panicked. He analyzed a situation and came up with the most logical solution. But nothing had been logical since the moment she'd shown up at Sugar Blitz. He couldn't go back to the way things had been. More importantly, he didn't want to.

"Jada," he pleaded.

At last, her eyes fluttered open. In one fluid motion, she pushed away from the wall and pressed a quick, hard kiss to his mouth, her soft lips clinging to his for a way-too-brief moment, then collapsed against the door again, her eyes fluttering shut once again, her breaths still coming fast.

What the fuck?

Panic beat at his chest. Was she in shock? He scanned her figure, looking for any signs of distress. Everything looked normal, but he knew not all wounds and scars appeared on the outside. "Are you okay? Did that dickwad do or say something out of pocket to you?"

Her eyes slid open. "Dickwad?" she murmured. "Have you been

watching *Animal House* or some other raunch com or something from the eighties? Or the nineties?"

"Jada." He wasn't in the mood for their banter to deflect from serious matters right now. He needed to make sure she was okay before he collapsed from worry.

"Do you realize the whole media circus is going to start all over again? Except this time, it's going to be all about a love triangle. Is Jada lording her womanly wiles over two men and luring them into her web of doom?" Her voice was light and airy, like she couldn't believe she was in this situation, but found it hilarious all the same. "My parents will have a fit."

"Jada, I don't care about all that. I care about you." He cupped her shoulders. "Are you okay?"

Her eyes locked on his. "I wondered what would happen if I ever saw him again. Would the butterflies come back? Would I feel that same spark I felt the first night we met? You know, I always wondered if that spark was real, or was it a result of producer manipulation telling us over and over again that we were about to meet the man of our dreams, who was looking for his wife? Would I be hit by a wall of regret when I saw him? Would I ask for another chance or would he drop down to his knees and beg for another chance because I was his dream woman?"

Donovan swallowed hard, trying to bring some moisture to a throat that had gone desert-dry, and forced out the question as she gave voice to the fears he hadn't wanted to acknowledge. "What did you find out?"

A small grin pulled at her perfect lips. "The whole time he was talking to me I couldn't stop thinking about you. I wanted it to be you. I *want* to be with you. Only you. For real."

Again, her lips landed on his with a clear purpose—to seduce. He'd always approved of having a plan. She nibbled at his bottom lip until his mouth fell open. Then she was inside, letting him taste the sweetness that was Jada Townsend-Matthews. He happily lost himself in her.

Their tongues met in a slow, sensual glide. He crowded closer. Close wasn't close enough. He cursed the clothes separating their bodies. He wanted to see and worship the soft breasts pressed against his chest. He wanted to lay her on a bed of roses and explore every inch of her delectable body with his hands and mouth. He'd never wanted anything more.

She pulled away. He held back an undignified whimper by the skin of his teeth.

Her eyes searched his. "Wait. Do you feel the same way?"

"Yes. So much." He'd never had to think less about an answer in his life.

Her stunning smile stopped his heart for two full beats. He'd never seen a more beautiful sight in his life than a happy, confident Jada. "Okay, good. Back to kissing."

Donovan grinned. "My pleasure."

He captured her lips with his. Their tongues tangled together as he explored her mouth. Her scent surrounded and intoxicated him. She entranced him. He couldn't get enough. Would never get enough. He rocked against her and swallowed her whimper when she registered how hard he was. Moaned when she snagged her hand in his belt and pulled him closer.

Desire coursed through his veins. This is where he wanted to be. With Jada, locked away from the outside world.

Wait. He pulled back, although it took every ounce of his willpower. "Does that mean you told him to kick rocks?"

He wanted to make sure there were no more misunderstandings. That she was with him in this, whatever this was.

"You wanted me to use those exact words, didn't you?" She bit her lip. Wait. That was his job. He leaned down for another kiss, paying special attention to the plump bottom lip that had been tormenting him since the day they met.

Reluctantly, he pulled away and gave a quick nod. "I wouldn't complain if you did."

She caressed his cheek. He leaned into the embrace, craving her soft touch. "Well, I didn't use those exact words, but I did let him know that he and I would never be an us. There's someone else in my life I'm dedicated to."

Exultation filled his every pore. "Perfect." He lowered his head again.

Chapter Nineteen

*E*ventually, Jada grudgingly came up for air. Her heart was racing out of control, but she gathered her faculties enough to swipe a thumb across Donovan's hard jaw and speak. "I like doing that."

"I know."

She rolled her eyes. "Don't act all macho. I'm the one who made a move."

"I was going to, but you beat me to it!"

Now she was intrigued. "Oh, really? What did that move entail?"

"Well, I planned to demand that you come talk to me in my office when your shift ended." He leaned down to nibble at her neck.

It only made sense for her to tilt her head to give him better access. "Of course you would have."

"Then I planned on telling you that I've been reconsidering our relationship," he murmured against the hammering pulse at the base of her throat.

She snorted, though she struggled to keep up with the thread of the conversation. His mouth was extremely talented. "Of course. In that perfectly logical way."

When he lifted his head, she barely held back a whimper. "And you would have said in your bougie way, 'What does that mean?'"

"No, I wouldn't have." She slapped at his chest, then decided to linger because it was a very nice chest. Hard muscles flexed under her seeking fingers. *Very* nice. "Okay, yes I would have," she added at his snort.

"And I would have said, 'I'd like to discuss the situation over dinner in a more private setting.'"

"And I would have said, 'Donovan Dell, are you asking me out on a date?'"

"And I would have said yes and then jumped up from my chair to catch you as you fainted and slid to the ground." He trailed his mouth up her throat to her right ear, teasing her with his lips and tongue.

Jada tried to marshal her thoughts, which had scattered to every corner of the earth. His lips really were masterful. "So, basically, I screwed everything up."

"No, you did everything right."

And just like that, her heart stopped. How in the world did she think she ever stood a chance at resisting him? At resisting the feelings he stirred in her?

She rose on her toes and angled her mouth to his. A perfect fit, just like all the other times they'd kissed. Pleasure and desire flowed through her body in an unyielding stream. It was her turn to groan when Donovan stepped back.

"As much as I'd like to stay in the cozy confines of my office and kiss you for hours on end, I do believe my initial plan still has some merit."

"Dinner?" At his nod, she grinned. "I like food. Think we can sneak out of here? I'm sure everyone is out there waiting to see how we'll react to John's visit."

"They're going to be disappointed." He reached for her hand. "We'll go out the back. I'll text Nicholas that we've flown the coop."

Look at that logical side of him coming in handy. "Sounds like a plan."

He pressed one more kiss to her lips. "Follow me in my car. I'll send you the address for your GPS in case we get split up."

"Where are we going?"

"My place."

* * *

Donovan reached for Jada's hand as soon as she stepped out of her car. Touching her never got old. If he was honest with himself, a feeling he could only describe as pure joy had swept through him when her car pulled up behind him. This was real. "Ready for our date?"

She squinted. "Is *date* a synonym for *more kissing*?"

He laughed. She never failed to amuse him. "Probably."

She clapped her hands. "Then let's get to it." She tugged him toward the front door.

Once inside the house, he led her straight to the kitchen. She turned and lifted on her toes. Thrilled to accept the invitation, he cradled her chin and lowered his head. He wanted to go slow, take his time in hopes he'd remember every moment. He patiently sipped at her luscious lips, content to savor her sweetness. Until she moaned. That sound, so sexy . . . what she did to him without even trying. Her lips parted, and he pulled her closer for a long, intense kiss that rattled his brain.

He chuckled slightly when her hands went wandering, yanking

at the hem of his shirt. Then he sucked in a breath when her hand met his skin underneath the polo. Who knew such small hands could cause so much havoc? Her palms trailed along the sensitive flesh of his stomach, leaving goose bumps in their wake. How would it feel to have those greedy hands touching a more sensitive, yet eager part of him?

"I want to touch all of you," she murmured against his mouth, seemingly reading his mind, the yearning in her voice ramping up the fire in his blood.

Then a loud, unwelcome sound joined the fun.

Reluctantly stepping away from her intoxicating touch, Donovan grinned down at her. "Your stomach disagrees."

Her lips pulled into a pout. "But, but—"

"But I promised you dinner and I'm not going to have you fainting on me."

"But, but—" Again, her stomach made its opinion known.

His eyebrows rose. "You were saying?"

Jada lifted her chin. "Fine. You promised me food, so where's the food?"

Yeah, there was no denying it. Her bougie tone got him hot as hell.

* * *

Twenty minutes later, they were settled on his massive sectional couch, close enough for Jada to touch Donovan whenever she wanted. Close enough to lay out on if the mood struck.

It was cute that he wanted to take care of her. She still couldn't believe she was here with him and they weren't fighting, unless coming dangerously close to tearing each other's clothes off counted. An activity she planned to return to in the near future.

"Stop looking at me like that," he growled.

"Like what?" she asked with her most innocent voice. "I'm simply enjoying this fantastic meal your chef made." She gestured toward the plate on her lap that contained perfectly roasted chicken, fingerling potatoes that practically melted in her mouth, and the best asparagus she'd ever tasted.

When she'd expressed surprise that he wasn't cooking since he loved baking, he'd reminded her he didn't have much time to cook, with the bakery and his other full-time career of playing football, and his chef was more knowledgeable than he was about what he needed to keep his body in peak condition.

Jada perused his fine form one more time. She couldn't wait to get her hands on him again. Oh, yeah. She definitely needed to give her compliments to the chef.

He side-eyed her. "I'll bet. Wanna tell me what happened with John?"

Jada choked on a bite of that perfect asparagus. After taking a swallow of water, she glared at the man she'd been fantasizing about doing all kinds of wicked things to. Now those wicked things included murder. "Way to bring the mood down."

His expression remained unfazed. "Need I remind you that you only realized you wanted to be with me after he showed up?"

"You said we were going to end up here anyway," she immediately countered.

He ducked his head for a second. "We were, if you agreed, but I didn't anticipate having to wait to see if he could win you back first."

She was in so much trouble. He was entirely too cute. "That wasn't going to happen." While it was nice to know she hadn't left John with any lingering damage, the rush of attraction hadn't materialized. Neither had the overwhelming need to be in his presence.

No, that feeling was only reserved for the man sitting a few inches away, currently scrutinizing her face.

"Did he take it well?"

"Yeah, for the most part. He was disappointed, but he took it like a gentleman. He said he had to give it one last shot, but he hoped we could remain friends."

Donovan grunted. Then he shocked the hell out of her. "I watched the show."

This time, a piece of chicken had the honor of getting stuck in her throat, sending her into a coughing fit. He reached over with a long arm and whacked her on the back. When she was done embarrassing herself and could breathe again, she glared at him. "You can't say stuff like that."

He had the audacity to smile. "Why not?"

Jada threw her hands up. "Because you've always acted like you barely knew what the show was!"

"Which is why I watched. Reality TV isn't my thing, but I felt like there was a huge part of you I didn't know or understand."

Which was really sweet, and not simply mortifying. He'd watched the show? Her brain was having a hard time accepting the fact. She'd assumed he'd read an article and that's why he knew who John was.

He held up a finger when she groaned. "I'd like to hear the story from you though. You done eating?" When she nodded, he deposited both of their plates on the coffee table and tugged her closer until her back rested against his hard chest. "Don't worry. I got you."

I got you. Such a simple phrase, but it did the trick. Had anyone, other than her grandmother and her best friend, ever really had her back? Certainly, no romantic partner for any length of time. Or her parents.

Jada filled her lungs, then exhaled. "I was contacted by the show through Instagram to ask if I was interested in being on it. I'd just bombed another audition in L.A. and said yes. I had nothing else going on." She shrugged. "I'd seen an episode or two over the years. I did some research on the show and the contestants and discovered people had essentially turned being reality show contestants into full-time careers. I figured I could use the exposure to launch a lucrative career as a social influencer."

"What happened on the show?" He drew circles on the back of her hand with a surprisingly soft index finger.

Finding it soothing, she concentrated on that motion as she went down memory lane. "I thought it would be a once-in-a-lifetime experience. An adventure. And it was! I never expected to fall in love."

Donovan's circling motion stopped. "And did you?"

Jada was glad she didn't have to look him in the eye. "I thought I was, or could be. I mean I liked him. The dates were fun. We laughed a lot. Some of the other contestants told me I was a shoo-in. That I was clearly his favorite. I always tried not to get ahead of myself, to take each step as it came. That attitude actually worked to my benefit. I made things easy for him. He told me he could relax around me."

He resumed stroking her hand. "But you turned down his proposal."

That decision had changed her life forever in ways she'd never been able to imagine. Jada sighed. "Yeah."

She held her breath, her whole body tensing. Was he going to ask why? That was always everyone's next question. The question she still had trouble answering.

"Did you realize the reaction was going to be so brutal?" He shifted to cradle her body even more, causing her to sink into him. His strength buoyed her.

Jada shook her head. "Not at first. When the show started airing, my social media follower numbers blew up. Which was good. Viewers were rooting for us and messaging me to tell me they couldn't wait until the final episode because they knew I was going to win, and we were the cutest couple. As the weeks went on and I got more and more messages, I knew it was going to be bad." She grimaced. "But I still wasn't prepared for the backlash. Or maybe my skin isn't as thick as I thought it was."

"Thick skin can be overrated."

Jada twisted to meet his gaze. "Yeah, my therapist always tells me I'm allowed to feel what I feel. It's sometimes hard to remember, let alone take that advice. She has me do affirmations when I really start to beat myself up. Apparently, I'm not supposed to be so hard on myself."

"You're not. You're amazing." He squeezed her waist. "One more question—why did you say no?"

Ah, there it was. But she wasn't upset. He made her feel safe. Understood. Unjudged. She scoured her brain to conjure up her emotions and thoughts from that night. She wanted to give him as honest an answer as possible. She settled back against his chest, letting his heat soak into her. "Something wasn't right. He and I weren't right together." Her voice quieted. "It wasn't any one thing I could point to, but my gut was screaming at me to get away."

"You followed your gut. Nothing wrong with that."

Jada let out a mirthless laugh. "Except when you have producers in your face constantly asking what went wrong. Lila, the one in charge, wasn't trying to hear gut instinct. So I invented someone at home."

Donovan pressed a kiss to her temple. "You sound like you're not too fond of your instincts."

"You already know my parents aren't that tolerant of my dyslexia.

They want me to find a real job. A job that makes sense to them. They're very analytical. Humanities as a major made no sense to them. Being a deejay in Europe made no sense to them. Going on reality TV made no sense to them." She huffed out a laugh. "They're not very understanding of things that don't make sense to them."

"You have a hard time getting their voices out of your head."

She faced him again, taking comfort in the understanding in his expression. "Yeah. They've been there for twenty-five years." She ducked her head. "They cut me off as a result of going on the show and further embarrassing them. According to them, I needed to grow up."

He frowned. "What do you mean they cut you off?"

"It means I'm lucky to have a job to buy groceries and pay my electricity bill. They didn't kick me out of my condo, at least, but only because they own it outright."

Shock flashed across his face. "Wow."

"Yeah. And I can't tell Grams because she would be furious with my mother, and why am I protecting my mom again?" She chuckled. "In my own way, going on the show was listening to them. It made sense to use what I'm good at—being personable—to launch a new career. Then it all blew up in my face because I couldn't control my natural tendencies."

"Your natural tendencies make you you."

A small smile pulled at her lips. "I seem to recall someone calling me impulsive."

He entwined their fingers. "I might have been a little hasty in that assessment."

"At least you're giving me that. I am impulsive."

"You are, but I'm learning that's not all bad."

Jada maneuvered herself so that she was straddling his hard thighs. She looped her arms around his neck and scooted forward until her breasts brushed against his chest. Oh, yeah. She liked this position. Should have done it earlier. "What else isn't so bad about me?"

"You want compliments?"

She eyed the up and down movement of his Adam's apple as he laughed. She wanted to track that movement with her tongue, followed by her mouth. Soon. Very soon. After the compliments. "Yep. Sure do."

Donovan tilted his head to the side, then snapped his fingers. "You brought more customers to the store."

She punched him on the shoulder. "Really?"

"Okay, fine. How about you're funny, quick on your feet, good with the customers, a great event planner? Gorgeous."

She thought about it. "Okay, that's better."

He squeezed her waist with strong, sure fingers and drew her forward another precious inch until only a breath separated their bodies. His gaze locked on her parted lips. Her breathing quickened. Was he going to kiss her now? It had been about thirty minutes since she'd last felt his mouth on hers. A lifetime. Her eyes drifted shut and she leaned forward.

"What about me?"

Her eyes flew open. "What?"

"Where are my compliments?" His eyes twinkled.

Lust was rampaging through her veins, and he had *jokes*? She narrowed her eyes. Fine. She twisted around and surveyed the large living room with its light, airy feel and ocean view outside the big bay window.

"I like your house. It's not what I expected."

"What did you expect?"

She dropped a light kiss on the tempting brown skin of his throat. "Something modern. A high-rise."

His throat vibrated with laughter under her seeking mouth.

"You're not that far off. When I first signed with the team, I did buy a high-rise. Lived there for a few years."

She was vaguely paying attention to what he was saying. His lips, the bottom one so full and lush, were drawing most of her focus. "What happened?"

He grinned. "I sold it for a tidy profit."

She playfully punched him in the arm. "Seriously?"

"Yes, but that's not all," he added when she lifted her hand again. "I wanted somewhere quieter. More space. An actual house, not a condo."

"This is quite a house, though. Big."

He shrugged. "I like my space, but more importantly, it's on the beach. The neighbors aren't too close. I like surfing."

Okay, now that caught her attention. Her mouth dropped open. "You surf?"

He grinned. "Don't you?"

Jada wrinkled her nose. "I tried it once in high school. I fell off the board before I could actually stand up, got hit in the head with the board, and decided to head back to dry land." She grinned. "I listened to my gut telling me it wasn't for me."

"Maybe you needed a better teacher."

"You offering?"

"You gonna listen?"

Jada lowered her head to nibble at his delectable neck again. "Maybe. How did you get into surfing?"

"In college. One of my coaches suggested it as a way to relax. I thought he was crazy, but he basically forced all of us to take a lesson as a team-building exercise."

"How did it go from being a mandatory activity to a desirable activity?"

"I liked being on the water in the sunshine with the quiet

surrounding me. I could think or not think, whatever I needed in that moment."

"You were good at it right away?"

He laughed. "No. In case you hadn't noticed, I'm pretty big. I had to learn how to find my center of gravity on a board that's not steady. But I did eventually, and never looked back. I'll show you how great surfing is."

Enough talking. "Okay. Sounds cool, but I'm more interested in what I can learn tonight."

"Like what?"

"Like if you kiss as good as I remember." She nipped at his lips until the sound of his ragged breath filled the air. "Like whether you look as good as you feel." She slipped her hands under his shirt and reacquainted herself with his amazing abs, her fingers tracing the hard lines and ridges. Good Lord. Better than she imagined. She rocked against him and made contact with his rapidly rising erection.

Victory!

She rocked again. Moaned at the contact. It wasn't enough. She wanted more. She wanted it all.

"Jada." The heat in his eyes singed her. She was ready to be burnt.

His hand slid up her nape and sank into her hair, tugging her closer until their lips collided. The kiss was wild and incendiary. Uncontrolled. Jada sank headlong into the feelings of wonder and lust sweeping through her. This was where all the arguing, flirting, teasing had been leading.

Their lips meshed perfectly as their tongues dueled, sliding, tangling against each other in a hungry, unbridled dance. She was greedy and would never get enough. Arousal charged through her. She pressed against his erection, desperate to get closer, wanting to feel his hardness between her legs. Longing for the moment when he would fill her.

He dragged his lips down the sensitive skin of her throat, his teeth making the barest, yet oh so powerful contact. The sting thrilled her. He swirled his tongue at the base of her throat, causing her pulse to skyrocket. Then his mouth was on hers again, seeking, then demanding a response, his hands sweeping across her body, frustrating her with the fleeting touches. She wanted his rough hands on her with nothing in between.

"Jada." He sounded tortured. Desire swirled unchecked in his dark eyes.

There was no question how this night would end. How it had always been destined to end. Her voice came out sure and proud. "Yes."

Chapter Twenty

The hunger on Donovan's face thrilled Jada. The heat in his eyes fried her nerve endings. She couldn't wait to combust.

His eyes never left hers as he slowly, so slowly undid the buttons of her Sugar Blitz polo. He slipped a finger inside and brushed a finger across her sensitive flesh. She gasped as goose bumps rose along her skin.

He pressed a hard kiss to her neck a second before her shirt was whisked over her head. She barely registered the motion before his mouth landed on her bare collarbone. Jada gasped for some much-needed air as he dragged his lips across her flesh until he met the strap of her bra. He slowly followed the line of the lace material down over the swell of her breast, teasing her. Tormenting her. Thrilling her. She shivered. Her head lolled back, silently offering him more. A chuckle rumbled from deep within his chest, but soon her bra met a similar fate as her shirt.

The light touch of his blunt fingers on her nipples was enough to have them puckering into tight balls.

"You are so beautiful." He sounded enthralled by the sight of her.

Jada growled when his hands slipped away. She wanted his hands, his *mouth* on her. Now. "Donovan."

"Hmm?" he murmured against her throat, his hands now at her waist, climbing higher, over her quivering flesh, but not quite touching her where she wanted. She dug her nails into his wide shoulders to get his attention.

Jada gathered her scattered thoughts as best she could. "Please."

"Is that what you want?" His tongue and teeth scraped along the outer swell of her breast, so close to where she wanted him, but still so far. He repeated the action on her other breast. All she had to offer was a desperate whimper. She clutched at the back of his head with unsteady hands, needing the anchor and hoping to draw him closer.

"Or this?" He drew her breast deeper to his mouth, his tongue licking across her hard nipple, finally giving her the solution she'd sought. She cried out at the heady sensation. He didn't stop, his tongue swirling over her again and again, adding a hint of teeth every now and then, keeping her teetering on the edge. Just when she thought she couldn't take any more, he switched breasts and started the torture all over.

An intelligible answer was beyond her at the moment. She was barely hanging on to reason as lust twisted inside her, building to a feverish pitch. She rocked against his dick, seeking some release from the torture, but he didn't seem interested in offering her mercy.

She was barely aware she was chanting his name until he drew away from her. His eyes were wild. She'd done that to him. Still, he took care with her, gently laying her on her back against the soft leather like she was precious cargo.

"You are so beautiful," he murmured.

The compliment sent warmth cascading through her. "You said that before."

"Because it's true."

She reveled under his ardent gaze. She couldn't stop herself from arching her back a little. Preening a bit when his eyes greedily tracked her every move.

A light smile broke his across his serious face. "You think you have me wrapped around your little finger, don't you?"

"Yes." He'd left her defenseless. She wanted to have the same effect on him. She lifted herself up to nip at the hard line of his jaw. Smiled when he shivered. "Take off your shirt. It's only fair."

"True." He obliged her.

She bit her lip to keep another whimper from escaping when she got her full, unvarnished look at his chest. She was a lucky, lucky woman. Scrumptious brown skin she couldn't wait to taste. Soft swirls of black hair covered hard pecs. The hair tapered in the most intriguing way into a line that went down his well-defined abs to his waist.

She'd given her compliments to the chef earlier. But if good, healthy cooking led to those abs, she hadn't given the woman her due enough. Her mouth watered with the desire to follow his happy trail to the promised land with her mouth. Soon. Very soon.

She beckoned him toward her with a crooked finger. With an arrogant eyebrow lift, his hands bracketed her body. He covered her body with his, pressing her into the soft cushions, settling in between her legs. The most wonderful predicament she'd ever found herself in. He was all heat and hardness against her welcoming softness. Jada exhilarated in the contact. The hair on his chest tickled her breasts. She turned her head into his neck and inhaled a lungful of Donovan.

He boosted himself up on his hands and looked down at her, wonder in his eyes. Wonder that matched her own.

"Wow," they whispered together.

"We're really here, huh?" she said.

He nodded. "We are."

She knew how he felt. She wasn't in this alone. She lifted her head, greedy for another kiss, while her hands went wandering, striving to touch every inch of the smooth, brown skin she could reach. The ridges and planes of his body fascinated her.

He thrust against her, sending another rush of sensation cascading through her.

"Again," she said, part demand, part frustration that clothes still separated them. He repeated the action. Jada moaned her approval. She wanted him there where she was so soft and wet.

Then he lowered his mouth to hers. Another mind-blowing kiss followed. When he finally wrenched his mouth away, his chest heaving, she pressed hungry, desperate kisses to the strong line of his neck and wide, muscular shoulders. Anywhere her lips and tongue could reach.

Then he was gone and she didn't try to stop an undignified whine from escaping. She wanted him back now. She rose up on her elbow. The view was spectacular. Muscles rippled in all their glory as he divested himself of his pants and underwear. She'd wanted to do that, but she'd allow it. Next time. He was magnificent. Long and hard. Her mouth watered again. A pulse throbbed between her legs. Yes.

He perused her figure, then lifted an arrogant eyebrow. Oh, right. She needed to return the favor. She stood and quickly got rid of her pants and panties.

He swept her figure from head to toe, leaving a trail of heat in his wake. "It bears repeating. You are so beautiful."

Before she could respond to or bask in the compliment, he swooped down, swept her up over his shoulder, and strode out of the room. Good Lord, the man had a world-class ass. Round and tight and biteable. Which was *not* important at the moment. Later, though. She pounded on his hard-as-a-brick back. "Put me down."

He continued like he felt or heard nothing, not stopping until he turned into a room and promptly dropped her. She bounced on the bed, then raised herself up. "Hey!"

She would ignore how this was possibly the most comfortable mattress she'd ever been on with the most luxurious sheets. The man knew thread count. He bent a knee to the bed and crawled upward until he covered her body. She inhaled his scent, quickly becoming intoxicated again. Hints of cedar and ocean and Donovan.

She needed to taste him. She trailed her teeth along a tendon in his neck.

"You were saying?" he whispered against her ear.

She caressed his jaw, the soft hair of his five o'clock shadow scraping deliciously against her palm. How would his beard feel against the skin of her inner thighs? If there was any justice in the world, she'd know sooner rather than later. "Hush and kiss me again."

He shivered dramatically. "That bougie voice just does it for me."

He cut her laugh off with his mouth. Then she was drowning again in him, in how he made her feel. Cherished. Desired.

His talented mouth slipped down her body, his destination clear, though he took several detours, first to her collarbone, then to her breasts again, then the curve of her hip.

Jada gripped the magnificent sheets with both hands and held on for the ride. Then he was between her legs, worshipping her like she was a goddess. She felt like a goddess.

His mouth and hands were magic. First, there were the gentle kisses to both thighs with quick nips of his teeth, followed by soothing licks of his tongue. The soft scrape of his beard on her skin heightened her pleasure, as she'd suspected. Gentle circles of her clit with his thumb and index finger had her arching her back and gulping for breath. Then his tongue joined the action on the sensitive flesh. Jada panted, unsure she would survive the delicious assault to her senses.

"Baby, you're so wet," he whispered against her. Wonder and desire filled his tone.

She knew. She knew.

But he wasn't done.

He slipped a finger inside her, then another, working her while he thumbed her clit in a rhythmic motion. New flames built inside her. He swiped a tongue down her sensitive folds once, twice, before returning to her clit.

Jada cried out, her throat arching. Aching.

He didn't stop.

Not when she pleaded. Not when she begged. Thank God. She panted for more. Implored him to release her from this torture. To keep going. He took his cues from her, alternating between slowing and quickening the pace of his fingers and tongue as she responded. "Yes. Like that. Please. Donovan."

She looked down as he looked up. The expression on his face dazzled her. Determined. Intense. Focused on her. Making sure she was taken care of. Turned on. Wild. "Anything you want, baby."

He lowered his head and continued to feast on her like she was a banquet. Strong glides of his tongue were followed by slower swirls. Right when she was about to explode, he gentled his touch. The torture continued until she couldn't take it anymore. "Donovan," she pleaded. "I . . . can't . . ."

"I got you, baby."

A gentle squeeze of her clit with his teeth and she soared over the edge, tumbling straight down into the abyss.

"You okay?" he whispered close to her ear, sometime later. He lay next to her, cradling her hand, rubbing his thumb over her palm.

Aftershocks continued to sweep through her. But she had just energy to swing a leg over his hip until she straddled him. "Never better."

Giving in to the craving that had never been far from the top of her wish list, she slid her hands up his body, starting at his fabulous abs bisected by his happy trail and working upward. His curly chest hair was soft and springy beneath her palms. She thumbed his nipples and grinned at his strangled gasp. Delighted at how they hardened under her eager hands. She loved that she affected him as much as he affected her. She wiggled her eyebrows. "But here's the thing. I'm not done. We're not done. Not even close."

"I was hoping you'd say that. Why don't you open that drawer?" He jerked his chin toward the mahogany nightstand.

"Say no more." Jada dove for the piece of furniture and came back triumphantly holding up the holy grail—a condom. "Do you mind if I do the honors?"

"Knock yourself out."

She ripped the package open and scooted down his magnificent body until she straddled his hips. She stared at his dick, licking her lips. She really hadn't given the appendage as much attention as she would have liked, but flames of desire couldn't be ignored, and she needed him inside her now. He hissed out a breath when she gripped him, then stroked him up and down, his flesh hard and warm, but he quieted as she carefully rolled the condom down his length.

Bracing herself on his flexing abs, she eased down on him, flutters of desire quickening at every flex of her inner muscles. They maintained eye contact the whole way, their connection unguarded and true. When he was fully inside her, her eyes drifted shut at the sensation of finally being one with him. She swallowed hard. Nirvana couldn't be this good. They fit like they'd been made specifically for each other.

His grip on her thigh tightened. "Jada." He was trembling beneath her. "I want to make this good for you, but I need you to move, baby."

Jada lifted, gasping at the shock of arousal that bolted through her. With his hand at her waist, he guided her back down, and they quickly found a rhythm that worked. Their simultaneous gasps confirmed it. His dark eyes held hers, refusing to let her go. Not that she wanted to. It wasn't just their bodies that were connected. So were their souls. She tightened her inner muscles around him, feeling his swift inhalation of breath at the movement. Then his magical fingers joined the action at her clit.

"Oh, my God." Jada could no longer concentrate. Could no longer maintain that careful, measured rhythm. She could only feel as the storm raged through her as she raced toward the end.

She yelped in surprise when Donovan flipped them. Never stopping the glorious motion of his hips, he guided her leg over his hip and amazingly reached deeper inside her with an expert thrust. She held on for the ride, the sparks flying high and bright throughout her entire body, as his pace quickened. He rolled his hips, pressing against her clit, and his mouth swallowed her cry as she fell headlong over the edge.

At her encouragement, he pistoned a few more times, shocking another climax out of her before finally throwing his head back in a hoarse shout as an orgasm claimed him.

* * *

Donovan was having trouble catching his breath, but at least his body had cooled. He slid his hand through Jada's hair and pressed a kiss to her forehead. He smiled when she snuggled up against his side. His brain was a whirlwind, bits and pieces of the past hour floating in and out of his consciousness. But there was one thing he had no trouble grasping. Jada was here. With him. He'd never been more content in his life.

"You have the best bed," she muttered.

Donovan laughed. How could he not? "That's what you're thinking about?"

She rolled over, propped herself up on his stomach, and stared down at him, tousled strands of dark hair falling all around her shoulders, her luscious lips now bare, but no less tempting. He caught his breath. Her beauty never failed to stun him.

"I mean yeah." Her lips stretched into a teasing grin. "What else am I supposed to be thinking about?"

"What about this?" He tugged her upward and did his best to push all rational thought out of her mind. He started by teasing her lips, keeping the kiss light until she murmured her disappointment, then he gave her what she wanted. What they both wanted. It was the furthest thing from a hardship. Jada tasted like sunshine, like everything he could ever want and more. What he would never get enough of. He wanted to offer her the same pleasure. When he leaned away, she was panting with a dazed expression on her face.

He knew the grin on his face screamed arrogance. He didn't care.

She did because her eyes narrowed. Jada sniffed. "So you can kiss. In the words of the inimitable Shania Twain, that don't impress me much."

His lips twitched. "Shania Twain? Really?"

She slapped him on the arm. "Yes, really. She's a legend. Get into it."

He side-eyed her. "If you say so. If my kissing skills don't impress you, then what will?"

She considered the question for a second. "Food. I seem to have built up quite an appetite."

"You have, huh? Then let's get you some food. Dessert work for you?"

"Absolutely, but first this." She captured his lips with hers and gave as good as she got, deftly exploring his mouth with considerable skill, her lips and tongue working in tandem to drive him out of his mind. He was panting for breath when the kiss ended.

"You all right?" she asked, arching those perfect eyebrows, her tempting lips curved into a knowing grin.

"Never better." He climbed out of the bed and stood on legs that weren't quite steady. He grabbed some sweatpants off a chair and stepped into them. "Will a T-shirt work for you?"

"Yes, please."

He retrieved two from his walk-in closet and returned to his bedroom. "Here you go."

He struggled not to roar like a Neanderthal when she raised the Knights shirt to her nose and inhaled. He smiled to himself at her little grumble when he donned his shirt.

When they entered the kitchen, Jada clasped her hands together. "What do you have? A cheesecake? Dutch chocolate cake?"

"Nothing."

Her smile fell. "What do you mean nothing? I thought you had a personal chef."

"I do, but she doesn't make desserts. I get enough of that at the store. And I'm not breaking my promise to provide dessert. We're going to make cupcakes."

Jada blinked. "Oh, you mean you're going to make them, and I'm going to watch."

"Nope. Don't think I've missed you dodging every opportunity to get back into the kitchen at Sugar Blitz."

"That's because I was a disaster."

"You were not a disaster."

She sent him a get-real look. "We had to start over three times. I kept spilling stuff. You kept glowering. And then I almost blew up the kitchen. Pretty sure that counts as a disaster."

"Stop. I can't have someone working for me afraid to step in the kitchen. I'm here to help and guide, not glower."

Jada sniffed. "Are you capable of not glowering?"

"You're not distracting me. We're only going to make a half dozen chocolate cupcakes. Simple. No large mixers. No professional-grade oven."

"Yeah, you have real bargain-basement equipment here." She gestured toward the decidedly upscale stainless steel appliances.

Donovan shrugged. "It's still a simple oven."

"I don't cook." Her pout was adorable. Everything about her was adorable. He was in so much fucking trouble, and he didn't give a damn.

"You're not cooking. You're baking." He looped his arms around her waist and peered into her eyes. "In any case, I believe in you."

"Thanks." Jada scanned the kitchen with wide eyes, then turned back to him. "Okay, yes. I want to try. Good idea."

He jerked back in surprise. "Really?"

She squared her shoulders in her very Jada way. "Yes, I'm determined to be a better me and believe in myself more. I even promise not to give you an opportunity to say I tried to burn down your kitchen."

"Hey, I apologized for that."

She poked him in the chest. "With Crocs! That's what you should be apologizing for. Gifting me those fashion abominations."

"You love those shoes. You're wearing them right now." They'd detoured through the living room on the way to the kitchen so she could get them.

Jada stared down at her footwear. "Well, yes, but still."

He crossed his arms. "But still what?"

Her chin lifted. "But still I have to complain because your head is already big enough."

"You like my big head."

She rolled her eyes. "Maybe."

"Definitely."

"Whatever." She balled her hands into fists, punched the air, and bounced on her toes. "So are we doing this?"

He lifted an eyebrow. "What? Boxing?"

She narrowed her eyes. "I'm ignoring you."

"You can't. I have to show you what to do."

"Ah, there's the control freak."

"You want to bake or insult me?"

She wrinkled her nose. "Both?"

"Why do I put up with you?"

"My dazzling, sparkling wit?"

"Yeah, something like that. Or maybe it's the way you're not afraid to speak your mind and stand up for what you believe in, no matter what."

The smile that bloomed across her face made his heart stutter. "Really?"

He drew her closer. He no longer had to resist the temptation to touch her whenever he wanted. "Yeah, really. You're brave and you make me laugh."

She buried her face into his chest. "You mean cry?"

"Hey, I'm trying to give you a compliment. Take it." He searched her eyes until he found what he was looking for—belief in what he was telling her.

She nodded. "Okay. Thank you. You're not so bad yourself."

"Thanks. But please understand I'll take back every word I said if you burn down my kitchen."

Jada froze. "You're the worst."

"You meant the best, I know. It was a slip of the tongue. It happens to the best of us." He dodged her playful shove and retrieved eggs and milk from the refrigerator. He jerked his chin toward the counter behind her. "Flour and sugar are over there."

He walked her through the process. She concentrated fiercely, matching him step by step. The intense look on her face was sexy as hell. They only stopped twice—okay, three times—for long, lingering kisses and for him to slide his hand under her shirt to feel that soft skin he loved to caress.

"See, that wasn't so bad," Donovan said as he slid the cupcake pans into the oven. He dropped the towel on the countertop. "What are you doing?"

She was poring over her phone, not paying him any attention. "Setting my phone alarm."

Donovan blinked. "Why? I already set the oven timer."

She looked up. "I'm not taking any chances. You know what's better than one alarm? Two alarms. And you know what's better than two alarms? Three." She took a few steps to the microwave and set its timer. "It's going to be great when my batch turns out better than yours."

Donovan crossed his arms. "Oh, yeah?"

"Oh, yeah."

She was so busy smirking at him, she never saw the flour headed her way. He landed a perfect strike. The ingredient hit her square in the chest right over the San Diego Knights logo. She gasped. "Donovan!"

He laughed, throwing his head back. Big mistake. Just as his head returned to its natural upright position, clumps of flour landed in his mouth. He sputtered and turned to face the counter, hacking.

Jada laid a hand on his back. "Donovan, are you okay?"

Sugar smacked her on the cheek. She gasped. "Oh, it's on now."

Donovan hurried around the island and crouched. If his friends and family could see him now, their jaws would permanently detach from their faces. This was not like him. But he wanted it to be.

What had come over him? Jada. It was all Jada.

He never relaxed. There was always another mountain to climb, another goal to reach for that elusive feeling of security, a feeling that had been all too rare as a kid, but here tonight with Jada, his mind wasn't racing with thoughts of what was next, of how to make the shop or any of his other ventures more successful. He was being silly with the woman who'd invaded so many of his thoughts over the past few weeks and he'd rather be nowhere else.

Jada. It was all Jada.

Now he had a food fight to win.

The ingredients they'd been using were right above him. All he had to do was reach up and grab them. What was left? Chocolate chips, a couple eggs, sprinkles. Where was Jada? All he could hear was his own ragged breathing.

"Remember to keep my hair out of this, buddy," she warned. Her voice came from the other side of the island. She was over by the refrigerator.

He laughed. "I grew up with a Black mother and two sisters. I would never dream of committing such heresy. But the rest of you? Yeah, it's on." But he had to be stealthy and methodical about his attack. Make sure he attacked at the exact right time. He held his position, not moving a muscle, straining to hear if she moved.

"Donovan, Donovan, come out to play. You started this."

That's right. He had. He leapt and grabbed a handful of sprinkles in one smooth action. He launched his missile and watched them cascade down to the ground in a sad, sad spiral, never reaching their target. Jada grabbed some chocolate chips and threw them at him. Donovan sent sugar flying her way, then snuck up behind her when she turned away to keep the white stuff from hitting her in the face. He wrapped his arms around her waist. She yelped, then settled against his chest, covering his hands with hers.

"I think that means I won," he said.

She harrumphed. "Whatever, dude."

"Never change, Jada. Never change." Donovan laughed as he surveyed the damage. Flour, sprinkles, and sugar decorated the floors and countertops in the usually immaculate space. "Wow. We made a mess." He had no regrets.

"We? That was all you, sir. I got the best shot in though." Her sparkling laughter filled the room and his spirit.

"Feel better?" he asked, nuzzling the side of her neck. He couldn't get enough of touching her. Of being with her. The lightness she had brought to his life could not be overstated. He hadn't even realized something was missing until she came roaring into his world, insulting him at every turn. She smelled so damn good, even through the flour and sugar. Like sunshine and flowers. He was going to be an addict in no time.

"Marginally," she murmured.

"Marginally? I must not be doing something right. I have to try harder." He turned her in his arms and covered her mouth with his. Kissing her was a new, better experience every time. He couldn't believe he'd wasted so much time not doing it at every opportunity. Stubbornness had led him nowhere but feeling deprived of her sweetness.

He willingly drowned in her, in her taste, in her scent, in her essence. Their tongues twined together in a thorough, slow movement. Time ceased to have meaning.

It took him a few seconds to recognize the incessant beeping wasn't the pounding of his heart. He reluctantly broke away. Jada's eyes widened.

"The cupcakes!" they yelled simultaneously.

Chapter Twenty-One

"You have a little more pep in your step this morning," Nicholas said to Donovan the next morning.

"Pep in my step? Okay, boomer." Donovan poured a cup of coffee, added a packet of sugar, and took a deeply appreciative sip of the hot brew.

Nicholas leaned an elbow on top of the display case and leveled a hard look at him. "Don't try to distract me. You know it's true."

"If you say so." It wasn't that Donovan was ashamed of the new turn in his relationship with Jada, and he rarely, if ever, kept things from his best friend. But this thing with Jada was new and he wanted to protect and savor it for all its worth before they let outsiders with their unwanted opinions in.

"You and Jada snuck out of here like ninjas yesterday."

"I texted you. And stop watching those movies."

"Donovan, come on," August said, joining them. They'd decided to double-team him. Great. Wasn't he lucky to have *two* best friends? And there were no customers waiting to order to distract them.

He went with his only option—stalling. "What?"

Nicholas sighed. "At least tell us what happened with Dr. Asshole."

Donovan's hand tightened around the mug as he recalled what Jada told him. "He said he wanted to get back together. Jada told him no."

"Then why are you grinding your teeth?"

"Because he had the goddamn nerve to show up here when he knows she's in a relationship."

"She is?" Nicholas exchanged a knowing glance with August.

Fuck. He'd stepped right into that one.

"But we can tell you're not ready to talk about it, so we'll leave you alone," August said.

"We will?" Gossipmonger Nicholas curled his lip in disagreement.

August fixed a hard look on Nicholas. "Yes, we will."

Nicholas sighed, his shoulders slumping. August didn't put his foot down very often, but when he did, people listened. "Okay, fine, but when you're ready to talk, we'll be ready to listen."

Donovan tapped him on the chest. "Thanks, man. I appreciate it."

"You look happier than I've seen you in a long time." August offered up that observation, then did his usual disappearing act, mumbling something about needing to fix a leaky faucet in one of the bathrooms.

The bell over the front door dinged, and there she was, looking more beautiful than any woman had the right to, even in her "blah" uniform, as she referred to it, of a Sugar Blitz teal polo, khakis, and Crocs. His heart skipped a beat like a pimply faced ninth-grader seeing his crush standing near his locker before school started.

Nicholas smacked his hand on the counter, drawing Donovan's attention. "August was right, you know. It's good to see." Then he, too, headed to the back of the building, after calling out a greeting to Jada.

"Hi," Donovan said, rounding the counter. He sounded like a besotted fool. Probably looked like one, too. There wasn't much to be done about it. He was. He glanced around. More than ever, he was aware of the bakery's patrons watching their every move. It had never bothered him much because they hadn't been dating for real. But now they were, and he wanted to protect the relationship. He wanted to protect her. He'd seen and heard her hurt last night as she talked about the vitriol she'd faced on social media.

"Hi," she said, offering up a tremulous smile. She didn't know how to act, either. The whispers and phone camera clicks hadn't abated since she walked in. Might as well give them something to talk about. Why the hell not? They wanted to know how things had ended after Dr. John showed up, right? And everyone thought they were dating anyway.

He looped an arm around her trim waist, pulled her toward him, and lowered his head. She met him halfway. Desire punched him in the gut as soon as their mouths met. He sipped at her lips like a man dying of thirst, savoring the taste of her. Her tongue slid inside his mouth and he gathered her closer, barely containing a moan that threatened to slip out.

Starting this was a very bad idea because he couldn't finish it. He reluctantly backed away when the hoots and hollers from the bakery's customers became too loud to ignore.

"Get a room," Mr. Till grumbled on the way to his favorite table in the back, the one he claimed gave him the perfect view of the action in the store.

Donovan shook his head at the old man, then focused on the woman who commanded his attention. "Hi."

She laughed, a flirty grin stretching across her pretty face, all previous traces of nervousness gone. "Hi."

He drew her forward for a hug. Yep, this real relationship thing was pretty damn fantastic in his book.

* * *

"So, what do you have planned for tonight, Jada?" Ella asked in what she undoubtedly thought of as an innocent way. She'd been snooping and asking leading questions for the past two hours of her shift. Jada had dodged and weaved as much as she could, unsure of how much Donovan wanted her to divulge about the new status of their relationship. Unsure of what she herself wanted to reveal.

It didn't help that Donovan was sitting at a table nearby with Nicholas and could hear Ella's question.

She didn't want to assume she was spending the night with Donovan or announce it to anyone in case he wasn't comfortable with it, but given the incendiary looks he'd been giving her when he thought no one was paying attention, she didn't think it was presumptuous of her to believe her presence would be welcome.

"Since we don't have an event tonight, I planned to go look for a birthday gift for my grandmother."

"Oh." Ella's face fell in disappointment. Jada met Donovan's amused gaze over the teen's head. "Hold strong," he mouthed. She bit her lip to stop herself from laughing.

"Why don't you go with her, Donovan?" Nicholas asked.

Jada choked on her lemonade. His friends were truly world-class, Olympic-gold-medalist meddlers.

Donovan kept his cool, merely stroking his chin. "Why do you think I should do that?"

Nicholas eagerly straightened in his chair. He picked up his phone and waved it. "You're not the only one who can do analytics when the mood is right. Our social media hits and impressions were off the charts yesterday when Dr. John showed up. People are wondering what's going on with you two. Photos of #JaDon in the wild will boost interest. Need to get that hashtag trending again. And stop for dinner while you're out. Sit on the patio of whatever restaurant you choose so people walking by can see you. Oh, yeah, and you have to go through the whole restaurant on your way in and out so those people see you, too."

Jada exchanged another glance with Donovan before he cocked his head to the side and stared at his co-owner. "When did you become so diabolical?"

Nicholas flashed the smile that caused so many to swoon. "I learned from the best."

* * *

Donovan held open the door to Burberry. "What do you get the woman who can buy herself anything she doesn't have?"

Jada stepped through the entrance, accidentally on purpose brushing against Donovan. "A question I've asked myself a million times."

"Have you found the answer?"

Fond memories came back to Jada in a rush. "I went through a phase in my teens where I thought I had to go big or go home." She wrinkled her nose. "I became a little too aware of how much money my family had. I thought I could get the attention of the adults in my family if I bought them something grand. My parents are a little . . ."

Donovan stepped next to a trio of mannequins dressed in the brand's legendary plaid coats. "A little what?"

Jada fingered the sleeve of one of the coats. Expensive. Chic. "A little—make that a whole lot—not like me. They accepted the gifts, liked them even. Who doesn't like a private, behind-the-scenes tour of the winery that makes their favorite wine? After they thanked me, they then asked why I didn't get an A on my math and science exams, and if I needed more tutoring."

Donovan laid a hand at the small of her back. "I'm sorry."

"Thanks." Jada leaned into the comfort for a moment before walking toward a display of scarves that had caught her eye.

"What happened with Mrs. T?"

Jada held up a plaid scarf. "I probably bought her something similar to this scarf for her birthday, if not this exact same scarf. She said it was pretty, but I could tell she wasn't blown away, so the next year, I tried harder. Credit cards are evil enablers. She set the gift aside and asked to see me alone. She said and I quote, 'Jada, I thought I raised you better than this. Wasting money so you can show off is *not* the way."

Donovan's shoulders shook with laughter. "I can so see her saying that. What did you do then?"

"I wanted to make her proud, of course. I had a year to think about it. I thought about it *a lot*. I realized she values family time. And the Knights winning. But family always comes first. The next year I gave her a gift certificate that said she and I would have lunch together, just the two of us, once a month, outside our normal family gatherings." Jada smiled at the memories that never failed to warm her heart. "You'd thought I'd given her the keys to the *Vogue* fashion closet or number one draft picks for the next ten years."

He held out his arms wide, his brow wrinkling. "So what are we doing here?"

Jada shot him a look. "I like looking at the pretty clothes, duh." And looking was all she could do. Her parents hadn't changed their mind about her credit cards. But she had a roof over her head, a job she loved, and a man she . . . adored. She had no complaints. And honestly, she hadn't missed shopping much. Yeah, she was enjoying being in the store, but she'd discovered other things that gave her— dare she say it—more pleasure than buying clothes. "I can take a minor detour before I get down to business. I deserve a reward. I've been working very hard at a certain cupcake shop."

"Have you?" he teased.

"I most certainly have." She lifted her chin and marched out of the store. Donovan caught up with her in a few strides. Damn him and his long legs.

Laughing, he took her hand and entwined their fingers. "Are you really going to buy Mrs. T a present?"

"Absolutely. I always give her a gift. I haven't done my job if I don't make her groan, the louder the better."

"Give me your greatest hits."

Jada rubbed her hands together. "There was the time I got her a Raiders hat."

Donovan guffawed. "You got her a hat from our biggest rival? That's brilliant."

Jada preened. "Thank you. I've never seen her so outraged. I mean I don't follow football, but I've heard her disparage them enough over the years to know the gift would be perfect. I ran out of the room to stop my giggles from giving me away while she opened the gift. Then she yelled for me to get my butt back in the room. She said, and I quote, 'Now that I've calmed down, I recognize this was a gag gift, so in that vein, I approve. Don't ever bring this crap into my house ever again.' Then she started up the fireplace and threw the hat inside. It went up in a glorious ball of flames."

Laughter rumbled from his chest. "What else?"

Jada giggled as one particular memory came to mind. "She loves the landscaping around her estate. It's her pride and joy. Award-winning variety of flowers and trees, with a nice pond to balance things out, all carefully selected by her, as far as the eye can see. She loved when *Home and Garden* came calling a few years ago. Whenever we talked, that's all she could talk about. I bought her a whole family of inflatable flamingos, garden gnomes, and a nice, inflatable pool for them to drink out of. I had them delivered and set up a few days before the photo shoot. That was greatness."

"You put a lot of thought into her gifts."

"I try. The trick is to have fun with it. Sometimes, the right gift presents itself like the garden gnomes. Other times, I think about it for months, and I end up walking around a mall waiting for inspiration to strike. Like today. I've been a little busy, if you haven't noticed."

She suddenly stopped. "That's it. It's perfect. Grams is always busy, and as her granddaughter, it's my duty to help her in any way I can." She grabbed his hand. "Let's get out of here. Grams is going to love her membership to singlesoversixty.com."

* * *

After dinner, during which they followed Nicholas's directions to a T by eating at a restaurant that placed them in full view of the other diners and passersby, they headed back to his car. Donovan pulled out his phone when it beeped with an incoming text. He studied the screen, his face going carefully blank. He shook his head, then stuffed the phone into his back pocket.

"Everything okay?" Jada asked.

"Yeah, no worries."

She didn't believe him. He sounded distracted, a million miles away. But she couldn't force him to tell her. And it wasn't the first time he'd gotten that look on his face after a text.

He was keeping secrets. It was the reminder she needed to guard her heart and not just hand it over to him like she'd done in all her previous relationships. What they had was new, so she needed to take her time.

"This whole situation has been so strange for me," he said a minute later, nodding at a woman who called out their names from across the street.

"How so?" Jada studied his profile.

"I'm used to people recognizing me and wanting to talk about football, but now I'm that guy dating Jada from *My One and Only*. I'm getting recognized more than I've ever had before."

Jada nodded. "Yeah, that's the power of social media."

Donovan shook his head. "And gossip."

They stopped at his car. Jada didn't want their time together to end. But the truth was they didn't have any plans for the night. He could drop her off at her car at the bakery and go on his merry way. She looked up at him curiously. He hadn't produced the key fob to unlock the door. "What's up?" she asked, hitching her purse up on her shoulder.

His head tilted to the side. "Here's the thing. I had a good time tonight."

A teasing smile played across his lips. She should stop staring at said lips. Act like she had some chill. But they were so stareable and biteable. And lickable.

Chill. Right.

She cleared her throat and pointed at herself. "Here's *my* thing. So did I."

He leaned down. "Those people over there with their cameras out, not even trying to pretend they're not taking photos and videos of us, are waiting for us to kiss," he whispered in her ear. She shivered. She couldn't help herself. His deep voice did something to her. Something really, really nice.

Jada nodded. "I am aware."

"Now, we could give them what they want."

She nodded again. "We could."

"But I want you to know that I would be kissing you because not kissing you for the past two hours and fifteen minutes has been killing me. I don't give a fuck about who's watching or what ends up on Instagram." His eyes had darkened with interest as his hungry gaze lingered on her mouth. She licked her lips, smiled to herself when he moaned.

The ball was in her court. He wasn't going to pressure her. He'd laid out his position. How she responded was up to her. Though there were cameras trained on them, this kiss was for them. Only for them. Last night didn't have to be a fluke.

Jada lifted her hand and curved it around the back of his neck while she rose on her toes. The first touch of his lips sent a sigh cascading through her body. Or maybe that was the sound she made. His lips tasted better than she remembered, and she had a crystal-clear memory.

Her eyes drifted open as the kiss came to an end.

"How was that?" he murmured against her lips.

She pretended to give the question serious thought. "A strong nine out of ten."

He slapped a hand across his chest. "Wow. Okay. A dagger to the heart, but I can take it."

"I was thinking we need a little more practice."

Donovan made a face. "Really? I think I'm gonna go home and chill for the rest of the evening. Work on my kissing skills. Alone."

Jada tilted her head to the side. "Oh, really? Yeah, me too. Actually, I don't need to. My skills are on point."

"Eh." He waved his hand back and forth, a smile playing at his lips. "They're all right. But you know, my house is kinda quiet, and I've kinda gotten used to having a talkative woman around. One who's never afraid to express her opinion and doesn't give a shit about sparing my feelings."

Jada rolled her lips inward to keep a smile from taking over her face. It was going to take some time to get used to these warm and fuzzy feelings he inspired in her. "Really? She sounds cool. I'd like to meet her."

"You remind me of her, actually." He snapped his fingers as though some profound idea had just occurred to him. "Hey, would you like to come over? Just to keep that momentum going of having an opinionated woman around. I'd be cool with that."

"What woman can resist an invitation like that?"

"I'm hoping one who realizes how much I enjoy spending time with her and don't want this day to end."

Her heart melted. Damn, he could be charming when he wanted to be. She'd think he'd been taking lessons from Nicholas, but bullshitting wasn't Donovan's way. If he said it, he meant it. And the absolute certainty of that made her heart skip a couple of beats. She grinned. "I'd love to."

* * *

Jada's phone trilled out a peppy greeting. Donovan smiled. The ringtone was so Jada.

They'd arrived at his house a few minutes ago and settled on his sofa.

She pulled the phone out of her purse, checked the screen, and blew out a breath. "Sorry. I have to take this." She didn't look or sound thrilled by the prospect.

"Hello," she said, injecting some clearly fake cheer into her voice. She stood and moved a few feet away, but he could still hear her side of the conversation. Not that she was doing much talking.

Mostly "yes" and "no" and "mmm." Whoever was on the end was clearly directing the chat.

She sighed and dropped her head into her free hand. He didn't like her body language. Stooped shoulders. Defeated. That was not the Jada he knew. The Jada he was coming to . . . care for.

"I don't—" she started, then quieted. Her shoulders squared. "Right. Yes, of course. See you soon."

"You all right?" he asked after she ended the call with a pointed stab of her finger at the poor, defenseless phone screen.

Her lips stretched into a smile that more closely resembled a tortured grimace. "Guess who's coming to dinner."

* * *

The look of bewilderment on Donovan's face would have been funny if her life wasn't a classic comedy of errors.

He rose from the sofa and drew her into a hug. "What are you talking about? Are you okay?"

She dropped her head forward on to his strong chest and inhaled the fresh cotton scent of his shirt under the smells of vanilla and chocolate and sprinkles, scents that now signaled comfort. "Never better."

Donovan rubbed her back. "Somehow I doubt that. Who do I have to beat up, or at least have a stern talking-to?"

That prompted a more genuine smile out of her. She sighed. "That was my father, with my mother making a special cameo appearance."

"I see," he said, his voice indicating that he did, in fact, understand the seriousness of the situation. "What did they want?"

She leaned back to look up at him. "My parents, or rather, several of my parents' business associates, saw us on *Good Day, San Diego* and burned up the telephone lines to ask my parents about our relationship."

"Oh," he said, blinking, clearly not expecting that response.

"Yes. Oh." Jada wheeled and began to pace around the living room. "My parents are morally opposed to feeling uninformed in any and every situation and were thusly embarrassed. Not knowing something, whether they actually care about it or not, is tantamount to evil to them. They're scientists and enjoy knowledge. They were further appalled to learn that your mom has met me, while they have not met you. Their friends were thrilled to show them photos of your mom from her visit to the shop that ended up on social media."

That simply would not do. They didn't care about Donovan or any relationship she found herself involved in, but not knowing about it when someone asked—that was the sin. "You have been commanded to accompany me to Grams's birthday dinner."

"I see." Now, he sounded calm. Even looked it. But how could he be?

Oh, God, now embarrassment was starting to claw its way into her heart to sit next to the mortification over her parents' command. Would he think she'd engineered the invitation and was putting expectations on a brand-new relationship? Yes, they had fun together and had some terrific sex, but they'd been in a fake relationship less than forty-eight hours ago.

Maybe he thought she was already planning a trip down the aisle. Oh, God. Panic sunk its tentacles into her skin and spread like a fast-acting rash. She slapped her hands over her eyes and groaned. "I'm sorry."

"Am I Sidney Poitier or Ashton Kutcher in this scenario?"

That reaction was enough to make her peep through her fingers. "What?"

"You said guess who's coming to dinner. I assume that was a reference to one of the versions of that movie."

She dropped her hands. "Oh, right."

He pointed at himself. "I mean I don't think I have pasty white boy energy, but who knows?"

A snort of laughter burst from her chest. He definitely did not have pasty white boy energy. Donovan was all Donovan. Hot and amazing and fine. BD energy all the way. "You're safe on that point."

He let out a loud whoosh and dramatically wiped his brow. "Great, but that leaves Mr. Poitier, but everyone involved in this scenario is Black, so I'm not sure that fits either. Although, I do share the same suave debonair flare as the esteemed Mr. Poitier, if I do say so myself." He stroked his chin.

She laughed. "Of course you say so yourself." She quieted. "Honestly, you're not Sidney or Ashton. I'm the black sheep returning home to a skeptical crowd ready and willing to judge my every move and word. It's gonna be a joyful time, let me tell ya."

"Why didn't you say no?"

She brought a hand to her chest in mock shock. "One does not say no to the esteemed Townsend-Matthews parental units. It would never occur to them that one of their offspring or their subordinates would do such a thing." She rubbed her temples hoping she could conjure up some magical solution if she thought about it long enough. "I'm sorry for dragging you into this."

He pulled her hands away from her face. "No need to apologize. We're in this together. We said that from day one. Now that we're us for real, I mean it even more."

Jada stared at him. She was in so much trouble. She was starting to fall hard for her not-so-fake boyfriend.

Chapter Twenty-Two

"Ready to do this?" Donovan asked.

They'd arrived at her parents' house five minutes ago, but Jada had made no attempt to exit his SUV. She'd stared out the window like she'd never seen the Spanish-style house with its stucco roof before. When she didn't respond, he placed a hand on her knee. "Jada."

She jumped like she'd been stuck in a trance. She blinked two times. "No, not really. I'm freaking out, but yeah, let's go."

She got out of the car without further comment and strode toward the house with quick steps. He caught up with her at the door. "Let's go over the plan one more time," she said without looking at him.

"We are dating," he said by rote. "Fake dating will never enter the conversation. You came into the shop before you went on the show. There were sparks, but you'd committed to the show and didn't think it could be real, so you went, but because I'm the best thing ever, you couldn't stop thinking about me while you were on the show, and we reconnected when you came back. We dated in secret until after the finale when we could go public."

"Perfect." She raised her hand to knock but stopped before her fist made contact with the wood. "Still freaking out, by the way."

"I know, but I'm here."

She glanced over her shoulder at him, then nodded. Without further ado, she knocked, and a few seconds later, a woman who looked like an older, more conservative version of Jada answered. Her mother, clearly. Her dark brown hair, lightly streaked with gray, was pulled back into a neat bun. She wore black slacks and a blue lightweight sweater. Nothing obviously fancy, but Donovan recognized quality clothing when he saw it. Her dark eyes, so like her daughter's, were assessing and missed nothing. "Jada, so happy you could make it. Please come in."

Donovan placed a hand at the small of Jada's back and followed her inside. Shit. She was trembling. His hand tightened at her waist. He wished he could draw her into a hug and tell her everything was going to be okay. But her mom was in earshot, and Jada had expressly forbidden any public displays of affection. Her parents were not fans. Still, he couldn't resist a quick squeeze of her waist.

Jada leaned back against him slightly. "Mom, this is Donovan Dell."

He held out his right hand. "It's nice to meet you, Dr. Townsend-Matthews."

She shook his hand in a simple, businesslike gesture and inclined her head in his direction. "Points to you for using my title, but please call me Nina. My husband and other daughter are waiting in the living room."

Out of the corner of his eye, he saw Jada raise her wrist to glance at her watch. He squeezed her waist again. They weren't late. She could relax on that front. But on other fronts? Well, the jury was still out.

He'd done a bit of research before coming here tonight. Her parents were both doctors and scientists, as was Jada's sister. Those credentials could intimidate the most secure of individuals.

The home was spacious and well-appointed without being ostentatious. These were people who had money but wouldn't dream of blinging out their home. The house was decorated with expensive, yet understated items, as though professionals had been called in for the job without much input from the home's residents. Wood floors, tasteful splashes of blues and greens mixed in with the neutral palette of grays and white. The warmth he so closely associated with Jada was missing.

They passed a spiral staircase and entered the living room located toward the back of the house. A man and woman stood from the sectional sofa dominating the space. Jada's father and sister, clearly. Like her mother, Jada's dad was dressed simply in a well-tailored blue button-down shirt and slacks. He had close-cropped salt-and-pepper hair and a medium build. Jada's sister eyed him with curiosity. Unsurprisingly, she and Jada bore a striking resemblance to each other, though she had a few inches on Jada.

"Jada, I'm glad you could join us this evening," her dad said. "Why don't you introduce us to your young man?"

Jada gripped Donovan's hand. "Donovan, this is my father, Walter. Dad, meet Donovan Dell, and as I'm sure you know, he plays for the Knights."

Her father's eyebrows drew together. "Of course I know. You think I'm going to let someone date my daughter without finding out everything there is to know about him, especially when we didn't know he existed three days ago?"

Donovan took it as the threat it was obviously meant to be. And the fact that her father cared little about his wife's family business.

Jada sighed, a vee of stress appearing between her eyes. "Donovan, this is my sister, Patrice."

Donovan nodded at them. "It's nice to meet you both. Thank you for inviting me."

"This should be fun," Patrice said, eyeing him with speculation. "I can't wait until Grams gets here."

Nina checked her watch. "She should be here any second now. My mother is never late, especially when we're celebrating her birthday. Why don't we have a seat while we wait for her to arrive? We can get to know each other."

Donovan and Jada sat at one end of the large sofa while her parents took the other. Patrice sat in a matching chair across from Jada.

Donovan reached for Jada's hand. She looked at him, her lips slipping into a tremulous smile. That familiar twinkle in her eyes had returned. Good. There was the woman he . . . cared about.

Shit. A fist squeezed his heart, cutting off his ability to breathe. Yes, he cared about her, enjoyed being in her company, but what if it was something more? But it couldn't be. Not yet. You didn't fall in love with someone you'd known for less than a month. It didn't make sense. It wasn't logical. His brain rebelled at the thought even as his heart leapt at it.

A pealing bell cut into his riotous thoughts.

"That must be my mother," Nina said, rising. "I'll get the door."

"Hello, everyone," a familiar voice drawled from the doorway a minute later. Mrs. T stood there, quite content to have all eyes on her, looking regal as usual, despite her diminutive size.

"Grams," Jada and Patrice exclaimed simultaneously.

Walter stood and took the few steps to meet her.

"Joyce, welcome. Happy birthday!" He placed a hand on her elbow and guided her to the empty chair next to Patrice.

"Thank you, but let's remember, I stopped counting birthdays years ago."

His brow wrinkled in confusion, clearly not understanding that logic. "Right."

Nina took her husband's place, exchanging polite kisses on the cheek with her mother. "Happy birthday."

Mrs. T turned her hawklike gaze on her daughter. "I labored for twenty-six excruciating, never-ending hours before giving birth to you, and that's all I get?"

Nina smoothed her hair back, though not a hair was out of place. "Mother, really. Must you be so . . . colorful?"

Mrs. T shook her head. "I knew I shouldn't have sent you to the fancy private school for gifted students. They filled your head with all kinds of science and math and sucked all the humor out of you."

"I love you too, Mother," Nina said dryly. "And no, a happy birthday wish isn't all I have for you. I got you a gift, and I'm happy you're here."

Mrs. T patted her on the cheek. "That's more like it. Love you, honey." Mrs. T waved her hand when her granddaughters made to stand. "You're already sitting, and I know you love me as much as I love you."

Mrs. T clasped her hands together. "Well, well, what do we have here?" she asked like she hadn't spied Donovan the moment she stepped foot in the room. "I guess the dating rumors are true."

Donovan grinned. "Nice to see you, Mrs. T."

"Look at my worlds colliding. I never thought I'd see the day. A player from my team in my daughter's home alongside the rest of my family, who couldn't possibly care less about football."

Nina groaned. "Mother."

"I'm only speaking the truth." A smile stretched across her face. "Donovan, I hear congratulations are in order. We've agreed on a new contract with your agent."

Jada gasped, slapping him on the arm. "What? You didn't tell me! That's great."

He shrugged. "Tonight wasn't supposed to be about me."

"Which is very sweet, but unnecessary."

Mrs. T nodded. "My granddaughter is right. We can celebrate more than one thing today. Now let's get to eating. I can smell my favorites, and the food won't eat itself."

Jada's parents exchanged a bemused look before leading the way to the formal dining room.

* * *

Jada was doing her best not to freak out, but having Donovan there was worth its weight in gold. He radiated calm.

She smiled at him as he held out her chair for her. He took the seat next to her, while her sister and grandmother sat across from them. Her parents sat at opposite ends of the table.

Grams was right about one thing. Her parents had spared no expense on the food. A veritable feast was spread across the table. Prime rib, roasted vegetables, garlic butter mushrooms, risotto, Cobb salad, and soft French bread. Truly all Grams's favorites.

"Donovan, I'm sure you're aware our daughter didn't tell us you two were dating," Walter said as the food circulated around the table.

Jada's stomach cramped. What she wouldn't give to be somewhere—anywhere—other than here.

"I've learned it's best to leave the when and where to reveal that kind of info up to my partner," Donovan said, clearly trying to be as diplomatic as possible. She should have known he would have the perfect answer. Her stomach settled the tiniest bit.

Her mom cleared her throat. "A very tactful answer. How did you two meet?"

Grams straightened in her seat and ensnared Jada's gaze. "Yes, Jada, tell us how you met."

Jada exchanged glances with Donovan. It was one thing to lie to her parents, which technically wasn't good, she supposed. It was another thing to lie when her grandmother, who knew the truth and could blow their cover in a heartbeat, was sitting less than five feet away. She hadn't thought this through, obviously.

Jada took a deep breath and basically blurted out the story she and Donovan had concocted.

"Is that so?" Grams said when Jada took a pause to catch her breath. Humor filled her voice.

"Yep," Jada said without looking at her grandmother. She stuffed a piece of bread into her mouth. Hopefully, they could move on to some exciting research her sister and parents were working on. The latest happenings in the mayor's office. The weather. Whatever.

Grams studied them over her wineglass. "Donovan, what did you think when you first saw my granddaughter?"

Jada forced the bread down a tight throat. She should have known better.

Donovan's lips split into a wide grin. Jada's breath caught. Damn, he was fine.

He looked her way. "She came into the shop in her heels and perfect, expensive outfit and perfect hair. I thought she was the bougiest person I'd ever seen in my life."

"Hey!" Jada slapped him on the arm, while her family members laughed. He didn't have to tell the *whole* truth.

"But then I really looked at her and thought she was the most beautiful person I'd ever seen." He lifted her hand and pressed a gentle kiss to her wrist, then the back of her hand. Her heart stuttered once, then twice, then sped up to twice its normal rate. What was he doing to her? "Ever since then, I've learned that her outside pales in comparison to her inside."

"Well, well, well," Grams murmured, shooting Jada an approving glance.

"Wow," her sister said. "Be still, my heart. I wish someone would talk about me like that."

Jada stared at Patrice in shock. Her genius sister was jealous of Jada? No way. Though they didn't have an acrimonious relationship, they'd never been particularly close. They didn't have much in common. Patrice had always been very studious and career-focused, her head buried in a book while Jada's was stuck in the clouds.

Her parents said nothing, no doubt stunned into silence. They didn't really deal in emotions or public displays of affection.

Her rumbling stomach relaxed. Grams clearly found the whole situation amusing, and if it wasn't Jada's life, she would think it was funny, too.

"Where did you attend school, Donovan?" her mom asked.

"UCLA."

Her mom's eyebrows lifted. "I see."

Jada's hand tightened on her wineglass. "Mom, UCLA is a perfectly respectable university."

"I didn't say it wasn't, dear."

That tension headache that had started to creep up on her the closer they got to her parents' house hit like a sledgehammer now.

Her father spoke up. "You went on a football scholarship, I assume, given that you are a professional football player?"

Donovan nodded. "I did, although I got my degree in business economics."

"With all due respect to my in-laws, I've never been much into sports. I met Nina at the college library on a Saturday afternoon because it was the quietest place on campus."

Donovan's demeanor didn't change. "Sports aren't for everyone, but I've learned tons of life skills from playing organized sports, like problem-solving and teamwork."

Her father's face twisted with perplexity. He truly didn't understand why people wouldn't major in the sciences in some way. "I see. Well, at least that's useful. Much more sensible than humanities." Jada's food settled like lead in her stomach. Of course, her father didn't notice. He kept talking.

"We own and run a medical research firm. The science, we love. Sometimes, the business side gets tiring."

"Humanities is a great major, but yes, Jada told me about your business. What do you research?"

Her dad perked up. There was nothing he liked more than discussing his research, even if ninety-nine percent of the population had no idea what he was talking about. "Biomedical research on pulmonary hypertension. Heart disease is the leading cause of death in the US, but Black Americans are thirty percent more likely to die than white Americans."

"That sounds like important work you're doing."

Her dad took a sip of wine. "Thank you. We tried to get Jada to come work with us, but she has persistently rejected our job offers."

Her mom leaned forward. "Yes, gallivanting all around New York, Europe, and L.A. was much more important to her than having a steady career doing meaningful work helping us better the world's scientific knowledge. I'll never understand it."

Jada wished she could be mad. Maybe she should be mad. She'd never hurt anyone because of her choices in life, had actually brought humor to some, but her parents didn't care or understand.

They liked facts and figures. Theories that could be proven or dis-
proven. Science didn't care about feelings.

Her dad nodded in agreement with her mom. "Yes, we wanted
her to come home, but she decided a reality show was a better option.
Have you seen the show, Donovan?"

Donovan squeezed her leg under the table. "I have."

"I can't understand why or how anyone thinks they can find a
partner, let alone a spouse, on a reality show."

He shrugged. "Stranger things have happened. In any case, we
love having her at the shop."

"Yes, a cupcake shop, is it?" her mom asked.

"Yes, it's a bit of a labor of love for me and my business partners.
We hoped to bring a bit of whimsy and good sweets to San Diego."

Jada stuffed a mushroom in her mouth to stop a sigh from escaping. Her mom and dad were in tag team mode. Time for her dad
to speak. "Did you do business analyses on opening the store? The
property is in a popular part of town. You could sell the building
for a tidy sum. I'm not sure of the profit margins for cupcakes."

Donovan, because he was who he was, handled the interrogation
like a pro. "I did do quite a bit of research about the best use for
the property, and then my business partners and I decided you can't
put a price on dreams. We're doing well, thanks in no small part
to Jada's influence."

"I see." Her mother turned her way. "Jada, we saw you two on the
morning show. Was it really necessary to bring up your dyslexia?"

Jada carefully set her fork down. There was no longer any use
pretending she was enjoying the food or could even eat. Her parents always did this. Made her feel that none of her choices were
good enough. But she had to stand up for herself. She had to try.
"It's the truth, and I wanted her to understand why if I stumbled
over the words on the cue cards."

Confusion settled on her mom's face. "Why would you have done that? We got you the best tutors and therapists money could buy to help you."

"Money can't cure dyslexia," Jada muttered.

Her dad harrumphed. "Of course not. We know that. We are doctors, after all. However, we didn't see the relevance in that moment. You were doing just fine."

"Actually, you should be proud of your daughter for bringing it up," Donovan said quietly, but forcefully. "We've had several people reach out to us to thank her for mentioning dyslexia and the therapies and work-arounds she has learned to employ. A mom said she asked her son's doctor about them, and it's already helped him in the classroom. And I haven't gotten into how much she's helped us increase business at the shop in her short time there. She's been a godsend."

"What exactly are you doing, Jada?" her mom asked, undoubtedly more than happy to leave the discussion of dyslexia behind.

Jada lifted her chin. "I'm planning events."

"Oh. I see." She didn't find this news impressive.

"Nina," Mrs. T warned.

"I don't think you do," Donovan said. "Her vision is incredible. She has her pulse on the community and instinctively knows what they're looking for."

Jada's chair scraped back against the wooden floor. "Donovan, don't bother. Excuse me. I've lost my appetite."

* * *

Jada paced around the kitchen, hoping, praying she would tire herself out enough that the anger driving her motions would drain from her. Coming here had been a big mistake. But she'd done it anyway because she was a hopeless fool. Her parents were never going to accept her, be proud of her. How silly to think they would. Planning events at a cupcake shop? That, in no way, compared to saving mankind.

Footsteps sounded behind her. "Don—" She turned. It wasn't Donovan. "Grams, what are you doing here? You're supposed to be out there eating cake and opening presents. I got you an epic gift."

Grams stepped forward and wrapped her arms around Jada. "I'll do that after I make sure my granddaughter is okay."

Jada dropped her head to her grandmother's shoulder. Comforting hugs from her were how she'd survived her childhood with her mental and emotional well-being mostly intact. "I'm okay."

Grams stepped back, grasping her hands. "You're not, but you will be."

Jada wiped at the stupid tear that refused to stay in the duct. "How do you know?"

"Because you come from hearty Townsend stock, strong enough to withstand those weak Matthews genes."

A snort of laughter bubbled up in Jada's chest. Her father would not be pleased. He'd done his genetic map sequencing for funsies and had been extremely happy with the results.

Grams leaned against the counter. "But that's not the only reason. The only person I've ever seen defend his partner as fiercely as Donovan did you is your grandfather, God rest his soul, when those old white men in the league office couldn't fathom a woman taking interest in running a team, even with her husband as her partner. He put them in their place more than once."

Jada shrugged. "Donovan's a good guy. He would have done that for anyone."

"Perhaps, but would he have looked like he was half a second away from leaping across the table to tackle your father like he was the opposing team's quarterback instead of a fifty-seven-year-old nerdy scientist?"

"Grams . . ."

"Don't Grams me. Now, I know for a fact you and Donovan weren't dating when you met in my office. You could barely stand the sight of each other. I don't know what scheme you two cooked up with this whole dating thing, but I do recognize a man and woman in love."

Every muscle in Jada's body froze.

Yep, Grams had done the unthinkable—gotten her to stop obsessing over and seething about her parents. Now, thoughts about her feelings for her date crowded every corner of her brain.

Donovan couldn't be in love with her, the eternal screwup, could he? She couldn't be in love with him so quickly, could she?

Chapter Twenty-Three

"Penny for your thoughts." Donovan settled his large frame next to Jada on the beach towel and held out a wineglass. Jada gave serious thought to grabbing the wine bottle out of his other hand and swigging straight from it, but that seemed like overkill. She reserved the right to change her mind, though.

"My thoughts are worth at least ten cents." Jada gratefully accepted the glass and took a deep, fortifying sip of the excellent Chardonnay, then returned her attention to the gently lapping waves of the ocean.

They'd come back to his place after the dinner from hell and, after a brief detour to the kitchen for wine, headed straight for the beach. Moonlight cast an otherworldly glow on their surroundings. There was no other soul on the beach. Jada was grateful. She needed the tranquility.

He placed a hand over his heart. "I stand corrected. Do you accept credit cards?"

A brief smile touched her lips. He could always make her smile even when she felt like crap. "Cash only, but for you, I'll make an exception."

He looped an arm around her waist, and she lay her head on his hard chest. His heart beat steadily and sure underneath her ear. Unfortunately, calm remained out of her grasp. So many thoughts were rioting through her head.

"I'm willing to pay anything, you know," he said quietly.

Why did he always know the right thing to say? What had she done to deserve having this man in her corner, who supported and encouraged her at every turn despite everything she'd put him through?

"I know." Jada sighed. Her parents, what Grams said. It was a lot. Thoughts on all of it kept pinging around in her head. She went with the safer, less scary, more immediate concern. "My parents are my parents and expecting them to change is a fool's errand. Sorry I put you through that."

"Don't apologize. I was there of my own free will." He tucked a strand of hair whipping around her face behind her ear.

"Yeah, but . . ." She cringed, remembering the things her parents had said.

"Hey, don't worry about me. I'm sorry you had to go through that. Parents can put you through hell, I know."

A strong man, but he had his own demons, and if she could, she wanted to be there for him like he was for her. Jada lifted her head and looked up at him. "Can I ask you a question?"

His gaze was intent on her. "Sure. Go for it."

"What happened to your dad? You don't talk about him."

Donovan sighed like he'd been expecting the question. Or maybe the situation with his father had made him weary. He raised his wineglass to his mouth and turned his dark gaze to the ocean.

"He's still in Oakland. My parents divorced when I was a sopho-more in high school. My mom finally had enough, but times were tough. We didn't have a lot to start with, and then the little support he offered disappeared. My mom and Sloane moved down here permanently when I got drafted. Shana came shortly afterward."

Jada laid a hand on his thigh. "Do you have a relationship with him?"

"Guess it depends on what you mean by relationship."

A chime sounded. Donovan pulled out his phone and stared at the screen. He huffed out a breath. "His ears must be burning."

He held out the phone. Jada took it and quickly read the text from someone listed as Guy in the phone.

Hey, son, I need an extra 5K, just to get me through the next month. Rent's due and money's tight.

Jada passed the phone back to him. "Does he ask for money often?"

Donovan's jaw tightened as he stared at the ocean. "I send him money every month. My mom doesn't know—the only one who does is August. I thought if he had a decent financial base, he could get his life back together."

Jada rubbed the tense muscles of his back. "And?"

"It worked for a while, but gambling addiction is real. I don't think I fully understood that until I was in the league and sent him enough money to live a comfortable life. He got pulled back in, and yeah, I don't know. When he's winning, he flies high. When the losses hit, it gets ugly. Lately, he's been even more persistent than usual asking for more." He turned to face her. "All those texts and calls I've been ignoring? They were from him. Leaving him in the lurch seems cold-blooded, but I don't know what to do."

The moonlight cast a shadow over his face, but it didn't hide his uncertainty, his unease. Jada laid her head against his shoulder and stared, unseeing, at the water. She wished she had some words of wisdom to offer. Wished she could take on his hurt. "You're a good son."

"It doesn't feel like it a lot of the time."

They sat in comfortable silence for a few minutes. Though the night had been heavy, there was nowhere else she'd rather be. No one else she'd rather be with.

Donovan squeezed her thigh. "Let's talk about something else."

Jada nodded, eager to shake off the weight of the evening. "Sounds like a plan. You know, you promised me a surfing lesson."

His lips curved. "I haven't forgotten, but seeing as it's dark now, that's going to have to wait. I have some good news."

Jada clasped her hands together. "More good news?" She held up a palm. "Wait. New rule. Whenever you have good news, you must share immediately. Congrats again on the new contract, but I'm still mad you didn't tell me earlier, by the way."

He chuckled. "I'd planned on telling you after dinner, but Mrs. T spoiled the surprise. Adam finally got his head out of his ass and negotiated like the world-class agent he is."

They shared a look, remembering the agent's initial asinine requests that either Donovan break up with her or Jada sweet-talk Grams.

"So, yes, congrats on the contract." She slapped his arm. "What's the other good news?"

"I've been in contact with Rose."

The photographer from the book club meeting?

Jada's mouth dropped. Of all the things he could have said, that was nowhere close to her top ten contenders. "Why were you in contact with her?"

"Because I wanted her to send me the photos she took of us." The "duh" was unspoken, but very much implied. Jada's heart flip-flopped in her chest. "Anyway, we've been texting back and forth, and she agreed to do a photo shoot for the store."

She'd barely picked her chin up. Now he'd shocked her again. "A photo shoot? Are you serious? Why?"

His eyes twinkled. "I don't know if you remember, but the first time you were in Sugar Blitz, you said the place was stale, and for some reason, I've never been able to forget it. Rose is going to come and take photos of our cupcakes—fun, lively photos—we can hang on the walls."

Excitement zinged through her. Jada gasped. "And she can also take photos of you, August, and Nicholas baking and interacting with customers and joking around. It'll be perfect!"

Donovan grimaced. "Yeah, I'm not sure August is going to go along with that."

"Why not? I'll talk to him. He likes me. Yay for good ideas!"

"Thanks." A dangerous, sexy light entered his eyes. "I have another good idea."

She set aside her glass, the blood already thickening in her veins. "Do tell."

He set his glass next to hers, then leaned down and pressed a soft kiss to her neck while he slid a hand under her dress. "How about I show you instead?"

* * *

While Donovan provided an excellent distraction from her parents and their opinion of her and her life choices, the next day Jada was still obsessing about what Grams said. And the way she'd felt when he said he'd sought out the photos they'd taken.

So she did the only thing that made sense when she got home from work. She called her best friend over to eat ice cream.

"Then he defended me to my parents." Jada set aside her bowl and hopped up from her couch. Pacing would calm her. Maybe. Hopefully.

Olivia's spoon clattered into her bowl as her mouth dropped open. "He defended you to Dr. and Dr. Townsend-Matthews? Bet they reacted well to being told they were wrong. They always have facts on their side."

Jada reached the end of the room and headed back toward her friend. "Well, Donovan speaks their language. He runs on logic and so do they, so he knew exactly what to say to get them to stop lecturing me. It was quite impressive."

Olivia wiggled her eyebrows. "Was it now?"

Jada stuck her tongue out at her best friend. "Stop."

"I will not. Only one of us has anything remotely resembling romance in her life and it certainly ain't me. I'm not the one having wild, passionate sex with a ridiculously attractive man, who went out of his way to get some photos y'all took. My life is all about should we open a new hotel? What new employees will that entail? I'm living vicariously through you."

Jada's mouth twisted. "Yeah."

Olivia's head cocked to the side. "What? What is that look on your face? What aren't you telling me?"

Jada reached the couch and plopped down. "My dad asked him what he thought of me when we first met and he said I thought I was bougie."

Olivia took another bite of her Rocky Road and shrugged. "You are. Nothing new there."

Jada glared. "Do I need to audition for a new best friend?"

Olivia snorted. "Like you could do better than me."

Absolutely true, but she wasn't going to swell her BFF's head by verbally agreeing. "Anyway, he then said he thought I was beautiful and I was more beautiful on the inside than I was on the outside."

"And you haven't declared your undying love yet? Girl. *Girl.* I admire your fortitude and resiliency. Couldn't be me."

The ice cream in her stomach started to curdle. "I've been impulsive my whole life, which is how I ended up with a fake boyfriend in the first place."

Olivia stared at her, clearly confused. "But there's nothing fake about what's going on now."

Jada jumped up from the couch to take another lap around the room. "But shouldn't I be taking things slow? Not rushing things? I was supposed to work there so I could gain control of my trust fund and decide what I want my life to be, not find a man to distract me. I'm on the right road. I've found something I'm good at, and I don't want to mess that up."

"He's not distracting you. You're doing great. He said you were."

"But what if things don't work out? My relationships don't work out!"

Olivia pointed her spoon at her. "You've never dated Donovan Dell."

Truer words had never been said. And wasn't that the crux of the problem? He was definitely one-of-a-kind and made her long for things she'd never known she'd wanted. But everything could work out—as long as she didn't mess it up.

* * *

"You met the parents? Wow. This relationship is moving fast," Nicholas said.

Donovan lowered a dirty pot into the sink, hissing as the hot water hit his skin. "Is it? I haven't thought about it." Which was not like him, admittedly, but when he was with Jada, he was fully engaged. He didn't feel the need to analyze every aspect of their relationship because everything was so natural between them. That didn't mean they were moving fast. Right?

Nicholas, ever the best multitasker out of the group, measured out ingredients for his latest cupcake experiment, raspberry chocolate crunch, while he talked. He claimed his multitasking skills came in handy as he juggled multiple women. "Let's recap. You had dinner with her parents."

"Only because they heard that she met my mother and sisters."

"Which does not negate my point. During this dinner, you told her parents and her grandmother, who happens to be our boss by the way, that she's more beautiful on the inside than she is on the outside. Am I correct or am I correct?"

Donovan scrubbed the pot like his life depended on it. "You're correct."

"And you weren't lying when you said this, am I correct or am I correct?"

"You're . . . correct," Donovan said through gritted teeth. If he wasn't elbow-deep in dishes and suds, he'd give serious thought to clocking his best friend.

"Sounds like you're in love to me."

The towel slipped out of his hand, splashing water everywhere. Donovan barely noticed. Air rushed out of his lungs in a whoosh. Donovan did the only thing he could do. He deflected. "What do you know about being in love?"

Nicholas cracked open an egg and added it to the bowl. "Nothing, but I've watched a lot of sappy romcoms on my Netflix-and-chill dates and the dudes in those movies always end up looking like you do right now."

"Oh, my God, are you serious right now? I'm not listening to you." Logically, it didn't make sense. He couldn't be in love. Not so soon. What he and Jada had was great, but it was new. Football and Sugar Blitz still came first. Right?

"Well, Pretty Boy Nick may not know anything about love, but I have been in love before and I recognize the real signs, not the movie kind, and you've got it bad," August said from where he was restocking the refrigerator.

Donovan groaned. "Really? You too?" So much for brotherhood. "Did you bet on that?"

"Nah, 'cause that would have been a sucker bet." August shrugged. "I call 'em like I see 'em."

That he did. Always. Donovan stared at the man he'd known since he was a cocky eighteen-year-old determined to take on the world and win at any costs. Both he and Nicholas were so certain about Donovan's feelings. Hell, they didn't even know he'd tracked Rose down for those photos.

Donovan stumbled. Shit.

He was so screwed. He'd fallen in love with Jada Townsend-Matthews, the most unpredictable person he'd ever met, who lived to shake up his carefully ordered world.

And he was *happy* about it? When was the last time happiness had factored into his decisions?

* * *

Jada turned in a circle, glee pumping through her veins. Everything was ready. Who said adults couldn't have after-hours birthday parties in a cupcake shop? Not her.

Amanda Spencer, the CEO of a very successful local tech company and the daughter of a former San Diego mayor, wanted to have a bit of whimsy for her fortieth birthday party. If Jada did a good job, she was sure other business would follow.

At the request of the birthday girl, who considered herself San Diego royalty, purple and silver streamers hung from the light fixtures. A HAPPY BIRTHDAY banner, again in purple and silver, was strung along one wall. Each table had a personalized centerpiece along with party favors at each seat. Jada chuckled. Basically, she'd designed a wedding reception for Amanda's birthday.

She checked her watch. Guests would start arriving in a few minutes. Fifty people, who would all be looking to have a good time, and she would give it to them.

Games, drinks, food, music—she'd thought of it all.

Amanda loved karaoke, so Jada had, with Donovan's permission, bought a machine and rented a small stage. That decision had brought home the booking. Amanda had been considering having the surprise party at a karaoke bar, but the birthday girl also enjoyed Sugar Blitz's fare, so Jada had jumped in with the offer.

Freshly baked cupcakes—chocolate, red velvet, and Oreo—spelled out Amanda's name. A nice touch, if she did say so herself.

The bell over the front door tolled. Putting on her best hostess-with-the-mostest smile, Jada turned to greet the first partygoers. The smile died a sad, sudden death. The blood in her veins curdled.

What in the hell?

Somehow, she got her vocal cords, which had seized up in shock, to work. "What are you doing here?"

"Hi, it's nice to see you again too, Jada," Lila Patterson said with an arch of a razorbladed eyebrow. She was a tall woman, which didn't stop her from wearing killer high heels. Her concessions to the long hours of filming were to slick her dark brown hair back into a sleek, stark ponytail, a style that drew attention to her sharp cheekbones and pale skin, and wear three-inch heeled boots, designer silk T-shirts, and jeans.

Jada shook her head. "Sorry. I'm stunned. You are the last person I expected to come through the door." The texts and calls had pretty much stopped over the past week or so. Jada had hoped that meant Lila had moved on.

Lila nodded. "Understandable." She sank gracefully into a chair like she owned the place and took a quick look around. She probably thought she did. Nobody said no to Lila Patterson, certainly not at the network on which *My One and Only* aired. The show was a bona fide hit, and Lila was considered a genius mastermind. Jada was sure she missed nothing in her scan. Her sharp green eyes returned to Jada. "Nice decorations."

"Thanks." Jada grimaced. "I don't mean to be rude, but you can't stay. Maybe we can catch up tomorrow. The store is closed for a birthday party. The guests will be arriving any minute."

"I know."

Jada blinked. "You know? You know what?"

Lila crossed her right leg over her left thigh. "That the guests are supposed to arrive for the birthday party for Amanda Spencer. Amanda's a good friend of mine. It's always good to have contacts in all walks of life when you're in the biz."

Jada collected herself as best as she could. "Oh, so you're one of the guests? That's great."

"No, I'm not one of the guests. I am the guest."

Composure was becoming harder to grasp. Jada's brain scrambled to keep up with the shocking revelations. "I'm sorry, what?"

Lila gestured for Jada to take a seat across from her. Jada took the lifeline. She felt like her world was about to be turned upside down, and she needed all the support she could get to keep from sinking to the floor in an undignified heap after she fainted from shock. But maybe she was being dramatic. Time to get it together. She squared her shoulders and took a deep breath.

Lila searched her eyes. She must have found what she was looking for—evidence that Jada wasn't going to pass out—because she nodded. "I am your only guest. There is no birthday party."

Jada pressed her fingertips to her temples, hoping to stave off a rapidly approaching headache. "What? Why?"

"Don't worry. You'll still get paid."

Jada shook her head. "That's great, but that's not my immediate concern. Why would you go through all this subterfuge to book a birthday party and give very specific instructions for its execution, only for it all to be fake?"

Lila shrugged. "I admit part of it was for my own amusement. But I also wanted to see if you could execute my vision, which you did, so good for you."

Jada shook her head, hoping the action would cause everything to make sense. "But why? Why would you care if I can plan a party?"

Lila spread her arms wide, as though the answer was obvious. "I've been following you since the finale aired. Word on the street is that you've matured since your time on the show. I had to see for myself. I could've called, but you haven't been in contact with anyone else from the show. You certainly haven't been answering my calls and texts."

Jada refused to feel guilty about her decision to divorce herself entirely from the show's contestants and crew. The toxicity she'd experienced online and sometimes in person did not make for a healthy desire to maintain contact with anyone who reminded her of that time. She'd started over and was in a much better place. So much so that she didn't feel like she deserved the good that had come her way—a new career and a man who cared about her as much as she cared about him.

She wasn't going to let Lila spoil the dream world she was living in. She would chitchat for a few more minutes, then get her out of here. She could be polite for five minutes. "You're correct, but you're here now, so how have you been?"

Lila chuckled. "I'm fine. Now. I don't think I need to tell you that I was furious that you turned down John's proposal, but it turned out to be the best thing to happen to the show in years. Everyone is *still* talking about it, even those people who believe they are too good for reality TV. No one is too good for some juicy gossip."

Jada tilted her head to the side. "Yes, I know. I'm living it. Happy I could oblige though that was never my intent."

"What I've come to appreciate about you is your honesty. John wasn't the right guy for you, and you didn't settle."

"Thanks." Compliments were always nice, but her gut told her not to trust this one.

"But you're not always honest, are you?"

Lila's voice could cut glass. Or at least slice through Jada. Only a lifetime of dealing with her parents saved her from flinching and showing her hand. "I don't know what you're talking about."

Lila braced her elbows on the table and steepled her fingers. "Well, after your revelation, and after I calmed down enough to stop being angry, I thought about everything I knew about you. About the background checks we do on all contestants, and frankly, it didn't make any sense that you would have someone at home. You told us your last relationship worth mentioning ended a year ago. Your background check confirmed this."

She would not wince. She would not give Lila any ammunition. Jada stared straight ahead at Lila and infused as much confidence in her voice as she could muster. "Donovan and I were not in a relationship before I went on the show, but we had met. I didn't violate the rules of the show."

Lila's eyebrows rose. "Yes, I am aware that is the story you've told everyone."

"What do you want, Lila?"

Lila pursed her thin, red lips. "What do I want? So, so much. *My One and Only* has been great and made my career, but what I really want is to expand my empire. And I need a new show—a can't-miss prospect—to make that happen. That is where you, my dear Jada, come in."

Calm. Stay calm. "What are you talking about?"

"You're a natural. The fans love you. Well, when they're not hating you."

Jada would not be deterred, even if the room felt like it was spinning faster and faster around her. "What are you talking about, Lila?"

"I'm talking about the fact that I originally had a redemption arc in mind for you, involving a personality I'm already familiar with." Lila leaned forward, her evil vibe spreading through the air like a deadly virus. "I asked John to see if he could get back together with you, with the thought of you starring in a new show together, but he couldn't close the deal. So I had to go to Plan B, which I actually like better. What am I talking about, dear Jada? I am talking about the fact that your relationship with Donovan is a lie."

"No, it's not," Jada said through stiff lips. She'd always thought the phrase about your blood running cold was hyperbole. Now she knew it wasn't.

Lila scoffed. "Don't bother denying it. I'm not stupid, and you're not that great of a liar. I saw that kiss when it hit Twitter. Dissected it three ways to Sunday. He was stunned when you kissed him.

You can deny it, but I'm much better in the publicity game than you are." She waved her hand. "But all that unpleasantness can be avoided if the two of you agree to do a show together about your relationship and this wonderful little cupcake shop you have here. If you don't, I will expose your lie, which will make your initial lie feel like a tiny fib and dwarf the negative reaction you received from the public. The backlash will be, I'm guessing, at least three times as worse. I want to help you avoid that fate. America loves #JaDon."

Lila shrugged a shoulder, like she was offering Jada a chance to go to a spin cycling class, if she wanted. "I just want to give them more."

The buzzing in Jada's ears refused to abate. Lila's words—no, Lila's *threat*—played nonstop on a loop in her head. She had to protect Donovan. He'd done nothing wrong.

This was all her fault. If she'd never opened her mouth, not once, but twice, none of this would be happening. Lila couldn't rise to the occasion as the Wicked Witch of Reality TV if Jada hadn't inadvertently led her straight down the yellow brick road. Everything Jada touched turned into a tornado, destroying everything in its path.

She should have known the good vibes couldn't last.

Chapter Twenty-Four

Donovan had always assumed nothing would ever make him more furious than when he found out his father had gambled away the little money Donovan's mother had managed to save for a rainy day. He'd made the discovery that fateful afternoon during his sophomore year in high school, when his mother had been laid off from her job and they needed that money to pay the rent. That had been the final straw for his mom, who filed for divorce soon afterward. However, they had come dangerously close to being kicked out of their home. Only the kindness of family friends had stopped that from happening.

He'd resisted the urge to smash his fist into his father's smug, unremorseful face because ultimately, that would solve nothing. Instead, he'd vowed right then and there to never be that vulnerable again and to always be there to protect and support those he loved. He'd succeeded. Until today.

He'd failed, and because of his failure, Jada had been hurt.

Fucking unacceptable.

Fury rampaged through his veins as Jada recounted her encounter with Lila, the TV producer who'd decided to moonlight as a black-mailer. He was absolutely livid with Lila. How fucking dare she?

He channeled his emotions—his desire to win, his desire to be there for his teammates and coaches, his desire to make his family proud—into his play on the field to bring the destruction and chaos the game called for. Off the field, he reined in his emotions to make sure his life followed the path he had laid out. Now that was being threatened, and he didn't know how to stop it. "I can't believe this. This is utter bullshit. She thinks she can come here and upend our lives unless we give in to her demands. Even if we do, something tells me she won't stop there.

"She wants to destroy our lives. Who does that? Why would someone do that?" His breathing was coming fast and furious. His fingernails dug into his palms as he fought back the urge to smash something.

His world was spinning out of control, his emotions getting the best of him. He didn't know what to do or how to slow his whirring brain to come up with a solution. What the hell was he going to do about this? "What the fuck is her problem?"

"I'm sorry," Jada said in a small voice.

Donovan came to a halt, then whirled. His heart plummeted to his feet.

Where had the bold and brave Jada gone? She was slumped in a chair. Her eyes were downcast, her shoulders hunched in like she was trying to protect herself from something. From someone? From him? He took two long strides toward her and leaned down to cup her shoulders. He'd been a selfish prick, only thinking about how this affected him. She was the one really suffering. "Baby, what are you sorry for?"

"For putting you in this position." Her voice came out small and timid.

"You didn't put me in this position. Lila did."

She raked a hand through her hair. "But it wouldn't have gotten to this point if I hadn't lied about having someone at home."

Donovan shook his head. "They were hammering you on why you turned down John's proposal and wouldn't stop until you gave them a satisfactory answer. And don't you dare say you shouldn't have turned down that jackass's proposal, given the stunt he pulled."

She rubbed her face with a shaking hand. "I know, I know, but then I compounded the lie with another lie about you being my boyfriend."

He squeezed her shoulders. "A lie I went along with, by the way."

Jada was already shaking her head before he finished speaking. "It doesn't matter. She doesn't care that we're a real couple now. She probably wouldn't believe us even if we told her. I wish I could disappear. Make all this go away. I'm so sorry I put you in this position. Everything I touch turns to trash."

He pulled her out of her chair and into a hug he needed just as much as she did. He sighed as her soft body contoured to his. They were a perfect fit. Always would be if he had anything to say about it. "Hey, we're in this together. I refuse to let you shoulder all the blame. Look at what you've accomplished. In case you didn't notice, the shop wasn't doing that great until you came along and insulted me and the shop, and then bullied me until you got your way to make improvements."

A very welcome bubble of laughter spilled out of her. "I did not bully you. I just made a few suggestions." She stepped back and looked up at him. Tears pooled in her beautiful eyes. "Thank you for being so nice. I don't deserve it."

He knew where this was coming from. Her parents making her feel like her accomplishments were never enough. That she was never enough. "Come with me." He grabbed her hand and tugged her behind him into his bedroom. He stopped when he reached the back wall and tugged her in front of him to stand in front of the mirror. "Affirmation time."

She looked at him askance in the mirror. "Affirmation time? Now?"

"Yes, now. Let's go. You're the one that said they helped you."

"You're not supposed to listen to what I say!"

He shot her a look. "Jada. Stop procrastinating."

"Fine. Bully." She squared her shoulders and stared at her reflection. "Oh, my God, I look awful. Crying is not helpful when one is trying to maintain that dewy glow."

"Jada . . . ," he warned.

"Okay, okay. I am Jada Townsend-Matthews, and I am enough."

He snorted. "That was pathetic."

"Hey!"

He was resolute. "Try harder."

She braced her legs apart and stared at her reflection. "I am Jada Townsend-Matthews, and I am enough."

"Better. Again."

"I am Jada Townsend-Matthews, and I am enough. I am Jada Townsend-Matthews, and I am enough." With each recitation, her voice got stronger and clearer. The tension in his shoulders abated a small bit. His breathing calmed. This was better. Much better.

"My name is Jada Townsend-Matthews, and I am enough. My name is Jada Townsend-Matthews, and I am . . . going to beat her ass!"

Oh, shit.

* * *

Jada was pissed. Pissed like she couldn't remember. When the finale aired and people dogged her out on social media, she took it, believing she'd let everyone down and hoping that disappearing would make the hate end sooner. She'd gone on the show hoping to find a way to take control of her life. That hadn't worked out, but it had led her on a path to discover who she wanted to be and what she wanted to do. She wasn't going to let anyone take that away from her. Not now. Not ever.

She was ready to fight. She was ready to take control of her life one more time.

Jada crossed her left leg over her right knee, placed her elbows on the table, and steepled her fingers. "Thank you for agreeing to see me."

"I was surprised, but happy to get the call." John graced her with the smile that had caused countless women in the country to get the vapors. Once upon a time, she'd been affected as well. That time was long gone. Now she recognized it for the practiced tomfoolery it was. Her gut had known, even if her mind hadn't.

She'd wanted to handle this on her own. The calm certainty and logic she'd absorbed from being around Donovan gave her peace in the situation. She wanted to give John a piece of her mind—he deserved a piece of her mind—but she wanted answers more. Or at least first. Donovan had objected—no doubt because he thought she'd kick John's ass and do damage to the furniture in his office, but she'd held her ground.

She'd come prepared wearing her best armor—a black, custom-tailored Gucci suit that hugged her curves and her favorite red patent leather Louboutin stilettos. She loved those shoes. She'd strolled down the streets of Paris and New York in those shoes. She missed her Crocs and the polo and khakis she'd become accustomed to wearing, but she needed to fight fire with fire. After a trip to the hair salon and an hour in the mirror carefully applying her makeup, she looked fabulous and was armed for battle.

John raised his gaze from where he'd been ogling her legs. "Dare I hope this means you've given more thought to my offer?"

Jada's eyebrows arched. "You thought I'd ask you to meet me in my boyfriend's office if I planned to dump him and run off to Hollywood with you?"

A muscle in his jaw, which wasn't as steely as she'd once thought, spasmed. "Stranger things have happened. I just thought you wanted a quiet place to talk."

She inclined her head. "I did." There was no way she was inviting him to her condo, and they couldn't meet in the shop within earshot of customers and shop owners/employees, who all had opinions they'd want to share. "Did you feel anything for me ever, John, or was it all for show?"

Dr. John's face smoothed into the pleasant I'm-such-a-good-guy expression he'd perfected. "Of course I did. I loved you. Do you think I'd come back here for more possible rejection if I didn't?"

He was good. She had to give him that. The angst, the uncertainty in his voice sounded top notch. Maybe he did have a future in Hollywood. Too bad she didn't give a shit. She knew the true depths of his character. "Stop the act, John. Lila told me about the little scheme you two cooked up."

Shock, then a hint of anger, flashed across his face before he again smoothed out those unpleasant emotions. "I'm not sure what she told you—"

Jada held up a hand. "Cut the crap. We both know it's true. Did you ever care about me, *actually* love me?"

He deflated against his chair. "Yes, Jada, I cared about you. Love? We looked good together. I knew you were a star the moment I met you. Together, we can fly."

"So the answer to that is no."

A dangerous light entered his eyes. "Don't act all innocent. You made me look like a fool on national TV! Why did you turn down my proposal?"

"Because I didn't love you, and it didn't feel right." Now that she knew what right felt like, she couldn't believe how close she'd come to making a colossal mistake. "I didn't mean to embarrass you, and for that I apologize. I let things go too far."

John sucked his teeth, the unpleasant sound reverberating in the quiet room, drawing her emotions closer to the edge. "I take it you didn't invite me here to tell me you changed your mind about us?"

"Got it in one," she said, pointing at him. "You're a doctor, so I figured the smarts were in there somewhere. I was wrong for running out on you on the show, and you deserve to hear that from me. I was unsure of my feelings and was too cowardly to confront them until it was too late. For that, you have my apologies. But trying to blackmail me? That's low, really low and underhanded."

He sighed. "I thought you would say yes. We were good together, Jada. Opportunities like this don't come along very often."

"You have a good career as a doctor!"

John made a face. "An anonymous doctor in an anonymous hospital in Minnesota. I like attention. I like the opportunities and money coming my way. I like people calling my name when I walk down the street."

Yep, all those opportunities she'd thought she wanted. She sighed. "Well, good luck. But if you ever pull something like this again, my mercy won't be so sweet."

He studied her for a second. "You're fierce, much fiercer than I gave you credit for."

Jada glared at him. "Compliments ain't gonna get you nowhere, buddy, but thanks. I feel fiercer than I ever have in my life." She stood and took a few steps to the door. "And because I am feeling that way, I have one more surprise for you."

She opened the door. John jerked back in his chair when Donovan stepped inside.

She shouldn't take delight in the scared look on John's face, but she did. She'd work on that later. "You know how I said we were done? I lied. Hi, Lila."

John's eyes, already widened, turned into saucers when Lila stepped from behind Donovan. She inclined her head. "Jada. John."

Jada nodded at Lila. Lila had only been too eager to meet with her and Donovan, undoubtedly thinking she would agree to Lila's Plan B.

Jada had wanted the meeting on her own turf, the better to set the tone and be in a familiar, powerful spot. She didn't know or care about football, but she had learned a thing or two from her grandmother over the years.

Lila's smug smile dimmed when she spotted John. "What is he doing here?"

"Oh, we're going to get to that in a bit. Have a seat, please."

She and Donovan sat across from the Terrible Twosome. Having him there calmed her. She'd never believed she'd find someone who had her back like Donovan did. She didn't know what she did to deserve him, but she was grateful nonetheless. "Thank you for coming, Lila."

Lila's thin lips curved into a caricature of a smile. "My pleasure. I'm assuming you called us here because you either changed your mind about doing the show with John or you like my new show idea with you and Donovan. John and I are here for your final answer, right?"

"You would think, but no," Donovan said, his hard gaze cutting between Lila and John.

Lila sat up straight. "Then why are we here?"

Jada pasted on a saccharine smile. "To talk, of course. Now, from what I remember, your working theory is that Donovan and I aren't really dating, and you're going to expose us for frauds if we don't do what you say."

Lila's gaze darted to John for a second. "That sounds . . ."

"Accurate, I know. Well, joke's on you." Jada silently added the *bitch*. "Because we are very much a couple."

"We are." Donovan raised her hand and laid a gentle kiss to the back of it.

The last of Jada's nerves faded away as righteous anger took its place. "Of course, it's our word against yours, I know. In order for you to believe me, I could describe the location and shape of a scar from his childhood on a part of his body not on display right now, but I'm sure you can use your imagination as to why I know it exists. I haven't mentioned the part where our friends and families will back us up about the status of our relationship."

"If you insist on 'exposing us,'" Donovan said, his voice hard as ice, using air quotes, "we'll have to do some exposing of our own. Certain people, like network executives, probably aren't too keen on their employees engaging in blackmail. Besides, Jada is beloved. You know it, and I know it. I'm sure her fans would love to fill your Twitter mentions with all kinds of creative replies if they knew what you were attempting to do."

"You have no proof of blackmail." Lila's eyes spat fire.

Jada held up a manicured index finger. "Oh, but I do. You know how you kept calling and leaving messages? Silly me, I thought you were asking me to do interviews. Which you were, I guess, technically. I finally got around to listening to the voice mails."

She wrinkled her nose. "Wow. Really creative vocabulary you have there, Lila. That last voice mail was quite a doozy. I wasn't expecting the threats about how you were going to destroy me, how you were going to leak damaging rumors about me, how you'd been behind a lot of the hate I received online with bot accounts." Jada grimaced. "Ugly stuff. You sounded drunk or high when you admitted that, so you might not remember saying all that, but you did."

Jada kept her gaze trained squarely on Lila. She ignored John's gasp.

Lila's already pale skin turned ghastly white. "I don't know what you're talking about."

Jada sniffed. "Oh, I think you do. Really, I'd hate for those messages to fall into the wrong hands."

Lila sneered, her veneer finally cracking. "You wouldn't dare. You're a spoiled, rich girl. You don't have the balls."

The courage of her convictions swept through Jada. "Keep telling yourself that."

Jada turned to the other member of the blackmailing crew. "As for you, John, I'm sure people would love to know their perfect Mr. America has slid into the DMs of no less than three contestants from *My One and Only* with a woe-is-me story, trying to get back together with them, *all at the same time.*" Jada snapped her fingers. "Did I forget to mention I ended my social media hiatus to check my DMs? I do so love it when women have each other's backs."

Jada gave the cowards a moment to respond. When none came, she offered up the kill shot. "If none of that reasoning convinces you, and I can't imagine why it wouldn't, please remember this spoiled, rich girl has a billionaire grandmother who loves her very, very much. If I tell her what you both attempted to do to me, she will ruin both your lives, barely lifting a finger. Contrary to what you believe, Lila, I don't make idle threats. I suggest you both slink away and forget you ever knew my name."

Lila and John exchanged a glance and jumped up at the same time. John yanked open the door and stumbled back. Nicholas and August filled the doorway, both wearing expressions of impending malice. John swallowed, then pushed past them with Lila hot on his heels.

Chapter Twenty-Five

Donovan shut the door on his best friends' beaming faces and turned to the most important person in his life. "We did it, baby! You were so badass."

He wrapped his arms around her waist, picked her up, and spun in a circle.

Laughing, she smacked him on the shoulders. "Put me down."

"Not before I do this." She was at the perfect height for him to kiss and he took immediate advantage. Kissing her was a new, better experience every time. He lost himself in the taste and scent of her. He kept the embrace soft and languid, wanting to savor the moment. Savor her. Connect with her.

He loved her. And he was going to tell her. Now.

Donovan ended the kiss, his chest heaving, the blood roaring in his veins. He reluctantly set her on her feet, hating to lose the connection.

Jada took a step back—away from him—her hands twisting together at her waist. "We need to talk."

Donovan's brow furrowed as he wrestled to bring his rioting senses under control. "Talk about what?"

Her throat worked up and down. "About us."

Donovan fought to keep calm. "What about us?"

"We need to . . . end things."

Donovan stumbled back. "What? What the hell are you talking about? We just told Lila and John we're a real couple because we are!"

"I know, but we can't . . . shouldn't continue."

"Why the hell not?"

He took no solace in the fact that she looked miserable. Panic was ripping his insides to shreds, obliterating his ability to think straight. The woman he loved, the only woman he'd ever loved, was telling him that not only did she not feel the same way, she didn't even want there to be a "them" at all. "Is this because I was thinking about myself when you first told me about Lila?"

Jada vigorously shook her head. "No, no, no. This is all about me."

He didn't believe her. He'd been so worried about himself that he hadn't taken the time to immediately check on her. And he was doing it again. He knew her. He knew he hadn't been in this alone. Knew the kiss they'd just shared was more than mutual lust.

He went to her and cradled her cheek, his thumb smoothing over her soft skin. "Baby, tell me what's going on."

"I need to do this for me." She shied away from his touch, ripping a new hole in his chest where his heart used to reside.

"Do what?" He wanted her to say it. To put into words the action that would destroy him.

"Not work here." She pressed her eyes tightly closed, like she was giving herself a pep talk to continue. "Not be with you."

"Why?" He heard the pleading in his voice. He didn't give a shit. Now was not the time for pride.

Her eyes fluttered open. "I came to work at Sugar Blitz to convince my grandmother that I was responsible enough to gain control of my trust fund. I've always been a screwup, someone who couldn't stay with anything for long, twisting in the wind from here to there, from impulse to impulse. I thought I found what I was looking for here, but again I nearly brought disaster to your doorstep because of one more impulsive decision I made."

Donovan gathered her hands in his and squeezed. "But we weathered that storm together."

Jada nodded. "I know we did, but it's hard to forget that I was the cause in the first place, and I don't want to ever put you in that position again." A tear slipped down her cheek. He reached out to wipe it away. He couldn't help himself. Her pain was his pain.

Jada squared her shoulders. "To truly be the adult I want to be, I need to be on my own, not at a job my grandmother picked out for me, even though I've had the time of my life here. I don't want to be that impulsive screwup for the rest of my life. I refuse to be. We've moved so fast, and I've come to rely on you. I need to figure out who I am and what I want and stand on my own two feet before I commit to someone. I need time."

Her eyes pleaded with him for understanding. But he couldn't. Love for her consumed him, and he wanted to tell everyone every damn day how he felt.

But that's not what she wanted from him.

If he thought about it rationally, logically, he could understand. It took everything within him, but he reined in his emotions. If she needed time, if she didn't see a future with him, then he would respect her decision. No matter how much it ravaged him.

But he'd been through plenty of emotionally draining, soul-crushing events in life, and he'd gotten through them by concentrating on what came next and making sure he was never vulnerable again. This would be no different.

He swallowed his hurt and lifted his chin. "Okay."

* * *

Jada followed Stacey into Grams's office. Her grandmother stood and made her way toward her. "Jada, what a wonderful surprise."

She held out her arms and Jada gratefully fell into the embrace. She'd never felt worse. Being an adult sucked. She missed Donovan more than she'd ever thought possible. It had been less than two days, but it felt like a part—an integral part—of her was missing. She didn't know if she'd ever feel whole again. But it was a necessary step for her. She needed to figure out who she was outside of a relationship, outside of a job handed to her. But it hurt so much not seeing him every day. Not being able to kiss him whenever the mood struck. Not being able to tease him when he got too serious.

"Jada, honey, what's wrong?" Grams led her to her seating area.

Jada sank into one of the plush chairs and took a deep breath. Time to rip off the bandage. "I quit my job."

Grams settled into the other chair. "Why? You love working there. You love working there with Donovan."

"Because it's time for me to grow up and take control of my life. And no, I don't want to talk about Donovan."

Grams studied her, concern filling her eyes. "Okay. We don't have to talk about him if you don't want to, but what do you mean it's time for you to grow up?"

Jada's shoulders deflated. "I worked at Sugar Blitz because you set me up with a job there."

Grams reached for her hand. "And you flourished. I've never seen you like this. You're more determined. You're more focused. You're joyful. I've always been proud of you for keeping a stiff upper lip no matter what gets thrown your way and powering through and maintaining your sense of self, but now I'm *happy* for you."

Jada nodded, barely holding back the tears. "I enjoyed working there, planning events and getting to know the regulars, and converting people to regulars."

"Then what's the problem?"

"I don't want to have a job because my grandmother handed it to me. I liked what I was doing at Sugar Blitz, but I need to continue to move forward, planning events on my own." She lifted her chin. "I want to do this. Prove to myself that I can."

Grams sighed. "Jada, I know your parents took away your credit cards and stopped paying your bills. Your mother assumed you had told me, which you should have. She and I had some words about that, believe me."

Jada made a face. "Which is why I didn't tell you."

"Hmmph." Grams's lips twisted with disagreement for a moment, but then she held her hands up in supplication. "Well, now that you're no longer working at the cupcake shop, I can give you access to your trust fund."

Jada shook her head. "No, you can't."

"Why not? You need money to eat. And it is your money."

"That I'm not supposed to have until I'm twenty-six if I can prove to you that I can keep a job, which I've failed at admittedly, but I have a plan."

Grams scrutinized her face, opened her mouth like she intended to argue, but then she sighed. "Okay, if you're determined to do this, then I support you. How can I help?" She snapped her fingers. "I know. I can give you a job in our marketing department planning events. I've always wanted someone in the Townsend bloodline working for the team."

Jada laughed for the first time in what felt like forever. "Grams, that's exactly what I don't want!"

"I just want to help you, honey. I worry about you."

Jada covered her hand with her heart. Her grandmother's love and support meant the world to her. "I know you do. A month ago, you asked me if I had a plan. I didn't then."

"But you do now?"

Jada nodded. "I do. I'm not sure how good it is, but I do. I've made some contacts while working at the cupcake shop. I have a few leads on event-planning jobs. They're small, but I have to start somewhere. I'm hoping if I can prove to you that I'm serious about it and good at it for the next few months, you'll give me access to my trust fund on my birthday so I can put more money into my business."

She lifted her chin, ready for her grandmother's response, no matter what it was.

Grams squeezed her hand. "Jada, I love you, and I'm here to help in whatever capacity you need, whether that's emotional or financial support. As it happens, I do know a thing or two about running a successful business. I'd love to add mentor to my grandmotherly duties."

Jada's lips lifted into a tremulous smile. Even if her heart was splitting open, at least one area of her life could be on the upswing. "I accept."

* * *

"Where's Jada?" Mr. Till asked as he stepped up to the counter.

Donovan sighed. "You ask that question every day."

Mr. Till shrugged in the universal sign for *And?*

Donovan sighed and opened the display case to retrieve the red velvet cupcake, the only cupcake they served worth a damn, according to Mr. Till. He snapped the case closed with a little more force than necessary. "She no longer works here, which you know."

When he gave that response to inquiring customers, he usually followed it with, "We're still dating, but we've decided to be more private about our relationship," partly because he wanted it to be true, and partly to protect her. He would never intentionally cause her distress. He'd rather cut off his arm with a rusty saw.

Mr. Till made a face. "Son, I'm going to give you some advice. You're not that bright, but maybe it will sink in somehow." He pointed a bony finger at Donovan's chest. "If you let a woman like that go without a fight, then you're a dumbass."

Donovan slid the cupcake across the counter. "Are you going to pay for this or not?"

He didn't give a damn that he was being rude to a customer. At this point, Mr. Till was family, coming in here every day and sticking his nose into everyone's business like a patriarch. Besides, he was not in the mood. Jada had left of her own volition and had not been in touch once in the past three months. He checked his phone, his email, and even his DMs on social media accounts every two minutes to make sure. She wasn't ready. Maybe she would never be ready. Hell, maybe she was done completely and didn't think about him a million times per day like he did her.

And he couldn't escape her, even here at work. Even if customers weren't asking about her, all he had to do was look up and see her handiwork everywhere.

He'd gone through with the photo shoot. Rose was a brilliant photographer. The original boring, stale artwork had been replaced with Rose's photos—artistic, fun shots of the store's offerings, along with photos of customers sitting around the tables, laughing and eating. Their regulars had been thrilled to be asked to participate in the photo shoot. He and Nicholas had even cajoled August into taking a few shots of the three in them in the kitchen, laughing and baking. The photos were displayed to perfection against walls that had been painted a soft, welcoming yellow.

More importantly, business was booming. Sugar Blitz was now a neighborhood hangout, where community members could grab a cupcake and catch up with friends. A new full-time manager was set to start next week.

None of that would have happened without Jada's influence. Damn it.

Mr. Till harrumphed. "Yeah, yeah, I'm going to pay. Don't shoot the messenger just because I'm right." He paid, then shuffled away to his table, where a few of his chess buddies waited. He only shot one "you're a dummy" look over his shoulder. An improvement. Usually, he got three good head shakes in.

"He *is* right, you know." Nicholas came up, carrying a sheet pan of freshly baked cupcakes. August trailed him, holding another pan, nodding.

Donovan sighed, weariness pressing on his shoulders. He'd heard all this before. But what the fuck did they expect him to do about it? Jada was the one who left. She was the one who said she didn't want to be with him. "Can we not talk about this for the millionth time?"

Nicholas and August exchanged a glance, then nodded in unison.

"Did you get your tux cleaned for the Knights in Shining Armor event?" Nicholas asked.

Thrilled at the change in topic, Donovan gave the sigh and eyeroll Nicholas undoubtedly expected. "Yes, Dad, I did."

The Knights in Shining Armor event was a fundraiser benefiting the local Boys & Girls Club. Donovan and some of his teammates who volunteered with and donated money to the organization were being honored. Ordinarily, he'd be looking forward to the event, but lately he looked forward to nothing. At least his mother, who could always be counted on to cheer him up, was acting as his date. He'd assumed Jada would fill that role, but he'd assumed a lot of things, so . . .

Nicholas slapped him on the back. "Great. See you there. And try to learn what a smile is before you show up. You don't want to scare the kids."

* * *

Five hours later, Donovan stepped into the ballroom at the US Grant Hotel in downtown San Diego with his mother at his side. He'd done his best to pretend that all was well. She knew he and Jada were no longer seeing each other but had respected his wishes not to go into detail.

"Wow. This place is fancy," his mom said.

It was.

Donovan had been here several times before, but he was always taken aback by the room's sheer opulence. Multiple gold and diamond chandeliers hung from the ceiling. Elegant, extravagant flower centerpieces dotted every table. The carpet underneath their feet was sumptuous. All the attendees wore their best, fanciest gear and were ready to open their checkbooks for an excellent cause. All he had to do was smile and shake the hands of donors, promise the Knights would win the Super Bowl next season, and accept a plaque when his name was called. Any other time, that task would be easy. Even enjoyable.

Tonight, he felt like shit.

But no one cared or needed to know. His pain was his alone, to be dealt with later at some indeterminate period in time. He held out his hand. "Shall we?"

They stepped into the room and were immediately swept into a world of photos and small talk with teammates he hadn't seen since the season ended, team employees, and eventgoers.

The room was packed to the gills. He only got brief glimpses of Nicholas and August, barely long enough to exchange nods before they were swept away. Time dragged on as a headache dogged his every step. He repeatedly reminded himself to smile.

A familiar noise cut through the general chatter filling the room. Donovan whirled. A flash of red caught his eye. He stepped around a couple chatting at a high table and stopped in his tracks. His heart leapt into his throat.

Jada. She was here. It had been her effervescent laughter that caught his attention. She was chatting with a guest and hadn't seen him yet. He took immediate advantage to look his fill.

She wore a shimmery red floor-length gown that hugged her terrific figure, dipping in at her waist and flaring to cover her hips. Her dark hair cascaded over one shoulder in soft waves. She looked sophisticated and stunning. Her bold eye makeup drew attention to those amazing chocolate-brown eyes.

What was she doing here? This wasn't an official team event, though many of his teammates and team officials were here, so she couldn't be here at the command of Mrs. T.

His mother moved into his line of sight, blocking his view of Jada. He took a step to the right, but it was already too late. She was gone, swallowed up by the crowd.

Damn it. Should he go after her? And say what? She'd dumped him, after all. More than likely, she was here as a donor like almost everyone else here. She wasn't here for him.

At the sound of a clearing throat, he dropped his gaze to his mother, who was watching him with entirely too much interest. He'd successfully dodged any and all questions about Jada. Looked like his good luck was about to run out.

"You know, I can tell you're hurting. You've looked miserable the entire night. I've been pretty patient, respecting your privacy, but I'm your mother, so that comes to an end now." She laid a hand on his sleeve. "Let's go somewhere quieter to talk."

He followed her to a corner, away from the chatter and the orchestra providing the musical backdrop. His mother didn't waste any time.

"Donny, what's going on? Why are you here with me instead of Jada?"

Donovan pushed the answer past a tight throat. "We're no longer seeing each other. You know that."

His mother nodded. "Yes, I do. The question is why." When he remained silent, she sighed. "Can I let you in on a little secret?" She looked around, presumably to make sure no one could hear them. "I knew you and Jada weren't really dating the day I stopped by the shop." She held up a hand as shock swept through him. "Now, I know you and your sisters think I don't know how to keep a secret, but I do. I was married to your father, after all. I know you really well, and I could tell things were a little off between the two of you, but I could also tell you really wanted it to be true, and I wanted you to figure it all out. Obviously, you did, but then you screwed it up."

Donovan worked his jaw side to side, the emotions still so raw and jagged. "I was prepared to tell her I had fallen in love with her, but she ended things before I could."

"And you let her go."

Donovan scraped his hand against the back of his neck, frustration tearing him apart. "What else was I supposed to do?"

"Not let your father continue to rule your life."

He staggered back at that sucker punch to gut. "What's that supposed to mean?"

His mother was resolute. "It means that I know he still calls you for money, *and* that you respond. I talk to people from the old neighborhood all the time. They let me know what foolishness your father is up to so I can protect my kids as much as possible." She sighed. "Your father hurt you, he hurt all of us, and I'll forever be upset with myself that I didn't get us out sooner."

He'd heard enough. "You did the best you could. You're a terrific mother. Never doubt that."

She patted his arm. "Thank you, my favorite son, but it's true that your parents influence you, for good or for bad. The lesson you learned was to concentrate on eradicating any surprises and upheaval from your life. If you could be financially stable, then life would be smooth sailing."

Donovan kept quiet, unable to deny her claims.

"Then Jada came along. She shook you and your world up and you fell hard. But then she hit you with the biggest surprise of all by ending things and you retreated. Yes, your sisters told me what happened."

Donovan sighed. He couldn't be mad at his siblings for spilling the beans. He should have known. They were too close-knit for secrets.

"What was I supposed to do? I can't make her be with me."

Anguish still ate at him, still dogged his heels at every turn. He wasn't sure when it wouldn't. If it ever would.

"No, you can't, because Jada is her own woman. But I also know this is the first time you've been in the same room with her in three months. Are you really prepared to leave it at that?"

No, he wasn't. Not by a long shot. It was time to stop living in the past and fight for his future with everything he had in him.

Chapter Twenty-Six

*T*heoretically, Jada was having a good time. Tonight was proof that following her dreams was paying off. As she'd told Grams, she'd used the connections she'd gained by working at Sugar Blitz to secure several small event-planning gigs. That had led to more events, which led to her being here tonight. A client recommended her services to the event organizer, Sydney, when Sydney's assistant had to go on bed rest for the last two months of her pregnancy. As far as Jada was concerned, any experience was good experience, and she'd readily accepted the new gig.

She'd happily done the grunt work asked of her, from blowing up a million balloons to organizing myriad spreadsheets, to make sure this event was a success.

They were raising money for a worthy cause. All around her, people were having fun, thanks, in a small part, to her efforts.

So yes, theoretically, she was having a good time. But she couldn't stop thinking that Donovan was somewhere in this packed room. She'd damn near hyperventilated when she learned he was one of the night's honorees and gave a moment's thought to quitting. But she'd quickly come to her senses and realized that was impulsive and something the old Jada would have done. Instead, she'd put her head down and gotten back to work.

That didn't mean she didn't think about him approximately a million times per day. She'd even tried to rehearse what she would say if she saw him tonight, but could never come up with anything that did justice to how much he had meant to her. What he still meant to her. Would she even have the courage if she did have the chance?

Earlier, she thought she'd caught a glimpse of him, thought this was her time to find out, but then someone called her name, and by the time she returned to the spot, he was no longer there, if it had even been him in the first place.

Anytime anyone asked about him, asked about *them,* she smiled, nodded, and said she was working tonight, so they couldn't spend much time together, but she'd surely pass along their congratulations. All in a day's work.

And her heart ached all the more for it. It had been aching for ninety-two days, three hours, and twenty-seven minutes. But who was counting?

She missed him. There, she'd admitted it. But she'd done the right thing, saving him from her chaos. She'd done the right thing, focusing on herself.

Then why do you go home every night and spend the time wondering what he's doing? Wondering if he's thinking about you too?

"Jada!"

She turned to see Sydney coming toward her. "Jada, we need to start tallying the winners of the silent auction."

An hour later, Jada found a loveseat in an out-of-the-way corner of the hotel lobby and collapsed. This event-planning business was no joke. She'd been running around nonstop, putting out little fires that popped up every three minutes. She was exhausted. Exhausted, but happy.

Mostly happy.

Other than watching as he'd accepted his award, she hadn't seen Donovan. That was probably for the best. Bursting into tears in the middle of a ballroom didn't exactly scream professionalism.

She tipped her head back and closed her eyes, exhaling. She needed this break. She needed the quiet.

Donovan filled her thoughts. His smile. His Principal Dell–ness. His patience. His determination. The way he looked at her. She missed it all. She missed him.

The ache had only gotten stronger.

She'd walked away to discover her place in the world and to protect him from her and the chaos she brought to his life.

You're a coward. She shook her head, but the treacherous thought remained.

You let the best man you've ever known get away because you were afraid you wouldn't be enough for him. That he would realize she wasn't smart. That he would get bored.

Where had that gotten her?

Even though she'd found what she was looking for in her professional life, she wasn't as fulfilled as she'd hoped. But she could do something about it. If she had the courage.

Was she ready to claim what—who—she needed in her personal life?

Yes, she was. Tonight. Now. Before he had a chance to leave.

Jada's eyes flew open as she leapt out of the chair. She ran toward the ballroom, nearly careening into a group of tourists and their suitcases.

"Sorry," she called back over her shoulder, never slowing down. She was a woman on a mission to get her man.

She ran headfirst into a brick wall and bounced off. "Oof."

No, not a wall. A human body. She glanced up, preparing to apologize. The words died in her throat, surprise rendering her mute.

"Jada." Donovan was there in all his handsome, not-imaginary glory. His eyebrows arched, a grin teasing at his full lips. "Going somewhere?"

She shook her head. "Not anymore."

"Good. You are a hard woman to track down." His deep voice rumbled, laced with a thread of humor. He was so handsome, so perfect. Her fingers itched to trace the line of his clean-shaven jaw, but she didn't have that right anymore. She'd turned her back on that right. "From what I hear, you have a lot to do with tonight being such a success."

"Thanks. What are you doing out here instead of in the ballroom?" she whispered in case she was dreaming. Hoping he would say . . .

"Looking for you." His dark eyes were trained squarely on her.

"Why?" Hope, that ever-optimistic being, bloomed in her chest.

"Because it was never an option that I wouldn't."

Her heart stuttered. Maybe she *could* make this right. He grasped her arm to guide her out of the way as someone almost bumped into her. Jada barely noticed the other woman. She only had eyes for Donovan.

"You okay?" When she nodded, he gestured to a sofa a few feet away. "Sit with me?"

As she followed him, she tracked his every movement with greedy eyes. It had been so long since she'd seen him. Since she'd been close enough to touch him. She sucked in a breath when he sat next to her, with only a small cushion separating them. "You look beautiful."

"Thank you," she said. Her pulse was thundering loudly in her ears. "You look nice, too."

His body—his wide shoulders, trim waist, and hard thighs—had been made to wear a tuxedo.

His lips twisted into a brief smile. "Thanks."

Here was her chance. Time to corral all the thoughts rioting around her brain and let him know what he meant to her.

He spoke before she had the chance. "I'm glad we're both here tonight. When we were in my office that last time, the conversation didn't go how I expected it to. You said what you had to say, and I just let you go. At the time, I thought I was doing the right thing, but the truth is I was scared."

Her mouth dropped open. "Scared of what?"

"The feelings you inspire in me. I was coasting through life, sure I had the perfect, logical, predictable plan in place, and you came and blew it all up, and it was exactly what I needed. I want to thank you for that."

"You're welcome." Her heart rejoiced at his admission, but she had to know. "Is that all?" Was he here to get that off his chest and to tell her goodbye forever? Her heart plummeted to the marble floor.

"No." He rested his arm on the sofa back, so near to her body. She longed for him to close the distance. "I need to apologize to you."

Jada shook her head, her mind still spinning. "For what?"

"I heard what you were saying, and I wasn't there for you. I don't like emotions and feeling out of control, and when things start getting real, I retreat. Instead of offering my support to you, I shut down and pretended I was fine. I don't know if I'll ever forgive myself for that. You were doubting yourself, and I didn't say any-thing to reassure you. I should have reminded you that you were amazing at the cupcake shop. I should have told you that I love the unpredictability you bring to my life. I love how you make me feel so much, and you made me realize I don't want to go through life thinking that financial success is all that matters, because it's not. You saved my business, but more importantly, you saved me."

Tears welled in her eyes. He wiped them away with a thumb. "Don't cry yet. I'm not finished."

She laughed. "My bad. Please continue, sir."

"You bring joy and love to my life. I love your supposed imperfections. I should have told you I believe in you, and I want you to do the same. I should have told you that you have so much to offer to the world, and I want a front row seat to your continued blossoming."

Jada couldn't breathe. Finally, finally, he touched her, linking their fingers. He dropped a gentle kiss to the back of her hand. She witnessed it all through the tears blurring her vision. Thank God for waterproof mascara.

"I should have told you that I love you, and I'll go to the ends of the earth for you."

"Really?" she asked, still a little unsure that she, Jada the impulsive screwup, could be so lucky.

"Yes, really, baby. Do you love me?" The touch of shyness in his voice, on his face, melted away any lingering doubts. He'd laid it all out on the line. This man would be there for her always, and she planned on being there for him.

She nodded, then touched her forehead to his. "When I ran into you—sorry about that, by the way—I was rushing to go back into the ballroom to tell you that I love you so, so much. You have no idea. I'm sorry I got scared. I can't promise that it won't happen again, but I do promise not to run again. Thank you for being the steadying force I need in my life. Thank you for believing in me when I didn't believe in myself. I wouldn't be experiencing all the good in my life if you didn't come into my life. Thank you for being you. You are the best man I've ever met. You are Donovan Dell, and you are enough, just the way you are." She caressed his strong jaw, thrilled she no longer had to deny herself the pleasure. "Yes, I love you with all of my heart. I even love you more than my shoes."

Jada lifted the floor-length hem of her dress to reveal the Crocs she'd changed into midway through the night. She cut off his laughter with her mouth. It had been ninety-two days, four hours, and approximately twenty-three minutes since she'd last kissed him. She was not throwing away her shot. Now or ever again.

Epilogue

"**D**amn, woman, you look good," Donovan said as Jada stepped onto the patio at his house.

"Thank you. Thank you." Jada did a little twirl, squeeing as the thigh-high slit in her teal dress opened to reveal her right leg and her silver Louboutin stilettos. "You don't look half bad yourself."

Donovan stroked his chin. "I try."

He did more than try. He wore a custom charcoal gray suit that hugged his wide shoulders and showed off his powerful legs. His crisp white shirt contrasted perfectly against his skin. His teal tie matched her dress exactly.

He was the handsomest man she'd ever seen, and he was all hers.

In a few months, they would stand in front of their family and friends to make it official, but today, they were taking engagement photos. She couldn't wait.

He tugged at his tie. "Was it really necessary for us to get all dressed up for this? We could've worn Sugar Blitz polos for old time's sake."

Jada shot him a look. "Sir, first of all, we already incorporated

Sugar Blitz with the teal. More importantly, these are our engagement photos, not an ad for your business."

Donovan snorted. "You just want to flex on Instagram."

She lifted her chin. "No, I want a symbol of our love immortalized on film. This is a full circle moment for us. Rose did our first photo shoot, and she's doing this one. It's perfect."

He side-eyed her.

"And okay, yes, I want to flex on Instagram for all the #JaDon haters. Besides, can you blame me? We look so good."

Donovan's shoulders shook with laughter.

Joy swept through her at the carefree sound. She'd never get tired of seeing him happy. She'd never get tired of knowing she brought him as much joy as he brought her.

Things with his dad weren't perfect—they probably never would be—but Donovan had returned to Oakland for a heart-to-heart chat with his dad, and his father had agreed to get help for his gambling addiction. He'd even followed through a few months later, and so far, so good.

"I love you," she murmured. Sometimes, she still couldn't believe she could say that whenever the mood struck.

"Come here," he murmured, wrapping an arm around her waist and drawing her toward him. Jada eagerly rose on her toes to meet his descending lips.

"No, no, no," Rose said, joining them on the patio. "Save that for the photos."

They groaned, but broke apart and followed her to the beach.

"Don't say a word," she said to Donovan as she stumbled over the sand. Maybe the Louboutins weren't the best choice given the location, but she loved them.

"I wouldn't dare," he whispered back. "I value my life too much."

Jada endeavored to side-eye him even as she snickered. She loved how much he made her laugh. She blew out a breath when they reached the designated spot. Jada shaded her eyes and studied the location. The sun would be setting in an hour, creating a fantastic glow of light. Water crashed on the beach. The perfect backdrop. They couldn't have chosen a better spot.

She couldn't have chosen a better man. Eight months had passed since the night they got back together. They hadn't been apart since. Life had only gotten better every day.

Business at Sugar Blitz was so good that they were preparing to open a second location. She'd gained access to her trust fund and put the money to good use, starting JTM Events. Business had been brisk ever since. Wonder of wonders, her parents had attended an awards banquet she'd planned for a local hospital and complimented her on a job well done. Jada had almost fainted.

"Okay, this is perfect," Rose said, checking the lighting. "Get into position. Y'all already know what to do."

Jada met Donovan's dancing eyes. Indeed, they did.

Donovan circled her waist with one arm and pulled her close. At Rose's direction, Jada laid her left hand over his heart, the better to show off the solitaire diamond ring.

"Perfect," Rose said, as her camera clicked. "Look deep into each other's eyes. Think glamorous drama."

"Yeah, Donovan. Give me glamorous drama," Jada said, snickering. "Give me smolder."

He smacked her on the butt, then picked her up, surprising a gasp out of her, and swung her in a circle. He cut off her laughter with a lingering kiss.

"You two really are adorable," Rose grumbled when they came up for air. "If I didn't like you both, I'd hate you with every fiber of my being."

"Thanks, Rose," they said in unison.

Chimes and beeps filled the air in an unyielding cacophony of sound, interrupting the idyllic setup. Their phones, which were lying innocently on a blanket a few feet away, were the culprits.

"What in the world?" Donovan lowered Jada to the ground, then walked over to grab the devices. He handed Jada hers.

She scrolled through the texts and social media notifications that were coming in a torrential flood. She opened one text from Olivia.

HAVE YOU SEEN THIS?

A link to a tweet was attached. Donovan looked over her shoulder while she clicked.

"No way," Donovan said, as the video in the tweet played. "He's going to be *pissed.*"

Jada shook her head. "Yes way. August has gone viral!"

Acknowledgments

To my mama and my family, I love y'all forever and ever. Clydell, thank you for encouraging and sharing my love of sports.

To the Destin Divas, I'm so happy I have y'all and thank God all the time that Farrah forgot that I didn't fully commit to our first retreat because I was being cheap and held a spot for me anyway. Y'all inspire me every day and this book wouldn't exist without your support. Special shout-out to Synithia and Sharon for reading the book proposal that started it all.

Piper Huguley, my sister at heart, thank you for always being a sounding board and for making me laugh and clutch my pearls at your fierceness.

Thank you to my agent, Sara Megibow, for guiding me through this crazy process. You're way more positive than I am, which is a good thing (for me anyway). Lol.

To my editor, Jennie Conway, who believed in this story from day one. Thank you for understanding my vision and being patient with me. Trust me, I know I don't always make it easy. Special thanks for the title! It's perfect.

To everyone at St. Martin's who had a hand in shepherding this book into publication, thank you for loving books and doing what you do. I am forever grateful.

When I attended my first RWA meeting all those years ago, I made a decision to sit next to the woman who looked like she, too, was alone and around my age. I was right on both accounts. Roni Loren, thank you for all your years of friendship.

Mariah Ankenman, thanks for reading this book and letting me know it didn't suck. Everyone should be so fortunate to have a cheerleader like you in their corner.

To all romance readers, we authors couldn't and wouldn't do what we do without you. If you've read my other books or if this is your first one, thank you from the bottom of my heart.

I'm sure I've forgotten someone, and I'm sick to my stomach about it. That doesn't mean I don't love and thank you, because I do. I'm just a woman in her forties, whose memory isn't as good as it used to be. And we shan't speak of age again, okay?

About the Author

Kim Campbell

Jamie Wesley has been reading romance novels since she was about twelve years old, when her mother left a romance novel that a friend had given her on the nightstand. Jamie read it instead, and the rest is history. When she's not writing or reading romance, Jamie can be found watching TV, rooting for her favorite sports teams, and/or planning her next trip to Walt Disney World.